Praise for Veronica Henry

'It's a glamorous and absorbing read, a well-written romp with a cast of believable, empathetic characters whom you'll be fascinated by from the start' *Daily Mail*

'Compulsive reading' *Woman & Home*

'Glam yet emotionally astute . . . a sparky absorbing read which fizzes with life and zip' *Mslexia*

'A perfect summer delight' *Sun*

'The book is first-class chick-lit and a great beach read' *Sunday Express*

'A great and absorbing read with a storyline that will certainly keep you hooked until the final page' *Chicklitreviews*

'Warm and brilliantly written' *Heat*

'A riotous summer romp' *Closer*

'This sweet book would be a great beach companion. ****' *Star*

'A great summer read. Veronica Henry's creation of a clever web of characters, each with their own story to tell, makes this a real page-turner' *Cornwall Today*

Veronica Henry worked as a scriptwriter for *The Archers, Heartbeat* and *Holby City,* amongst many others, before turning to fiction. She lives with her family on the coast in North Devon. Visit her website at www.veronicahenry.co.uk or follow her on Twitter @veronica_henry

By Veronica Henry

Wild Oats
An Eligible Bachelor
Love on the Rocks
Marriage and Other Games
The Beach Hut
The Birthday Party
The Long Weekend
A Night on the Orient Express
Christmas at the Crescent: A Novella
(*ebook exclusive*)

THE HONEYCOTE NOVELS
Honeycote
Making Hay
Just a Family Affair

VERONICA HENRY

Love On the Rocks

An Orion paperback

First published in Great Britain in 2006
by the Penguin Book Group.
This revised paperback edition published in 2014
by Orion Books,
an imprint of the Orion Publishing Group Ltd,
Orion House, 5 Upper St Martin's Lane,
London WC2H 9EA

An Hachette UK company

Typeset at The Spartan Press Ltd,
Lymington, Hants

Printed and bound in Great Britain by Clays Ltd,
St Ives plc

The Orion Publishing Group's policy is to use papers
that are natural, renewable and recyclable products and
made from wood grown in sustainable forests. The logging
and manufacturing processes are expected to conform to
the environmental regulations of the country of origin.

www.orionbooks.co.uk

To Val and Araminta

One

Lisa Jones was struggling desperately to minimize her cleavage. Breathing in only enhanced it; hunching her shoulders had a similar effect. No matter how hard she tried, sixty-five per cent of her bosom was on display. Which wasn't surprising, as she was a 36DD and her jacket was a size ten.

She was convinced Milo had done it on purpose. The single-breasted red jacket with matching skirt was a departure from the usual skimpy outfits promotions girls wore at motor shows, but Lisa refused to conform to the stereotype. That wasn't what she was about any more. If Milo wanted her on his stand, then he had to accept that she would dress like a businesswoman, not a glamour model. On her thirtieth birthday, six months before, she had decided she was too old to have everything on display. Those days were over. From now on she was to be fully clothed, on or off camera, and if her clients didn't like it they could choose someone else to promote their wares.

Milo obviously disagreed with her decision and bringing her an outfit two sizes too small was his idea of forcing her into a compromise. Once she'd managed to squeeze herself into it, Lisa decided she looked more voluptuous and inviting than if she'd been wearing one of the gold bikinis sported by the girls on the next stand. The jacket acted like a corset, squeezing her waist in and her breasts out. Had Lisa had time she would have gone and bought a polo-neck jumper to go underneath, but thanks to the traffic on the motorway she only had fifteen minutes to get ready before the show opened.

She struggled with the skirt zip, tutting as she discovered that the skirt only just reached mid thigh. She was grateful that she had worn tights and not hold-ups, otherwise she would have spent all day tugging the hem down to cover the tops of her stockings. She surveyed her reflection in the mirror and narrowed her eyes at Milo, who nodded in approval.

'You look gorgeous,' he reassured her. Milo had a large showroom on the outskirts of Coventry, selling 'previously enjoyed' prestige motor cars. This show was the high point of his year, his chance to show off to the general public.

'Don't think I don't realize you did it on purpose,' Lisa retorted, tying her mass of brunette ringlets back into a ponytail in a vain attempt to look businesslike. Even wearing flat shoes wouldn't help. Lisa sighed as she slipped on her black suede courts with the three-inch heels. She didn't want the clients towering over her. There was nothing worse than having to look up at someone who was leering at your décolléte.

Lisa was used to men staring. She was only five foot two, with creamy, luminescent skin, wild dark curls, dancing brown eyes with incredibly long upturned lashes, and rosebud lips that were generally curved into a smile guarded by two of the deepest dimples. That she was ravishingly pretty was the icing on the cake, however, for her real attribute was her hourglass figure, the ultimate glamour girl proportions. It might not be fashionable to have such generous curves – she would never in a million years make the catwalk or the pages of a fashion magazine – but for promotion work, she was ideal: she attracted custom like a magnet. And of course the warmth of her personality, her infectious laugh, her irresistible charm combined with her total professionalism meant she was much in demand.

Despite her misgivings, ten minutes later she was on the stand, smile at the ready, leaflets in hand. The exhibition hall was boiling hot and airless, and she could barely breathe in her restrictive clothing. The bones of her bra were digging in; there was sweat trickling down her back. A burst of music from a neighbouring stand blared out as four dancers writhed around a low-slung black sports car to rapturous applause, drawing an instant audience of middle-aged men who weren't sure which to lust after more, the motor or the girls. Sadly for the majority of them, both were out of reach. The show peddled wares attainable by only a few, but dreaming, as everyone knows, is free. Thus men strode around the exhibition hall looking knowledgeable; surveying the vehicles with arms crossed, nodding their heads sagely in agreement as they debated their various merits, pretending to themselves and those around them that they could actually afford what they were looking at; that it was just a question of weighing up the pros and cons before making their final choice. It was for the most part a charade. Ninety-five per cent of the people attending the show couldn't come close to affording as much as a spare tyre. But that didn't matter: it was the remaining five per cent the exhibitors needed. The five per cent who stood back and kept their counsel, not wishing to look too eager. Although there was always one who couldn't resist showing off, doing a deal in full view of the other visitors, anxious to display their usually new-found wealth and revelling in the envy of passers-by.

By midday, Lisa was dealing with just one of those. In his late fifties, wearing a petrol-blue washed-silk shirt under a leather waistcoat and sporting a neatly clipped grey beard, he was hustling Lisa for a price on a mouthwatering navy-blue Maserati.

'There's no point in trying to negotiate with me. Mr Sweet will be back in a moment,' she said politely, willing Milo to reappear. He always spent most of the show networking, bartering with other dealers. They swapped cars like little boys in a playground swapping Dinky toys, apparently oblivious to the sums of money involved.

'Come on,' he persisted. 'If you can get me some discount, I'll see you right.'

He leaned right in to Lisa, and she breathed in a noxious layer of aftershave.

'I'm sorry. But I'm nothing to do with negotiations. I'm just here to hand out leaflets.'

'Now don't do yourself down. I'm sure you've got influence. And I bet a bit of extra cash wouldn't go amiss, would it?' His eyes gleamed behind his tinted glasses as he gawped at her chest. 'Get yourself something nice to wear.'

Lisa smiled a smile that anyone but a fool would see meant 'back off'.

'Mr Sweet will be back in a moment.'

The man pursed his too-red lips into a little moue of disapproval. Then he gave Lisa another appraising glance. He obviously liked what he saw, as his apparent sulk dissolved and he gave her what he thought was a charming smile.

'Why don't you come out for dinner with me after the show finishes?'

'I don't think so. But thank you.'

'Come on. Admit it. That's why you work here, isn't it? So you can meet someone rich? You'd love to go out in one of these, wouldn't you?'

He indicated the Maserati. Lisa tried hard to bite her tongue, but she'd had enough. Enough of being ogled and propositioned.

'Not if it meant being seen next to you.'

The man stared at her in disbelief.

'What?'

'If I wanted a car like that, I'd buy it. I don't need to prostitute myself.'

'There's no need to be uppity.'

'Yes, there is. You seem to think that I'm for sale.'

'Hold on a minute. I only offered you dinner.'

'And what were you expecting back? A quick grope in return for steak and chips at the nearest gastropub?'

The man opened and shut his mouth like a goldfish. Lisa

4

realized that people were staring, but she was in full flow. Nothing was going to stop her now.

'Why don't you go to that stand over there? I know for a fact that some of those girls aren't fussy, if you're that desperate.'

By now, Milo had reappeared.

'What's going on?'

The bumptious little man turned on his heel to confront Milo. Lisa stood her ground patiently.

'You've just lost yourself a sale. I was about to buy one of your motors, and if this jumped-up little cow hadn't been so rude to me—'

He turned to glare at Lisa, his eyes baleful. She stood with her hands on her hips, knowing that her stance was probably accentuating her embonpoint more than ever, but she was beyond caring. She'd had enough. Enough of peddling dreams to people who couldn't afford it or, worse, to people who could and thought she was part of the package. She didn't want to dress up any more, spend half an hour doing her face before a job because, although she didn't need it, full make-up was expected and you could never look anything less than done up. She didn't want to be a slave to fake tan and pedicures and leg waxing, because you never knew what the job might entail and an even tan, painted toes and smooth skin were expected. Even fully clothed, she was still being treated like a piece of meat.

'I'm sorry, Milo.' Her voice was calm. 'I can't do this any more.'

Milo, desperate to retrieve his sale, smiled at the two of them, poised like prize fighters either side of him.

'I'm sure it's just a misunderstanding. I'm sure this gentleman didn't mean to be rude.'

'Me? Rude? I just wanted to buy a car. I didn't expect to be insulted.' The man looked self-righteously indignant. 'Not that I'm going to buy it now. No bloody way.'

'Don't be rash.' Milo was alarmed. Selling the Maserati

would cover several of the rather disconcerting invoices piled up in his in-tray. 'We can talk about it. That's a beauty, that is. It's got a host of added extras and only eighteen thousand on the clock. I'm sure we can do a deal.'

'I'm sure we can. But I want an apology first.'

Triumphant that he had the upper hand, the man squared his shoulders and tilted his chin, challenging Milo, knowing that extracting an apology from Lisa was less likely than the Maserati sprouting wings and flying out of the exhibition hall. There was no doubt he was enjoying the scenario.

Milo looked pleadingly at Lisa.

'Lisa . . .'

'No way.'

Milo took her by the elbow and led her out of earshot, speaking sotto voce.

'I'll make it up to you. I can't afford to lose this sale.'

'I'm sorry, Milo.'

'Please, Lisa. I can make the best part of fifteen grand. Just apologize.'

'You can't be serious.'

'Oh yes I can.'

'You're expecting me to grovel to that patronizing, lecherous lowlife?'

Milo swallowed. 'Yes.'

Lisa took a deep breath in. The situation encapsulated everything she hated about her job. The bullshit, the posturing, the egos. The fact that money was the driving force, that all morals were jeopardized in its pursuit. That Milo, who she'd done shows for on and off for nearly ten years, cared more about his profit margins than her feelings. Yes, she could have swallowed her pride and apologized. But she would have felt degraded and belittled and worthless – even though Milo would have bunged her a couple of hundred quid as a sop.

Lisa decided that she was worth more than that. She shook her head defiantly, her curls springing loose from their ponytail.

'I'm off.'

'You can't just leave.'

'I can.'

'You won't work for me again.'

Lisa looked him in the eye.

'Milo,' she said gently, 'I don't want to.'

Milo blinked once as he debated how to retrieve the situation. Bribing Lisa wasn't going to work, so he tried a threat.

'I'll do you for breach of contract. And loss of business, if I don't get this sale.'

'I'll do you for sexual harassment.'

'I've never laid a finger on you!'

'Expecting me to wear this uniform is degrading and humiliating. I'm sure a good solicitor would find a case.'

Milo looked shocked.

'Lisa – I didn't mean to offend you. I never knew you felt so strongly—'

'Well, I do. I'm a human being, you know. Not just an impressive cleavage.'

She took off her jacket and threw it at him, well aware that now she was in full view of the entire hall in just her best Rigby & Peller bra and a tiny skirt.

'There you go. Is that what you want?'

Milo's mouth was hanging open. Lisa put out her arms and did a twirl for the audience that was gathering round his stand.

'Happy? Now you've got everyone's attention?'

A flash went off, followed by another, and Lisa struck a Page Three pose to tumultuous applause, then turned on her heel and stalked through the screens at the back of the stand to the tiny cubicle which acted as both changing room and office. With shaking hands she pulled off the red skirt and tugged her jeans and T-shirt back on as quickly as she could.

'Well, Lisa Jones. I think that's called making an exhibition of yourself,' she said to her reflection, before putting on her coat and dashing for the exit.

*

Twenty minutes later, she flung her parking money at the startled attendant and was out of the car park before the barrier was fully raised. As she drove back down the motorway, her mobile chirruped into life. She pushed the hands-free.

'Hi.'

'Lisa. What the hell do you think you're playing at?'

As she'd expected, it was her agent.

'I'm sorry, Tony. But I've had enough.'

'You can't just walk off a job. You'll never work again. You know what this business is like. I want you to turn your car straight round and get back on that stand.'

'Not if you paid me a million pounds.'

'What happened?'

Lisa knew that being ogled by the entire exhibition centre wouldn't be a good enough reason. She sighed.

'Nothing. I've decided to jack it in, that's all.'

'You could have picked a better moment. You could have picked a less important client to do over. Milo Sweet's one of my best customers. And he's got the biggest mouth in the West Midlands.'

Lisa felt a momentary pang of guilt. But then she recalled how Tony had strong-armed her into the job against her will in the first place. She wasn't going to be manipulated any longer.

'Get one of your other girls to help him forget,' she said tartly.

'You won't get paid.'

'Of course I won't. I'm not that stupid.'

'And you're off my books. You're fired.'

Never mind that it was the first time she'd let him down since she started working for him when she was seventeen. Never mind that she had stood in for his less reliable girls time and again, when they hadn't been able to make it in because they had drunk too much the night before or needed to rush to the chemist for the morning-after pill. She knew that when

8

he'd calmed down he would remember this, that he would be back on the phone pleading with her.

She grinned, revelling in the sweetness of the realization that he needed her more than she needed him.

'Actually, no, Tony. *You're* fired.'

She cut him off, turned on the CD player and flipped through the changer until she found her favourite Fleetwood Mac album. The music was of another age, soothing and re-assuring. She put her foot down, eager to put as many miles between her and the exhibition centre as possible. On the other side of the motorway she saw an Aston Martin zip effortlessly past all the other vehicles. The driver was obviously on his way to the show, perhaps to choose a replacement for his status symbol. Well, good luck to him. She'd be home by four. Just time to nip into Marks & Sparks for something to eat. Not to mention a bottle of wine to drown her sorrows.

Before she sat down and decided what she was going to do with the rest of her life.

In his office, George Chandler had his head in his hands. He was on speaker phone. The tone in his boss's voice was not to be argued with.

'You're not to make any contact at all. Don't phone the hospital. Or his wife. We don't want to make any move that will incur liability.'

'For heaven's sake, Richard, that's totally callous,' George protested. 'He's worked for us for over ten years, and we're not supposed to show concern?'

'You've got it in one.'

'You mean the guy might die and I can't even call his wife? Give her my condolences?'

'George. You know the score. Lawsuit. Litigation. Liability. It's the world we live in, I'm afraid. Anyway, you're going to have enough to deal with. We'll have the insurance guys swarming all over us before we know it. And Health and

Safety. Questions will be asked and it's your head on the chopping block.'

'But he wasn't wearing his safety harness.'

'That's not the point. The balcony gave way. Our fault. Or to be more specific, your fault. I'm sorry.'

Richard hung up. George put his head on his desk in despair. He felt sick. What a perfectly hideous situation.

It was George who was responsible for the maintenance of all the commercial buildings his company managed. Colin, currently lying in hospital with severe head injuries, held the contract to clean all their windows. Flouting all the safety guidelines and regulations, he had failed to wear a safety harness while cleaning the windows of a fourth-floor office. He had slipped, fallen and grabbed on to the balcony which, being merely ornamental, had given way. Colin had plunged four storeys on to the concrete below. And George, it seemed, was liable. He should, it turned out, have ensured that every ornamental balcony they owned could take the weight of a falling man.

When he thought about Colin, he wanted to retch. He had three kids, George knew. The stupid man. Why hadn't he worn his harness? He'd be here now, instead of a bloody mound of broken bones and teeth waiting for a brain scan. Meanwhile, George couldn't even go down and comfort Colin's wife in the hospital corridor while she waited for the results, in case he inadvertently admitted liability. It was a mad world.

George rubbed his hands wearily over his face. Then he picked up his jacket from the back of his chair, scooped up his car keys and walked out of the office. It was only half past two, and he had an important meeting scheduled for three, but he didn't care.

'Cancel my three o'clock,' he said to his secretary, with an uncharacteristic lack of warmth. 'I'm going home.'

'Don't you feel well?' she asked, concerned.

'No,' he said. 'I feel sick. Sick to bloody death of it all.'

Traffic in Bath on a Friday afternoon was notoriously horrendous. Whether people were trying to get in or out of the city, George couldn't be sure. He only needed to cross from one side to the other, but he had sat in a jam for fifteen minutes now, rather detracting from his dramatic exit as it gave him too much time to reflect on whether he had been wise to flee the office like that. He realized that it was the first time in his life that he had skived. Well, adult life. At university skiving had practically been part of the curriculum. Now, he wasn't sure how he felt, knowing he'd left chaos in his wake. His absence at this afternoon's meeting would be a major irritant. Richard would be livid.

But did he care?

On balance, he thought probably not. Over the past few months he had become increasingly overwhelmed by boredom. Disillusionment. Stagnation. After four years in the job, a pattern had set in. He was doing the same things over and over again, following the same old routine. The names and the places might change, but the motivation never differed. The only alteration was the rules and regulations, which became more and more complicated, petty and impossible to work to. Which was why a situation like today had evolved. To George, Colin's accident and its repercussions summed up his frustration with where he was in life.

The future had once been exciting; the world his oyster. At eighteen, he was brimming with promise, and getting into the school of architecture was widely regarded as a ticket to success. He'd be able to do whatever he wanted. Visions of glittering skylines peppered with the curves of his masterpieces filled his dreams. He imagined iconic museums, headquarters that were the jewels in the crowns of international conglomerates, developments that represented the status of the entrepreneurs whose businesses they housed. He foresaw awards and accolades; respect and awe; waiting lists . . .

Reality was somewhat different. He graduated with an

underwhelming second-class degree. The world he had moved into was tough, competitive, and he hadn't lived up to his original promise. Too much partying, maybe. Together with a lack of ruthlessness. An inability to think laterally and provide the spark of originality needed to make him stand out from the rest.

And so now here he was, not someone whose name was bandied about in hushed, reverent tones, but a salaried hack worrying about disabled access; wrangling with the local council over green-field and brown-field and change of use; bartering with them over low-cost housing and mixed development, which he knew meant pleasing no one. Colin's accident epitomized how he had found himself repeatedly compromised and unable to follow his heart, penned in by policies and red tape and EEC directives. It was the last straw.

George knew that, on closer analysis, he was being rather a spoilt brat. In most people's eyes, he would be perceived as successful. His job allowed for quite a few nice lunches, and being dragged round a golf course occasionally. His salary was generous. He found the job easy, if tedious. What was there to moan about?

As he finally made his way past the roadworks that had amplified the Friday traffic jam, and sped up Lansdown Hill, he came to the conclusion that what he wanted was freedom. Freedom to make his own decisions. Creative freedom that wasn't held in check by the whims of bureaucracy. Where he was going to find that, God only knew. George knew he'd be tempting fate by jumping ship – especially when he didn't have another ship to jump to. But today's events highlighted the fact that he owed it to himself to make a decision. Put up and shut up. Or take a risk. And one thing he did know. This was his last chance. He was soon going to be nearer to forty than thirty. Only just, but that made him no spring chicken. If he didn't make a bid for freedom now, he would be trapped for ever.

By three thirty he had reached his house. Amazingly, there

was a parking space not far down the road – one of the benefits of coming home earlier than usual. By the time he got back the spaces were usually taken up and he often had to park two or three streets away. He reversed neatly into the space, knowing that it had probably been vacated by a mother on the school run who would spit tacks when she got back and found it gone.

The house was in a terrace of Georgian houses that were typical of Bath. The street was by no means as grand as the gracious proportions of the Royal Crescent only a few hundred yards away – the most prestigious address in Bath and one George had long aspired to, but that was definitely out of reach. He consoled himself that the houses there were far too large for a single man, and he wouldn't have wanted a mere flat. He'd bought the house in Northampton Street when he'd moved from Bristol five years ago, and it had been badly in need of some tender loving care. Over the years he had given it just that, restoring it to its former glory, obsessively replacing the period detail but at the same time incorporating mod cons. The project had taken up most of his spare time and a large proportion of his wallet, but now he was safe in the knowledge that he had an immaculately restored home that purchasers would be falling over themselves to buy.

He opened the pale grey-green front door, deactivated the essential CCTV and burglar alarm that was sadly all too necessary, even in supposedly genteel Bath, and made his way through into the kitchen. Sparkling stainless-steel appliances were softened by the lustrous cherrywood of the units, built square and no-nonsense and chunky with outsize bun handles and topped with a high-gloss work surface. He pulled open the refrigerator, took out a bottle of Tiger beer and sat down on a chrome bar-stool at the island, swinging his legs casually as if to convince himself that he was relaxed and off duty. In fact, he was as tense as a piano wire.

He wondered about picking up the phone to Lisa, then remembered she was working at some motor show. It was a pity. He felt like taking off somewhere for the weekend, somewhere he might be able to forget the day's dreadful events. If he stayed at home he would be waiting for the phone to ring with news. Or he might be tempted to call the hospital, or even sneak in there to see how Colin was. He'd have to be inhuman not to care about the outcome. And what on earth would his wife think? He couldn't even call her to explain that he couldn't call her.

The trilling of the phone suddenly broke the silence. George didn't answer it in case it was Richard ordering him to come back to the office – he'd already switched his mobile off. He let the answerphone intervene, and was surprised to hear Lisa's voice cut through the silence. Her accent was tinged with a Gloucestershire burr that she always protested she hated, but George thought was charming. It summoned up images of milkmaids dropping curtsies. Or *Cider with Rosie*, which had always been one of his favourite books. But she thought she sounded like a Wurzel.

It brought a smile to his face now, to hear her.

'George! It's me. I just phoned your work and your secretary told me you'd walked out. She seemed to think you were upset about something. What's going on? Give me a ring as soon as you get this message—'

George crossed the room and picked up the handset.

'Hi. It's me.'

'George! What happened? Did you really walk out?'

'Yep.' He quickly filled her in on what had happened.

'What bastards!' She was suitably outraged. 'I don't blame you for walking.'

'No. And I'm tempted not to go back either.'

'Well, you can join the club. It's you and me both.' Lisa sounded defiant. 'I've just told Tony to stick it up his Prada jumper.'

'You're kidding?'

'No. I've had enough. I'm not putting up with it a minute

longer. I've had enough of dirty old men gawping at my chest and thinking I'm easy—'

George chuckled. He knew for a fact that wasn't the case. He should know. He'd been dating Lisa for nearly six months before they'd finally ended up in bed.

'Don't laugh at me. I mean it!' She sounded indignant. George could imagine her eyes sparking dangerously, her chin tilted in the air.

'I'm not laughing at you. I'm laughing because I know you'll have given them what they deserve,' he reassured her swiftly. 'And you're quite right not to put up with it. What are you doing now?'

'I'm still on the motorway. Heading back home. Stuck in the Friday-afternoon traffic.'

'Why don't you carry on and come straight here? We could go away for the weekend. Somewhere we can reflect on our rash behaviour. Sounds like we've both got some thinking to do.'

'That sounds great. I think I'd go mad if I had to stop at home all weekend.'

'Where do you fancy going?'

Lisa thought about it for a moment.

'The seaside. I'd like to go to the seaside.'

'Why not!'

'But I'll have to go home first. I haven't got any clothes with me.'

'Don't bother. I can lend you some stuff. You can sleep in one of my T-shirts. We can buy you some clothes in the morning.'

Lisa giggled. He loved her giggle. It was an elixir. A tonic. If you could bottle it and sell it, it would lift your mood quicker than any prescription.

'I'll borrow a pair of your boxers. I'll be with you as soon as I can.'

As soon as she finished speaking to George, Lisa put her foot down and swooped into the fast lane. She felt better already. It was as if she and George were partners in crime, the pair of them sneaking off, skiving. Instead of turning off for Stratford, where she lived, she stayed on the motorway, grateful that now she was away from the outskirts of Birmingham, the traffic was less heavy. She could be in Bath in less than two hours.

While he was waiting for Lisa, George changed into jeans and a thick olive-green ribbed sweater. He ran his hand through his hair, inspecting it in the mirror. Had he been staying in Bath for the weekend, he would have taken a trip to the barber the next day – he kept it cropped fairly short nowadays, even though it was still thick, because he knew from his friends that once you hit your thirties, hair had a habit of suddenly thinning without you noticing, and the longer it was the worse it looked. So to preclude that ghastly eventuality he went with the regular precision cut, experimenting with his sideboards to ring the changes – long, short, pointy, blunt. He had a special razor for keeping them in trim. This weekend, however, he toyed with forgoing a shave as well as a haircut, going for the unkempt look. Wow, thought George. He was really rebelling.

Casting his appearance to one side, he swiftly packed a leather holdall, sticking in a couple of extra Fruit of the Loom T-shirts for Lisa to sleep in, then got out his road map of Great Britain to look for inspiration. It would be five by the time Lisa got to him, so if they wanted seaside, they'd have to step on it. He traced his finger along the coastline, until it finally came to rest in North Devon.

Mariscombe. He remembered it from his childhood, and he immediately felt a flutter of fond nostalgia. He'd gone there one summer, when he was about eight or nine. Not with his parents, for his mother wouldn't have been seen dead somewhere like Mariscombe. It was far too working class, full of caravans and string vests and chip shops. She wanted yachting types and delicatessens and tasteful pubs – Salcombe or

Lymington were more her scene. It was his uncle and aunt and his noisy brood of cousins that had taken him there, in their clapped-out old camper van, the summer it became clear to George his parents really weren't getting along. Up till then, holidays to him had meant gîtes in the Dordogne, thoroughly boring for a boy of eight who had to plough through plates of unspeakable innards mixed with bitter salad leaves while his parents burbled their appreciation.

So Mariscombe, with its miles of golden sand, the diet of chips and ice cream and the occasional crab sandwich, had been bliss. They'd pitched their three sagging, smelly tents on a gloriously unspoilt cliffside campsite. The farmer who owned it had gone round all the pitches on his bike each morning, bringing fresh eggs and foaming milk. George had put on weight that week, gorging himself on the cooked breakfasts rustled up on the calor gas stove, cream teas, packets of crisps and 99s. A real bucket-and-spade holiday, with sandcastles and rock pools and fishing nets. Even the downside – sunburn and jellyfish and torrential rain – hadn't marred his memory.

Of course, his holidays now were more sophisticated – city breaks in Prague or Budapest, scuba-diving in Egypt, skiing in Canada. Resorts like Mariscombe held few charms for a sophisticated man about town. But seeing it now on the map jogged his memory about an article he had read in the *Sunday Times* only a few weeks ago. An article that was pinpointing property hot spots, predicting what was on the rise, and Mariscombe had been top of their list for holiday investment.

'Surfers' paradise and guaranteed family fun,' the article had proclaimed. *'Mariscombe is rapidly shedding its kiss-me-quick image; the old Victorian guest houses are being transformed into chic apartment blocks, presumably by those developers who can't afford Sandbanks or Rock. It's hot, it's hip. Get in now before it's too late. Mariscombe is next on the map.'*

In his head, George was an entrepreneurial property developer with interesting projects dotted all over the countryside. In reality all he had was the house in Bath – although to say 'all' was to diminish its worth, which was probably tipping three quarters of a million. Not a bad return on his money. Nevertheless, he liked to keep his eye on which areas of the countryside were flourishing, just in case he one day decided to throw caution to the wind and extend his mortgage.

The article about Mariscombe had intrigued him. And there was no doubt it was the perfect place for him and Lisa to blow the cobwebs away. He imagined long, bracing walks along the beach and the clifftops, scrumptious cream teas by a roaring log fire in some cosy tearoom, a gourmet supper somewhere followed by sweet dreams in a luxurious four-poster bed . . .

Suddenly the doorbell broke his reverie. Lisa was on the step – he could see her red Mazda MX5 double-parked outside.

George opened the door with a wide smile.

Lisa threw her arms round his neck.

'It's so good to see you. I want to get away. Shall we go in my car? I filled up with petrol.'

'Sure. But you better let me drive. You must be exhausted.'

He picked up his bag, his Australian wax jacket with the nubuck collar and cuffs, punched the code into his security system and led the way out. Lisa followed him.

'So where are we going?'

'Mariscombe. I used to go there when I was a kid. I read an article in the *Sunday Times* about it the other day. They predicted it as the Next Big Thing. Property hot spot.' He chucked the map at her. 'It's on the North Devon coast. It'll only take us a couple of hours to get there, with the wind behind us.'

'Do we need to book a hotel?'

'No. Let's just wing it. There's bound to be places to stay. We'll take pot luck when we get there.'

He turned the key in the ignition, suddenly excited. This felt like a real adventure, and the fact that they had both walked off their jobs that afternoon gave it an extra frisson. Next to him, Lisa pulled her seat belt across her chest.

'Drive on!' she commanded. 'I'll put on the Beach Boys.'

'It's not exactly California Dreamin',' warned George. 'It's the British seaside in February.'

'I don't care,' said Lisa. 'Anyway, that was the Mamas and Papas.'

George took it steady on the motorway. Rain began in earnest as they inched past Bristol in the rush-hour traffic. By the time they drove down the hill into Mariscombe two hours later, the wind was howling, the rain was lashing the windows and neither of them could see a thing.

'We'll try the Esplanade first,' decided George. 'There's loads of hotels along there.'

They crawled past the houses that lined the seafront, peering to see if there was a vacancy, but there wasn't a glimmer of welcome anywhere.

'I suppose it is off season.' George upped the speed of the windscreen wipers but it had no effect; the rain was coming down faster than the blades could cope with. They were now heading up the steep, winding hill that led from the centre of the village to Higher Mariscombe. George knew from memory that there was a treacherous drop to their left-hand side, and strained his eyes to ensure they didn't leave the road.

'There!'

Lisa pointed excitedly to a white sign with 'The Rocks' badly painted on it, and underneath another notice proclaiming 'Vacancies'. George drew to a halt and they peered out of the window in vain.

'How do we know what it's like?'

As they hesitated, the rain redoubled its efforts. Lisa shrugged.

'I really don't care. Let's go for it. It's either that or sleep in the car park.'

George pointed his car cautiously up the vertical drive.

'Are you sure? It doesn't exactly scream Rocco Forte.'

'How bad can it be?'

George didn't answer. The trio of gnomes peeping out from behind the gatepost said it all.

The car park of The Rocks was empty, apart from an ancient Peugeot presumably belonging to the owner. The hotel loomed in front of them, a large Victorian house, grey and forbidding, but a light gave them a glimmer of hope. They stood in the porch, unable to see through the frosted glass, and rang the old-fashioned brass bell.

'It's like a Hammer Horror movie,' whispered Lisa, clinging to George's hand. 'And nobody knows we're here. We might never be heard of again.'

'Come on. Let's drive back to Exeter. We'll get the number of a decent hotel. We can phone ahead and book a room—'

'Too late. There's someone coming.'

A shadow had indeed appeared through the glass and someone fumbled at the locks before flinging open the door triumphantly.

'There we go. Sorry, ducks. Didn't hear you. I had the telly turned up that loud to drown out the sound of the rain. Come in, come in – you'll catch your deaths.'

Lisa and George exchanged dubious glances. Their prospective hostess loomed in the doorway, nearly six foot tall and three foot wide, a rose-pink quilted dressing gown wrapped round her and held in place with a mismatched towelling belt. Her iron-grey hair was enveloped in a net which met an enormous pair of spectacles halfway down her forehead. Her grin was welcoming; her tombstone teeth leaned at alarming angles.

'Are you . . . open?' faltered Lisa, hoping fervently the answer would be 'no' and they could revert to plan B.

'My dear, I'm always open. Nearly everyone else closes after the Christmas break till Easter, but not me. No skin off my nose. I'm here anyway, after all. No point in turning good custom away. What do you want, a double room for the night? Or two?'

'Um, just the one.'

'Come on in. I'm Mrs Websdale. But you can call me Webby. Everyone does.'

She ushered them inside. George and Lisa followed uncertainly in her wake. The entrance hall was cavernous, the floor covered in acres of brown and orange patterned carpet, the elaborate wallpaper barely visible behind items that represented a lifetime of collecting: stuffed fish in glass cases, a shelf full of reproduction Victorian dolls staring blankly into space, a display of silk fans, all illuminated by the stingy glow of some heavily tasselled wall lights. In one corner stood a large, ugly grandfather clock; in the other a suit of armour.

'It's the Addams Family,' whispered Lisa.

'Freaky.' George shuddered. He couldn't cope with kitsch that wasn't tongue in cheek.

'I always keep the two main bedrooms made up, in case of passing trade,' Mrs Websdale informed them cheerily as she climbed the stairs. 'I'll give you the one with the best view.'

She stopped outside a door with a white plastic number three stuck on and threw it open dramatically. The room was extremely large, but somehow made to feel small because of the overpowering decor. What really frightened George was that someone had given it considerable thought. The wallpaper was green and pink embossed stripes up to dado rail height, above which was a profusion of flowers which matched the curtains. The buttoned Dralon headboard was green and the eiderdown pink, trimmed with some of the material left over from making the curtains. The attempt to coordinate everything stopped at floor level, however, as the carpet matched the one in the hallway, clashing swirls of brown and orange. The furniture was large, heavy and ugly – salerooms all over the country were groaning with similar items that never got a bid.

'The bathroom to this room isn't technically en suite, which is why I can't charge as much as some of these places that'll give you a room no bigger than a shoebox.' Mrs Websdale tutted. 'The tourist board have got funny ideas. But, anyway, it won't matter to you because there's no one here tonight to share with, so you'll have it all to yourself. Unless you want me to come and scrub your back.'

She winked at George and gurgled with laughter as she led them further down the corridor to a door. An enamel sign depicting a lady reclining in a mound of bubbles hinted that this was the bathroom. Firmly in line with the house colour scheme, the suite was pink, the carpet tiles on the floor green. At the bottom of the bath lurked a plastic mat, and clinging on to the surface with suction cups was a blow-up pillow. A curling bar of Wright's coal tar lay in the soap dish. There was a shagpile bath mat in luminous shrimp.

'There's constant hot water so feel free to have a bath each, deep as you like. And help yourself to bubbles.'

Mrs Websdale proudly held up a supersize bottle of supermarket own brand bubble bath.

'Lovely,' said Lisa faintly.

She escorted them back to their room. Moments later the door was shut behind them, and George and Lisa looked at each other in disbelief.

'Don't say I don't spoil you.'

Lisa grinned.

'Listen, I'm so exhausted I could sleep on a clothes line.'

'I'm sorry it's so awful. We should have carried on looking. Or perhaps we should have just stayed at my place.'

Lisa put her bag on the bed and looked round the room.

'Don't be silly. I've stayed in worse places than this.'

George looked horrified.

'Really?'

'You should see some of the dumps they put us up in at exhibitions. At least this is clean.'

George looked at the white and gold melamine dressing table and shuddered. Lisa thumped him on the arm.

'You are such a snob.'

There was a tap at the door and Mrs Websdale popped her head round.

'I don't suppose you've eaten, have you?'

'We thought we might pop out. We wondered if you could recommend somewhere local. Perhaps a fish restaurant?'

George felt certain that, given Mariscombe's meteoric rise, the equivalent of Rick Stein's would be only five minutes' drive away. Mrs Websdale pursed her lips thoughtfully, as if mentally perusing the suitability of several local Michelin-starred eateries, before delivering her verdict.

'There'll only be the Mariscombe Arms open. But they stop serving at half eight in winter, and to be honest from what I've heard the cooking's not up to much at this time of year. The chef goes off to his villa in Spain come New Year. Or there's the Jolly Roger but Friday night's karaoke night and I don't think that's quite what you're after, somehow.'

'No . . .'

'I don't mind. I love karaoke.' Lisa was always one to look on the bright side, but George looked more than alarmed at the prospect. Mrs Websdale smiled at him kindly.

'Don't worry. I can do you a bit of supper if you like. I don't usually do evening meals but I've got a couple of chops left over.' She patted George on the arm reassuringly. 'Come down to the dining room when you've freshened up. I'll make sure you don't go hungry.'

The door shut behind her before they could demur. George picked up his bag with determination.

'Right. Let's just get in the car and go.'

'We can't offend her. She's been so sweet.'

'We can pretend we've had an urgent phone call.'

'It's not going to kill you to stay here. Just for one night. We can find somewhere extra special tomorrow. I'm too tired to go and find somewhere else now. And I'm ravenous.'

'You're not seriously going to eat her chops?'

'Yes, I am. You can stay up here and starve if you want to.'

George relented, putting his bag back on the bed.

'You're a hard woman.'

'No, I'm not. I'm a tired and hungry woman who doesn't want to hurt an old lady's feelings. So come on.' Lisa poked him mischievously in the ribs. 'Freshen up.'

The dining room was spectacularly dreary. And brown. Full-length brown velvet curtains fell to a brown carpet, and heavy brown furniture loomed in every ill-lit corner. More glass cases full of truculent fish were interspersed with amateurish seascapes and rather incongruous prints of African wildlife. The air hung thick with the smell of tinned soup, which duly arrived in mock earthenware tureens decorated with smiling root vegetables.

'There.' Mrs Websdale stood back proudly, then peeled the cling film off a plate of white sliced bread and butter. 'Lovely minestrone. That should warm you through. Would you like a nice sherry to go with it?'

George bit back the urge to reply that yes, a crisp, dry Monzanilla would be perfect, as it was obvious that his and Webby's idea of a nice sherry were two different things.

Lisa beamed at her, anxious to avert an incident.

'Actually, Mrs Websdale, what I'd really love is a nice cuppa.'

'Webby, remember.'

'Webby.'

'And I only do Typhoo. None of your herbal rubbish.'

'Good thing too,' Lisa assured her. 'Just a splash of milk and two sugars, please.'

'Strong and sweet, eh? Like your man?'

Webby waddled off, cackling. George raised his eyes to the ceiling, then wished he hadn't. It was Artexed to within an inch of its life, with a monstrous false ceiling rose from which hung a heavy wooden chandelier with red tasselled lampshades.

'Where are the taste police when you need them?'

Lisa kicked him under the table.

'Get real, George. You've been in Bath too long. You can't be surrounded by perfection all your life.'

'I don't see why not. You do realize there are proper encaustic tiles under this ghastly carpet?'

'For heaven's sake, just relax. We can find somewhere else tomorrow.'

George ploughed his way reluctantly through the lukewarm soup, then tackled the subsequent pork chops, boiled potatoes, frozen peas and puddles of Bisto as best he could. Lisa was beside herself with mirth. George, who was an inveterate foodie and had never touched a gravy granule in his life, tried not to mind that he was having the mickey taken out of him.

Webby cleared the plates away.

'The best I can do for dessert is tinned fruit cocktail.'

'My favourite,' said Lisa, before George could decline.

Moments later two metal bowls brimming with squares of peach, pineapple and the odd cherry were deposited in front of them, along with an aerosol can. George looked askance as Lisa picked it up and squirted a whirl of cream on to her fruit with a flourish.

'For heaven's sake, don't look so po-faced.' She brandished the can playfully. 'Do you think she'd notice if we took this to bed with us?'

She gave her best dirty chuckle and George managed a smile, despite himself. Although he didn't show it, he was grateful for Lisa's chirpy optimism. She'd managed to make him see the funny side of their situation, and he knew he deserved it when she teased him. She was right, after all. He did live in a perfect little world of his own making. He needed bringing down to earth from time to time, and she was just the girl to do it. He watched her spooning the fruit cocktail into her mouth, as if it was the finest selection of fresh tropical fruits prepared by a top chef. She ran her tongue over her bottom lip, licking away the last of the cream, and George felt his heart beat a little faster.

He put his hand over hers.

'Come on,' he said. 'Let's go and crash.'

She put down her spoon.

'Good idea,' she said. 'I'm exhausted. It's been a crazy day.'

Ten minutes later, he cuddled her to him. She was deliciously warm and snug. She smelt gorgeous, of the cocoa butter body cream she rubbed on religiously every night. He could feel her skin through his T-shirt. He ran his hand up her inner thigh, stroking her gently.

'How exhausted are you, exactly?' he whispered.

Two

Lisa woke the next morning with a racing pulse and a burning sensation in her stomach that could have been the indigestible supper from the night before, but was more likely to be stress. She felt a sudden onset of panic as her actions of the day before replayed in her mind. What the hell had she been thinking of, walking off the job like that? In the cold light of dawn, her resolution melted away, her principles faded, her righteous indignation dissolved and she felt rather sick. She'd completely overreacted.

She shivered as she imagined the sort of revenge that Tony and Milo might cook up between them. They were both the sort of people you wanted on your side, people who didn't take kindly to being crossed, and she'd heard tales about them that in the past she'd chosen to ignore. Only now the rumours became amplified in her imagination, and she pictured slashed tyres at best. Or a mysterious house fire. She tried to reassure herself – what had she done, after all? She hadn't committed a crime. But her performance would have made a fool of Milo, and he in turn would have made Tony suffer for it. She could imagine the two of them talking, planning their revenge . . .

What should she do? She must have been mad. Not only had she made enemies, she had a mortgage to pay, not to mention the loan on the car she'd taken out. Lisa hadn't overstretched herself, but she certainly couldn't afford not to work. It was too early to call Tony and give him a grovelling apology. But even as she toyed with this possibility in her mind, Lisa knew that a situation like yesterday's had been brewing. Her heart hadn't been in her work for a long time. She couldn't backtrack, or they would win. Nevertheless, she felt slightly unsettled at the thought that she might have burned her bridges.

She slid out from between the sheets as quietly as she could and pulled on her jeans from yesterday. George was out for the count, and she didn't want to worry him. She knew that this was the time when fears were imagined, and that it might all seem better in the light of day. She crept down the corridor, down the thick carpet of the main stairs. A cuckoo clock informed her that it was ten past seven. Not as early as she thought. What she needed was a cup of tea. She pushed open the door of the dining room and was surprised to find that the heavy brown curtains had already been pulled back. Fingers of early morning light were tentatively filtering through the windows as Lisa threaded her way through the tables to look outside.

What she saw made her gasp. The view was absolutely breathtaking. She hadn't realized last night that The Rocks was perched on the edge of a cliff, only separated from a vertiginous drop by twenty yards of sloping lawn. Fifty feet below, giant waves hurled themselves against the eponymous rocks, the force throwing up rivulets of spume like celebratory champagne shooting from a bottle. The sea was grey. No, green. No, surely blue? It moved through the spectrum with the ever-changing light, impossible to pin down. Clouds were scudding furiously across the sky, like a flock of sheep frightened by a wayward dog, and as she watched they parted to reveal a patch of brilliant blue sky. To the east, around a thick finger of land that obviously separated Higher Mariscombe from Lower, she could see the golden sands of the resort, the spectacular surf rushing in with an enthusiasm that belied the time of day, for anyone with any sense must surely still be sleeping. And to the west, a rocky cliff jutted far out into the sea, still shrouded in the last of an early morning mist that was gradually receding.

Lisa shivered as the cold air insinuated its way through the flimsy fabric of George's T-shirt. She spotted an electric fan heater. Bending down as surreptitiously as she could, she flicked the switch to full.

'That's it. You make sure you're warm enough. I'm used to this bracing sea air, but I expect you're used to central heating on all night. Mine doesn't kick in till half seven.' Webby sailed past, still in her rose-pink dressing gown, bearing a metal teapot. 'Lovely cup of tea for you.'

'Thank you.'

'You're up early.'

'I'm terrible. Once I'm awake that's it. And I wanted to start exploring.' Lisa indicated the view. 'Isn't it amazing?'

'You never tire of it, I tell you. You can stand here and see every sort of weather. It might be bright sunshine in one corner and thunderclouds in the other.'

'How long have you been here?'

'Fifteen years. Since my husband took early retirement from the electricity board. We bought this place with some money he had from when his old mum died.' She made a face. 'Wouldn't be able to afford it now, mind. Prices have gone through the roof. Not that I mind.' She gave a mischievous grin. 'I shall cash in all right.'

'Are you selling?'

Mrs Websdale nodded vigorously, her fleshy cheeks wobbling.

'Bill passed away last autumn.'

'Oh, I'm sorry.' Lisa looked stricken, but Mrs Websdale flapped away her commiseration with a hand that sported a surprising amount of gold jewellery.

'Don't be, love. He went quick enough. Didn't know a thing about it. I struggled on last year. I don't mind the breakfasts and the bed-changing, but it's the maintenance. I can't be running up ladders at my age, changing light bulbs and cleaning out gutters. And I'm not paying any other bugger to do it. No, I'll cash in my chips and get myself a nice little flat somewhere warm. Should leave me enough to finance a toyboy.'

Lisa looked rather startled as Mrs Websdale collapsed into gales of wheezy laughter, not sure whether to take the old bird seriously or not.

'In fact,' Mrs Websdale struggled to continue through her mirth, 'he's just my type. If it wasn't for the fact he's obviously spoken for, he'd have to watch out.'

She pointed a fat finger and Lisa turned to see George in the doorway. She had to admit he did look divine, still sleepy with his hair sticking up, in a blue sweatshirt and jeans. She couldn't help but join in the laughter at the prospect of Webby toying with him.

'What's the joke?' he asked indignantly.

'Nothing, duck,' Mrs Websdale reassured him. 'You're quite safe, it's all right. Thirty years ago it might have been a different story.'

George looked at Lisa in bewilderment, but she beckoned him over to the window.

'Come and look at this incredible view.' She turned back to Webby. 'You must get tired of people saying it.'

George came to stand by her, as Webby poured him a cup of tea.

'Wow.'

'If you want to go for a quick stroll, I'll do you a nice cooked breakfast for when you get back,' Webby offered as she passed him his cup. 'There's a little path at the end of the garden that leads down to a small beach.'

'Come on! Let's go, while the weather's still fine.' Lisa was dancing up and down with impatience.

What George really wanted was a pot of fresh Costa Rican coffee and the Saturday *Times*, but that seemed unlikely, so he submitted to Lisa's pleas with as much grace as he could muster. He gave a long-suffering grin.

'I'll go and get our coats.'

As he left the room, Mrs Websdale followed him hungrily with her eyes.

'He's gorgeous, isn't he?'

'He's not bad.'

'You going to marry him?'

Lisa was slightly taken aback by the directness of the question.

'No,' she replied carefully. 'Actually, I'm not. I'm not going to marry anyone. I don't believe in it.'

Webby sucked in her breath through her teeth, showing disapproval.

'Lovely girl like you?'

Lisa turned to look out of the window, her hands curled round her mug.

'There's only one way to go once you're married,' she replied carefully. 'And that's down.'

'That's very cynical.' Webby looked rather upset by this diagnosis. 'Mr Websdale and I worshipped each other until the day he drew his dying breath.'

'Well, you're lucky then.' Lisa was brisk. 'Personally, I'm not prepared to take the risk.'

She put her mug back on the table to indicate that the conversation was over. Then she smiled, wondering if perhaps she'd been a little abrupt.

'We'll just go for a quick walk on the beach. We won't be long.'

Webby nodded.

'I'll keep your breakfast warm.'

She watched Lisa weaving her way back through the tables. She was such a beautiful girl. Not stick thin, like most women these days. Curvaceous, rounded. Webby wondered what on earth it was that had given her such a hard attitude. Perhaps she'd been jilted by some bastard. Badly treated. Webby couldn't imagine why anyone would want to treat a gorgeous creature like Lisa badly, but people were strange. And selfish. She'd seen enough horror stories unfold under this very roof – last-ditch attempts to come on holiday in order to save a floundering marriage. She'd seen everything, from stony silences to blazing rows. But there'd been happy endings too . . .

She gathered up the dirty cups and trotted back to the kitchen. From the back window, she could see Lisa and George, hand in hand, crossing the lawn, and she smiled. Maybe the sea would work its magic. It often did.

Lisa had grown up over the family chip shop in the rough end of Gloucester, near the docks. Not near enough for it to be interesting, just so that the dregs passed by on their way back home from the pub. It was run by her dad, Bob, who'd been in the catering corps and so knew a thing or two about cooking for hordes of people. And her mum, Julie. Warm, sparkling, pint-sized Julie, who knew enough of everyone's business to keep a witty banter going when they came in for their chips. Who could stop a fight with one word, if the customers got lairy. Who could memorize the order for a queue of fifteen and time their haddock or cod's roe to perfection, so that it emerged crisp and golden from the oil just as they reached the counter.

From the potato delivery at five o'clock in the morning, to the last cone of chips scooped out at about half eleven at night, it was a tough life. And the Joneses had learned the hard way to keep it in the family, because with a cash business you couldn't trust anyone else. It was incredible how people just couldn't resist doing you, even if it was as simple as not charging their mates for a portion of mushy peas. As Bob said, look after the mushy peas and the pounds will look after themselves. They had become adept at spotting all the tricks, but in the end it wore you down. In the end it was easier not to employ anyone. You couldn't diddle yourself, after all.

So from the age of thirteen, Lisa was hands on. Her parents hadn't forced her into it by any means, but to her it seemed obvious that she should help, and it gave her money to spend at a time when she was starting to long for fashionable shoes, make-up and music; stuff she didn't want to fleece her parents for. Home from school by four, she just had time to change and grab something to eat before she put on her apron and took her place behind the counter. The chippie opened for the evening at five, and apart from the odd lull when the soaps were on and just before the pubs shut, it was non-stop.

For a few years, they were on the gravy train. The Joneses took pride in their chips being the best in town, because they changed the oil regularly and only used the freshest fish. There was no room for soggy batter, reheated chips or lukewarm curry sauce in The Happy Plaice. The salad for the pitta kebabs was never limp. And the place was scrupulously clean. The white tiles gleamed, the steel counter sparkled, and from the sound system trickled out the mellow sounds of Joni Mitchell, Carly Simon and Neil Young – a fan of the seventies, Julie was well known for her impromptu solos as she sang along to her favourites, and her regulars would smile and listen for a moment before putting in their order.

Despite the hard work, Lisa and her parents enjoyed their time off. Sundays were sacrosanct and always spent together – they would go to the countryside, for lunch in a pub. Or Lisa and her mum Julie would go off shopping to one of the big malls while Bob messed with the motor. And once a year they would go to Spain, while Julie's sister Andrea and her husband came to look after the chippie for a week – a much-needed rest.

They loved Spain. Julie and Lisa were both sun-worshippers. They stayed in the best hotel they could afford and ate out every night, wallowing in the luxury of someone else having to do the hard work for a change. And every time they went, they talked about emigrating, buying a little bar. They knew people who had done it. The last summer they went, they viewed a development of villas clustered around a swimming pool, the air heavy with the scent of orange blossom.

'We could do it,' Julie would say wistfully. 'One of these villas. Not a big one, but maybe with a sea view. Running a bar here can't be any harder work than The Happy Plaice. And at least it would be sunny.'

'Five more years,' Bob promised. 'We'll do it when we've got enough cash.'

'That'll be never then.' Julie sighed. 'It's the bloody winters that get me down.'

Lisa had looked at her mum with new eyes. She'd never realized she got down. Her mum was always so cheerful, so quick with a smile and a hug, always laughing and singing. But she sensed the weariness in her that August. Maybe it was because her mum had just turned forty. Some hormonal change that was sapping her strength.

By October, it became clear to everyone that it wasn't just middle age that was creeping up on Julie. She became overwhelmed with tiredness, headaches, blurred vision. She never complained, but it was evident to everyone who saw her that she was suffering. She looked pale, exhausted, with dark rings under her eyes. And she had no zest for anything. She didn't sing any more. She couldn't even bear the noise of the sound system.

Lisa eventually forced her to see the doctor. The speed at which the medical profession reacted told them everything was not well. Within a fortnight, Julie had been taken in and operated on, the majority of her insides scooped out like the seeds from a melon. And even though the operation was technically deemed a success, the prognosis wasn't good. The malignant cells had seen fit to take themselves off on their own journey, exploring Julie's body for somewhere else to settle and grow, and had made themselves comfortable in various other hiding places where the surgeons couldn't get at them.

Bob went into denial. Tight-lipped and silent, he carried on running the shop. Lisa redoubled her efforts, even though no one expected a fifteen-year-old to take on the responsibilities. But someone had to, while her mother underwent the aggressive chemo necessary to blast the remaining tumours into oblivion. It was Lisa who went into Boots and bought a pair of clippers to shave off the remains of her mother's dark curls, then lovingly massaged her poor, sore scalp with sweet-smelling lotions until Julie fell asleep in her arms, exhausted and drained.

Lisa's head teacher eventually discovered what Lisa was going through. Lisa never cried at home, but after an assembly for the sick, incensed by the fact that most of her peers had whispered and laughed their way through it, she had broken down completely. Bob was called in. The head was as gentle as she could be, but she was also firm. Lisa could not be expected to shoulder the burden of her mother's illness, help run the chip shop and do her school work. Mr Jones was relying too heavily upon her. Surely there was other family that could help?

And so Aunt Andrea stepped into the breach.

Lisa had never trusted her Aunt Andrea. She was a tougher, harder version of her mother: the same features, but harsher, over-made-up, worked out, sun-bedded. Andrea was too ready with her demands and her opinions. She drank and smoked too much, her skirts were too short, her hair too blond. And Lisa didn't like the way Andrea touched her dad. All the time. She touched everybody – she was very tactile. But her hands seemed to linger that little bit longer on Bob. Lisa was suspicious. Especially as she knew that her Aunt Andrea's marriage to her husband Phil was rocky. Phil had warned her himself.

'Watch her,' he said. 'Andrea is only interested in one thing and that's money. Which is why she's gone off me. Being as my business has gone down the drain.'

He smiled ruefully at his own attempt at humour. Phil was a plumber – a wizard with a spanner but hopeless at running a business. Several bad debts had buggered up his cash flow and he'd ended up bankrupt. Andrea had been less than support-ive, apparently. Her eagerness to help her sister out could only be seen as questionable, in Phil's eyes.

'She's gone on and on about that bloody cabriolet,' Phil went on. 'As if I can magic one out of a hat.'

Bob had bought a second-hand soft-top Golf as a surprise for Julie's fortieth. It was their pride and joy, and Julie loved going out in it.

'I'm not being flash,' Bob had insisted. 'I've worked hard for it. But it's our little treat. What's the point, otherwise?'

Andrea obviously saw it as an indication that there was more where that came from.

When Julie became too ill to do anything other than lie in bed, Aunt Andrea moved in. She grafted, Lisa had to give her that, because as well as working in the chippie and running the house, she nursed Julie – before the doctor gently suggested that she be moved into the hospice. That was when they knew.

It was the most dreadful few weeks. How time drags when you are waiting for someone to die, thought Lisa. Half of you praying for a miracle, the other half praying for release, as you watch the person you love decompose, wilting faster than a discarded wedding bouquet. Lisa had to get the bus to the hospice, as Bob couldn't bear to visit. He used the chippie as an excuse, but Lisa knew he was being an ostrich, that for every day he didn't go he could kid himself that the next time he visited there would be an improvement, that Julie would be sitting up and laughing, scoffing her way through a box of Milk Tray brought by some other well-meaning visitor. Instead of lying, limp, exhausted, defeated, unable to even lift the remote to change channels on the tiny portable telly they'd brought into her room so she could keep up with the latest shenanigans in Albert Square.

One Tuesday, unable to face double maths because there really didn't seem any point – after all, she could add up five portions of fish and chips in her head quickly enough – Lisa went home and found her dad and Andrea in bed together. In the middle of the afternoon, with the curtains shut and George Benson on the stereo. She stood with her arms crossed while Andrea shot off to the bathroom and locked herself in and her dad pulled on his trousers.

'You could have waited until Mum actually died.'

'Lisa, love. A man has . . . needs.'

'You could have gone elsewhere for that. There's plenty enough places in Gloucester.'

Bob looked shocked.

'I'd never do that!'

'But you'd screw Mum's own sister.'

'I don't actually think she'd mind if she knew.'

'Don't you?' Lisa's eyes were hard. 'Shall we ask her, then?'

Bob went pale, not realizing that Lisa had no intention of taking what she'd seen any further.

'Please. Don't.'

He put out a hand to touch her, but Lisa drew back.

'It's your money she's after, Dad. Not your body.'

'Money.' Bob snorted disdainfully.

'There's the life insurance. Or didn't you know about it? I bet Andrea does.'

When the man from the insurance company came round once a month, Lisa watched her mother count out the premiums in greasy cash. She'd looked at the officious little weasel warily as he slid it into his document wallet.

'You'll be grateful enough if anything happens to either of them,' he'd said once as a parting shot to Lisa, disappearing off in his ill-fitting suit with the too-short trousers.

Lisa knew if it had been left to her father, he wouldn't bother with life insurance. He didn't even bother with car insurance. It was Julie who made sure everything was paid up. Before she went into the hospice, she'd gone through the paperwork with Lisa.

'I don't want to bother your dad. He can't cope with it. But these are the important ones – and don't forget the MOT. Sid from the garage will come and pick the car up and drop it back if you just tell him. Preferably before it runs out. I've marked it all up in the diary.'

Julie's eyes had been bright that day, and Lisa felt a surge of hope that perhaps she was on the turn, that perhaps Mother Nature had had a change of heart. But she hadn't.

Andrea stood next to Bob at the funeral. Lisa wore a red dress that she and her mum had chosen on their last shopping trip together. And when she saw her aunt's fingers close around her father's, Lisa felt sick. Phil had been at the funeral, because he had always got on with Julie, but he lingered at the back and made his escape before he came face to face with his wife. Not before he'd given Lisa a hug, though.

'I'm so sorry,' he'd managed to croak gruffly, and she wasn't sure if he meant about her mum, or about her dad and Andrea.

Lisa moved in with a friend from school, so she could finish her exams, though she felt rather halfhearted about them. She missed her mum so much she felt ill, and seeing Andrea take her place made it worse. Her father couldn't talk to her about it. He couldn't defend his decision, but it was obviously his way of coping. She realized how weak he was and she despised him for it. How could he possibly view Andrea as a replacement for Julie?

The chip shop soon ran itself down. Andrea cut corners, changed suppliers, didn't have the warmth or the charm or the rapport with the customers. And although Bob toiled away in the background, trying to keep it all together, his heart wasn't in it. The place was dirty – the tiles coated in grease, the floor muddy, the air thick with burned oil. Where Julie had made sure there were freshly laundered and ironed overalls for each shift, they were now worn for days on end.

And all the while, that long hot summer, Andrea drove around in Julie's car, with the roof down and the stereo blaring, her peroxide curls ruffling in the wind, tapping her painted nails on the steering wheel.

Lisa didn't have the energy to remonstrate with her father. To try and open his eyes to what was happening. She knew she had to get away from Gloucester, make a new life for herself somewhere else, before she was eaten up with resentment. She was getting harder by the day. And she wanted to be like her mum. Happy, optimistic, warm, generous to the last. Not like grasping, cold, hard-hearted Andrea. The final blow came when the news filtered through to her that The Happy Plaice had been sold. Bob and Andrea had bought a bar in Spain. Courtesy of the insurance pay-out. Courtesy of her mum's cancer, actually, when you looked at it closely. Now Lisa knew she could never forgive her father. For not allowing her mother to fulfil her dream. And giving it instead to Andrea.

From that day on, Lisa was determined never to rely on anyone else for her happiness. Or to give too much of herself away. That way she could never be compromised. No one could ever do to her what her father had done to her mother. Bob had loved Julie with all his heart, yet he had still found it within himself to betray her. If that was true love, thought Lisa, then who needed it?

On the surface, she was everything her mother had been. Warm, affectionate, vivacious. You had to dig deep to get to the hard core, but it was there, steely and immovable, like the stone of an avocado buried at the centre of its soft, inviting flesh. And as long as you just wanted the outside, that was fine.

That was why Lisa's relationship with George was so perfect. They'd met nine months ago, when she'd been employed to work on a riverside development he'd been over-seeing just outside Stratford. The company had decided to hire specialist promotions girls to do the sales for the first few weeks, as the apartments were targeted at wealthy bachelors. Lisa had mistaken George for a prospective client and had proceeded to escort him around the show apartment, giving him such a beguiling spiel that he'd almost started believing in the complete flummery he'd written himself. He had to come clean, because he was enchanted: by her incredible enthusiasm, her complete conviction in what she was doing, her effervescent charm. And, of course, the amazing body that was evident underneath the low-cut cream trouser suit she wore.

And now, they were both entirely happy with the status quo. They didn't live in each other's pockets. They were two people with their own lives who enjoyed each other's company. Who made each other laugh. Who had fabulous sex. But if one of them wanted a weekend alone, the other didn't fall into a sulk or a frenzy of insecurity. It was easy. And Lisa was happy. With George, she could be the person she wanted to be. He didn't push her. He didn't ask for too much. And she didn't think he would. George seemed just as happy with the way things were as she was . . .

The path down to the beach was incredibly steep. As they scrambled the last few yards and dropped on to the shingle, George saw you could walk around the finger of rocks to the main beach, but it wouldn't be long before you were cut off again, so getting back to The Rocks would entail walking all the way back up the main road, adding a good extra mile to the journey.

The two of them crunched their way over the shingle that soon gave way to sand. The wind took their breath away, whipping Lisa's curls into a mad tangle and making George's eyes water. He thrust his hands deep into his pockets. He was surprised that, when he woke up, he hadn't felt a sense of doom at his behaviour the day before. If anything, he felt more resolute. They sat on a rock at the water's edge, the two of them contemplating the scene in silence. In front of them the sea stretched interminably. The rise and fall of the waves was almost hypnotic.

'This was a really good idea,' said George. 'It's so exhilarating here. It's as if the real world doesn't exist. Yesterday seems like a lifetime ago.'

'I have to confess, I panicked a bit when I woke up,' admitted Lisa. 'But now I just think bollocks to them. There's got to be more to life than standing around in your stilettos handing out leaflets.'

'My sentiments entirely,' agreed George. 'Not that I stand

around in stilettos, obviously. But I think if I have to make another phone call to Bath City Council . . .'

'So are you going to go back to work on Monday?'

'I don't know.' George shrugged his shoulders. 'I can't just walk out without a plan, can I?'

'Why not?' demanded Lisa. 'You've got no responsibilities.'

'I'm not programmed like that. I'm not a risk-taker.'

'Nor me. Not really. But you know what they say. Life's not a rehearsal, is it? And wouldn't you be annoyed with yourself if you died, and realized you'd spent your whole life compromising? That you'd never fulfilled your dreams?'

'I wouldn't be annoyed because I'd be dead,' replied George, ever the pragmatist. 'But I get your drift.'

He looked at Lisa, who was gazing out to sea, her eyes fixed on the spot on the horizon where the water joins the sky. He was startled to see her eyes suddenly fill up with tears.

'Lisa?'

She turned to look at him.

'I can't think of anything worse.' Her tone was vociferous and George recoiled slightly, alarmed by this uncharacteristic venom. 'It happened to my mum, and I'm not going to let it happen to me.'

George pulled her to him and she snuggled into his chest for a moment, taking comfort.

'Hey.' He stroked her curls. 'It's OK.'

'Sorry.' She pulled away, embarrassed by her display of emotion, but he pulled her back, tucking her under his arm, and she relaxed. 'It's just . . . it's so stunning here. So clean and pure. It makes you realize what it can be like. That maybe you've been wasting your life.'

'You haven't.'

'I have. I've spent too long doing something I don't really want to do. And so have you.'

'Not everybody has a choice, Lisa.'

'Who's to say we don't?'

Lisa turned and looked up the cliff towards the hotel. A mischievous smile spread over her face.

'Why don't we buy The Rocks?'

'Yeah, right.'

'Seriously. It's for sale. Webby's selling up.'

'Is she?'

George looked up at the building with interest. Lisa nudged him.

'What do you think?'

'Don't be ridiculous.'

'Why not? It would be great. You could do all the design stuff. You love all of that. And I can be front of house. I'm great at being nice to people.'

'I thought you wanted to get away from that.'

'It would be different if they were *my* customers. I'd be selling something I believed in.'

George allowed his eyes to wander up the cliff again, then shook his head.

'Everyone comes to the seaside for the weekend and dreams about running a hotel. It's such a cliché.'

'Doesn't mean we can't do it,' retorted Lisa.

'You're mad.' George grinned.

Lisa made a mad face, crossing her eyes. George looked at his watch.

'We better hurry back,' he said, 'or Webby will have burned the bacon.'

Breakfast was a pleasant surprise – not too greasy, with endless rounds of warm toast. George decided to stick with tea, as Webby's idea of coffee was putting a teaspoon of brown dust in a cup and adding hot water. As she proudly brought out yet another pot for them, George smiled his thanks.

'By the way,' he said casually, 'Lisa tells me you're thinking of selling this place.'

'Not thinking. I am. It's on the market already.'

'Have you had a lot of interest?'

'From property developers. Yes. But they all want it on the cheap. They think I'm dumb. They come round here with bottles of sherry and try and make me cash offers. Try to cut out the agent.'

'That's pretty normal,' said George.

'They all want to turn this place into apartments. It seems to be the way things are going round here. Running a hotel or a guest house is too much like hard work. And people want to make a quick profit. Most of the big houses have already been converted. And most of them are second homes, not holiday lets.' She pursed her lips in disapproval. 'What these developers don't realize is how damaging it is to the local economy. These second-homers come down for the weekend bringing their own food. They don't use the shops. It's bloody selfish.'

'So you want to sell to someone who wants to run it as a hotel?'

There was a gleam behind her spectacles. She wasn't as dim as she looked. Or as principled as she pretended.

'I don't care who I sell it to or what they do with it. But I'm not doing anyone any favours. Whoever makes the best offer gets it, at the end of the day.'

'It would be a shame to see it spoilt, though. It's a lovely house.'

'It is. And Bill and I spent a fortune having it done up. We gutted the place. It's all been done top of the range, you know. New roof, new heating, rewired, new windows. No expense spared. But nobody wants my style of B and B any more. They expect muesli and croissants and fresh coffee.'

Too right, thought George, stirring his tea.

'What this place needs is somebody young. Like you two. Someone with a bit of energy.'

Lisa kicked George gently under the table. He deliberately didn't look up. He wondered if Webby had been briefed to say that, but no – there hadn't been a moment when Lisa had been out of his sight. Why did he feel as if he was being stitched up?

'It's a little goldmine, but personally, I shan't be sorry to see the back of it,' Webby went on. 'I've been very happy here, but I'm too old now. I'll bugger off somewhere hot on the proceeds.'

Lisa had a sudden vision of Mrs Websdale stretched out on a sunlounger in Benidorm and wanted to giggle.

'Any chance of more toast?' she managed to gasp.

'Course.' Mrs Websdale picked up the metal toast rack and made her way to the kitchen. Then she turned. 'Will you be wanting the room again tonight? Only I'll need to get some more bacon and eggs in if you are.'

Lisa looked at George meaningfully. It would give them a chance to have a good mooch round. Get a feel for the place.

'Yes,' sighed George. 'We'll stay another night.'

After breakfast, they walked down the winding hill that hugged the shoreline and went to explore the village. A sweeping row of Victorian houses painted in ice-cream colours led to a cluster of shops and cafes, most of which defiantly stated that they were closed until Easter. There was a post office, with an optimistic display of beach balls, kites and buckets and spades. A juice bar, a bakery and a chippie. Several boutiques sporting surfing gear. An art gallery, the window crammed with seascapes and paintings of upturned boats. At the far end perched the Mariscombe Hotel. Originally a Gothic folly commissioned by a Victorian entrepreneur for his beloved invalid wife, it was built to resemble a castle, with four castellated towers, one at each corner. Between the hotel and the sea was an expanse of lawn fringed with monkey-puzzle trees, beyond which were the dunes.

In front of the public car park was a relatively new shopping mall, built in a New England style and painted a weathered cream, with pointy gables and a big clock. Here was an ice-cream parlour. And, to George's huge relief, a cappuccino bar. It was warm enough to sit outside, for the balcony was sheltered from the prevailing wind and the clouds had parted to reveal a shining sun. Sitting there, it was hard to believe it was February.

The reflection of the sun off the sea was almost blinding; the foam of the surf as bright white as polar ice. The surface of the water shone like glass, reminding George of the Fired Earth mosaic tiles he'd installed in his bathroom – shimmering turquoise, cobalt and silver. The sand stretched out in front of them in a crescent of gold. From a distance it looked as if you could run from end to end without getting out of breath, but in reality it was probably a good half hour's walk, longer if the wind was against you.

'Busy?' George asked the waitress politely.

'For the time of year.' The girl put down their mugs of steaming latte. 'You wait. Come Easter you won't be able to get a table in here for love or money. And to be honest, it's getting busier all year round. We always used to close after autumn half-term, but there's enough surfers and walkers to keep us going off season.'

Lisa had insisted on calling in at the estate agents to get the details of The Rocks. George perused them with an architect's precision, working out the square footage.

'The thing is,' said Lisa, 'Webby and her hubby have done all the hard work. The place is sound. It just needs all their horrible stuff ripping out.'

'What gets me,' replied George, quailing at the memory, 'is that bloody awful carpet costs a fortune.'

'No expense spared,' Lisa reminded him impishly. 'Top of the range.'

They had several refills as they watched the beach gradually fill up, with dog-walkers and joggers, young families with three-wheeled off-road buggies, fathers and sons with disobedient kites. And surfers decked out in neoprene from head to foot, leaping into the waves with eager abandon despite the sub-zero temperatures.

'This is a happy place.' Lisa put down her cup defiantly.

'People come here because they want to be here. You can feel it.' She looked at George. 'Why can't we have a bit of that?'

George smiled wryly.

'You're being idealistic. You're romanticizing.'

Lisa thumped the table.

'No, I'm not!' she insisted. 'It would be bloody hard work. Probably harder than what I'm doing now. But a lot more rewarding. And imagine waking up to that view every morning.'

George pulled a tenner out of his pocket to pay for their coffee.

'Come on, then,' he said. 'We'll go and have a proper look round.'

On the way back they passed a house that advertised fresh fish and seafood for sale, on a chalked-up board. George went and bought two lobsters. From the local mini market they bought a loaf of granary bread, some West Country butter, a brace of lemons and a bag of salad, and a bottle of Chablis. For lunch, they picnicked in Mrs Websdale's dining room, and she happily brought them plates and cutlery.

As they ate, Lisa's eyes darted around, taking in the detail.

'Can you imagine this room with the carpet pulled up and all that wallpaper ripped off? It wouldn't take much . . .'

George nodded thoughtfully.

'You could have folding glass doors the whole length of the room, so you could push them right back in the summer.'

Lisa gave a gasp.

'Perfect! You see, you're a genius. This is your *raison d'être*!'

George smiled.

'Some simple decking, with uplighters,' he continued. 'Imagine sitting out there with a glass of wine, looking at that view as the sun goes down . . .'

Lisa smiled in triumph.

'There you go, you see. You're wasted at that bloody company.' She sucked lasciviously at a lobster claw, then waved it about to emphasize her point. 'Just think of all those people out there like us, who want to escape for the weekend and recharge their batteries. Be pampered for twenty-four hours. Or forty-eight.' There was butter running down her chin. She wiped it away with a piece of paper towel Webby had thoughtfully provided. 'Come on, George. Give me one good reason why we shouldn't. Because I can think of hundreds why we should.'

George tipped back in his chair and took a satisfying slug of Chablis. Its steely aroma made him shiver with delight. Lisa was right. He couldn't think of one good reason why not.

'OK,' he agreed. 'Let's do the maths.'

Three

On Sunday evening, once back in Bath and away from the euphoric glow provided by too much Chablis and hotel-room sex, George felt a huge sense of anticlimax. Tomorrow he'd have to pick up the pieces, defend his hasty departure of Friday afternoon, find out how Colin was, discover the extent of their liability . . . It was amazing how he'd been able to forget his troubles in Mariscombe. But then, it was easy to daydream away from the confines of reality.

Suddenly, he didn't want Lisa to go.

'Why don't you stay tonight?'

'There's no reason why not. I haven't got to get up for work in the morning.' She stretched her arms over her head luxuriously. 'I can cancel my nail appointment. I don't have to shave my legs. Or pluck my eyebrows.'

George looked faintly disgusted, and she laughed.

'It's all right. I'm not going to turn into a total slob overnight. But it will be a luxury, not having to be perfect all the time in case you get called upon.' She put her head to one side and surveyed George, who was rummaging about in his enormous fridge for something to eat. 'Have you decided what to do?'

'Scrambled eggs? Or I've got a carton of vichyssoise.'

'I don't mean about supper and you know it.'

George sighed.

'I can't just quit without having something to go to.'

'You're getting cold feet about our idea, then?'

George decided on the soup. It needed eating. He pulled a

saucepan from the *batterie de cuisine* hanging overhead, opened the carton and poured in the pale green liquid.

'I can't help feeling it's a monumental risk. We'd both have to sell our houses. We don't know if we can work together. And what do either of us know about running a hotel?'

'It can't be any harder than running a chip shop. And lots of people who buy hotels don't have a clue. They have to learn the hard way.'

George gave the soup a swirl with a wooden spoon. It was the one thing he hated about himself. Being cautious was so unsexy. He looked at Lisa, eager to throw caution to the wind, her eyes sparkling.

'Don't you think it was meant to be? Don't you think fate led us there? Both of us walk out of our jobs on a Friday afternoon and end up in a seaside hotel that's crying out for a makeover? It's . . . what's the word?'

'Serendipitous.'

'That's it. Serendipitous.'

She pulled the details out of her handbag. They were looking rather worn already, they'd been pored over so many times.

'It's so beautiful.'

'It's a dump.'

'Hang on a minute. You're the one who was having orgasms over the tiles under the carpet in the hall.'

She looked so indignant George had to laugh.

'I know. It's just that I know how much hard work it's going to be.'

'Well, if you don't want to get your hands dirty . . .' Lisa tossed the details back on the counter top.

'It's not that.'

'What's the problem then?'

There was a small pause as George took the soup off the heat.

'I'm scared,' he admitted.

'In that case I should potter back into work tomorrow

49

morning, apologize to everybody and carry on paying into your nice, safe, sensible pension fund. Because you'll be stuck there for the rest of your life. But at least you won't be scared.'

This last word was dripping with vitriol. George blinked in surprise. He hadn't known Lisa could be so scathing.

'OK,' he rallied. 'Let's do the maths again, shall we?'

Lisa smiled and picked up the details again. George threw her a pencil from the leather pencil pot by his phone.

'OK,' she said. 'I can get three and a bit for my place tomorrow. And just under two for the flat.'

Lisa had a small town house on an estate just outside Stratford, and had astutely bought a flat on the same development three years ago, which she rented to a student.

'You'll have capital gains to pay on that,' George pointed out.

'So let's say that by the time I've paid off my mortgage I'll clear four hundred.'

'If I can get five and a half for this, then I'll have about the same.'

'And the guide price for The Rocks is seven.'

'Which only leaves us a hundred grand to do it up.'

'Only?' Lisa squeaked.

'Come on. Be realistic. I know we're only talking about a cosmetic refurb, but we've got to rip up all those carpets and pull off all the wallpaper. And preferably redo the bathrooms. Then we have to furnish the place. A hundred grand won't go far.'

'Then we borrow some more. That's what people do, George.'

George pulled the ciabatta out of the oven, just as the doorbell rang.

'Who the hell could this be on a Sunday night?'

He stood stock-still in the middle of the kitchen, clutching the loaf in his oven gloves. Lisa slid off her stool.

'I'll go.'

'No!'

George dropped the bread on to the work surface and rushed out of the room. Lisa watched after him, frowning slightly. George seemed tense all of a sudden. She supposed he didn't like being cornered. In a way she was calling his bluff. To her, the plan seemed logical. What was the worst that could happen? That they tried and failed? She picked up the details once again, wondering what she could do to persuade him that this was the perfect project for them, when George came back into the room with a tall, gaunt figure in tow.

'It's Justin. He's just got back from skiing.'

'Six weeks in Morzine. It was absolute hell.' Justin loped across the room and gave Lisa a kiss on both cheeks. Lisa could never decide if Justin was attractive or not. He looked like Antoine de Saint-Exupéry's Little Prince – thin, slightly startled, with a cap of wispy silver-blond hair and wide blue eyes that seemed to look right into you and lift every bit of information he needed from the depths of your soul. He was usually incredibly pale, but his spell in the Alps had turned his complexion golden brown. 'Are you about to eat? Fantastic. I'm starving.' He sat down at the island. 'I haven't had a square meal for weeks. Man cannot live on fondue alone.'

'I don't know how you put up with it,' said George, tongue in cheek, sawing up the bread and serving out soup for everyone.

'It was exhausting,' Justin protested. To sustain his skiing habit, he'd taken on the management of a young cover band, who performed nightly at various different hotels in the French Alps. And a nice profit he'd made from it too. 'I was networking like fury all day. Lining up gigs for the band for next season. Then I had to make sure they turned up every night. And get them back on the bus afterwards when they were totally bladdered. I had to play nursemaid seven nights a week. I need a holiday!'

'Well, you're in luck. We might have the perfect destination for you.'

George tossed the details of The Rocks over to him, holding his breath for his reaction, for Justin's was the only opinion he really cared about. George was fairly certain that he was Justin's only real friend, and he wasn't sure why. He didn't feel interesting enough to be granted the privilege. They'd met at university, where Justin had been the star of the English faculty, supplementing his grant by writing brilliant essays for wealthy students who couldn't be arsed to work. One day, somebody grassed him up. Someone who had no doubt caught the rough end of his acerbic tongue, or someone who was envious of the fact that every female was madly in love with him, even though he wore the same pair of jeans and the same dark green V-necked lambswool jumper every day, a Paisley scarf wrapped round his neck on cold days, a red spotted bandana when it was warmer, accessorized with an ancient wind-up Timex and white lace-up plimsolls. Justin hadn't been fazed by his subsequent sending down. Now, his lifestyle was legendary. He blew whichever way the wind took him, usually some international hot spot, and he always seemed to find a way of subsidizing his trip. Essentially, Justin was everything that George wasn't. Capricious, devil-may-care, a risk-taker. A maverick. Impossible to categorize or pigeon-hole. And infuriatingly successful. So Justin's opinion was of paramount importance to George.

'We've been to the seaside,' explained Lisa. 'Daydreaming about buying a hotel.'

Justin perused the contents thoughtfully.

'It's a complete nightmare at the moment,' said George. 'Formica and melamine hell. Swirly carpets, Artex, coving.'

'Perfect,' said Justin. 'So what would be the plan?'

'A sort of boutique hotel by the sea. *Swallows and Amazons* with a bit of Soho House thrown in. Think Famous Five go to Nantucket.'

Justin nodded.

'I think I'm getting the picture.'

Lisa decided it was time to put her oar in.

'George is making it sound complicated. It's pretty simple, really. You don't need to do much because the setting does it all for you. Light and airy bedrooms. Yummy breakfasts with proper fresh coffee—'

George shuddered.

'Not that awful muck she tried to serve us.'

Justin tossed the details back on to the work surface and picked up his wine.

'So what's stopping you?'

George gave a wry smile.

'Simple question of money. No matter which way we do it, we can't raise enough to do it properly.'

Lisa topped up everyone's glass.

'My bank manager's pretty friendly,' she said.

'Quarter of a million friendly?'

Lisa shrugged.

'I always get a Christmas card.'

George shook his head.

'There isn't enough time to get investors on board. It's best and final offers at the end of the month.'

Justin ran his crust around the rim of his bowl and chewed thoughtfully.

'I'll bung in a couple of hundred if it will help. I could do with losing a bit of capital.'

Lisa and George looked at each other, not quite able to believe what they were hearing.

'A couple of hundred . . . ?'

'Thousand, obviously.' Justin clarified his position casually.

'Are you serious?' George knew that Justin wasn't the type to make jokes, but he had to be sure.

'Deadly. But I want a third share of the business in return. As a sleeping partner.'

George did some rapid mental calculations. That was a big share, considering he and Lisa would be putting in four hundred each, not to mention their time. But he knew that if Justin was interested, then he would make it happen. And it would certainly save them time, not having to go through tedious meetings with bank managers. Plus, George knew full well that there was more where it came from. If Justin had a vested interest, and they needed more capital, he would be forthcoming, George was certain. He decided to push his friend a bit further. He didn't feel guilty. You couldn't pull a fast one on Justin. It wasn't possible.

'Call it two hundred and fifty.'

Lisa looked at him in surprise. George hadn't struck her as a tough negotiator.

Justin grinned.

'I admire your cheek,' he said. 'It gives me faith in you. Two fifty it is.'

George looked down at his piece of paper, calculations scrawled all over it. He added on the two hundred and fifty, and underlined the total with three thick black lines.

'Almost starts making it look like a possibility.'

'Don't think about it too much,' said Justin. 'Or you'll never do it.'

Lisa felt a little swirl of excitement in her tummy.

'Come on, George. What have we got to lose?'

'Um – a few hundred grand each? And our livelihoods?' George tried to make his tone light.

'I've lost that already,' said Lisa.

'I think it's about time you took a risk, George.' Justin was playing devil's advocate. 'Or else you are in grave danger of becoming the most boring man in the universe.'

'Thanks a lot!' George feigned hurt.

'Fine.' Justin shrugged. 'Put on your grey suit in the morning and go back into the office. For the rest of your life.'

'That's exactly what I said!' Lisa wasn't sure it was fair to take sides, but George needed a push.

'We can't all be crazy risk-takers.'

'I'm not crazy, actually. I've never taken a risk that wasn't considered. And I wouldn't be offering you my money now if I didn't think you could make a success of it.'

'You haven't even seen the place.'

'If there's one thing you've got, George, it's good taste in buildings. And you know your locations.'

'True.'

'It has got a lovely feel.' Lisa felt the need to put in her contribution. 'Even though it was hideous inside, the view is just amazing. And it's virtually got its own private beach. It's perfect for romantic getaways. Or girly weekends. You couldn't not enjoy yourself.'

'Let's not get carried away,' George intervened, putting his hand up. 'What we need to do is a proper business plan.'

'Rubbish,' said Justin. 'I've never done one in my life.'

'You don't want to protect your investment?'

'A business plan isn't protection. It's no guarantee of anything. If you ask me, it's restricting. I'm quite happy to write you a cheque here and now on the basis of what you've told me.'

'Seriously?'

'As long as I get my own room when I come and stay.' Justin grinned. 'I quite fancy surfing.'

George looked around his kitchen, thinking of the five years he had spent getting the house just as he wanted it. It had been an incredibly hard slog; he had put his heart and soul into the project. The very last tile had only been laid two months ago. Did he want to enjoy the fruits of his labours? Or did he want to profit from them and move on?

Fate, he thought, was a strange thing. If Colin hadn't fallen off his ladder, he wouldn't be debating this upheaval.

'Let's give it a go,' said Lisa. 'The least we can do is make an offer.'

'A sealed bid is legally binding,' George warned. 'You can't just pull out.'

'For goodness sake, George. When will you stop being the harbinger of doom? Let's just get on with it.'

*

Just over three weeks later, with the phone clamped to his ear, George held his breath and looked round at the others waiting in his kitchen.

Justin's brow was furrowed under the wispy blond fringe that had fallen over his left eye ever since George had known him. His anxiety was tangible, which was rare. Nothing usually fazed Justin. His disquiet was unnerving, and George wondered what the reason was behind it. He wasn't to know that Justin felt sure that this project was going to be the making of his friend.

Lisa was chewing on her plump bottom lip. Neither had discussed what they would do if the deal fell through and George felt a sudden twinge of responsibility. He didn't need to, of course. Lisa had her head more than screwed on. He hadn't talked her into it, by any means. It had been her decision to leave the agency, after all.

In the line of duty, George had been involved in sealed bids countless times – on behalf of clients. He had it down to a fine art, guesstimating rival offers, working out exactly how much was cost-effective to lose, when to be bullish and when to be cheeky. He'd learned never to get emotionally involved. Only this time, it was different. This time it was him. As he awaited the outcome, his heart was hammering, his mouth was dry, his stomach was flipping over and over like a pancake being tossed by an exuberant chef.

He listened to the estate agent's verdict, and carefully put down the phone.

'Right,' he said flatly. He paused for a moment for dramatic effect, then as the others looked at him uncertainly his face broke into a broad grin. 'You'd better go and pack your buckets and spades. We are officially the proud new owners of The Rocks.'

Seconds later, George found himself enveloped in Lisa's flying embrace. Justin paraded the room, his arms held aloft as he stabbed the air in triumph.

As George bent to pick up his briefcase, he reflected that

the estate agent had been rather cool in his congratulations on the telephone. But then maybe they didn't take kindly in Mariscombe to out-of-towners trumping locals with their cash. They'd be grateful in the long run, thought George. Between them they were going to put Mariscombe back on the map. George felt a tingle of excitement and drew out the bottle of champagne he'd put into his fridge earlier.

'How did you know?' exclaimed Lisa.

'I just did,' smiled George, peeling away the foil and easing the cork out gently. It had all been worth it. Three weeks of adrenalin, sleepless nights and number juggling. The legwork, the surveys, the legal work, the lengthy debates with the council, the maths, the meetings with the bank for the hideous bridging loan in case the sales of their houses didn't correspond with the completion of the purchase. And most important of all, the design: the breathtaking, radical renovation that was going to turn The Rocks from a gloomy, old-fashioned seaside hotel into a chic beachside retreat.

His boss, Richard, had been surprisingly sanguine when he had gone to tell him that he was going to hand in his notice. George had expected him to be peevish, but he'd seemed almost more excited by the project than George was.

'Best of luck to you. I can't pretend I'm not envious.'

'We haven't got it yet.'

'Don't worry. You'll pull it off.' Richard seemed confident. 'And remember, any help you want. With surveying. Or contractors. Any of that bollocks. Just get in touch.'

For a moment, George felt guilty.

'Shit. You're making me feel bad now. I feel as if I'm dumping you in it.'

'Listen, mate. You go for it. You're living our dream for us. Go and show us it can be done. Then maybe we'll all have the nerve to leave this bloody rat race.'

Richard's encouragement had given George the stamina for the last push. Up until that moment, he'd always known he could bail out; it was almost as if he was playing a game, going through the motions safe in the knowledge that if it didn't come off he could be back at his desk the following Monday. But at the last minute, with Lisa and Justin's agreement, he'd upped their offer by ten thousand. He wasn't going to lose out for the sake of a few extra quid. And the gamble had paid off.

'To The Rocks,' he now proclaimed, holding his glass high. His elation was only pricked for a moment, as his conscience whispered to him that actually all he was doing was running away. As he swallowed down the bubbles, George wondered if North Devon was far enough.

Four

Bruno Thorne was sitting with his feet up on his desk, one arm curled around the back of his head, the other holding the phone to his ear. He didn't like what he was hearing.

'I don't think I understand,' he said slowly, his tone threatening, his black brows meeting in the middle.

'The other side upped their offer by ten grand at the last minute.'

'You should have got back to me.'

'You told me categorically that was your best and final offer!' The estate agent was indignantly defensive. 'Anyway, it was sealed bids. I'm not supposed to know what's in the envelope, remember?'

'Come off it,' Bruno laughed. 'At the end of the day all you want is the best price for your client, surely?'

'I'm sorry, Mr Thorne. There's nothing I can do about it now. It's a done deal.'

Bruno sighed.

'Any idea what their plans are?'

'I've no idea.'

'Come on!' Bruno couldn't hide the impatience in his voice. 'You must have shown them round. It's off the record. I'm going to find out sooner or later.'

'They're no real threat to you. They've got eight beds max. And between you and me I don't think they've got much of a clue.'

'Then let me know when it comes back on the market,' Bruno replied smoothly and put the phone down.

Bruno swept through the foyer of the Mariscombe Hotel, raking his hand through his black curls. He should have played it straight. If he'd just made a decent offer, The Rocks would have been his by now. He was pretty sure he could have second-guessed the top offer, then added on a few thousand that, let's face it, he could afford to lose. But old habits die hard; Bruno was used to getting a bargain. He'd never paid over the odds for anything in Mariscombe. But it looked as if the tide was on the turn. People in search of a lifestyle were moving in with cash. The fiasco with The Rocks meant the goalposts were moving, and Bruno wasn't quite so sure of the rules any more. He needed to take stock.

A cleaner dodged out of his way, dragging an ancient vacuum in her wake. He watched her with distaste – no one should be cleaning in the middle of the day, for heaven's sake. She'd vanished through the double doors that led to the dining room, and something made him follow her. He stood in the doorway, surveying his surroundings as if for the first time. The carpet was a deep maroon, showing up the crumbs from breakfast that still hadn't been cleared away even though it was nearly lunchtime. The white tablecloths still displayed coffee rings and splodges of ketchup from the full English breakfast enjoyed by the coachloads of pensioners who filled the hotel in the winter months. Although full English implied something generous and satisfying, Bruno knew it consisted of a shrivelled piece of bacon, a slender sausage, a tinned tomato and a spoonful of watery scrambled egg. He sighed and walked back through the foyer to the receptionist.

There was no doubt about it, things had slipped badly. He hadn't kept on top of the hotel at all. Looking around it now, he couldn't imagine why anyone in their right mind would want to stay there – apart from the staggering view, of course. It was tired, old-fashioned, dreary. Until recently, he'd been able to get away with it. But people expected more these days. Facilities. Luxury. Design. Skin peels and seaweed wraps, fresh mango for breakfast and Wi-Fi in every bedroom. Not eighties chintz curtains and a portable telly.

The bookings spoke for themselves. According to the Mariscombe tourist board, they were inundated with requests for accommodation and made hundreds of bookings on behalf of people eager to indulge in the currently fashionable British bucket-and-spade holiday. But analysis showed it was young families heading for self-catering apartments, or over-worked couples keen to de-stress by indulging in the myriad physical activities the coastline offered: surfing, kite-flying, walking, kayaking, paragliding – the opportunities were end-less. For what it offered, the Mariscombe Hotel was expensive, and didn't pass muster. It was a dinosaur, redolent of a bygone era. Its very atmosphere sapped your energy. It just didn't appeal to the new breed of visitors. They didn't want three-course dinners in a stuffy, formal dining room. They wanted casual suppers where they could sit down with a beer or a glass of wine, unwind and enjoy the view.

Bruno ran an expert eye around the foyer. The furnishings and the fixtures were all heavy and old-fashioned; the air was stale. The occasional guest crawled through en route to morning coffee on the terrace. Two or three others sat behind the *Telegraph* by the fireplace. Outside, a wintry sun shone, valiantly attempting to lure the inhabitants of the hotel into its rays.

Bruno knew he only had himself to blame. He'd deliberately stayed away from Mariscombe over the past two years, apart from the occasional duty visit to his parents, when he'd slipped in and out of the village unannounced. But he couldn't bury his head in the sand any longer. If he carried on neglecting the hotel it would start to fall down around his ears. And it should be the jewel in his crown. It was a prime piece of real estate, the best position in the village. He owed it to himself, and to Mariscombe, to restore it to its rightful place before it became a laughing stock. Before he lost so much money that he wasn't in a position to do anything positive, and the decision-making process was taken out of his hands.

He walked behind the reception desk and settled himself down at the computer. There were no staff in evidence, but Bruno was familiar with the system. He clicked rapidly on the mouse, moving the cursor over the bookings for the next three months, muttering softly under his breath as he did some rapid mental arithmetic, his brows drawing further and further together. The advance bookings were even more dire than he had imagined. He knew that people's holiday habits had changed, and that they were leaving it later and later to book in order to assess the weather or take advantage of late deals, but even taking that into consideration, surely by now there should be a healthy sprinkling of rooms taken up?

Bruno picked up a nearby pencil with 'The Mariscombe Hotel' stamped in gold along its length, and started doing sums on the back of a brochure. If there was one thing Bruno was good at, it was thinking on his feet. Working as a bond trader in his twenties had given him the power of his convictions; the ability to put his head on the chopping block and stand by his decisions. He'd missed that thrill recently. Now he was an independent financial adviser, working from the capacious basement of his house in Kew. Of course, there was always a risk involved in financial advice, but the stakes weren't as high as they were on the floor, when millions could be lost in a split second, when a moment's hesitation could cost one dearly. Nowadays his risks were calculated, spread, considered. The work was rewarding, but not necessarily exciting.

It was time for a change.

Now, in a split second, Bruno made a decision. If the Mariscombe Hotel wasn't going to become a millstone round his neck, he had to do something positive. He could sell it, but it went against the grain to sell something which was clearly on its knees. Even if he went down that route in the long term, he had to fatten it up first. He wasn't going to let somebody else have a bargain at his expense, no way. He put his pencil down decisively as the receptionist walked back into the foyer, clutching a mug of coffee. She started in surprise when she saw Bruno behind the desk.

'I'm sorry, sir. I didn't know you were here.'

'Lucky I wasn't trying to book a room.'

He smiled up at her, but his eyes were hard. Granite grey. Unforgiving.

'There's a bell.' Hannah pointed it out, determined to stand her ground. 'I would have heard it.'

Bruno waved a dismissive hand.

'Don't worry about it. I want you to phone everyone who's unfortunate enough to have booked in here. Tell them there's going to be building work going on over the next few months and that some of the facilities might not be available. Give them the chance to cancel, but if they still want to come tell them they can't complain about the noise and the mess because they've been warned. If they really kick up, offer them a discount.' His eyes narrowed thoughtfully. 'Twenty per cent. No more. And anyone else who books, tell them the same.'

He strode out from behind the desk. Hannah was still staring at him in disbelief. She knew he was the hotel owner. She'd seen him once or twice before – and let's be honest, once you'd seen Bruno Thorne, you didn't forget him in a hurry. Even in a polo shirt and jeans, he had presence. There'd been a rumour in the staffroom that he was back – the staff were all jumpy. And it seemed they were right to be nervous.

'What's happening then, exactly?' Hannah wasn't one to beat around the bush.

'Let's just say the honeymoon is over.'

He gave a ghost of a smile, looked her cursorily up and down, then turned on his heel and walked back through the reception area, through the revolving door and out on to the steps that afforded him a panoramic view of the bay. He breathed in the salty tang, felt the ozone hit his lungs and immediately felt exhilarated. God, he loved it here. Whenever he had so much as a glimpse of the wild, craggy rocks, contrasting with the softness of the sand, with the sea either crashing or lapping, depending on its mood, he wondered why he'd ever left. The place was stunning. What had he been doing, stuck in the city, penned in by traffic and pollution and people? Why had he ever gone away? This was where he belonged.

He looked out across the water, as if seeking a sign that what he was about to do wasn't utter madness. On the other side of the bay, tucked on the edge of a far cliff, he saw the outline of The Rocks. For a moment he tensed as he remembered his earlier conversation with the estate agent, but then he relaxed. Perhaps it was a good thing that he hadn't won the bid. He was going to need all the money he could get his hands on, if he was going to turn this place round.

He marched back inside, along the corridor, past the dining room and the kitchens, which smelt of over-boiled soup, then ran lightly down the back staircase that led to the laundry area that doubled as a staffroom. He pushed open the swing door to find seven startled faces staring up at him. Three chamber-maids, two waiters and the kitchen porter were sitting round a baize-topped table, drinking coffee, smoking cigarettes and looking in awe at Hannah, who had wasted no time in running down to deliver the latest bombshell. In the background, industrial tumble-dryers whirred.

'Cigarettes out, now. If I catch you smoking again in here, you're fired,' Bruno snapped, sweeping an open packet off the table and crushing it in one hand.

'Hey!' One of the waiters dared to protest, leaping to his feet, ignoring a warning glance from one of the chamber-maids. 'You can't do that.'

'I think I can,' replied Bruno mildly. 'Who wants their sheets smelling of stale tobacco? Where's Caragh?'

'Um . . .'

There was a panicky exchange of complicit glances. Bruno raised an eyebrow, looking from one to another. One of the chambermaids looked down at her fingernails in confusion, obviously not wanting to split. Bruno analysed her. She was a pretty little thing. She didn't look much older than fourteen. He peered at her name badge.

'Molly?' he asked gently.

The girl blushed, self-conscious at being picked out.

'Sorry. I don't know. I saw her first thing, but . . .'

She trailed off. Bruno, secretly admiring her loyalty, turned his gaze to Hannah.

'Hannah?'

Hannah glanced momentarily at her colleagues, then squared her shoulders.

'It's her coffee break.' She straightened her cuffs before looking up defiantly. 'So you'll probably find her in one of the Tower Suites.'

Raising an eyebrow, Bruno nodded his thanks, pulled a pass key off one of the hooks and was gone as quickly as he'd arrived. The others turned on Hannah.

'What did you go and tell on Caragh for? She'll go ballistic!' exclaimed Molly.

Hannah bit her lip, slightly worried about the consequences now she had let the cat out of the bag.

'Because it's about time somebody knew. She can't get away with the way she behaves for ever. And he ought to know . . .'

'Who was that bloke, anyway?' Ed, the young kitchen porter, pink with acne and confusion, was flummoxed by the exchange.

One of the waiters looked at him witheringly.

'Keep up, Ed. That's Bruno Thorne. He owns this place. And the chip shop. And the arcade. And the caravan park.'

'Oh. Roight.'

'Looks like he's on the warpath. I don't fancy Caragh's chances if he catches her with her pants down.'

Hannah looked pleased. Ed looked worried.

'Shall I phone up to the suite and warn her?'

Hannah leaned forward.

'You do that, Ed, and I'll shut you in the walk-in freezer.'

Ed blanched – as much as a boy with chronic acne could blanch – while the others fell about laughing. Except Molly, who looked rather pale.

'You OK?' asked Hannah.

'Yeah.' Molly bent down to tie up her shoelace, letting her hair fall over her face so Hannah couldn't see her confusion.

'You don't fancy him, do you?' The other chambermaids were already preening themselves, slapping on lip gloss.

'Course not.' Molly stood up straight and pushed back her shoulders. 'He's way too old.'

'Who cares, if he's rich? And he's well fit.'

Across the room, Hannah looked in the mirror on the back of the door and sighed. She was an ungainly girl, with a large nose and small eyes rather too close together, giving her a sly, untrustworthy look, although she was actually perfectly honest. In fact, she had a reputation for plain speaking – you didn't ask Hannah if your bum looked big if you couldn't cope with the truth.

'He'd never look at me, would he?' she sighed. 'It's no good. I'll have to try and get some overtime. I'm never going to save enough at this rate.'

Molly put a reassuring hand on her shoulder.

'I think you're crazy, Hannah. You don't want to go having plastic surgery. It might not look right. Anyway, it's person-ality that counts.'

'Oh yeah. That would be why Frank's shagging Caragh. Because she's got such a great personality. Not because of her looks.'

Hannah sounded bitter. Molly bit her lip. It was true. Caragh was gorgeous, and an utter cow, whilst Hannah had a heart of gold underneath her bumptious exterior. But the truth of it was, life wasn't fair. If anyone knew that, it was Molly.

*

66

There were two Tower Suites, east and west, one at each end of the hotel. The laundry trolley was outside the second. Bruno took out his pass key, unlocked the door and walked straight in. He didn't bat an eyelid as Caragh, skirt round her waist and stockings round her ankles, squealed and wriggled out from underneath Frank, the head chef.

'Haven't you heard of knocking?'

Bruno ignored her. Instead he tossed her a set of keys.

'I want you to open up my house. I want it cleaned from top to bottom. Fresh linen on all the beds. Towels, toiletries, light bulbs – everything double-checked and replenished. And the fridge and the freezer filled. I'll get you a list. And I want somebody to come in every day from now on to clean.'

Frank was fumbling, pulling up his trousers and tucking his shirt in. As Bruno turned to walk back out of the room he pointed a finger at him.

'And you're fired.'

'What?' Frank looked at him in outrage. 'You can't do that!'

'I just did.'

'I'll take you to an industrial tribunal.'

'See you there. As far as I'm concerned, having sex on my time on my premises is a sackable offence.'

Moments later the door clicked shut. Bruno was gone. Frank looked close to tears.

'He can't sack me, can he, Caragh?'

'He can do what he likes. He's the boss.' Caragh had an overwhelming sense of self-preservation and no compassion whatsoever. She smoothed her skirt down over her hips and inspected her appearance in the mirror, patting her auburn bob into place, then picked up Bruno's keys, suddenly the professional. Totally ignoring Frank's mews of panic, she ran down to the reception area, where Hannah had installed herself back behind the desk.

'I've got to go and open up your man's house,' she announced, jingling the keys Bruno had thrown at her. 'Want to come and have a snoop?'

Hannah turned to face her, trying not to look guilty.

'I don't think I'd better. I've got to phone all the future bookings. Warn them about the noise.'

'What noise? What's going on?'

'Sounds like we're having a refurb.'

'Nobody told me,' said Caragh indignantly. 'But then, why would they? I'm only the manager.'

'Probably because you won't be here.'

The deep voice behind her made Caragh whirl round. Bruno was standing there, gazing at her stonily.

'Unless you stop gossiping and get on with the job. Here's my grocery list.' He handed her a list, handwritten in black capitals. 'I want fresh flowers, too. No chrysanthemums, no carnations. And no yellow.'

Seconds later, he was gone.

'Bloody hell,' said Caragh. 'He doesn't take any prisoners, does he?'

'He could tie me up any day of the week,' sighed Hannah.

Caragh looked at her sharply for a moment, then looked down at the list she had been given. 'Serrano ham. Ice cubes. Limes. San Pellegrino – what's that?'

Hannah shrugged.

'Haven't a clue.'

'Vine-ripened tomatoes. Fresh coffee – coarsely ground. Blueberries.' She rolled her eyes in exasperation. 'I'm not exactly going to get this lot around here, am I?'

'You'll have to go to the supermarket in Bamford.'

Caragh puffed herself up like an angry cobra.

'I don't think this is my job. I'm management. Not some skivvy. I'm going to tell him to shove his shopping list.'

'I don't mind doing it.' Hannah stretched out her hand for the list, but Caragh suddenly thought better of it.

'Actually, no. You're right. It could be interesting.'

They both gazed outside, where they could see Bruno pacing up and down on the terrace, raking his hands through his black curls, talking into his phone. They both admired the broadness of his back, his athletic stride.

'Has he got a wife? Or a girlfriend?' asked Caragh casually.

'I don't know. I've never seen one. Or heard of one.'

'Maybe he's gay.'

The two of them surveyed his retreating figure, then looked at each other.

'Nah,' they chorused, grinning.

Later, Frank held court in the staffroom, complaining bitterly at his treatment. His jaw-length strawberry-blond hair looked the part when he was stripped to the waist with a surfboard under his arm, but at the moment the shock of the morning's events had made his skin pale and his eyes pink.

'What am I going to do if he really does sack me?' Frank was filled with righteous indignation. 'I'm not going to get another job round here, am I? Not without a reference, and he's not going to give me a reference, is he?'

Hannah put her arm round him.

'Listen, he can't sack you just like that. Not without a written warning. And, anyway, if he sacks you he has to sack Caragh too. It would be sex discrimination if he didn't.'

'Sex discrimination,' Frank echoed gloomily. 'Maybe I should have had a bit of that before I shagged her.'

'Well, don't say I didn't warn you,' answered Hannah briskly.

'She's just using me for my body.'

Hannah looked him up and down with hungry eyes and shuddered. She couldn't bear the thought of the rapacious Caragh getting her claws into him.

'Anyway, what are we all supposed to do while this place is being pulled apart?' he demanded.

'We're still open for business,' Hannah pointed out. 'And there's going to be staff training, apparently. And brainstorming sessions and stuff like that. All dedicated to putting the customer first.'

'Blimey. There's going to be big changes, then,' said Frank in wonder. 'I can't remember the last time anyone gave a toss about what any of our customers wanted . . .'

Satisfied with his morning's work, and mildly amused at the thought of the consternation he had caused inside the hotel – although he reminded himself that he must tell Frank that he was going to get a second chance – Bruno opened the boot of his Range Rover. Out trickled Hector, his Rhodesian Ridgeback, his sleek fur the colour of the golden sand, the ridge on his back that gave the breed its name bristling with the excitement of being released from his temporary jail.

'Come on, boy.'

Hector shot joyously over the lawn towards the path he knew led to the beach, even though it had been several months since his last visit. Bruno followed after him. Hector was another reason why his decision to come back was a good one. It was madness having a big dog like that in London. Although Hector was better than a burglar alarm, and although Bruno paid a local girl to take him out for walks twice a day, then took him for a quick run in the park every night whatever the weather, Hector needed freedom.

Within a minute, they were on the beach. The tide was on its way in and a few intrepid surfers stood up to their chests in water, waiting for the waves to pick up, but apart from that there was no one to be seen. Bruno strode across the sands, enjoying the sensation as his calf muscles stretched themselves further than they were used to. By the time he reached the little path that led up the cliff to Higher Mariscombe, he was breathing heavily. Far more heavily than he would have liked. He determined to get up every morning and go for a run on the beach. By the end of two weeks he would be fit again. The extra few pounds he knew he was carrying, courtesy of Christmas and the dull weather of January and February that took the edge off one's enthusiasm for anything involving exertion, would soon melt away.

At the top of the cliff was a stone wall, and set into it was a faded blue gate with a twisted iron handle. He hesitated for a moment before pushing it open. Inside was a tiny graveyard, belonging to the church at Higher Mariscombe. It looked out across the ocean towards infinity, the grass between the stones rustling in the breeze. For some, it would be too exposed, a cold, harsh resting place. But for others, with its magnificent view, its oneness with the elements, it was the perfect place to be laid to rest. And for visitors, it was the ideal spot to contemplate one's mortality, with the vastness of the sea and the sky, the gorse-covered cliffs, the mighty rocks beneath and the clouds scudding overhead.

Bruno and Hector wandered amongst the stones, Hector sniffing curiously, Bruno feeling the heavy dread he always did. It was at this point that he hoped he would arrive at the plot in the far right-hand corner and find that the huge granite slab was not there after all, that the whole thing had been a terrible dream. But no, as ever, there it was, standing square and tall and proudly proclaiming the reason for its presence in bold white letters: 'In loving memory of Joseph Mark Thorne [Joe]. A much loved son and brother. Sadly missed.'

How bald and insufficient those words still seemed.

Bruno stood for a moment, fists clenched. Hector somehow sensed his angst and sat down by his master's feet, nudging his calf gently with his nose as if to remind him he was there for him. Bruno had been hoping, naively perhaps, that the supposed great healer had done its job, and that this time his despair might have abated. Every time he was confronted by the stone, he was filled with rage and anger, incensed by his impotence. Furious that he couldn't express how he felt – for even if he could have analysed his feelings, Joe wasn't there to listen. Two years later, the urge to justify his actions was still as strong as ever.

He touched the stone gently.

'OK, mate?' he muttered, feeling foolish, for he knew Joe couldn't hear. Yet there was a part of him that hoped perhaps he could. It provided him with a crumb of comfort, the infinitesimal chance that Joe knew how much he had cared after all. The wind whipped, making Bruno's eyes water as he looked out to sea, trying to measure his pain. Was it his imagination, or was the knot in his stomach slightly less sharp than usual? It was three months since he'd last been here – had the suffocating tightness in his chest subsided? He took a shaky breath in and decided that perhaps it had.

And then, of course, felt guilty. He didn't deserve to recover. He deserved to suffer for the rest of his days. What right did he have for a reprieve, when Joe wasn't going to get one? Joe, after all, was six foot under, worm fodder, and unless you believed in reincarnation, which Bruno was fairly certain he didn't, had no hope of a second chance . . .

Growing up in Mariscombe had been idyllic for Bruno. His parents had a small farm, twenty-five acres of rolling fields that butted right up to the cliff's edge, overlooking Mariscombe one side and the wild Atlantic the other. They had a dairy herd, which gave the air a sweetness, and a flock of sheep. The farm, with its cream Devon longhouse, had been in the Thorne family for generations, and provided a lifestyle more than a living. There might not have been much spare cash, but there was good food aplenty, beautiful surroundings, a social life and, as the area filled up with incomers looking for a new life, they were afforded a certain respect for being genuine locals.

In the seventies, Bruno's parents made a decision to supplement their meagre income by letting out their fields for camping, which, given the spectacular location, had proved more lucrative and less responsibility than sheep and cows. Initially, all they provided was a single tap for water, but as the site became more and more popular through word of mouth, they gradually improved the facilities. By the eighties, they had converted one of the barns into a washroom, had hook-ups for electricity and had opened a small farm shop selling the very basics. Bruno spent his teens helping out on the site, mowing the fields, keeping the washrooms scrupulously clean, bringing round milk and eggs and fresh bread to each pitch in the morning. He also gave guests surfing lessons – his guarantee was that he could get anybody standing up on a board after half a day, and he generally succeeded. And all the time he built up a rapport with the customers, making sure they booked in for a return visit the following year before they left the site.

By the time Bruno was eighteen, he had a vision. The building of a new dual carriageway linking the North Devon coast to the motorway was imminent. He could see that the caravan site had enormous potential, and they had to strike quickly, before other developments overtook them and grabbed their market share of the tourists who would come down in their hordes once at least an hour was cut off their travelling time from Birmingham or Liverpool or London.

The expansion Bruno had in mind involved a significant sum of money for investment, but he had done his projections. It was a sound business plan. But his father was stubborn. He'd never borrowed any money in his life and he wasn't going to start now. No matter how many charts and graphs and diagrams Bruno thrust under his nose, outlining the potential for growth and profit, his father steadfastly refused to budge. And Bruno didn't have any experience or any track record to convince the bank by himself. In the end, he did a deal with his dad. If he could raise the initial sum over the next five years, his dad would hand the business over to him.

Bruno decided that going to university was only going to delay his ability to earn money. So he went off to London, where he invested in a smart suit and a good pair of shoes, and had his mop of wild black curls tamed by a Jermyn Street barber. He looked as stunning suited and booted and clean-shaven as he did stripped to the waist in his board shorts. He soon learned to lose his soft Devon burr and the quaint idiosyncrasies of the local speech. He understood figures: money didn't frighten him. To him, the world of high finance was no different to working a market stall, there were just more noughts involved. Looking back now at the risks he took, he shuddered. But maybe ignorance was bliss.

By the end of five years, he had enough cash accrued. His London friends had never understood why he chose to live so modestly, why he didn't have a flash car and a flash pad to go with it, but Bruno hadn't seen the point in conspicuous spending, preferring to invest wisely and quietly.

His father couldn't argue with his bank balance and his revised business plan. By now he had seen the light and agreed it was madness to stand still. In the intervening five years he had been approached countless times to sell the site, and had been rather shaken by the sums of money he'd been offered.

Over the next two years, they bought twenty static caravans, built a timber-framed club house and a swimming pool, a children's adventure playground, a new shower block and toilet facilities, and a designated barbecue and picnic area. Business boomed, for the site was large enough to have extensive facilities yet still retained an air of individuality and, thanks to Bruno's parents, a sense of being family run – some of the other sites were ruthlessly commercial and suffered from a lack of identity as a result.

Eventually, Bruno had enough money to buy his parents out, keeping his father on as manager. This gave them not only capital but a regular wage, which meant they had enough in the kitty to build themselves a new bungalow on the edge of the village. Living on the site was becoming too much of a hassle for them, so instead the old longhouse was divided up into self-catering apartments. With the business now officially his, Bruno had more than enough equity to borrow and increase his portfolio. In the next five years he added a chip shop and amusement arcade, both of which he immediately leased out. His *pièce de résistance* was purchasing the Mariscombe Hotel. By the time he was twenty-eight, he owned more freeholds than anyone else in the village. Not that he ever advertised this fact. Bruno was the soul of discretion, as were his secretly proud parents. He didn't come down and swank around. He knew he had to keep his trading job until he'd earned enough money to pay off a substantial amount of the loans that were propping up his deck of cards. By the time he was thirty-two, he had got his borrowings down to thirty per cent of his portfolio, a ratio he felt comfortable with.

It was at this point Bruno felt that the time had come to be more hands on in Mariscombe. The original leases on the arcade and the chip shop were coming to an end and he would have to decide whether to renegotiate or find new tenants. The manageress at the Mariscombe Hotel was leaving to have a baby, and despite her protests that she would return as soon as was humanly possible, Bruno suspected it was unlikely. He left his job on the floor, setting up as an independent financial advisor working from home, with a view to an eventual three-day London, four-day Devon week.

That June, he gave himself some time off to put an offer in on one of the much-coveted Art Deco houses perched on the dunes, appoint a new manager for the hotel and decide what to do with his other interests. It was only then, on spending more time than usual with his family, he realized that his younger brother had turned into something of a tearaway. Joe had been born when Bruno was ten – a late and unexpected arrival, but a most welcome one. Bruno was never jealous. By the time the baby arrived he had his own life – he was at school and had his friends – so he never resented him. By the time Joe was eleven, and starting senior school, Bruno had left home for London. Over the years, his mother had occasionally hinted at Joe's high spirits and lack of responsibility, but Bruno hadn't realized to what extent. Privately, he felt that Joe had been spoilt and indulged, never made to toe the line. Perhaps their mother feared an empty nest so much that she had clung on to Joe and made his life too comfortable, with the result that she'd spawned a monster.

Joe hadn't done particularly well at school. The lure of the beach was too great, and there was little discipline at the community college in Tawcombe where he had ended up. And his parents didn't push him. Besides, he was too useful on the site. He was good with his hands, was Joe, in more ways than one. At sixteen, his father put him in charge of maintenance – painting and decorating, mowing the fields, doing the little repair jobs that were inevitable with the amount of human traffic that passed through. And the work suited him. He got up early, spending the first four hours of the day working before the sun was too high. He had energy. He could do more in that time than most people achieved in a full day. By midday, he was done, ready for the pub or the beach, depending on the condition of the waves.

He became a familiar sight, in his baggy combat shorts and baseball boots, hair covered with a bandana pirate-style, his stepladder over one shoulder and a pot of paint in the other. He was always whistling, as well he might, for he was blessed with looks that casting directors and model scouts sought the world over. Light brown almond-shaped eyes, with dark lashes and brows. Lethal bone structure. A wide, full mouth, with a wicked smile that showed perfect, even white teeth. His hair was long, tousled, bleached by the sea and the sun. He was slight, but his chest and arms were toned from surfing and working. Even when he was in his scruffiest clothes, his hands smothered in paint, eyes followed him hungrily.

He should have come with a health warning. Girls who knew no better were warned not to fall under his spell, for it would only end in tears. But they never heeded the warning. He was utterly irresistible. For as long as his attentions lasted, his victims seemed to glow from within, radiating happiness, convinced that they would be the one to tame him, because at the time he made them seem so special, like the centre of his universe. But suddenly, without warning, his attention would wander, his eyes would fix on someone else, he would become infatuated. And then he would move on, leaving behind heartbreak and devastation. Yet he couldn't be criticized, for he never made anyone any promises. He was totally hands up about his inability to maintain a relationship or stay faithful. So there was rarely any sympathy for his victims. They had repeated warnings, not least from Joe himself.

The summer in question, nearly two years ago now, was glorious. The sea shimmered for weeks on end, its metallic surface almost too bright to look at with the naked eye. Mariscombe was a mini paradise, bathed in a permanent golden glow, a slight breeze keeping the temperature from being insufferable. The aura became sensual, sleepy, languid. The air hung heavy with the sweet scent of marijuana – the atmosphere was so chilled that people were smoking openly – and the sound of reggae. Skin turned gold, dark hair became streaked with blond, blond hair turned white. There was a gentle rhythm to the days. Rain seemed impossible: a distant memory from a far-off time.

Joe held court outside the Jolly Roger, the pub just off the main drag in Mariscombe. The landlord had him as well as the sun to thank for his meteoric rise in profits, as legions of girls hung around buying Reef after Reef, waiting for Joe to appear with his surfboard, wetsuit unzipped to the waist. And although no other male stood a chance with Joe around, he was popular with the blokes. They didn't seem to hold it against him; they were happy enough with his cast-offs. He reigned supreme, with no pretender to the throne.

The only person immune to his charms was Bruno. Mariscombe was small. There was gossip. Rumours. Plenty of people ready to stir things up. It wasn't long before Bruno was putting together a picture of his younger brother that he found disturbing. It seemed that he was something of a ringleader. There was a spate of impromptu raves on the beach, attracting an undesirable element – cars with booming bass zoomed up and down the hills, litter was left behind, there were camper vans in the car park overnight that disgorged unwashed, unkempt bodies who were off-putting to families pottering down to the beach. This was exactly what Mariscombe didn't want to become – a playground for decadent youth. Joe seemed to be at the centre of it. And it was generally acknowledged that if you wanted a bit of skunk for the weekend, or a couple of Es, then he was the person to ask.

To Bruno, Joe just seemed to cruise round oblivious to the chaos he left in his wake – the emotional fallout, the bad feeling. He seemed to have no regard for his parents' feelings, or the reputation of the family, something which Bruno regarded very highly indeed. The Thornes were one of the few families left to have been born and bred in Mariscombe – they went back at least five generations. Bruno felt pride in that, but Joe seemed happy to blot the family escutcheon at every opportunity.

Yet when Bruno confronted him, Joe was infuriatingly blasé.

'I'm not entirely sure what you're accusing me of. Seems to me you've been listening to local gossip.'

'Come on, Joe. There's no smoke without fire.'

'There is when people are jealous.'

'How do you think Mum feels, to know people are pointing their fingers at you?'

'She's got enough sense to know it's just tittle-tattle.'

'So why am I hearing these things about you?'

Joe shrugged, pushing his long shaggy fringe to one side.

'Dunno. I just want to work hard and play hard.'

Teenage girls who had been dragged on a camping holiday by their despairing parents soon snapped out of their sulk when they clapped eyes on Joe. They were like bees round a honey-pot. And how could he resist, when they threw themselves at him, these long-limbed, firm-skinned creatures in their tiny bikinis? It was inevitable that there would be trouble when he treated them so casually, and one afternoon Bruno was interrupted from his paperwork by an irate father threatening to call the police.

'I can't get her out of the van. She's breaking her heart in there. She's only fifteen. If I find out he's laid a finger on her, I'll have him locked up.'

It took Bruno the rest of the day to placate the father, coax the young girl out of the caravan to get her side of the story, and promise to remonstrate with Joe.

Joe was almost callous.

'What am I supposed to do, take her back out of pity? I never made her any promises.'

'At least talk to her, for Christ's sake.'

'What good would that do? It'll only get her hopes up.'

'You can't scamper through life acting like a flopsy bunny on Viagra. Getting away with it just because you're cute. It's not fair, Joe!'

'I can't help it if they throw themselves at me.'

'You can say no.'

'I'm a bloke!'

'They can't handle it, Joe. You can't just love them and leave them.'

'That's the point. I don't love them. I've never told anyone that.'

Bruno looked at him stonily.

'OK. I might not be able to force you to behave like a decent human being. But I can ban you from liaising with customers.'

'What do you mean, liaising?'

Joe leaned back in his chair insolently, chewing gum and looking at his brother defiantly. For a moment, Bruno knew how it felt to be a teacher faced with a class of uncontrollable adolescents. He tried to remain calm.

'Chatting up, flirting, touching up, snogging, shagging . . . do I have to spell it out in words of one syllable?'

'What if I meet her on the beach and don't realize she's a customer?'

Bruno grabbed Joe by the front of his T-shirt and pulled him up out of his chair. It was all he could do not to flatten him. He so resolutely refused to take anything seriously, to show even a modicum of responsibility.

'You know exactly what I mean.'

'Hey, chill,' said Joe, aggrieved.

'Just do as you're told or you'll find yourself out of a job,' growled Bruno through gritted teeth.

'I don't think Mum would be very happy about that.'

Joe was getting annoyed now, and was being uncharacteristically defensive. He never usually bothered – a smile was usually all it took to get him out of trouble. And Bruno didn't want to turn this into a bigger deal than it already was. He let him go with a sigh, not wanting their confrontation to get back to his mother. She would only be upset. And Joe was perfectly capable of telling tales, he was sure.

'OK. Have it your way. Forget I said anything. Just try and keep your hands off the customers if you can.'

Joe shrugged and sat back down.

'Plenty more fish in the sea.'

Bruno gave up trying to get his brother to see reason. And he wondered if perhaps he was acting out of jealousy. Joe had always been the apple of everyone's eye. The late baby. The cute one. Melter of the stoniest of hearts. While Bruno was working hard at school, Joe was garnering praise and attention by stumping round with his chubby legs, a sunny smile and a halo of curls. Maybe deep down Bruno envied him his freedom. He was living the perfect life. He had exactly the right proportion of sun, sea, surf, women, cash, free time and his mother to wait on him hand and foot. He didn't even have to get his dirty clothes as far as the laundry basket. When he came home from work, Joanie scooped them off the floor and popped them into the machine to wash while he ate the food she had prepared. Before he put on his freshly ironed going-out clothes. Meanwhile, Bruno was working his balls off, stuck in the city he had come to hate, to keep his empire afloat. He might earn a hundred times more than Joe, but he had no freedom to spend it, even though he was trying hard to adjust his lifestyle.

He thought his words had hit home, however, as before

long Joe seemed to be going steady, with an amazing-looking girl called Tamara whose father had done very well for himself. Bruno had to admire his choice, and in the back of his mind couldn't help wondering if it was Tamara's access to unlimited cash rather than her slender golden limbs that was the attraction. But he didn't comment, as at least Joe seemed to have settled down.

It was therefore another month before they clashed again. Bruno had come back down to exchange contracts on the house he was buying, and was staying with his parents. It was lunchtime and Joe was grumbling that his favourite shirt hadn't been ironed. Bruno was livid. In his eyes, Joe exploited their mother mercilessly. Expecting a meal at whatever time he came in. Expecting his clothes washed. His room kept tidy.

'This has got to stop, Joe. You can't treat Mum like this.'

'Mum doesn't mind!'

'Have you ever asked her if she minds? Have you ever stopped for a moment to think that there're other things she could be doing apart from picking up after a twenty-three-year-old?'

'I'm not a full-time job.'

'When's the last time you made her a cup of tea?'

Joe couldn't answer.

'You take the mickey out of her completely. She's not your slave, Joe. You can't just walk in and expect a meal whatever time of the day or night it is. You can't expect her to do your laundry and clean your room—'

'Why not?' Joe seemed genuinely flummoxed. 'She wouldn't do it if she didn't want to. Look, what's your problem, Bruno? Just because you're up in London and you have to pay someone ten quid an hour to clean up after you. She likes doing it, for God's sake. She likes looking after me.'

'And what does she get in return? Calls from the cop shop when you overdo it. Bills from the garage when you prang your car. Weeping girls on the doorstep. How do you think that makes her feel?'

'Not as proud as when she looks at you, obviously. With your Porsche and your Rolex. I'm sure she's very proud that her oldest son owns half of Mariscombe.'

'I've worked hard for it.'

'And don't we know it. Here he comes in his private chopper—'

Bruno had known that turning up in a helicopter would hardly go unnoticed, but it had saved him much-needed time on a couple of occasions.

'It wasn't mine.'

'Yeah, but you still have to make an entrance, don't you? Just so people don't forget how important you are. How loaded.'

Bruno pressed his lips tightly together. Joe had hit his Achilles heel. That was exactly how he didn't want to be seen. But of course people speculated.

'It's all very well you having a go at me about Mum,' Joe continued. 'But at least I'm here for her. At least I sit down and watch *Emmerdale* with her every night.'

This last remark pierced an arrow of guilt straight into Bruno's heart.

'Big deal,' he shot back. 'That makes up for exploiting her the rest of the time, does it? Try giving something back, Joe. You might find your life has more meaning.'

Joe just smiled his most infuriating smile.

'OK, let's see. What would Mum rather have? A big telly for the lounge? Or someone to watch it with every night?'

Bruno had indeed bought his parents a brand new television for Christmas, because he genuinely thought it was something they would get pleasure out of. Somehow Joe managed to twist his gesture into something flashy but meaningless. The last thing he wanted to do was lose his temper, but Joe had pushed him too far.

'You're a loser, Joe. A user and a loser. You milk Mum and Dad for everything you can get, without sparing a thought for how they feel. You please yourself twenty-four hours a day.

You trample over people, you exploit them. All for your own end. You're a disgrace to this family. Where would you be without us to provide you with a living and a roof over your head and twenty-four-hour room service? In the backstreets of Tawcombe with a dog on a string and a drug habit, that's where. You're twenty-three. We're not going to be around for ever to sponge off. Get a grip.'

'Maybe I'd like to.'

Joe's voice had dropped to a deadly hush.

'What?'

For a moment, Bruno stopped in his tracks. Joe looked up at him, his eyes bright. With what, Bruno wasn't sure, then realized later it had been unshed tears.

'Maybe I'd like to get a grip. But I don't know how. It's pretty hard following in your footsteps, I can tell you. Bruno the genius. Bruno the dutiful son. Bruno the entrepreneur whose cash is going to save us all. It's a pretty tough act to follow.'

Bruno looked at Joe warily. He seemed chastened, his previous air of insouciance evaporated. Or was this just an act? Another way of getting at him?

'I was a dunce at school. No one took an interest in me. No one gave a stuff if I didn't turn up. So what was the point in bothering? And no one expects much now. So they don't get anything. I'm certainly not capable of delivering anything on your scale.'

His bitterness seemed genuine and for a moment Bruno wondered if he really had suffered from being in his shadow. Then Joe gave a twisted smile.

'But who cares? Why should I bother? I'll get all of this when they're dead. They're bound to leave it all to me, being as how you've got so much already. So I don't really need to worry too much, do I?'

Bruno looked at him witheringly. The moment of doubt he'd had, when he'd felt a flicker of pity, switched to disgust.

'You really are a fool, aren't you?' His tone was mocking,

merciless. 'Who do you think owns this place? I bought Mum and Dad out years ago. It's me that pays their wages. And yours. So you needn't bank on being left the site, because it's not theirs to leave.'

He waited for a moment for the impact of this information to sink in.

'Just think,' he finished. 'You might have to get a proper job. When they're not around to run after you.'

Joe didn't reply.

Tight-lipped, Bruno left and called a cab to take him to the station. He had to zip back to London for a meeting the next day. He'd decided to take the train, as he had a mass of paperwork to look through. He could come back down on Thursday night in time to interview potential managers for the hotel on Friday – there were three contenders, two of them excellent, one of them a wild card. He decided to put Joe out of his mind, concentrate on his own business. Maybe Joe was right. Maybe their mother wasn't bothered by her youngest son's behaviour. Maybe it was worth it to have him at home. Bruno felt stung. Why was it that the encounter had made him end up feeling the guilty one? He had only ever done his best to be dutiful.

As the taxi arrived, Bruno jumped in. For a moment he wondered if he should have locked his Porsche up in the garage. But no. This was Devon, not London. It would be perfectly safe . . .

Nothing had quite beaten the sensation of turning up to the Jolly Roger in a bright red Porsche that night. Joe had nudged the bonnet right up to the tables that nestled outside and had revelled in the ensuing uproar – squeals of excitement from the girls, groans of envy from the boys. He totally looked the part, like some wild Hollywood star who'd hit the big time. Glamorous, dangerous. Too fast to live. Too young to die . . .

*

84

It was Leonard Carrington, landlord of the Mariscombe Arms, who had spotted the car at the foot of the cliffs the next day when he went for his ritual dawn swim.

At the inquest, the barman of the Jolly Roger gave evidence that he hadn't given Joe anything to drink. He might turn a blind eye to underage drinking, but he had enough sense not to let someone with a high-powered vehicle like that get hammered. Especially Joe Thorne. But what no one knew at the time was that Joe had already drunk the best part of a bottle of Jack Daniel's. He just didn't show it. He was smiling, lucid, calm. Only one girl, who'd kissed him on his way out of the toilets, reported that he'd tasted of booze. She'd pleaded with him to take her with him in the car. 'You don't want to go where I'm going,' he'd said darkly, and she thought he meant he was off to play pool in Tokyo Joe's, a seedy club in the backstreets of Bamford.

In the end, the verdict was accidental death. Even though it was generally agreed that to drive a car like that with the amount of booze the post-mortem showed in Joe's body was suicide.

The funeral was an extraordinary testament to Joe's popularity and the Thornes' standing locally. All the shops and cafes in the village closed for the afternoon out of respect. The heat was almost unbearable as the coffin bearing Joe's surfboard was carried in amidst muffled sobs from hordes of distraught young girls, their arms round each other. And the drinking at the Jolly Roger went on late into the night with no complaints, as toast after toast was raised by his friends and his favourite songs were pumped out again and again on the jukebox. It was unconventional yet dignified nevertheless, an apt celebration of a young life cruelly cut off in its prime.

Afterwards, Bruno felt paralysed. He couldn't tell where his grief finished and the guilt began. The two emotions churned together in an endless cycle that tortured him from the moment he woke up. To his shame, he took the coward's way out.

Jettisoning all the plans he had made, he couldn't face staying in Mariscombe, with the ghost of his brother taunting him at every turn. He swiftly arranged managers for all his business interests, left the house he had just bought in preparation for his return locked and empty, and slunk back to London.

He should never have been so harsh and so judgemental with Joe. He should have recognized his vulnerability in that small moment when his brother had tried to open up and confess. But Bruno hadn't wanted the responsibility of being in the wrong. He could have given Joe his support, some encouragement, even just listened. But no, he had chosen to believe the swaggering bravado and not look underneath. He'd taken the easy way out.

Would it really have hurt him that evening to sit down and talk to his brother? Have a real heart-to-heart? Dig a little deeper and find out if there was some ambition lurking there? No. He'd chosen to kick him down. He'd rubbed his brother's nose in his own success and crowed over him without a hint of compassion. Bruno had no idea how it felt to be a failure, a misfit, a black sheep. He hadn't had the grace to step down off his platform, come down to Joe's level and listen for just five minutes. Because he'd had a train to catch. He felt entirely responsible for his brother's death. He'd driven him to drink, he'd left the keys on the table, he'd swiped away any self-esteem Joe might have had in order to feed his own self-importance.

Self-importance which had swiftly metamorphosed into self-loathing.

To the outsider, Bruno functioned. He went back to work, his decision-making ability seemingly unaffected, and for eight hours in the day he was able to displace his grief temporarily. But outside the office, the pain was intolerable. There was no distraction. Food was tasteless, like sawdust in his mouth. Drink was bitter. Music was a white noise that drove him demented; television filled with talking heads issuing meaningless drivel he couldn't begin to follow. His relationship didn't survive. His girlfriend, Serena – sharp, clever, glacial on the outside but buttersoft at heart – insisted she could wait, but Bruno insisted on releasing her from the bond of her relationship with him. Sex was out of the question – not just physically, but because he knew he couldn't cope with the emotional intensity. And sleep provided no escape. In the end, Bruno had to resort to sleeping tablets, for he felt sure he could feel insanity approaching. It was either that or drink himself into oblivion. For nearly two years, he operated on autopilot, accepting that his torture was in some way his atonement.

Today, however, as he looked down at the hotel, he felt a little prickle of something that bordered on optimism, a little shoot of green after an endless winter. And this time he didn't try to suppress it. He'd wallowed about in negativity for long enough. Guilt was self-indulgent. And one thing was certain – it wasn't going to bring Joe back.

He called Hector and together they walked out of the graveyard back into Higher Mariscombe, following the road back up past the Mariscombe Arms, then turned off down the winding lane that snaked through several fields before arriving at his parents' bungalow. He walked into the kitchen, just as his mother drew the cosy over the teapot. Bruno smiled. Joanie had an instinct for people's arrival that bordered on the uncanny. He went over to hug her, holding her to him a fraction longer than usual, his little mother whom he had inadvertently caused such pain. The spark inside her had died with Joe, and he knew she was never going to get it back. His father, too, would never be the same. He never spoke about his pain, but there was a grimness in the set of his mouth that hadn't been there before. Bruno imagined the pair of them sitting night after night, staring at the television, locked in their grief but unable to share their feelings.

'Mum,' he said. 'I'm coming back. To Mariscombe. To live.'

Something flickered in her eyes, but it was only fleeting. Had it been joy? Bruno wasn't vain enough to think that his return could make up for Joe's loss, but he did hope she would be pleased.

And she was. 'Good,' she said, with feeling, and Bruno was reassured at his decision. It was his duty to come back. He should never have left in the first place, but he'd needed time to heal at his own pace. Now he felt strong enough to live among the memories. It was time to look to the future . . .

Five

Realistically, what chance does a forty-six-year-old man have against two scheming seventeen-year-olds? Especially when he is a vain, wealthy forty-six-year-old man convinced he is devastatingly attractive to women?

Miranda Snow, commonly known as Mimi, strolled out of the back gates of Lansdown Academy for Girls, linking arms with her best friend Yasmin. In deference to the spring, the two of them had already ripped off their ties, unbuttoned their blouses and rolled up the waistbands of their green pleated skirts to reveal slender, cellulite-free legs. Over-the-knee socks and clumpy-heeled shoes completed their outfits: two terrifying Lolitas with their hair in loose plaits, their eyes ringed with black kohl, their lips smeared with sticky lip gloss.

Yasmin was lolling against Mimi, trying to extricate a piece of Wrigleys from its wrapper.

'He is such a total lech. I still don't get how your mum can fancy him.'

'Dosh.' Mimi stated the fact baldly.

'Well, he's gagging for it. I can tell you.'

'Are you sure you want to go through with it?'

Yasmin looked sideways at her friend as she popped the gum in her mouth.

'Hey – isn't that what friends are for?'

'I guess.' Mimi, usually so resolute, was having a moment's doubt.

'It's perfect timing. I mean, he nearly crashed the car three times when he dropped me home last night. He couldn't stop looking at my legs.'

Mimi made a disgusted face.

'I know. He does the same to me. It turns my stomach.'

'I'm just going to have to shut my eyes and think of somebody old but attractive.'

'Why don't you just think of the money? Like Mum does?'

'Do you really think that's the only reason she's with him?'

'It's not for his looks, is it?'

'The trouble is he thinks he's gorgeous. He's such an eighties throwback!'

'He has his back waxed, did you know that?' Mimi convulsed with laughter. 'And he's got a special colour chart that he carries everywhere with him. So he knows what colour clothes to buy.'

Mimi looked at her watch, suddenly serious. The bus was due in five minutes. She prayed it wouldn't be late. Or, worse, that it wouldn't turn up at all.

'OK. Here's the schedule. Mum's taking the afternoon off work – she promised. She should be back around two. Nick usually gets back around one so he can play golf. If we time it right, get him all relaxed so he doesn't suspect anything . . .'

It was Yasmin's turn to look doubtful.

'Your mum is going to wig.'

'Listen, you're doing her a favour. Come on, Yas. She needs rescuing from that creep. This is the only way to do it.'

Mimi's tone was urgent. She didn't want Yasmin chickening out now. She was usually up for anything. If Yasmin didn't do it, she'd do it herself, even though the fallout would be much, much worse. But Mimi was desperate. She really couldn't stand it any longer.

Yasmin was leaning against the wall with her arms crossed, contemplating the deal.

'Two hundred and fifty,' she said.

'What?'

'Two hundred's not enough. I'll do it for two hundred and

fifty. You've got to make it worth my while. It's my reputation. And then I can get those boots from River Island as well.'

'Jeez!' Mimi grabbed her friend's arm. 'What is it about women and money? Have you no integrity?'

She dragged Yasmin towards the bus stop. They were going to miss the bus at this rate and that would mean blowing the whole plan. It was now or never. Mimi couldn't bear it another day.

Mimi's friends were all green with envy that she had such a trendy mother, who wore really cool clothes and listened to music at full blast with the roof down on her sports car. Who swore like a trooper and didn't care if Mimi and her friends smoked, and let them pinch her cigarettes because she had boxes and boxes of duty-free, so afraid was she of running out. But personally Mimi wasn't impressed. She longed for a normal mother. She wanted to be able to rebel! There was nothing she wasn't allowed to do; nothing she was forced to do against her will. Victoria never chased up her homework, or pored over her report demanding why her grades weren't better, or threatened to collect her hideously early from a party. In fact, she didn't bother collecting her from parties at all – Mimi had the number of a cab firm and she just had to call. She didn't even have to pay – it was all on account. She didn't bother telling her mother she was home. Victoria would either still be out, or zonked out in bed. 'You are so lucky!' her friends would groan. They all had curfews. But Mimi thought it would be fantastic to have someone expecting you home at eleven o'clock, demanding to know where you had been if you were five minutes late.

Saturdays were another case in point. Mimi longed for riding lessons, or tennis, or piano – all the activities her friends seemed to get locked into on a Saturday and moaned about. Instead, she had to go into town with her mother. Victoria usually booked the two of them into the hairdresser – Mimi was the first girl in her form to have highlights – for trims, touch-ups and blow-drys, in readiness for some social function that evening. Then they would spend an hour in Space NK, while Victoria tried out all the new products and demanded makeovers from the long-suffering assistants, desperately in search of some magical potion that would roll back the years.

'Try not smoking, Mum.' Mimi would roll her eyes. 'Try drinking loads of water. If you look like an old hag, it's because of what you do to your body.'

Then lunch, where Victoria would definitely drink too much white wine, would wave and greet and kiss people, who she would then tear apart, safe in the knowledge that she would probably see them again several hours later at one or other dinner party. In the afternoon, the hunt for a new outfit would begin in earnest, with Victoria moaning that Bath was parochial, behind the times and boring. This wouldn't stop her from buying, however. Then she'd come back home, try on everything that she'd bought again and shove it all back in the bags in disgust. But somehow they'd never find their way back to the shops. Her walk-in wardrobe was stuffed with things she'd never worn. Mimi never had to buy any new clothes. She just plundered her mother's cast-offs and gave it her own style, mixing designer rejects with her own teenage tat.

At six Nick would open champagne, for Victoria to drink while she had her bath and got ready. Mimi would be called upon to dry her hair, apply her fake tan (only a smidgeon, to give her skin a glow) and generally tell her she looked gorgeous. Which she did, her skin youthful and dewy, her hair glossy, her eyes bright. After three glasses of champagne, when she was perfectly done up and immaculately dressed, for a short while Victoria would be confident, ready to take centre stage. Victoria thrived on attention. At social gatherings she was the life and soul, a sparkling party animal. Only Mimi knew the angst she went through getting ready, both internally and externally. She was shored up by booze. And, Mimi suspected, something harder at times, though she never actually witnessed her mother indulging. But those pupils and that gushing, bubbly, extrovert exterior definitely weren't natural.

Then Nick would emerge in his black designer jeans and his tight, silky long-sleeved T-shirt that was supposed to show off how much time he spent in the gym but actually just showed his nipples. For a moment you could believe they were Bath's golden couple, him the media mogul, her the PR whizz, as they shared the rest of the bottle of champagne in the kitchen, some happening album on the sound system. (Nick was very serious about keeping up with music trends. He could bore for hours about how he'd discovered the latest band six months before everyone else.)

Ten minutes later, they would be gone. And Mimi would spend all evening praying that there would be a break in the pattern. She knew how it would go without even being there. Victoria would fizz and sparkle for the first half of the evening. By ten o'clock she would be three sheets to the wind. Then Nick would start winding her up, subtly, so no one could hear. And she'd take it out on other people. She would be provocative and argumentative. Then, when people fought back, told her to shut up, she'd end up in tears. And Nick would drag her out, apologizing to all and sundry, with no one realizing he had provoked her behaviour and done nothing to save her from herself.

Mimi would usually be in bed when they got back, and she would lie tense under the duvet, hearing Nick telling Victoria she was a waste of space. A raddled old drunken has-been who was riding on his coat-tails. She'd been virtually washed up when he'd found her. If he hadn't come along and rescued her, she'd be nothing. She could hear him, his voice low and vicious, as he ripped her apart. Then Victoria would retaliate. Mimi could imagine her lunging for him. Then the part that she really hated. Muffled thuds. Her mother's voice, high, hysterical, shrieking harsh expletives. The sound of a body falling to the ground. Hideous silence for a few long seconds and then more thuds. Something crashing against the wall. Her mother threatening to call the police and Nick laughing. Mimi had never dared interrupt. She was too afraid. She didn't want to humiliate her mother. And she suspected that if she did intervene, her mother might turn on her. She had a curious loyalty to Nick that Mimi could never quite fathom.

She had never seen physical evidence of any violence. The only proof she had was what she heard. On Sundays Victoria would be unabashed. As would Nick, up and about with a spring in his step, perfectly able to look Mimi in the eye, off to the gym followed by golf. Sometimes they all managed to have dinner together. Mimi would find herself carrying on a false, animated conversation with Nick, hating herself for her hypocrisy but as desperate as everyone else to pretend things were all right, while Victoria toyed with her food and drank water.

It wasn't just the violence Mimi hated Nick for, especially as she sometimes suspected her mother invited it. Victoria could be extraordinarily belligerent, and was an expert at pushing the wrong button, needling people. What Mimi really couldn't stand was the way he subtly tried to run Victoria down. Little digs about her appearance, which she knew her mother couldn't take. About looking a little tired, or old, or overweight, knowing that would get to her. And he constantly questioned her judgement at work. If there was one thing Victoria was brilliant at, it was her job. But Nick, media mogul extraordinaire, seemed to think she was merely playing at it. With one cutting remark he could rip her efforts apart. And Victoria just seemed to take his criticism. It was as if she believed every word he said. Without a drink inside her, she had no fight at all.

Gradually Mimi realized that Victoria was falling apart before her very eyes. Not that she'd ever been exactly stable. But even Mimi could see she was heading for a breakdown. Her confidence was fading; she had everything out of perspective. There was nothing for it. Nick had to go.

The bus arrived. Mimi took a deep breath and checked her

watch again, praying that the bus would keep to its schedule. If they were late, if Nick had been and gone by the time they got back, then they'd have blown it.

Crossways Farm was a total misnomer. There was no hint that anything had ever been allowed to grow and flourish within its environs. There wasn't a blade of grass that hadn't been slabbed over or manicured to within an inch of its life. There were towering remote-control gates, ornamental brickwork and enough automatic security lighting to illuminate Colditz. The house had been completely renovated, with UPVC leaded windows and shiny plastic drainpipes. Needless to say, there were no animals in sight.

At five past one the enormous gates slowly parted. Moments later a black Mercedes sports car zipped through them and headed straight into the centrally heated garage, whose doors had also opened as if by magic. 'Living on a Prayer' by Bon Jovi was suddenly cut short. Nick Taverner checked his appearance in the mirror, adjusting his trademark Wayfarer sunglasses, and leaped out.

Crossways Farm was Nick Taverner's pride and joy. A testament to his wealth, success and good taste. Everything had been done to his specification and it made him feel like a king. He bounded into the kitchen.

'Hi, Mr Taverner!' Yasmin was perched on a cowhide stool, swinging her legs and sipping Coke out of a bottle.

'No school?'

'Teacher-training afternoon.'

'Nice work if you can get it.'

Nick pulled open the huge American fridge and surveyed the interior, nodding his head and clicking his fingers to the music that was blaring.

'Mimi and I were just going to take a jacuzzi?'

'Yeah?'

'Why don't you join us?' Yasmin looked at him from underneath her fringe.

Nick hesitated. He was due on the golf course in an hour's time. But he would have to be clinically insane to turn down this offer. He'd seen Yasmin eyeing him up. He felt sure there was more than just a thread of attraction between them. And she was a smart enough kid. She knew how to play the game. He knew that by the way she'd hitched her skirt up in the car last night. She was sending him signals; strong signals.

He pulled a beer out of the fridge, turned and looked Yasmin in the eye. She stared straight back at him boldly. He flashed her a knowing smile.

'Give me five minutes to get my trunks on.'

It was all Yasmin and Mimi could do not to burst into howls of derisive laughter as, ten minutes later, Nick appeared in a minuscule pair of black trunks. Luckily, he'd not long had a back and chest wax at the health club, and he gave himself a quick run over with some Lancôme *Auto-Bronzant* which hopefully wouldn't wash off. As he sat down he discreetly checked to see if there was an incipient spare tyre, but felt reassured that his stomach was as flat as could be realistically expected. All those merciless sessions with the ab machine had paid off.

Mimi and Yasmin sat opposite him. He tried not to gawp. He didn't lech over Mimi; she was too close to home even for him. But Yasmin was something else. With her long dark hair and her eyes like sloes, that dusky skin, those peachy bosoms barely covered by her teeny bikini . . .

Suddenly, Mimi stood up.

'You know what? I'm actually starving. If I stay in here my blood sugar's going to drop way too low. I think I'll go and make us some pasta.'

'Cool.' Yasmin nodded her agreement. 'I'm going to stay in a bit longer. This is really chilling me out.'

Nick cleared his throat.

'Um – me too. I can feel my muscles starting to relax. But pasta would be great.'

Mimi climbed out of the tub, pulled a towel round her and padded out of the pool area. Nick sat back with his eyes shut, enjoying the sensation of the warm bubbles caressing his body. Suddenly he felt something next to him. A thigh rubbing against his. He opened one eye to see Yasmin looking at him with a dreamy expression in her eyes.

'You don't mind if I sit next to you?'

'No . . .'

Mind? Of course he didn't mind.

'I'm sitting right on this jet,' she breathed. 'I can't tell you what it's doing to me.' She arched her back in pleasure.

Nick swallowed. What the hell was he supposed to do? He wasn't sure if it was an invitation. Yasmin put her hands behind her head and pulled the string at the back of her neck. The two tiny triangles fell away.

'That's better.' She smiled. 'How are you feeling?'

'Um . . . well. Very . . . relaxed.'

'Just relaxed?' Her mouth twitched in amusement. It was perfectly plump, pink with gloss. She rolled her bottom lip between her teeth, surveying him, her eyes twinkling.

Nick gave a little laugh, not quite sure of the next move. He was being cautious. He didn't want to come across as a dirty old man. As long as she took the lead, he could justify his actions. He wasn't going to force himself on her. Suddenly she was sitting on his lap, straddling him, her face up close to his, her breasts perilously close. Her breath smelt minty from her gum, which she was still chewing. He could see specks of gold in her hazel eyes.

'Golly,' she said. 'Hel-lo, Mr Taverner.'

Nick tried a modest, self-deprecating grin. 'Hello,' he managed.

Yasmin starting moving herself against him. He thought about absolutely everything in his life that was boring. Recited all his pin numbers and security codes to himself . . .

'Nick?'

He opened his eyes with a groan, to find Victoria staring straight at him.

'I didn't actually touch it,' said Yas afterwards. 'I just had to pretend. It never came out of his trunks. I deserve an Oscar. It was all I could do not to laugh in his face. Where's my moola?'

Mimi counted out her birthday money.

'I can't believe your mum has been so calm about it.'

Victoria had just ordered Yasmin out of the jacuzzi, told her to get dressed and called her a taxi. Nick had made some pathetic excuse, about Yasmin being upset and him trying to comfort her, and Victoria had laughed a rather nasty, ominous laugh.

'Don't worry,' said Mimi confidently. 'It'll all kick off when you've gone. I'll keep you posted. And thanks.'

She hugged her friend, as the entryphone buzzed. The taxi was at the gates. Mimi pushed the button to open them.

'I better go,' said Yas. 'Listen, call me if it all gets out of hand. But you know what, you've done the right thing. Major creep.' She stuffed another piece of gum in her mouth. 'But he's very well endowed. Maybe that's why your mother's hung around so long . . .'

Later that night, Mimi felt slightly sick with guilt, not to mention panic. Her mother was totally distraught. Mimi was shocked that she was so surprised. To her, even at seventeen, it was blindingly obvious that Nick was a womanizer: Yasmin was by no means the first he had fallen prey to. A stupendous two-hour screaming match had ended up with Victoria shrieking her final ultimatum.

'I want you out of this house!'

Nick's eyes were flinty. He smiled mirthlessly.

'But this is *my* house,' he pointed out reasonably. 'If you've got a problem with my behaviour, you're the one who has to go.'

'Where are we supposed to go?'

'I'll phone a hotel. I'll book you in for a week. That should give you enough time to find someone else to live off. You're a fast worker.'

And so it was that Victoria and Mimi found themselves in a nasty hotel room with twin beds, orange eiderdowns and brown curtains. Victoria immediately popped two Temazepam and was out like a light.

Mimi sat in the semi-darkness, chewing the already ragged flesh at the edge of her nails. At eleven o'clock she finally summoned up the nerve to pick up her phone and dial the number that she had never forgotten.

'Sorry, but the number you have dialled is no longer available.' The woman from BT sounded firm and authoritative. Mimi dialled again, thinking she must have made a mistake in her haste. But the message was the same. Her heart racing, Mimi put the phone down. She looked over at Victoria, the slight rise and fall of the bedcover the only indication that she was still alive.

Her mum had put all her eggs in Nick's basket. Mimi wasn't totally familiar with her business affairs, but she knew her PR company had been taken over by Nick's conglomerate, and that Victoria worked exclusively for him now. He wasn't exactly going to expect her in the office first thing in the morning.

No job. No money. Nowhere to live. And the lifeline Mimi had been depending on, from the moment she hatched the plan, had been cut off.

Maybe the number had just been changed. She tried directory enquiries.

'I'm sorry – it's ex-directory,' the operator informed her.

'Please. It's terribly important. It's a matter of life and death.'

'I'm sorry.'

Mimi slammed down the receiver and put her head in her hands. She should have thought this plan through. She should have guessed there would be a hiccup. Everything had gone so smoothly until now. Nick had taken the bait; her mother had reacted just as predicted. But the plan was nothing without the final piece of the jigsaw.

She stood up and reached decisively for her coat. She couldn't give up now. She scribbled a note for Victoria on some hotel paper, though she was pretty certain her mother wasn't going to wake up until the morning. Then she went out to reception to order a taxi. Luckily Nick hadn't got round to cancelling their cab account, though she didn't think it would take him long to cut them off without a penny – mobiles, cashpoints, slates in their favourite bars, the petrol. They had a stream of tabs around town. At least Victoria's car was still in her name, even though she was rarely sober enough to drive it.

The cab glided into Bath and Mimi watched as the pubs emptied, envying the revellers their carefree, drunken journeys home. It was going to be all right, she assured herself. Now she'd proved to her mother just how awful Nick was. That had been the hardest part.

'Could you wait for me?' she asked the cab driver as they pulled up outside an elegant three-storey house in the middle of a terrace. There were lights on. Thank goodness someone was in. The seconds felt like hours until the door opened. A woman stood there, short dark hair, slim, attractive. She was frowning, suspicious. As one would be if a distraught-looking teenage girl appeared on your doorstep. Wary of some elaborate scam, she instinctively stood in the crack of the door, in case she was stampeded by a herd of thugs.

'Yes?'

'Is George in?'

'I'm sorry. I think you've got the wrong address.'

The woman made to close the door. Mimi stepped forward.

'No, I haven't. This is his house. George Chandler?'

'Oh. George. Of course.' The woman smiled in realization. 'I'm sorry. We've bought this house off him. Didn't you know he'd moved?'

Mimi stood rigid with shock.

'Moved?' she croaked. 'Where to?'

'Sorry. I don't think I can reveal that information.'

'You must have an address for him? Or a number?'

'I'm afraid not. He didn't leave it. He's had all his post forwarded.'

The door closed. Mimi walked back over to the cab slowly, as if to the guillotine.

'I'm going to need some money if you want me to take you back.' The cabbie was eyeing her suspiciously.

'It's on account.'

'Sorry, love. I've just had a call through from the boss. The account's closed.'

'But I haven't got any money on me.'

The driver put his car into first gear, as if he was about to drive away.

'Then it's tough.'

Mimi, who was a pretty cool customer, felt an unfamiliar panic. The evening was going from bad to worse.

'Take me back to the hotel,' she begged. 'My mum's got money.'

'I've heard that one before.'

'You can't just leave me here. I'm underage.'

The cabbie looked her up and down.

'Yeah, right.'

Mimi stamped her foot, foiled by her own attempt to look more grown up than she really was.

'If I'm found dead in the gutter with my throat cut, it'll be your fault. Could you live with that?'

The cabbie rolled his eyes. The kid did have a point. On reflection, judging by the way girls dressed these days, she probably was only about fourteen. And he wouldn't have thanked anyone for leaving his teenage daughter stranded miles from home at nearly midnight.

'Get in.'

Mimi slid on to the velour seat cover and pulled her coat

round her. She was shivering. Cold dread was seeping through her. As the car pulled out of Northampton Street and headed back through the city, she wondered what on earth she was supposed to do now.

Six

Lisa wasn't entirely sure what all the fuss was about, when people said that selling a house was near the top of the stress list. She'd found it remarkably easy, but then as the estate agent pointed out she had bought sensibly, maintained her properties well and priced them to sell.

'I wish we had more clients like you,' he said. 'Most of them expect to achieve sky-high prices when they can't even be bothered to vacuum the carpet before the viewers come round.'

Lisa made sure every surface was gleaming before anyone set foot over the threshold, which meant she got her asking price from cash buyers for both the flat and her house within a week of them going on the market. George was equally lucky as the agent he chose had a waiting list for property in his street, and found him a buyer straightaway. It had just been a question of agreeing a price.

'I could probably get more,' he told Lisa. 'But I want a quick, watertight sale. And I got a hefty discount from the agent as they didn't have to do any particulars, so I'm not going to complain.'

Luck, it seemed, was on their side.

There was only one moment when Lisa got cold feet about what she was doing. She went to say goodbye to the tenant in her flat, an earnest American girl called Dawn who was studying for an English degree at nearby Warwick University. They went to a local bar to share a farewell bottle of wine. Clutching a bottle of Pinot Grigio and two glasses, Lisa pushed her way through the jostling tourists who had recently spilled out of the RSC and were now discussing the finer points of the play in loud voices, hoping that whoever overheard them would be impressed. With the consummate skill of one used to crowded places, she appropriated a table that was just being vacated and beckoned Dawn to come and sit down.

After two glasses Dawn, slightly flushed, leaned forward with a conspiratorial smile.

'So – does this all mean wedding bells?'

Lisa looked rather startled.

'Not at all.'

Dawn drew back, mortified that she'd got the wrong end of the stick.

'Oh, I'm sorry. I didn't mean to be personal. It's just . . . well, it's kind of a big commitment, don't you think? Buying a hotel with someone? Even bigger than buying a house?'

Lisa thought for a moment.

'Yes, I suppose it is. But it's a business arrangement. I mean, there's someone else in on the deal.' She smiled tightly, feeling a trifle defensive. 'And I'm not going to marry him either.'

Dawn looked excruciatingly embarrassed.

'I shouldn't drink.' She put down her glass. 'It makes me say stuff I shouldn't.'

'Hey, it's no big deal.' Lisa was anxious that Dawn shouldn't feel bad. In fact, it was the first time she'd seen the girl relax. She hadn't meant to be snappy. But Dawn had hit a nerve. It hadn't really occurred to Lisa that this move somehow meant her relationship with George had moved on a step. They'd been so wrapped up in the machinations of buying The Rocks, and what they were going to do with it, that they hadn't really touched on their personal life.

Yes, when you looked at it closely, they were moving in together, technically. But only because it made economic sense, not because they'd made a conscious decision to do so. After all, there was only a small apartment in the hotel, with one bedroom. If they lived apart, it would mean one of them renting, or sacrificing a hotel room, which would eat into their profit margin.

She wondered if she should talk to George about exactly where they stood with each other. But then she decided to leave it. They had enough to worry about. And, anyway, if she started analysing where they were, he might think she was dropping hints, and that was the last thing she wanted. Dawn was being typically American, reading into it things that weren't there. From her reaction, she obviously thought Lisa was taking a big risk.

If there was any risk in what they were about to do, it was that neither of them had the first clue about running a hotel . . .

It was only later, in bed, her head swimming slightly from having drunk the lion's share of the bottle of wine, that she felt a slight panic. Lisa valued her independence. She had always clung to it fiercely. Had she sacrificed it unwittingly? Did George see this as some sort of commitment? She didn't think so. They'd always respected each other's space. That was why she was still with him, almost a year after they'd first met.

In the past, most men tried to crowd her after just a few weeks. They needed constant reassurance, bombarding her with presents in order to secure her undying love. They just didn't get it when she threw them back. Two weeks later it would be all over, Lisa backing off like a frightened horse being led into a box. George didn't shower her with meaningless gifts. He was more secure than that. And she trusted him. He was solid. She felt sure that whatever happened they could keep things on a businesslike level.

Reassuring herself she had done the right thing, she spent the next few days throwing herself into the task of packing up what she wanted to take with her, which didn't amount to a great deal. She'd sold most of her furniture with the house and the flat. And Lisa was always very careful not to accumulate clutter. At the end of every season she threw out any of her clothes that were worn or no longer fitted well or no longer pleased her, sent shoes to the cobbler for repair, suits to the dry-cleaners, then wrapped everything up in tissue paper and packed it away. She wasn't given to impulse purchases, never made mistakes. She knew exactly what suited her. Her wardrobe had to work, after all. She would be called upon at short notice for a particular job, and she needed to put her hands straight on the appropriate outfit and be safe in the knowledge that it was clean, pressed, fitted perfectly and had no loose threads or buttons missing.

The rest of her life was as streamlined and organized as her wardrobe. Her essential paperwork was always dealt with immediately and neatly filed away in colour-coordinated box files. She didn't keep personal letters. She threw them away. Or old photos – she put the few she liked (usually of places, rarely of people) in an album and chucked the rest. She dropped magazines off at the dentist or the recycling centre. It was as if she lived almost entirely in the present. She needed no relic from her past, either distant or immediate. Lisa had absolutely no sentiment. George was amazed that she kept no record of her modelling career – she didn't have a single photograph.

'What do I need them for? I'm not going to do any more work, so I don't need a portfolio. Anyway, I'd only look at them and get depressed.'

'No. You should be proud.'

She shrugged.

'It's hardly an achievement.'

That chapter in her life was definitely closed, and she didn't want to go poking about in it. As far as she was concerned, her erstwhile career had bought her a house and a flat, which in turn had enabled her to buy The Rocks. That was a sufficient memento.

George was absolutely staggered when she announced that she had finished.

'You'd better come and help me, then,' he said gloomily. He was rather overwhelmed by the undertaking, not least because he kept being distracted by emails and missives from the architect, by a flurry of applications for the various posts they had advertised, by articles and ideas in design magazines he fell across. This to him was far more interesting than sorting through his belongings. So Lisa came and stood over him.

By contrast to her, George was a spendthrift and a hoarder. His house was stuffed with clothes, gadgets, gizmos, works of art, CDs, DVDs, kitchen equipment, wine. And shoes – he was the king of shoes. Boots, brogues, loafers, trainers, from Patrick Cox down to three pairs of Timberlands in varying states ranging from pristine to distressed.

Lisa forced him to whittle his collection down to five pairs.

'You're moving to the seaside. What possible use can you have for black patent dinner shoes?'

Grumbling, George made his final selection, knowing that there would come a day when he would curse his culling. But time and again she reminded him that the owner's accommodation was only tiny. This really was the start of a new life, George realized eventually. He was downsizing, relocating, changing career. He looked at the boxes neatly stacked in the living room. Lisa had packed it all for him, labelled it neatly. There was nothing superfluous. They were ready to go. For the past month, George had kept on top of all the various estate agents and solicitors, snapping at their heels and smoothing out any possible snags almost before they had reared their heads. He knew how fragile property chains were, and as the purchase of The Rocks involved coordinating the sale of three properties, the likelihood of something going irretrievably wrong was pretty high. But eventually, just as a foul and blustery April transformed itself into a warm and balmy May, the day of completion arrived with no threat of the deal collapsing.

*

George stood on the pavement for a moment, then closed his front door for the very last time and posted the key back through the letterbox for the new incumbent. As he heard it thud on the doormat, he realized that this was the moment of no return. He loved Bath. It suited him. He understood how things worked; knew where to get things done, who to turn to. He had people who owed him favours; people he could do favours for. He didn't have a clue how things worked in Mariscombe. And George was no fool. He knew that every town, however small, had its own peculiarities, its own hierarchy. There were unwritten rules about what you could and couldn't do. Mariscombe, for all its superficial charm, wasn't going to be any different.

He looked at his watch. Five to twelve. The contracts were due to complete at midday; the monies would be transferred electronically. Theoretically, he could put in a phone call to his solicitor and stop the sales. For a wild moment, it was a possibility. He imagined the chaos, the uproar, the panic, all the other people in the chain standing on their pavements, waiting for the nod, then realizing it had all fallen through, that the removal lorries would have to be unpacked . . .

One minute to. The removal men were satisfied that everything was safely lashed up and covered over. They pulled down the back of the lorry, snapped up the lock.

'All right?' the gaffer asked George.

He took in a deep breath and nodded. Lisa appeared round the corner, with a carrier bag stuffed full of sandwiches and mineral water for the trip.

'Let's go.' She smiled, pulling her car keys out of her pocket. They had decided to keep her soft-top Mazda, as it seemed appropriate by the sea. George had sold his car, and to replace it they were going to buy a small van which would come in useful both during the renovations and when the hotel was up and running.

As he opened the door and slipped into the passenger seat, the minute hand on his watch slid smoothly on to twelve.

Midday. It was a done deal. No looking back. As Lisa started up the engine and followed in the wake of the removal lorry, George shut his eyes and put his head back, breathing deeply.

'OK?' Sensing his disquiet, Lisa looked at him sideways. George nodded, unable to vocalize exactly how he felt – elated but terrified. By comparison, Lisa seemed unfazed by the proceedings. She hadn't expressed a moment's regret at selling her house.

'It's just a house,' she'd shrugged. 'Four walls.'

He wasn't sure whether to admire her for her lack of sentimentality or pity her.

The further west they drove the warmer the day became. Once they left the motorway, Lisa pulled the roof back and they drove through the rolling Devon countryside, the hedgerows edged with citric yellow gorse, the velvet green fields sprinkled with an abundance of fluffy, bouncing lambs. And as they drove down the tortuous hill that led into Mariscombe, saw the golden crescent of Mariscombe Sands and the shining blue ocean stretched out as far as the eye could see, George found his fears and worries dissipating. As they pulled into the driveway of The Rocks, he smiled. How could this possibly be a mistake?

The removal men stood in front of their van, gawping in awe at the view.

'Bloody hell, mate. I can see why you've bought this place.'

George gave a disparaging smile that disguised how he felt.

'Yeah, well.' He tried to keep his voice downbeat. 'I'll probably be in debt for the rest of my life.'

'Who cares, with a view like that?'

Exactly, thought George, but he didn't want to come across as smug. It didn't seem fair, somehow, that he had this opportunity, this magnificent outlook to wake up to every morning, while these three guys had to trundle back up the motorway and go home to what were no doubt stifling little boxes on some faceless estate somewhere. But then he was taking a huge risk. If this venture failed, they would be homeless and broke. Their fabulous view came at a price. And the hard work hadn't even started yet . . .

He and Lisa spent the next hour directing boxes and furniture into various rooms, then made the removal men a cup of tea – Lisa had made sure to pack a kettle, mugs, tea bags, milk, sugar and a huge packet of Hobnobs into the boot of her car so they wouldn't be caught out. As soon as the removal van disappeared out of the drive, Lisa picked up George's hand and wordlessly they walked back inside.

Often when a property is stripped bare of its previous occupants, the new arrivals feel a sense of disappointment as dirt and imperfections are suddenly shown up. Rooms seem smaller or shabbier; pictures make themselves felt by their absence. But once The Rocks had been relieved of the Websdales' gloomy furniture and plethora of knick-knacks, it seemed to come to life. The atmosphere inside lifted, as if the house felt relieved of its shackles, and it seemed to have increased in size. They walked round silently, almost in awe. Finally, they came into the dining room. The hideous brown curtains had been left closed, hanging off the plastic rail that wasn't really strong enough to support their weight. The two of them looked at each other and, without a word, each took one end and pulled, until the entire rail collapsed, taking reams of dusty velvet with it. Light flooded the room. Outside, the sun sparkled in a periwinkle blue sky that bent down to kiss a cobalt blue sea.

George felt the hairs on the back of his neck prickle.

'It's even better than I remembered,' said Lisa softly.

'It's going to be fantastic,' said George. 'We hardly need to do anything to it. It's perfect, under all the crap they stuffed in it. Thank God they didn't put it on the market when it was empty. We wouldn't have had a hope.'

'Let's take our sandwiches down to the beach.' Lisa held up the carrier bag.

George hesitated. He wanted to look round the house properly, start taking detailed notes about what needed doing.

But outside the sea beckoned. He could feel its pull as strong as a rip tide.

'Come on, then.'

They sat on a rock, dangling their feet in a pool. The water was shockingly cold at first, but they found they got used to it. At the water's edge, a young couple held their toddler's hands as he took his first steps in the sea, squealing as the waves rushed in and broke over his toes.

'Our beach,' said George with a huge smile on his face, as Lisa stuffed their sandwich wrappers and empty bottles back in her rucksack.

'Race you,' said Lisa, leaping off the rock and on to the damp sand.

The tide had gone out quite a way in the time they had taken to eat their lunch, and they were both out of breath by the time they reached the water. They ran along the surf, whooping and hollering with excitement, breath taken away by the cold. Lisa bent down and splashed George, scooping up armfuls of water, drenching herself in the process. He retaliated by grabbing her, lifting her off her feet.

'No!' she protested as he held her over the water, then dropped her in. At the last moment she grabbed him and pulled him down with her. Gasping with the shock of the icy water, they wrestled like puppies. George rolled on top of her, smiling. They lay there for a moment in the shallows, the waves lapping over them.

'Is this really going to be our life?' she asked him. 'Can we do this any time we like?'

'Freeze our bollocks off, you mean?' he grinned.

'It's just brilliant. I feel so happy. When's the last time we did something mad like this?'

'There's going to be some hard work,' he warned. 'You won't always be able to frolic in the surf at the drop of a hat. In fact, we ought to get back. I've got a mountain of things to organize.'

He went to get up, but she pulled him back down on top of her.

'I've never made love in the sea,' she breathed.

George had a flashback to a Caribbean beach, white sand and a black velvet sky.

'Nor me,' he lied, effortlessly.

'Come on, then.' She smiled up at him.

'You've got to be joking. Those cliffs up there are crawling with birdwatchers. There's probably hundreds of people with their binoculars trained on us.'

'So what?'

George looked at Lisa askance. She put her hands up, amused by his apparent prudery.

'It's OK. I'm only joking.'

She scrambled to her feet, still laughing, and they walked back up the beach hand in hand, soaking wet, their clothes squelching, as a gentle sun beamed down. They looked up at The Rocks, towering benevolently over them.

'Good move,' said George. Any doubts he'd had earlier in the day had melted away. Even a house in Royal Crescent wouldn't come close.

At six o'clock that evening, Justin burst in through the front door with a fistful of character helium balloons.

'Our first guests,' he announced proudly, tying them to the newel post at the bottom of the stairs. Scooby-Doo, Tweety Pie and Homer Simpson bobbed around happily, looking quite at home.

'I've come to help,' he went on. 'And I want you to meet Enid.'

George's heart sank. Justin had a habit of scooping up flaky, zany girls who were usually deeply spiritual but hopelessly impractical – trust-fund chicks with elaborate names, like Biba and Ariadne. They were usually great at writing poetry or rolling joints, but unlikely to be handy with a paintbrush. One of Justin's hangers-on was the last thing they needed now, thought George.

'Enid?' he questioned, warily.

Justin pointed outside, grinning. In the drive, next to Lisa's car, was parked a pristine orange VW camper van. George was relieved, but rolled his eyes in fond exasperation nevertheless. It was typical Justin. Whenever he got involved in something, he had to go the whole hog. Whatever he took up – which over the years had included polo, skiing, sailing and shooting – he bought all the accessories and accoutrements. George imagined the attic at Justin's ancestral home in Bedfordshire, stuffed with guns and polo sticks and life jackets, all jettisoned when he had moved on to his next craze. Now here he was buying into the surfer lifestyle when as far as George knew he hadn't so much as stuck his toe in the water. He'd paid one fleeting visit to Mariscombe before he had signed on the dotted line with George and Lisa, and pronounced it paradise. Which from Justin was high praise indeed, as he moved from one international hot spot to the next in his quest for a new scam, a fresh buzz, the latest thrill. Now here he was, decked out in a pair of Hawaiian shorts, his floppy blond hair pushed back by a pair of titanium sunglasses. George grinned to himself. There was no doubt about it. Justin was barking.

'We'll make the most of it while he's interested,' George whispered to Lisa. 'I know Justin. He'll get bored after five minutes.'

That evening, the three of them wandered up the hill to the Mariscombe Arms, a long, low, thatched building painted a jaunty, nautical blue with a labyrinth of interconnecting white-washed rooms crammed with wobbly oak tables. In the height of summer there was no elbow room, but on a mild evening in early May there were just a few locals.

The landlord was a rather theatrical man with a leonine mane of grey hair. He surveyed the three of them with interest, as George and Justin decided to plump for a pint of cider each and Lisa ordered a Pimm's.

'Early holiday?' he enquired politely, in rich, plummy tones.

'Far from it,' joked George. 'In fact, I think we've just started a life sentence. We took over The Rocks today.'

'Ah.' Their host digested this news as he pulled the cloudy cider, then faffed about ceremoniously making a Pimm's for Lisa.

'You've put the cat amongst the pigeons, you know,' he announced, carefully slicing up an orange.

'Have we?'

'Bruno Thorne was after it. The word is he wasn't best pleased when he lost out to you lot.'

'Who's Bruno Thorne when he's at home?' asked Justin rudely.

'Local lad. He works up in London most of the time. Swans in and out of Mariscombe like he owns the place.' He smiled. 'Which, technically, he does.'

'Well, it won't hurt him to have some healthy competition then.' Undaunted, Justin took a slug of cider.

'Rather you than me. Last person that crossed him ended up over the cliff down there.'

He nodded his huge, shaggy head out of the window, towards the spit of land that separated Higher Mariscombe from the village below. It was lined with craggy, unforgiving rocks. Lisa shuddered.

'That's awful.'

'It was his younger brother. So you see, he doesn't take any prisoners.'

He put Lisa's glass on the bar top proudly. It was bursting with fruit and topped with a paper parasol.

'Well, neither do we,' Justin assured him.

There was a grave shake of the head.

'He's a tricky customer. Not averse to the odd backhander. And he's got a lot of people on his side.'

George looked annoyed.

'Why are you telling us all this?'

'Webby said I was to look after you.'

'Mrs Websdale?'

The landlord nodded, then leaned forward confidentially.

'Between you and me, I don't think yours was the highest offer. But she wanted you to have it.' He nodded his head to Lisa. 'She said you reminded her of her at your age.'

The look of horror on Lisa's face made him convulse with laughter.

'I know you find it hard to believe, but she was a looker once. I've seen the photos.' He gave a lascivious wink. 'She was the Face of Whitby in 1952. Miss Scarborough three years on the trot. It was only after her hysterectomy that it all went pear-shaped.'

George grimaced.

'Too much information.'

'She was a magnificent woman.' There was a wistful look in his eyes. Then he held his hand out. 'Anyway, I'd better introduce myself, as I'm sure you'll probably avail yourself of my hospitality now and again. Leonard Carrington.'

The three of them shook hands with him politely.

'How long have you been here?' asked Lisa.

'Twenty-five years,' answered Leonard. 'And I'm still regarded as a newcomer.' He smiled broadly. 'Welcome to Mariscombe.'

They sat on a bench in a big bay window and ate huge oval platters of scampi and chips.

'Perfect,' said Lisa, squeezing out tartare sauce from a sachet.

George wasn't so impressed. He prodded his garnish dubiously – cress and a tomato quarter.

'I don't think I'll be poaching this chef.'

'Pub grub. It's what people want by the seaside.'

'Not our guests,' contradicted George. 'At least I hope not. I'm after a more discerning clientele.'

'Don't be so snotty, George.' Justin poked him with his fork. 'You're a food snob.'

'Yes. I am. And this isn't scampi. It's never been anywhere near Dublin Bay.'

'Shut up and eat it,' ordered Justin, squirting ketchup liberally over his chips.

George managed a smile. He didn't like to admit it, but he was feeling rather daunted by everything that had to be done.

'Sorry,' he said. 'I guess I'm just a bit paranoid about the whole thing. What if I am wrong and people do want padded headboards and Neil Diamond piped through the dining room?'

'Listen, mate. We can't go wrong. So long as we market it right. There's always going to be people who want style and quality. And we've got the most stunning location. It's a winner.'

George tried to feel reassured. Justin was always confident. That's why he was so successful, with even the most madcap of schemes.

'I'm more worried about this bloke who wanted to buy The Rocks.' Lisa blew on a hot chip before eating it. 'Do you think he could cause trouble for us?'

George shook his head.

'The landlord's just stirring it up.'

'You'll always get someone who thinks he's top dog,' added Justin. 'You just have to show them who's boss.'

'Great,' said Lisa, not convinced. 'Turf wars already. It's exactly what I was trying to get away from.'

'This is Mariscombe. Not Chicago. I think we can handle whatever they throw at us,' said Justin, with the bravado of one who had once done three months inside, though nobody was quite sure what for. Rumours ranged from non-payment of council tax to driving while disqualified.

Lisa looked over at Leonard and giggled.

'Do you think he was having an affair with Webby?'

George nearly choked on a chip.

'What a horrible thought.'

'Hey!' Lisa nudged him with her elbow. 'If what Leonard

says is true, and I am the spit of her when she was younger, chances are I'll look like she does now when I'm older.'

'Can't wait. Remind me to buy you a quilted dressing gown for your next birthday.'

The mood lightened, the three of them had another drink, then wandered back down the hill. By now it was dark and all they could see were the twinkling lights of the village lining the shore below as they made their way down the inky-black road. Justin insinuated himself between George and Lisa and put an arm round each of them.

'This is going to be great for all of us. You know that?'

'Are you hanging around, then?' said George, surprised. 'I thought you'd be off to Rio or Fiji or Istanbul.'

'Bollocks to all of that,' said Justin. 'I need a rest.'

'You've come to the wrong place then, I'm afraid.' George shook his head. 'You got off lightly today. Tomorrow the hard work starts in earnest.'

'Work,' said Justin, a certain wonder in his voice. 'I've spent my whole life trying to avoid it. I wonder if I'll like it.'

Across the bay, Bruno stepped out on to his veranda, breathing in the cool night air, his hand curled round a heavy tumbler of Irish whiskey. He scanned the shoreline, picking out the familiar landmarks, recognizing each building by its own particular configuration of lights. He started with the Mariscombe Arms at the top of the hill, ablaze with multi-coloured fairy lights, past Atlantic Heights, the flash new apartment block whose car park was filled at weekends with identical black SUVs, then the youth hostel, then the shadowy outline of the church. Four buildings on, his eyes narrowed. There was a fresh set of lights. He counted down and calculated that it must be The Rocks. For weeks it had been shrouded in darkness, but tonight its sudden illumination reminded him that the new owners must have arrived. He felt a fleeting regret at the missed opportunity. Then thanked his lucky stars that his bid hadn't been successful. There was no way he could have fitted that into his schedule. Or his budget, come to that.

He took a gulp of Paddy's, appreciating its warmth, the way it seemed to permeate his muscles straightaway, allowing his shoulders to drop. They seemed to spend an inordinate amount of time up by his ears these days. He drained his glass and whistled to Hector, who shot eagerly out of the sliding door, ready for his bedtime stroll. The two of them made their way down the wooden steps that led from the house straight across the dunes and on to the beach. The long grass whipped at Bruno's legs; his feet disappeared into the soft sand. Ahead of him he could hear Hector snuffling, no doubt hot on the scent of the hundreds of rabbits who built their warrens in the dunes.

Bruno had been biding his time at the Mariscombe Hotel for the past couple of months, and was troubled by what he had found. Things had got so slack that, after the initial shock of his arrival, it hadn't even occurred to any of the staff to sharpen up their act now he was around. He had made sure to melt into the background, giving them a false sense of security so he could observe who the real slackers were. And he was disgusted by what he found. The service was atrocious, the housekeeping diabolical, the food was worse than he'd been given on the one occasion he'd found himself staying overnight in a NHS hospital. The staff clearly looked upon the place as a holiday camp, as they were noticeable more for their absence than anything, especially when the weather was fine. Its absolutely only saving grace was that it was a stone's throw from the beach.

Bruno chided himself for letting things slide. But then he'd only ever bought the place as an investment, bricks and mortar, a more interesting resting place for his cash than the pieces of paper he traded in. Yet despite the hotel's shambolic aura, Bruno felt certain that it was salvageable. The bare bones were there; it just needed re-dressing, shaking up, bringing to life. He spent time wandering round the hotel, absorbing its atmosphere – or lack thereof – and weighing up its strong points. Now, far from being disillusioned, he felt filled with optimism.

He'd already begun making improvements. The outside of the hotel, once a dreary battleship grey, had been painted the colour of Devon clotted cream, and now looked sunny and welcoming. The ancient plastic letters that proclaimed the hotel's name across the front had been removed, and replaced with a trendy lowercase font in petrol blue. The crumbling terrace that lined the front was re-laid with limestone interspersed with squares of gravel planted up with palms and ornamental grasses which, when combined with the steamer chairs and parasols he had ordered, would add an air of colonial sophistication.

But so far, the changes had been merely cosmetic. The heart of the hotel was where the real transformation had to be made, and Bruno hadn't wanted to rush in. It had taken him this long to assess his existing clientele versus the one he wanted, and how best to continue pleasing one whilst luring the other. In the meantime, he had been tying up the loose ends of his financial business, informing all his clients that he would now be operating from Devon. He would have to go back up to the city once a week, as some of them still liked to discuss their money worries face to face rather than by phone and email, and Bruno respected that, given that these were often the clients from whom he earned the healthiest commission. All in all, he felt certain his decision to move back to Mariscombe was the right one. And now he had an action plan. Tomorrow it was going to be gloves off.

As Bruno watched a cloud scud across the moon and felt the breeze from the ocean caress his face, he smiled. If he was still living in London, he'd be pounding the pavements with a plastic poop bag in his hand while he waited for Hector's evening evacuation, instead of the two of them roaming the deserted beach. Already both he and the dog were significantly fitter, and Bruno worked best when his body was finely tuned. He felt good. He almost felt like himself again.

There was really only one blot on the horizon. His mother. Bruno was furious with himself for assuming over the past two years that Joanie had got over Joe's death. She'd always made such a show of coping whenever he came down: it was amazing what a smudge of lipstick and a well-cooked lunch could disguise. His father was a man of few words who wouldn't have dreamed of hinting that anything was amiss. Graham's way of dealing with it was to bury himself in his work: the site demanded an enormous amount of physical attention, and as a result he was occupied during the day and slept well at night. But Joanie . . . Now Bruno was here all the time, now he could call in on her unannounced and see the truth behind the facade, he was desperately worried. Looking back, he could see that there had been a period when she genuinely had coped, on the surface at least. But now she had slipped back down into the mire. The first anniversary of Joe's death had been and gone; the second was approaching and perhaps it had now dawned on her that he really wasn't ever coming back.

How did you snap someone out of a depression when they had every right to be thoroughly miserable? Joe, after all, had been if not Joanie's entire life then a good fifty per cent of it. He had been her *raison d'être*, Bruno realized now, and more than ever he felt guilty that he had criticized Joe for exploiting their mum when it was he who gave rhythm to her days.

Bruno didn't fool himself that his return to Mariscombe went any way towards filling the hole left by Joe. He didn't need to be fussed over and mothered; it made him feel thoroughly uncomfortable. And it wasn't in him to give Joanie the cheeky, irreverent but undeniably genuine affection that Joe had lavished upon her. Bruno wasn't the demonstrative type. Now, he remembered Joe throwing his arms round Joanie in the kitchen and squeezing her for no apparent reason, ruffling her hair and kissing her whenever he left the house, pulling her into his arms and dancing with her to the radio in the kitchen. If Bruno ever hugged or kissed his mother, it was with good reason, and with a certain restraint. He couldn't dish out his affection spontaneously or impulsively. It just wasn't in him to swing her round the kitchen while Elvis sang 'Blue Suede Shoes'. Which was why her face didn't light up when he came into the room like it had done with Joe.

And like a flower that has no sun, Joanie was visibly withering without Joe's attentions. The rooms of their bungalow rang hollow and empty without the thud of music coming from his bedroom. Where once the laundry basket had spilled over with T-shirts and jeans, the pitiful amount of washing that she and Graham produced between them meant it was only worth putting on the machine twice a week. She barely had to clean for between them they made no mess, whereas once the house had been littered with empty cups and glasses, discarded newspapers, abandoned shoes. And Graham didn't bother coming home for lunch now; he grabbed a sandwich on the site. Once this had been the main meal of the day, with Joe joining them nine times out of ten, and she'd always prided herself on doing meat and two veg whatever the weather, and a homemade pudding.

Bruno had spoken to their GP, who had been sympathetic but made it clear there was little she could do.

'I've told her there is medication that could help, but she won't touch it. The problem with women of her generation is the stigma attached to antidepressants. I've no doubt it would help her enormously, but I can't force her to take it. And I don't suppose you can either.' She smiled at Bruno. 'I know it sounds trite, but give her time . . .'

Any other solution he had come up with also seemed trite. A holiday, a puppy. He tried to get her to start up playing bridge again, but she had just sighed and said, 'What's the point?' A question he couldn't answer, as he'd never seen the point of bridge in the first place, but she'd enjoyed it once. He tried to get her on to the golf course, even though he would really rather stick hot needles in his eyes than play, but she refused. Instead, she spent the day with the curtains half closed and an endless diet of mindless television booming at her as she drifted round the house in the same grey cardigan and shapeless trousers. Joanie had once been smart – not fashionable, perhaps, but she had an extensive wardrobe of linen skirts and trousers, cotton and silk knit sweaters, all coordinated in navy and coral and cream, which she wore with Italian shoes and the nice gold jewellery Graham had bought her on landmark birthdays. Her hair had once been cut and highlighted regularly, whereas now it was flat and dull and lifeless and grey. Inactivity was making her lumpy and misshapen. His mother, his bright, busy, sunny mother wasn't even a shadow of her former self. She was unrecognizable.

Every time Bruno went to see her he came away guilty and depressed, to the point where it became tempting not to go. The absolute grey dreariness of her life sapped his strength. Worst of all, he had no one to share his frustrations with. He didn't count the doctor. And he certainly couldn't discuss it with his father, who had never mentioned Joe's name since the day of the funeral, but seemed to be coping, functioning, making decisions, interacting. Common sense told Bruno he was doing everything he could, but he wasn't used to not being in control of a situation. And, of course, compounding it all was his guilt. The knowledge that if it wasn't for him, they wouldn't be in this ghastly situation. He looked out to sea, as if it might hold the answer in its depths, but all he could see was the twinkle of a lighthouse further down the coast.

He whistled for Hector, who appeared out of the darkness and nudged at his leg, indicating that he wanted to play. The two of them mimicked a fight, each knowing just how far they could push the other – Hector pretending to growl, Bruno fondling the dog's ears roughly as he jumped up at him. Bruno grinned wryly to himself as he realized that the most intimacy he had with another living creature these days was with his bloody dog. Maybe he'd add finding a woman to his To Do list, though it might be tricky to find his type in Mariscombe. Bruno liked his women to have a bit of an edge.

Resigned to sharing his bed with Hector for the time being, Bruno slid shut the veranda doors and locked them. He'd get an early night. He needed a clear head for tomorrow, for tomorrow his staff were in for a shock.

Seven

The next evening, Bruno sauntered into the kitchen at six fifteen. The Stereophonics were blaring out of a portable iPod dock, the sound tinny and distorted. Along one work surface were rows of prawn cocktails: metal bowls brimming with limp iceberg lettuce, a few pitiful prawns scattered on top dressed with a luminous pink gloop. Further along, on a stainless-steel warming shelf, were rows of plates covered with metal domes. He lifted one up. Underneath was a clump of yellow rice, some watery tomato-based slop and a dried-out piece of cod. It was at least an hour before this was due to be served. What the hell was it going to be like by the time it reached the table?

He pushed open the fire exit. Outside, Frank the chef and Ed the kitchen porter were having a fag, both dressed in their baggy black and white trousers. Bruno crooked a finger at Frank, who flicked his fag in the bin and, shooting a glance at Ed, followed him inside.

Bruno indicated the plate he'd been examining.

'Talk me through this, would you? What is it, exactly?'

'Roasted Mediterranean cod on a bed of golden saffron rice.'

Bruno raised a quizzical eyebrow.

'Define Mediterranean.'

Frank pointed at the sauce.

'Um, well – that's ratatouille.'

'Is that what it said on the tin?'

Frank looked deeply uncomfortable.

'Look, Tuesdays is always Mediterranean cod. It has been ever since I've been here.'

Bruno crossed his arms.

'I wouldn't feed this to my dog. And, believe me, he'd eat anything.'

Frank could feel himself colouring furiously. Why the sudden inquisition?

'I haven't had any complaints,' he said defensively.

'That's because everyone who stays here is practically lobotomized. But all that's going to change.' Bruno paced across the kitchen, looking round, taking in the grease stains, the peeling lino on the floor, the old, cracked margarine tubs filled with misshapen slices of cucumber and grated carrot ready for garnish.

'What would you do here? If you could? Given free rein.'

Frank scratched his head. He wasn't used to being questioned. He'd worked on automatic pilot for three years. If his career wasn't fulfilling, then his lifestyle was. He lived to surf, not cook. Even if he had once had dreams of thrilling people's tastebuds.

'I don't know,' he answered lamely.

Bruno pulled open the fridge, raking his eyes up and down the shelves, evidently not impressed by what he saw. He slammed it shut and turned to face his quarry. 'I want to turn this place round, Frank. I want this hotel to be fresh, vibrant, family friendly. And I want the food to match. There's not going to be any place for pre-packed crap with bought-in cook-in sauces crammed with additives. I'm not talking off-the-chart gourmet cooking. I just want decent, fresh grub and plenty of it.'

'I see.'

'The place is fossilized. I want to rejuvenate it. My target clientele is wealthy grandparents treating their family to a holiday – thirty-something sons and daughters with two or three young children. We need to work out a menu that will keep them all happy, so they can eat together if they want to.

Or use the babysitting service and have a romantic dinner *à deux*.'

His eyes bored into Frank.

'I need to know if you're the person to help me do it, or if I leave you to breakfasts and running the coffee bar.'

Frank opened his mouth to speak, recognizing that this was his one chance to get it right.

'I think it sounds great. I'd . . . really like the challenge.'

Bruno nodded curtly.

'Good. Because I think you probably had ambition once. But like everyone else here you've got lazy.'

'I do my job!' protested Frank. 'No one goes hungry. I'm never late. I'm here until the last dessert plate comes back in empty.'

'Frank. Please. Don't try and fool me. You've worked things out so you can get away with doing the bare minimum, haven't you?'

Frank squirmed, not sure whether to confess or deny Bruno's accusations. To his surprise, Bruno just grinned.

'Listen, I know how Mariscombe works. It might seem like heaven on earth. The ultimate playground. But it saps people's ambition. They end up drifting through life on a diet of dope and surf and sun. All they care about is the state of the waves and how quickly they can bunk off work.'

As Frank opened his mouth to contradict, Bruno put up his hand to stop him.

'It's a great lifestyle. If you have nothing else to offer the world. But I've been watching you, Frank. I've looked at your CV. Your references. You're not a drop-out. I think you've just lost your way. And I'm prepared to take some of the blame for that. This place is a dump. Why would you serve up anything better than the swill you've been churning out night after night? I'd do the same. Get the slop out on to the plates and get out of the kitchen and into the pub.'

By now Frank was writhing in discomfort. Bruno had put his finger right on it. It was true. Frank didn't care. Not any more. Of course, he had once. He'd had immense pride in his work. Bruno's voice cut through his thoughts.

'Let's be honest, Frank. You're twenty-four. In five, ten years' time, is it you the girls are going to be after? When you're my age –' Bruno smiled self-deprecatingly – 'you're not going to be such a babe magnet. You might be grateful to have something to fall back on. Like a career.'

He moved over towards the swing door, casting a dismissive look at the prawn cocktails; the sauce had now congealed and some of the lettuce was visibly brown at the edges.

'You've got one day to prove yourself. I want you to serve me dinner tomorrow night. The sort of meal you would be proud to serve here. Show me what you're capable of. If I like it, we'll work together. I'm no chef, Frank, so I need someone who can translate my vision for me; tell me what I can and can't do. I have to trust whoever it is. And admire them. So impress me.'

A moment later he was gone. The only evidence that he'd ever been there was the door swinging back and forth with the force of his exit. Frank leaned back against the work surface, shell-shocked. Who did Bruno think he was? Gordon bloody Ramsay? Bollocking him like that, laying down the gauntlet. He could shove his job. There were any number of places up and down the coast Frank could find another job. Woolacombe, Croyde – he didn't care, as long as he could surf and have his pick of the girls.

Frank went to pull his apron over his head. Then suddenly he stopped.

Once upon a time, he had cared. Once upon a time, it would never have occurred to him to open a catering-size tin of ratatouille, or use pre-spiced boil-in-the-bag rice. And there were times when he looked at the muck they served up and shuddered. When had he stopped being ashamed and accepted this appallingly low standard? Bruno was right. In the beginning, he had hoped to make a name for himself, like every young chef. But he'd been distracted. He'd lost sight of his original goal. He wasn't on a career ladder; he was on a downward spiral. The next rung down was the burger van on the beach. And Frank suspected that if he didn't rise to Bruno's challenge, that's probably where he'd end up. He remembered how proud his mum had been of him when he'd come top of his year at catering college. My little Jamie Oliver, she'd called him. But that was laughable. He wouldn't get a job washing lettuce in one of Jamie's kitchens, he knew that. And he was ashamed.

Frank looked at his watch. It was twenty past six and there was no one to be seen. That was typical. But tonight it suited him. He had some serious thinking to do. Bruno had given him twenty-four hours. And Frank knew in his gut that was his only chance.

What would you do here if you could? Bruno had asked.

Frank pushed his way through the swing door and into the dining room. The atmosphere was sombre, almost funereal. Dinner was served between seven and eight thirty, a set menu with three choices that varied little and featured cheap cuts of meat disguised by bought-in sauces. He looked at his watch. The first guests would start shuffling in in about half an hour. It would take them less than five minutes to polish off their prawn cocktails. If he got a move on, gave the waiting staff a kick up the arse, he could be out of here by quarter to nine. Usually after service, he'd bolt to the Jolly Roger and get as many pints down his neck as he could. But tonight he couldn't wait to get back to his room.

Frank smiled to himself. His blood was up. He felt excited for the first time in years. He was going to blow Bruno's mind.

By nine, he was hurrying back to his room. Many of the live-in staff at the Mariscombe Hotel were accommodated in a sprawling wooden chalet tucked away in the far corner of the grounds, shielded from public view by a high hedge of rhododendrons. There was a central living area and a kitchen, and a dozen small bedrooms. Outside, the washing line was hung with drying wetsuits, bikinis and towels; surfboards were propped up against the wall, along with bicycles and skateboards. It was nirvana; a student doss-house, the bins brimming with empty cans and takeaway cartons, a place where the washing up was never done and the sheets were never changed, because the inmates barely slept. Life was one long party, with a token nod to the work that paid for their lifestyle. With food and accommodation thrown in, the only cash they needed was for drink. Clothes didn't matter much here. No one needed a car. Music and movies were pirated and pooled.

Frank realized that Bruno had hit the nail right on the head. You could forget the real world existed in Mariscombe: status symbols, responsibility and ambition meant nothing. But could it last for ever? Without some sort of momentum, it would be easy to become totally dysfunctional. The archetypal beach bum. He'd seen them around the Jolly Roger and the Old Boathouse – sad fifty-year-olds with dreadlocks and tobacco-stained fingers, staring longingly at the firm young flesh on display, always eager to be in on a round but suddenly noticeable by their absence when it was their shout. Frank despised them. Yet there was nothing stopping him heading that way at the moment. This, he realized, was his wake-up call and he better get it right.

He pulled a cardboard box out from under his bed. Inside were his bibles. He couldn't remember how long it was since he had last looked at them; it wasn't very cool to be seen to take your job seriously at the Mariscombe Hotel. But things were going to change. Frank knew it wouldn't be long before he was inspired as he started leafing through. Gordon, Jamie, Rick – all the heroes of great English cooking. Just a few minutes reminded him what it was that had made him want to become a chef in the first place. Ideas flooded his mind, overwhelming him. He needed to write it all down, he didn't even have a pen and paper. Hannah would have some. She was bound to be in. She always was these days. He leaped off the bed, out of the door and ran down the corridor, bursting into Hannah's room without knocking. She was lying on her bed reading last week's *Grazia*.

'Have you got a pen? And any paper?'

She sat up, blushing.

'Course.' She burrowed in a drawer and pulled out a ring-bound notebook and a packet of scented gel-pens. Frank took them gratefully.

'Thanks.'

'It's OK. Any time.' She smiled at him quizzically. 'How come you're not out on the razz?'

Frank opened his mouth to tell her, then thought better of it.

'I've got a couple of letters I need to write.'

'Oh.'

Frank held up the notebook, backing out of the door.

'Cheers.'

Back in his room, Frank looked at the pens. There was purple, pink, green, yellow or orange. Dubiously he drew out the purple one and sniffed it. Grape, apparently. He wasn't quite sure of the point. He certainly wasn't in the habit of sniffing his correspondence, but perhaps some people did. Anyway, he was sure Bruno wouldn't care. Swiftly, he began to draw, sketching out ideas, the purple pen flying across the page as he drew tables and chairs, labelled boxes with arrows and drew little icons to illustrate his ideas.

In the room down the corridor, Hannah felt hot knowing that she and Frank were the only two people in the building. Everyone else was out drinking; they'd pile back around midnight, and the music would go on. Hannah didn't mind her self-imposed incarceration. After all, staying in meant saving at least ten pounds. Which was ten pounds nearer her goal. She pulled open her bedside drawer and looked at her latest bank statement. Only two hundred and forty pounds to go. When she lumped it together with all the money she'd got for her eighteenth, she'd have enough.

She'd researched it meticulously. She'd been on the Internet, trawled through all the cosmetic surgery sites. She'd read hundreds of before and after tales, and satisfied herself that the risk was worth it. That the rise in self-esteem was certainly worth a couple of weeks of pain. Or mere discomfort, if you believed some of the more reassuring accounts. Life-changing, they said. To a woman.

For the six million, trillionth time in her life, she looked at her profile. It was not so much the size of her nose, though that was considerable. It was the way it jutted out from between her eyes, far too high up, then bent suddenly in the middle, dropping down at a sharp angle so that the end hovered over her top lip. She stroked her nose thoughtfully, wondering just what size and shape she would end up with. She was realistic enough to know that she would have to have something that was in proportion with the rest of her; not a dinky little Meg Ryan number. She would have to go on the surgeon's advice. But at least it would be straight. And smaller, if not actually small.

Hannah flopped back down on her bed with her mirror, casting a quick look at the clock. It would be at least another hour before the others came back and she had some company. She loved working at the Mariscombe Hotel. It was like having a huge extended family – a mad, noisy rabble of brothers and sisters. She'd been brought up on a remote farm on Exmoor, the youngest daughter of elderly parents who had increasingly needed her help, meaning that at certain times of the year she had missed large chunks of school. And being so far off the beaten track meant that she'd had no social life to speak of. It had been a lonely existence, and a tough one. Working at the hotel was a holiday in comparison; when you'd stayed up all night lambing for two weeks on end, or broken your back rushing to get the hay in before the rains came, sitting at a hotel reception desk being polite was child's play.

Her parents had been disappointed when she'd decided to go and study travel and tourism at college. They'd somehow expected her to stay on and help them, but Hannah had found the courage to stand up for herself. She'd done her HND, then got herself a job at the Mariscombe Hotel, which was less than an hour away. That had been her only compromise, that she hadn't sought gainful employment further afield. She was near enough to get back if her parents really needed her, and she promised to take her leave at the times of year when they needed her most to help on the farm. So Hannah never really had a holiday, but she didn't mind. This was as close to a holiday as it got.

The only thing Hannah found difficult was being so ungainly. She was five foot ten, with large feet and hands. Growing up on a farm, where appearances didn't matter, with a mother who didn't even use face cream, meant that Hannah hadn't been self-conscious about her appearance for the first eighteen years of her life. In fact, her size and strength had been a positive attribute. But here, where so many of the other girls at the hotel were utterly gorgeous, and had so many opportunities to show off their perfection, her lack of physical beauty had become painfully apparent. Whenever they all went down to the beach, Hannah always stayed fully clothed, while the other girls stripped down to dinky little bikinis, their skin golden and flawless. No one had ever encouraged her to get undressed. It was as if it was obvious that she wouldn't want to inflict her hideous body on the rest of them.

But they all liked her. Adored her, in fact. Hannah was the mother figure, the one who looked after them all and clucked around them. She was in charge of the barbecue on the beach; she made sure they all put sun cream on; she made sure they picked up all their litter. They came to her with their woes and problems – something she found rather baffling, as what did she know of affairs of the heart? But somehow her advice was always sound. And, anyway, she was a good listener. Auntie Hannah, they called her, and she didn't mind, even though it was never reciprocated. She hadn't told anyone else about her unrequited crush. And they didn't seem to notice that she blushed furiously whenever Frank was near. But why would he look at her, when he had Caragh, lean and groomed, her chestnut hair gleaming, as sleek as a thoroughbred entered for the Derby?

But Hannah wasn't one to mope and feel sorry for herself. Ever practical, she had decided to take matters into her own hands. No one had to suffer ugliness in this day and age. She peered at herself in her mirror again. She would start with her nose and work her way down. Collagen next, to plump up her lips – they were rather thin, decidedly unkissable. Hardly even worth putting lip gloss on. Then a boob job. Ironically, despite her size, Hannah had rather small bosoms. Implants would do no harm, to plump them up a bit, and a lift to make them high and rounded. Finally, some judicious liposuction – those bloody child-bearing hips of hers that had never born any children, and were quite unlikely to unless she took drastic action—

There was a sudden rap on the door and she dropped the mirror guiltily.

'Come in.'

Frank poked his head round.

'I need you to tell me if you think I'm going mad.'

He came in tentatively, waving the notebook she'd lent him earlier.

'What is it?'

'My ideas for the new dining room.' He sat down on the bed next to her carefully. 'Bruno wanted my input.'

'Oh.' Hannah took the notebook off him and sniffed it. 'Grape.'

Frank nodded, impatient.

'Yeah. But what do you think? Do you reckon this would work?'

He was sitting right next to her. She could feel his body heat only inches away. The pages in front of her swam. Her heart was pounding. She could hear the blood rushing in her ears. She couldn't really take in anything he had written, but she had to concentrate. She had to give him a coherent answer. She took a deep breath and steadied the pages.

Intrigued, she leafed through his outlines and his sample menus. Unable to wait for her to read through it, he leaned over and started explaining his thought process.

'I think we should split the dining room in half. Have a grill on one side – traditional, waitress service with the tables properly laid up. We can just serve steaks or fish or chicken, with a selection of sauces. On the other side, for more casual dining, and for families with kids, we have a wood-burning pizza oven and burger bar. Then a huge salad bar down the centre of the room, dividing one area from the other. I don't mean pre-packaged coleslaw and slimy potatoes in salad cream. I mean Greek salad. Couscous with roasted vege-tables—'

He broke off, realizing he was ranting.

'Sorry,' he grinned. 'I'm just really excited. What do you think? Honestly?'

'I think . . . wow,' said Hannah admiringly. 'And I'm not just saying that. This would be fantastic. It's just what the hotel needs.'

Frank rubbed his chin.

'I'm still not sure about desserts. They can be such a fag. And we don't have a proper pastry chef.'

'Why don't you do an American ice-cream parlour type thing? Sundaes and banana splits and milkshakes? And brow-nies and cheesecake?'

Frank beamed. How easy would that be? They could bake the desserts fresh in the morning and have them available all day.

'You're a genius.'

Hannah felt herself go pink with pleasure as he patted her on the shoulder. As he stood up, her heart sank. Now she'd done her bit, given him reassurance and advice, he was going.

At the door, he stopped.

'Do you fancy a drink?'

He probably just felt sorry for her. Felt he had to offer.

'No, thanks,' she said. 'I'm trying to save money.'

'We don't have to go out,' he replied. 'I've got a few bottles of Beck's in my room. We can sit outside and chill till the others get back.'

'OK.'

'I'll just put this stuff away. I'll see you outside in five.'

'Great.'

He shut the door. Hannah hugged herself excitedly. She'd have at least forty minutes alone with him if she was lucky. She wished fervently she'd put on something more attractive than her old black velour tracksuit – it really had seen better days and it was decidedly saggy round the bottom. But he'd think she was weird if she got changed. At least her hair was clean. She pulled it out of its scrunchie and it fell to her shoulders. Mousy, but shining . . .

Caragh Flynn was a conundrum, decided Bruno. She was clever, cunning and spectacularly lazy. She reminded him of an exotic cat. Sleek and sly, confident in her supremacy, trading on her looks.

He'd asked her to come over for a drink that evening, to discuss the hotel. She'd arrived bang on time. Eight thirty. She was wearing a black skirt, just above the knee, with a white blouse, crisp and pristine, but just transparent enough to reveal the lacy straps of the white bra underneath. Court shoes – not high, but enough heel to elongate her already long, slender, lightly tanned legs. A smudge of grey eyeliner, a hint of lip gloss. The faintest trace of some light, fresh scent. Pearl earrings and a slim gold chain with a crucifix round her neck. This girl was no surfer chick. She was a consummate professional. Bruno guessed that it had taken her quite some time to dress. To look so businesslike and efficient, yet give the hints of softness and femininity that would leave most men putty in her hands.

Bruno led her through into the living room. He saw her eyes flick around the walls, appraising the contents of the room in a split second, but not giving anything away. Bruno smiled to himself. He could tell by the set of her shoulders, the way she was carrying her head, that it was a strain for her to keep up this cool nonchalance, to pretend as if she wafted in and out of million-pound pads every day of her life. This little girl from the west of Ireland, with her sherry-coloured eyes and her copper hair.

He gestured for her to sit on the sofa with the view of the bay, then planted himself on the one adjacent, crossing one leg over so his foot rested on his knee. She sat bolt upright, but she met his gaze boldly.

'So,' she said, in her softest, most beguiling Kerry lilt. 'You've had a while to suss everybody out. What do you think of the show so far?'

For a moment Bruno felt as if the tables had been turned, and he was the one under scrutiny. She was incredibly self-possessed, and he couldn't help admire her for it.

'Frankly,' he said, 'if I didn't already own the place I wouldn't touch it with a shitty stick. It's a dinosaur. The staff are delinquents. And before you start defending yourself, I know you're only the acting manageress. You took on a poisoned chalice, and you've had no direction, no support, no budget . . . frankly, I'm amazed you've stuck around.'

'I was going to give it till the end of the summer,' admitted Caragh. 'Then maybe go off to Dubai.'

'What brought you over here in the first place? I know your part of the world. It's incredibly beautiful. And not so different from here.'

'Small-town Irish life is ten times more claustrophobic than English. I'm not Doctor Flynn's daughter over here.'

'So you can behave as badly as you like?'

He was teasing her. She could have bristled, but she didn't. She leaned back in the sofa, tilted her head to one side.

'Not so much that. There're more interesting people to behave badly with.' She tucked her hair behind her ear, a habit Bruno had noticed. 'My brother's an equine vet just outside Bath. I came over to stay with him a few years ago, and it was like being able to breathe all of a sudden. I was already trained in hotel management; I'd been working at one of the big hotels on the outskirts of Killarney. It was pretty easy to get a job here.'

'Well, as you might have guessed, I want to shake things up.'

'You'll be bankrupt by Christmas if you don't.'

He laughed at her bluntness.

'Actually, I think this place could limp on indefinitely just as it is. But I think it would be much more of a challenge to turn it round.'

He began outlining his plans. She listened attentively. After a few minutes, she shifted forwards in her chair slightly, tipping her pelvis, then uncrossed her legs languidly. Bruno was left in no doubt that she was a natural redhead.

For a moment, he was tempted. She was, after all, his type: sleek and groomed and ruthless. She had that little bit of edge he liked. He imagined that she would be totally uninhibited, that she would go out of her way to impress him with her bedroom antics. Under all that crisp clothing she'd be a vixen, a wildcat. Bruno knew it would only take one click of his fingers. But he managed to restrain himself. That was exactly what she wanted. For him to fall for her charms and be put off the scent. He ploughed manfully on with his prosaic descriptions.

'I'm installing a new computer system. Each guest will have a card, like a credit card, and every transaction will be recorded on that card until they come to settle up. There'll be virtually no need for cash in the entire hotel.'

'Good idea.' Caragh smiled her approval.

'It will make fiddling well-nigh impossible.'

'Fiddling?'

Bruno nodded gravely.

'I've had all the figures examined by a friend of mine who's an expert in these things. He's trained to spot patterns. The books here just don't add up. The takings are totally erratic; the average spend per customer isn't at all consistent. Which suggests the staff are on the take. Whether some or all of them isn't clear at the moment.'

'Are you quite sure?' Caragh looked at him coolly. 'The weather can have a very strange effect on spending patterns down here—'

'Don't worry. That's been taken into consideration. It's a very sophisticated program I've used – it's quite terrifyingly Big Brotherish.'

For a moment they stared each other out, each knowing what the other was thinking. Caragh caved in first.

'It's a bit like loft insulation, then, really,' she said finally. 'You spend a little bit of money to stop the pounds flying out.'

'Exactly. And no one will be able to skim off the profits, even if I'm not around.'

They smiled at each other, both equally clear that the message had been received and understood.

Bruno leaned back and curled his arms round the back of his head, deliberately nonchalant, as if the answer to his question was of no matter.

'So. Where do you see yourself in the near future, Caragh? Sunny Dubai? Or are you going to stick around in sunny Mariscombe?'

Caragh looked at her watch and stood up.

'Work me out a package,' she said briskly. 'And we'll talk.'

She held out her hand for Bruno to shake. He got to his feet slowly, took it, shook it, then didn't let go, but looked her in the eye and spoke softly.

'By the way . . . Caragh?'

He hesitated. She tilted her head to one side enquiringly.

'Yes?'

He cleared his throat.

'I prefer my senior staff to wear knickers. If you don't mind.'

Bruno watched as Caragh stalked her way down the steps leading to the sands, her head held high, and marched back towards Mariscombe. He admired the straightness of her back, the square set of her shoulders and the way she didn't stumble once, even though her shoes weren't ideal for walking on the beach.

He was in two minds about her. In some ways, he would be mad to lose her. If she was channelled, she could be a great manageress. She had that Irish charm that always seemed to work wonders with guests, and she didn't need to be liked by the staff, which meant she could whip them into shape. But there was no doubt she was corrupt. Bruno had done his research and was quite satisfied that she'd been on the fiddle, even if he couldn't actually prove it. But then, he reasoned, anyone who'd been given the chance of running the Mariscombe Hotel as it was, and hadn't taken advantage of the fact that it was a complete shambles to line their own pockets, probably wasn't worth employing in the first place. He admired opportunism and initiative. And he didn't like doing the expected.

Was it worth taking the risk on her? Bruno thought he would probably enjoy breaking her. She'd fight him every step of the way and spit in his eye, he knew she would. There was something slightly dangerous about her; something slightly unhinged. But there was nothing he liked better than a challenge.

Hannah thought she was in heaven. Sitting outside like this with Frank, the pair of them sipping their Beck's, some chill-out music wafting out of the speakers Frank had propped up on his windowsill, chatting idly. She shivered slightly.

Although it had been a warm day, the air was dropping rapidly in temperature. It was still too early in the year for the night to hold on to the day's heat.

'Are you cold?' Frank jumped up, concerned. He picked up his sweatshirt, which was hooked over the back of his chair. 'Here, put this on.'

Hannah obeyed. She didn't need telling twice. As she pulled it on over her head, she breathed in the smell of him, then shivered as the soft lambiness of the fleece inside stroked her arms. To be this close was such sweet torture.

'So you reckon my proposal's all right?' Frank was asking her anxiously, for the seventy-fifth time.

'I think it's brilliant,' Hannah reassured him, for the seventy-fifth time. 'And even if it's not exactly what he wants, it shows you've thought about it. And you know what you're talking about.'

'Thanks for your advice.' Frank leaned over and kissed her on the head. 'You're a complete star, you know that?'

Hannah sat stock-still, her heart thumping. Frank had kissed her! Hastily, she picked up her bottle and drank from it to hide her confusion.

It was ironic that, despite the fact that she was always there for the others, she would have no one to share this moment of triumph with, no one to pick over its significance. Hannah knew she was taken for granted by the others, and usually she didn't mind. Day after day, night after night, she was always there for whoever had been injured in the ongoing battles for affection. Yet no one ever realized that inside her own heart was aching, that she was in turmoil, because she knew Frank would never look at her, with her super-size conk and her size eight feet. For a moment, she thought wistfully that it would be nice to have someone to chew over this development with. Sometimes she confided in Molly, one of the chambermaids, but Molly always shot off home and never came out for a drink. She'd told her about the nose job, but Molly thought she was mad. It was easy to say that when you had a cute little freckle-smothered button.

'Another beer? There's one left.'

'I don't know. I've had three already. And I haven't quite finished this . . .'

'Go on.'

As Hannah hesitated, a figure came striding towards them through the moonlight. Tall, elegant, businesslike – Hannah's heart sank. Caragh. There would be no more kisses now. And it brought her crashing down to earth.

'Fuckin' patronizin' twisted lowlife bastard!' Caragh's language was foul when she was riled. The nuns would have been horrified.

'What have I done?' Frank leaped to his feet, terrified that he'd stepped out of line.

'Not you, you eejit.' Caragh flopped into a chair. 'Bruno arsin' whatever his name is. He's blown it with me, I can tell you.'

'Drink?' Frank proffered a bottle of Beck's.

'I need something a bit stronger than that.' Caragh dismissed his offering with a wave of her hand. 'A glass of Archers or something.'

'I don't actually have anything else,' admitted Frank.

Caragh scowled.

'Go on, I'll have the beer then.'

Frank flipped open the last bottle, the bottle that Hannah had been about to drink.

'So what's he done?'

'Who?' Caragh glared at Hannah in the half-light. 'You mean Bruno? Only as good as accused me of being on the fiddle.'

'But you are,' Frank pointed out reasonably.

'We all are,' Caragh replied sweetly. 'Which means that if I go down, you all go down with me.'

'Not all of us, actually.' Three Beck's had given Hannah an uncharacteristic bolshiness. 'Some of us weren't given the chance to join your little Christmas club. And, anyway, haven't you heard of honour amongst thieves? You can't bring everyone else down. It's just not done.'

Frank shrank back into the shadows, cringing. No one had ever dared cross Caragh before. She shot Hannah a look of pure poison, then stood up.

'Come on, Frank,' she ordered. 'I've had that ol' pervert trying to look up my skirt for the past hour. I know what he wanted. He wanted me to sleep with him. I don't know what he thinks I am, I'm sure.' She stretched languorously and her blouse slipped up, showing her taut stomach. 'I need a massage. I'm totally stressed. He didn't seem to realize that I'm the one that's been keeping this dump together.'

Hannah watched the pair of them slip away into the shadows, Frank casting an apologetic glance behind him. Her heart sank as she sipped the last of her beer. She imagined the two of them on Frank's bed, his long, brown fingers caressing Caragh's skin, exploring her perfect body – high, rounded breasts, slender hips, toned thighs . . .

Hannah sighed. What hope did she have? Maybe she shouldn't bother. Maybe she should just give the money to starving children in Africa and be done with it. There wasn't a plastic surgeon in the world that could work the miracle she needed.

Eight

Less than a week after their takeover, The Rocks looked as if a bomb had hit it.

George and Justin were overawed at Lisa's drive. She'd refused to employ anybody to gut the place, arguing that the money would be much better spent on fixtures and fittings and that they were all perfectly able-bodied.

'You can't be expected to help. It's bloody hard work.' Justin, who was strangely old-fashioned when it came to what was expected of women, watched in horror as she kicked out a toilet cistern with a booted foot.

'Listen, I've lived on my own all of my life. I'm a demon at DIY,' argued Lisa. She'd proven this very fact by locating the stopcock earlier and turning off the water at the mains. 'I got fed up being charged a bomb every time I needed something doing. I just bought a manual and got on with it.'

She wrenched the pipes out of the wall as George and Justin exchanged grimaces over the top of her head. From then on she set the pace. She had them out of bed at seven o'clock every morning, stripping wallpaper and pulling up carpets. The skip lorry could barely keep up with them. But she was a fair taskmaster. She ran down the hill to the bakery at nine o'clock for croissants and *pains au chocolat*, then made them bacon sandwiches at midday. At six, they were finally allowed to stop, and they all went down to the beach for a swim, to wash away the dust and the filth. They floated on their backs in the water, gazing at the sky, allowing their aching muscles to relax.

By Friday the hotel was a shell, almost every vestige of the

Websdales' decor eradicated. The weather was glorious. From their vantage point they could see the village starting to fill up with visitors who'd taken advantage of the forecast and decided to make a long weekend of it. Justin had pleaded for a day off, but Lisa was adamant.

'But I've booked a surfing lesson,' he whined.

'Look, the sooner we finish this place the sooner we start making money. Those are all potential customers down there . . .' She waved her hand airily at the beach. 'It's only a few weeks until high season. If we miss that golden six weeks, we're screwed.'

'I've got to do some paperwork.' George was determined to stand his ground. 'I've got to work out a proper schedule and make sure everything we need's been ordered. Trust me on this, Lisa. It's what I do.'

'OK,' she agreed reluctantly. 'You can have the morning off, Justin. And you can spend the day in the office. I'll strip the banisters.'

She stomped off. Justin and George exchanged glances.

'She's scary,' said Justin.

'Yeah, but she's a great gaffer,' grinned George in reply. 'I've never seen a place demolished so quickly.'

'She's a slave-driver.' Justin produced his brand new wetsuit from a carrier bag and surveyed it thoughtfully. 'Are you supposed to pee in these or what?'

By midday, Lisa realized she was shattered. It was searingly hot and the smell of paint stripper was making her giddy. Maybe she'd have the afternoon off after all. What she really wanted was sleep. They'd stayed up till after midnight every night this week, and though there'd been a party atmosphere, with music blaring and plenty of bottles of beer, it had suddenly caught up with her.

She went into the kitchen and grabbed a glass of cool water. Maybe a drink would revive her. Or perhaps she'd pop down into Mariscombe for an ice cream; just take half an hour's break, then carry on. She went back into the hall to find her bag and stopped in her tracks.

There was a girl standing in the middle of the chaos, glancing around with an air of dismay. She was slight, almost too frail for the bulging crocodile-skin handbag slung over her shoulder. She wore a jade-green Chinese kimono, faded designer jeans and three-inch stiletto boots. On top of her head, tucked into her mane of toffee-coloured hair, was an outsize pair of white Courrèges sunglasses.

As Lisa got closer, she realized that she wasn't a girl at all: that she was well into her thirties, that despite her tiny frame and delicate features there were lines round her eyes and round the corners of her mouth that spelt years of hard living and late nights. Moreover, her clothes might scream limitless budget, but her nails were bitten to the quick, her skin was dull and lifeless, and she smelt of stale perfume and cigarettes. Whoever she was, she didn't stand up to close scrutiny.

'Can I help you?' Lisa enquired politely.

The woman's smile lit up what had been a lifeless face. It was obviously her tool, her weapon, the means by which she got what she wanted. She had very small, perfect white teeth.

'I'm looking for George.'

Her voice was surprisingly deep, and she managed to eke three syllables out of George's name.

Lisa raised an eyebrow.

'Who shall I say is calling?'

'Victoria.'

'And Mimi.'

Another figure stepped through the doorway, sporting a two-inch tweed kilt held together with outsize safety pins, a corduroy blazer smothered in heraldic badges and a back-combed bob, from the depths of which peered two faintly suspicious eyes ringed with metallic blue.

'Victoria and Mimi,' repeated Lisa faintly. She'd spotted a Hello Kitty suitcase and a huge carpet bag by the front door, which rather indicated that Victoria and Mimi hadn't just popped in for coffee. 'Do you . . . have an appointment?'

She was rewarded with another dazzling smile.

'I don't really think I need an appointment,' Victoria said. 'I'm his wife.'

Years of being on public display and dealing with obnoxious members of the public meant Lisa was adept at hiding her emotions. She didn't baulk at these words, especially as something in the triumphant look the woman threw at her told Lisa she was expecting a reaction. She certainly wasn't going to give her the benefit of seeing she was thrown. Despite the terrifying lurch she felt in her stomach, she smiled.

'If you wouldn't mind waiting, I'll just go and see if he's available.'

With her heart thumping, Lisa walked as graciously as she could out of the hall. As soon as she was safely out of sight, she leaned against the nearest wall. George's wife? It couldn't be true, could it? But why would this Victoria lie? About something that could be so easily disproved?

It was clear to Lisa that only one person had the answers, and that was George himself. She steeled herself for the confrontation. There was no point in dithering. Gathering herself together, she marched into the office, where George was going through the quote they'd had for the refurbishment with a fine-tooth comb.

'George. There's a woman for you in reception.'

George looked up from his paperwork, frowning at the interruption.

'What is she? A rep? I'm not expecting anyone.'

'No.' Lisa crossed her arms. 'She says she's your wife.'

'What?' George jumped to his feet.

'Thin. Beautiful. Oh, and there's a young girl with her.'

'You're joking.' He ran his hand over his face, leaving his hand clamped over his mouth.

A horrible thought occurred to Lisa.

'Tell me it's not your daughter.'

'No, no. Of course it's not my daughter. It must be Mimi.'

'Oh.' Lisa narrowed her eyes and made a rapid deduction. 'Your stepdaughter, then?' she asked brightly.

George didn't answer for a moment. He bit his finger in concentration, looked longingly at the window for a moment as if leaping through it might provide either an answer or an escape, then sighed.

'I'm sorry, Lisa. This wasn't supposed to happen.'

'No. I guessed as much.'

'I don't know how they found me.'

'It can't have been that difficult. It's not like you're under the government protection scheme or anything.' Her tone was dripping vitriol.

George ran his fingers through his hair, which he always did when he was stressed.

'I'd better go and talk to her.'

'So she is, then?'

'What?'

'Your wife. Not some crazy, deluded madwoman with an identity crisis?'

'Tick both boxes,' George replied drily, then came over and put his hands on Lisa's upper arms, squeezing her in what he hoped was a reassuring manner. 'Look, I'll go and see what's going on. The sooner I can get rid of her, the better. Will you wait here for me? Then I'll explain.'

'Fuck off,' said Lisa bitterly, then shook him away and strode off down the corridor. George shut his eyes, took a deep breath and followed. The last thing he wanted was a cat fight.

By the time he reached the reception hall, Lisa had disappeared and Victoria was smoking languidly. She pointed towards the front door with her cigarette as George walked in.

'She's gone. I asked her to stay, but she ignored me completely. Have I put the cat amongst the pigeons?'

'What are you doing here?'

'It's absolutely gorgeous, isn't it? I've sent Mimi down to the beach so we could have a chat.' Victoria held out her cheek expectantly. 'I got the feeling your girlfriend knew nothing about me. She seemed awfully surprised when I told her who I was. No kiss?'

She pouted, feigning hurt. George gritted his teeth.

'Get to the point, Victoria. I can't imagine you turning up here is just a happy coincidence.'

Victoria flicked her ash on to the floor.

'I must say, she's very pretty, but she has eaten all the pies.'

'Lisa is not fat,' George snapped.

'I think you've put on a bit of weight yourself,' Victoria taunted him. 'Georgy Porgy pudding *and* pie?'

Why was it Victoria always managed to find his Achilles heel? They were living off fish and chips and cream teas at the moment. He knew he'd put on a couple of pounds. Trust her to notice. Trust her to point it out.

'Victoria. Why are you here?'

Victoria clasped her hands together, touching her knuckles to her lips with a sigh. George noticed she still wore the rings he'd bought her. The outsize tourmaline glistening on her left hand. And the Cartier trinity ring she'd begged for her little finger.

'Where to begin?' she said huskily, shrugged, then smiled up at him from underneath that ridiculously long fringe that only someone without a grip on reality could wear. 'In a nutshell, Nick and I are finished. And I'm broke. Haven't got a bean. Mimi and I are homeless and penniless.'

George raised an eyebrow.

'And your point is?'

'You've got this gorgeous huge place. And we're only tiny and we don't eat much.'

No, thought George, but you drink like a fish. He didn't say it, though, because he didn't want to start a slanging match. Be firm, he told himself. Firm, ruthless. No compromises. It was the only way with Victoria.

'Sorry. I can't help.'

'You've got to.'

George was surprised to hear a tremor in her voice. Victoria was always so defiant. So definite. But she had gone very pale. The chocolate-dark freckles on her milk white skin, the ones she hated and the ones he had once loved, were darker than ever. He remembered tracing them with his fingers, playing dot to dot, in the days when her beauty had left him speechless with awe.

He didn't want her anywhere near him now. One touch and he would be tainted. He felt himself drawing back. He could smell her perfume and it made him shudder. The aptly named Fracas.

Victoria leaned forward, her voice low, pleading.

'I'm really scared, George. Mimi's in a terrible state. You're the only one who can talk any sense to her. You always were. I'm seriously worried she's going to go off the rails.'

'Like you, you mean?' George knew he was being harsh.

'Yes. Like me. It might surprise you, but I don't want her to turn out like me. A complete loser. A flake, who shat on the only man who was ever decent to her.' There were tears welling up in her eyes. 'So what do I do then, George? Tell me.'

There were all sorts of things he could tell her. That it was her own fault. That she shouldn't have been so greedy. So mercenary. So fickle. That the day she had slithered out of his arms and into the grasp of Nick Taverner, media mogul, entrepreneur and total snake, was the day he absolved himself from any responsibility for her whatsoever.

'Victoria, I have no idea what you're going to do. And, frankly, it's not my problem.'

'But you're my husband.'

'Estranged. Abandoned. Cheated. Or had you forgotten?' He didn't mean to sound bitter. He meant to sound cool.

'I made a mistake.'

'That's not what you told me. You told me that Nick

Taverner recognized your talents, which was more than I did. That he understood your needs. That he was going to nurture you.'

'You were stifling me. You were trying to control me.'

'I was trying to stop you killing yourself. I was trying to give you a sense of perspective. You told me I was boring.'

'I didn't know what I was talking about. I didn't know what I was doing.'

'Victoria, you were a grown woman. You made your choice.'

Victoria seemed to crumple before his very eyes. Her chin was trembling as she choked back a sob. George wondered just how much of this drama was a performance and how much was genuine. Victoria was capable of using every trick in the book to get her way. She wiped away a runaway tear with her fingers, and George tried to remain stony-hearted.

'Please. Just let us stay for a week. While we sort ourselves out. I've got to work out how I can get some money. I'm in a real mess, George.'

'What about your business?'

Victoria bit her lip.

'Nick bought me out.' She had the grace to look a little shamefaced. 'I'm just an employee. I can hardly go back and work for him, can I?'

'What about the money from the sale? You must have got a decent whack.'

'We undervalued it. So I didn't have to pay capital gains . . .'

'Jesus, Victoria.'

'I know. But I didn't think I was going to split up with him, did I?'

'You must have got something. Where's it all gone?'

She gave a minute shrug.

'You know . . .'

George narrowed his eyes.

'Shoes? Handbags? Cocaine?'

'You really don't think much of me, do you?' she flashed.

'Then what?'

'A new car. Stuff for Mimi. We went to Mustique . . .' She trailed off lamely.

George sighed heavily. Victoria's eyes were glassy with tears.

'Please. If not for me, then for Mimi. You wouldn't see her without a roof over her head, would you? I mean, I'm sure you couldn't care less if I ended up in the gutter, but you care about her, don't you?'

George shut his eyes. He was being stitched up. He knew he was. But Victoria had him over a barrel. Of course he loved Mimi. Even if she wasn't actually his, she was technically still his stepdaughter, and he cared very deeply what happened to her. And he knew jolly well that if he didn't take responsibility for her, no one else would. With Victoria adrift without the life raft of Nick Taverner's millions . . .

What choice did he have?

'I'll have to talk to Lisa first.'

That perfect smile. That little dimple. George turned sharply and went to look out of the window.

'This is an amazing place.' She came to stand behind him. He could almost feel her soft breath on his neck.

'It will be.' His voice was matter of fact.

'I can just see it. The walls painted chalky, matt white. Stripped floors. Curtains . . . ? Mmmm . . . Not blue; it's so predictable by the sea. Hot pink and burnt orange, maybe. Some massive canvasses – modern, minimalist. Distressed furniture, like driftwood. Beaten copper wall lights . . .'

Had she already been in and rifled through his ideas? She couldn't have. Yet what she was reciting was almost what he'd designed. Could she read his mind? Maybe she could. For George knew the truth. That in many ways he and Victoria were in sync with each other. That together they made a whole. That whole had somehow splintered, rotted, fallen apart. He had long thought it beyond restoration, that no amount of love and care could render them complete again. But her words had made him realize . . .

He had missed her.

Her very presence in the room was making his skin tingle. He had butterflies, and it wasn't nerves or fear – though they were there too. It was excitement. Every time he breathed in, her scent mingled with the oxygen in the air and hit his bloodstream. She was inside him already, taking possession, like some wraith from the other side. He clenched his hand, superstition making him long for some talisman to give him protection from her power. But he had nothing. All he had to defend himself with was common sense, which told him that the quicker Victoria was out of here the better for everyone.

'I . . . better go and find Lisa,' he said weakly.

She smiled, locking her eyes with his, and every molecule in his body crackled.

'Where shall I wait?'

George panicked. He certainly wasn't going to let her sit in his office. He knew Victoria only too well – she'd be through the filing cabinets and know his business before he'd even turned his back.

'Why don't you sit outside? It's a lovely day. I'll bring you coffee.'

'Just water will be fine.'

He looked at her askance. Victoria was held together by nicotine, alcohol and caffeine.

'Total detox,' she said, a little too brightly. 'My body is now a temple. Apart from the fags, of course. Got to have something to keep body and soul together.'

'Oh.' George couldn't help feeling his reply was insufficient, given the import of what she was saying.

'I've made quite a few changes. I've been looking at things. Trying to work out where I went wrong.' Her voice cracked slightly. 'I must have been hell on wheels to live with. It's only now, looking back, that I realize what you must have gone through.'

Help, thought George. If she was going to turn fragile and vulnerable, he wouldn't have a hope. He curled his toes and locked his knees in the battle not to bound over and scoop her up in his arms.

'Nothing I couldn't handle,' he said heartily. 'No need to feel guilty on my account. It's all turned out for the best.'

'Yes.' She swept her beautiful eyes around the room, her gaze like the arc of a lighthouse beam as she took in her surroundings. 'The thing is, George . . .' She dropped her voice a few decibels and he had to strain to hear her. 'If we can't come to some arrangement – something that suits all of us, of course – I'm going to have to start proceedings.'

'Proceedings?'

'For divorce.'

It was like a punch in the guts. George stood, dumbfounded, as Victoria carried blithely on.

'I know you don't own all of this, but I'm guessing by rights that half of what you do own should be mine?'

The witch! She was a total utter witch.

George strode angrily across the sand, his hands in his pockets. In the space of just five minutes, Victoria had aroused a host of conflicting emotions in him. Shock. Panic. Suspicion. Lust. Pity. And finally fear, mixed with a copious dollop of anger now that he was safely out of range.

He felt relief when he saw Lisa. As if his sanity was regained. Lisa was safe. Reliable. Manageable. She was sitting on a rock, her arms wrapped round her knees.

'I'm sorry.'

'I don't do married men. It's one of my golden rules. One I never break.' She paused for a second. 'Knowingly, anyway. I should have known you were too good to be true.'

'It is just a technicality. The fact that we are still married. We just haven't got round to sorting it out. Because we can never have a conversation that doesn't end in mud-slinging.'

'That doesn't explain why you never told me.'

George clambered on to the rock next to her and sat down.

'If I didn't mention Victoria it was as if she never existed. And then she could never destroy us.'

'Get real.'

The look Lisa gave him was bleak and disdainful. His stomach curdled.

'Can I tell you about it? Our marriage?'

'Feel free. Then I'll tell you about the seventeen illegitimate children I forgot to mention.'

George flinched. Lisa was never sarcastic.

'I don't blame you for being angry.'

'Bloody good thing too!'

She stood up and began bounding over the rocks, towards the sea. George scrambled to his feet and tried to follow her. His shoes were leather-soled and not suitable for leaping over slippery, seaweed-covered surfaces. Eventually she reached a rock pool that was too wide to leap across. She came to a halt. He drew up beside her, panting, and saw there were tears streaming down her face.

'I feel such a fool. You're a bloody fraud. And I've given up everything . . .'

'Victoria means nothing. I don't give her a thought from one day to the next.'

'You obviously mean something to her. Else why is she here?'

'Because I'm a soft touch. Or at least she thinks I am.'

'Has she gone?'

George hesitated.

'Not yet.'

'You've told her she can stay.' Lisa's voice was flat.

'No. I haven't. I've told her I need to speak to you.'

'You want my permission? For your ex-wife to move in with us?'

George knew the whole situation was preposterous. And it was largely his fault. If only he'd been straight with Lisa from the start. But it had been so much easier not to mention his past. As each day slipped by and the opportunity for confessions became more and more remote, it had just seemed easier to play the ostrich. How the hell could he have kidded himself? The likes of Victoria never faded obligingly into the background. He looked at the ocean stretching in front of him.

'I'm going to have to tread very carefully with Victoria,' he said. 'And I'm going to need your support. I know I don't deserve that, in the circumstances. But if you'll let me explain what we were all about, what happened, you might understand.'

Lisa gave a tiny, reluctant nod. Her curiosity was greater than her pride.

George picked up a nearby shell and lobbed it into the rock pool, before taking a deep breath and plunging straight into his story.

'I met her five years ago, just after I first moved to Bath. She had her own PR company. She organized a launch party for a development of luxury apartments we'd done. A conversion of an old lunatic asylum.' He gave a wintry smile.

George was entranced the moment he set eyes on Victoria working the room. She was wearing an emerald-green wrap dress spattered with tiny butterflies and incredibly high heels, in which she walked with the utmost grace. At one point their eyes met. His heart began to beat faster as she glided over to him and, plucking two glasses of champagne from a passing waitress, handed him one.

'You're George Chandler. You were the project manager on this. You moved here six months ago, from Bristol,' she told him, as if he might have forgotten.

George nodded his agreement of her precis. 'You've done your homework.'

'It's my job to know exactly who everyone is.' Then she smiled. A proper smile; not the polite, hostessy rictus she had been wearing all evening, but one which reached her eyes and melted George's heart. 'I'm Victoria Snow, in case you haven't done yours. Come and sit down with me for a moment. The room's working beautifully – I can take five minutes.'

She led him over to a cluster of armchairs by the window and they sat down.

'You've done a wonderful job,' George told her.

He wasn't just being polite – she really had. The room was heaving with local heavyweights. Two well-known faces said to have already signed up for their unit were present – one who played a dashing doctor in a popular television drama, and a jockey who was tipped for the next Grand National. They were surrounded by crowds of sycophants delighted to be in the company of celebrity, however minor.

Victoria smiled her acceptance of his compliment. With her slanting green eyes and her extraordinary cheekbones, she was like Lauren Bacall, decided George. Or Faye Dunaway. She oozed glamour and class and style. Totally unobtainable, he decided. He wasn't even going to belittle himself by trying. There was bound to be an equally glamorous Mr Snow some-where.

'Actually, it's not hard.' She was leaning into him confiden-tially. 'It's just a question of spending other people's money. I'm fantastically good at it.'

'It's not though, is it?' protested George. 'You've put a lot of thought into this. The guest list, the canapés, the freebies – it's very slick. But seemingly effortless. That takes skill.'

'Ah,' she said, tipping her head to one side and smiling at him. 'You've caught me out. I rather prefer people to think I'm a bit of a bimbo. You're very . . .' She put a finger to her lips as she sought the right word. 'Perspicacious.'

She crossed her legs and the emerald-green silk of her dress slithered aside, revealing a perfectly toned, slender thigh encased in a gossamer stocking. George tried desperately hard to look elsewhere, then realized she was laughing at him.

'What?' he asked indignantly.

'What are you doing afterwards?'

He frowned and bit his lip, pretending to give it some serious thought while he played for time.

'I don't know,' he replied.

She dipped a finger into her champagne and pressed it to his lips, tracing the bubbles over his cupid's bow with an intense concentration. Then her head darted towards his, swift as an adder, and she kissed the last traces of liquid away. A moment later she was smiling at him.

'I must go and circulate,' she pronounced.

And before he could respond, she'd slipped away and lost herself amongst the crowds.

George followed her progress for the rest of the evening, intrigued with her professionalism as she made small talk, introduced people, broke up little cliques and redistributed guests amongst the room, passed drinks and canapés, directed waitresses. He could see her eyes didn't miss anything. Dirty glasses weren't left for more than a moment. Drinks were replenished. Each guest was made to feel as important as the next.

As the guests started dwindling away, he sidled up to his boss.

'Tell me about Victoria Snow.'

Richard looked at him sharply. His lips thinned.

'Crazy, fucked-up, alcoholic nympho spendthrift.'

'Oh,' said George, somewhat nonplussed.

'Think Paula Yates meets Imelda Marcos with a bit of Sue Ellen Ewing thrown in. Don't go there.'

George watched Victoria across the room, unable to equate the person being described with what he saw.

'She's done a very good job here,' he protested. 'People are actually looking at the plans. They never usually do at these launches. They usually guzzle as much free wine as they can and bugger off.'

'Yeah, well – you haven't seen her bill.'

'I'd say it was worth every penny.'

Richard gave an infuriating, knowing smile.

'She does great PR. But her personal life is a disaster area. Trust me. I've seen the fallout.'

'Maybe she hasn't met the right person.'

Richard raised a sardonic eyebrow.

'And you think you might be?'

George gave a non-committal shrug. Richard shook his head.

'Trust me, George. She's virtually certifiable, if her reputation is anything to go by.'

'I've never been one to listen to tittle-tattle.'

'Don't say I didn't warn you.'

George took Richard's doom-laden warning as a challenge. As the crowds thinned out, he wandered over to her.

'Dinner?' he asked.

'No, thank you,' she answered politely, and his heart sank. Then she gave him a mischievous smile. 'I don't like eating. I think it's thoroughly overrated. What I would really love is a nice bottle of vintage champagne somewhere with comfy sofas where I can kick these ridiculous shoes off and not have to be polite for a minute longer.'

George assessed the alternatives as quickly as he could. He knew he had a couple of bottles of Veuve in the fridge – not vintage, but he didn't think she was really going to quibble. He certainly had comfy sofas and she could take off as many items of clothing as she liked . . . He stopped himself. Inviting her home was going far, far too fast.

'I can arrange that, no problem.' He hoped he didn't sound too smooth. He didn't want to come across as smarmy. 'You finish up here and I'll bring my car round to the front.'

Less than an hour later they were ensconced by the fire in the drawing room of the Queensberry Hotel, a champagne-laden ice bucket on the table between them, and Victoria's L.K. Bennett mules carelessly thrown to one side. George, who'd never fallen head over heels in love in his life, found his hand shaking slightly as he poured out the bubbles, wondering wildly if he had any chance whatsoever with this creature. She was an extraordinary mixture of wanton and controlled – her drawl was so measured, her body language was languid, yet every now and then her eyes would flash with wickedness.

'Before we go any further,' she confided, 'you should know I've got baggage.'

Visions of a set of Louis Vuitton suitcases flashed into George's head.

'Baggage?' he echoed, rather stupidly.

'She's called Mimi, short for Miranda, and she's the result of too many Cinzanos at a school dance. And me thinking that single motherhood was preferable to doing my A levels. In my typical misguided, pigheaded, I-know-best-even-though-I'm-only-seventeen fashion.'

George still looked slightly blank.

'I've got a daughter,' Victoria explained patiently. 'A twelve-year-old daughter.'

'Is that a problem?'

Victoria sighed.

'It is for most men.'

'Why?'

'Because I'm not a free agent. I have to think twice before I go out or go away anywhere. Because I have to look after her, ferry her round, feed her, deal with her problems, do her homework – basically put her first. And most blokes can't handle that. They like to come first.'

'They must be very selfish. I don't think I'd have a problem with it.'

'Ah. That's what they all say to begin with.'

George felt wounded. He wasn't that shallow. He wasn't going to be lumped in with all the superficial, self-centred men that Victoria had dated up until now. Clearly, this was some sort of test. He decided to rise to the challenge.

'OK. For our first date, we'll go ice skating. You, me and Mimi.'

He thought Victoria looked rather pleased. She smiled and looked at him sideways.

'Aren't you going to ask about her father?'

George thought about it. He supposed it would be best if he knew what he was up against.

'I presume you're not together any more?'

Victoria threw back her head and laughed. George found himself gazing at her white throat, longing to press his lips against it.

'Absolutely not, darling. He was the school handyman. He was supposed to be patrolling the grounds during the sixth-form dance, making sure no one got up to anything they shouldn't. I couldn't resist. He was completely gorgeous. Very Sean Bean – rugged and silent. And as thick as shit.'

She ran her finger round the rim of her glass.

'I've never had a fuck like it before or since.'

George met her sly glance square on.

'What happened to him?'

'Oh, I didn't even bother telling him I was pregnant. He was married, for a start. And he'd have been sacked if it had all come out. I'd have ruined his life if I'd squealed. There was absolutely no point.'

'But what about your daughter? Doesn't she want to meet him?'

'I've told her all about him. If she ever wants to meet him, I'll arrange it somehow. But at the moment she doesn't seem to want to.'

'People like to know where they've come from. Don't they?'

He saw her visibly stiffen, and realized that perhaps he had gone too far.

'As far as I'm concerned, he was a sperm donor. He'd have nothing to offer her. He lived in a council house, for God's sake.'

George recoiled at her frankness.

'What's wrong with that?'

Victoria stared moodily into her glass.

'Oh, nothing. I'm just being defensive. It always makes

me say things I shouldn't.' She slugged back the last of her champagne and grinned. 'Anyway, I'm a total hypocrite. I ended up in a council flat myself, when I had Mimi. My parents were absolutely horrified that I'd come out of my nice posh girls school with no qualifications and a bun in the oven. My father threw me out. After the school had. Then he cut me off without a penny. It was up to my mother to sort me out somewhere to live. She made the council find me a flat. She's quite terrifying, my mother – one word from her and I went straight to the top of the housing list. Mind you, the one person she had no influence over was my father. She had to sneak out of the house to come and visit, pretend she was off to play golf.'

'That's awful. What a terrible start in life.'

'Listen, it suited me, I can tell you. I couldn't stand my father. He was a snob and a bully. It was my only escape. And, actually, I loved it. Mimi was the most darling baby. I couldn't understand why everyone my age didn't have one. The only problem was money. I couldn't live on the mingy state benefits. So I started working for a woman who ran a travel agency from her house. She didn't mind me bringing Mimi to work. And I could take a lot of the stuff home. I ended up doing all her brochures and design work for her. Then I organized a party for her, promoting her skiing holidays. It was so easy. I had fake snow everywhere and Christmas trees. We served glühwein and a huge fondue. She ended up with a massive piece in the local paper and trebled her bookings. Then she encouraged me to set up on my own, doing PR. I could never have done it without her. She let me use a corner of her office to start with. Eventually I got my own office. And Victoria Snow Public Relations was born.' She spread out her hands. 'Ta-da.'

'So single motherhood isn't as difficult as everyone makes out?'

'I can only speak for myself. And Mimi was a little angel.

She's always been brilliant at entertaining herself. Well, she's had to be . . .'

She burst into laughter.

'Do you know what's hilarious? She's at the same school that threw me out all those years ago. They've got no idea she's an illegitimate brat who was spawned round the back of the tennis courts . . .'

She collapsed back on to the cushions, doubled up with mirth. George was a bit alarmed; she seemed almost hysterical. Then she stopped and looked at him, very serious, and he realized she'd drunk more than he'd thought.

'Take me home.'

Her meaning was very clear. But George wasn't going to fall into the trap of taking advantage of her when she was three sheets to the wind. If he was going to seduce her, he wanted her sober.

Less than a month later, Mimi and Victoria moved in and George found his masculine enclave invaded. The butter compartment in the door of the fridge was filled with bottles of Chanel nail varnish. There were knickers strewn around the bathroom, cotton-wool balls, plastic dry-cleaning bags ripped off garments and thrown on the floor. Toe separators. Gel-filled eye masks. Fake tan wipes. Hair straighteners. Hair curlers. Nail files. Victoria might look a million dollars when she walked out of the door, but she left a bomb site behind her.

George had never considered himself to be fanatically tidy, but had never realized what chaos one woman could create. A bit of mess, however, was a small price to pay for having this fascinating, luminescent, sparkling woman in his life. And rather than Mimi being a handicap to his relationship with Victoria, he found he adored having her in the house. He toasted her bagels for breakfast, and introduced her to Nutella and blueberry conserve. He dropped her off at school, as it was on the way to his office rather than Victoria's, and she gave him all the gossip about what her friends were up to – stories that made his hair stand on end, but he reasoned that it was better that she told him than kept it all secret. At night he helped her with her homework, because Victoria didn't have the patience or, she insisted, the intellect to cope with logarithms or French irregular verbs. And at weekends, if Victoria had work or a hair appointment, he was happy to provide a taxi service and be the official cashpoint machine. He supposed he could be accused of spoiling Mimi, but he suspected that she'd had a tough time of it over the years, and had probably endured a rather lonely, self-sufficient existence. It wouldn't hurt her to be indulged.

By the end of six months, he felt a desperate need to cement the relationship between the three of them officially. George was the type who needed things written down in black and white and rubber-stamped. And that was how he found himself on a beach in the Caribbean, the legs of his best linen suit rolled up as the waves lapped round his ankles, with Victoria next to him in a white silk slip, the two of them repeating their vows. Mimi, wearing bright pink parachute trousers and a fishnet hoodie, stood at the water's edge and watched.

'Hello, Dad,' she beamed, as George and Victoria waded out of the water hand in hand as Mr and Mrs Chandler.

They had a huge party to celebrate their marriage when they got back to Bath. Only George's boss Richard was lukewarm in his congratulations. George decided that perhaps he had once made a pass at Victoria and had been rebuffed. He'd noticed at work that Richard had a tendency to bear a grudge. His disapproval was obviously sour grapes.

From then on, George and Victoria were the king and queen of the in-crowd. They dictated what bar to hang out in, what restaurant to eat in, whose invitations were accepted and whose shunned. To enter their inner sanctum was to win a ticket to the high life, fuelled by champagne and exotic cocktails. At first George revelled in it. He loved designer clothes, he loved style, he loved being at the cutting edge of setting trends. He knew he was burning the candle at both ends, but he was still young enough to get away with it. Just. And he didn't want to waste one precious moment with Victoria. He feasted his eyes on her, hung on her every word, couldn't keep his hands off her. And the sex . . . oh God, the sex. Bliss, ecstasy – there wasn't a word that came close to describing it.

As the months slipped by, however, the novelty began to wear off. At first, it was the social whirl that began to pall. Gradually, the veneer became tarnished and George recognized it as tawdry and shallow. The conversations he had once regarded as stimulating, the repartee he had considered witty, were repeated again and again. The majority of the crowd had only one topic of conversation: themselves. And too many of them were dependent on getting high or drunk for their entertainment. George liked a drink but, in general, he kept his head.

Suddenly, he looked at his so-called friends and saw superficial peacocks filled with insecurity. And by mixing with them, he realized that Victoria was guilty of all the attributes he found so unattractive. She could be spiteful and two-faced. She would cold-shoulder people for the most trivial of reasons. And she craved centre stage. She flirted incessantly, seemingly for the sake of it, seemingly to reassure herself that she was a more attractive proposition than anyone else. She had to be irresistible. George began to see her with new eyes.

More worryingly still, George had noticed that Victoria seemed to be drinking more and more. And maybe worse: George knew a lot of the people she mixed with dabbled in harder substances. She certainly kept it hidden from him, as she knew he disapproved. Either way, whatever she was doing, it was starting to encroach on her everyday life. Sometimes Victoria wouldn't get out of bed in the morning, even on a weekday. George would give Mimi her breakfast and drive her to school, then phone home at about eleven, when Victoria had just about surfaced, groggy and incoherent.

Somehow by midday she got herself together. She would be back in the office, immaculate, radiant, ready to hit the phones. Did that miraculous recovery come about with a little bit of chemical help, he wondered?

Infuriatingly, somehow she managed to keep it together work-wise. She simply never made morning appointments – her working day began at lunch. She was still picking up new clients by the handful. Because say what you like about her, Victoria knew how to make a splash. Every time she launched a new product or a new venue it had a twist, a clever gimmick that made sure it was lodged in the psyche of its target clientele. She was tireless, innovative, professional and raking in a small fortune, which slipped through her fingers almost before it had hit her bank account.

Although she never let her clients down, her private life was disintegrating. With increasing regularity, George had to extricate her from dinner parties when she began to get obstreperous and obnoxious. She could be very outspoken and she was brilliant at sensing people's weak spots. She would home in on them with a ruthless cruelty. And woe betide any other woman who tried to outshine her. Victoria would knock them down, cut their feet out from under them. The next day, she didn't show a flicker of remorse. Meanwhile, George ran up huge bills with his favourite florist, sending not only their hosts extravagant bouquets, but anyone Victoria had offended. People often said 'It's just Victoria', but George didn't think that was a good enough excuse. You couldn't excuse appalling behaviour on the grounds that you'd always been insufferably rude.

There were times when George convinced himself he could save her. Sometimes, on a Saturday afternoon, if he could grab her attention before she was due to go out for lunch, he would pin her down and talk to her about the house, which he was gradually redecorating. They would sit down with a pot of coffee and a table full of magazines, and she would give him ideas – ideas that made him tingle with excitement, because they were usually so simple, but with that flash of inspiration that made her so good at her job. And if he was very lucky, they would spend the afternoon in Walcot Street, wandering amongst the reclamation centres and antique shops, the lighting emporiums and the interior designers, picking out pieces that would make the house a home. And it would always be Victoria who spotted the key feature – the statue to go beneath the window on the landing, the enormous abstract oil painting whose vibrant colours set off the drawing room walls to perfection, the French chandelier that needed completely rewiring but was, when you thought about it, ideal for the kitchen, albeit totally impractical. This was the Victoria he wanted all the time, but he always felt as if he was borrowing her, as if she was humouring him, as if she was counting the moments until she could be herself. And no matter how hard he tried to hold on to that Victoria, she always slipped away. By six o'clock, she was getting ready, putting on her costume, fortifying herself with a cocktail or a glass of champagne, and by eight o'clock she had disappeared completely.

Eventually, he steeled himself to tackle her about the fact that her drinking had got out of control. It was a Sunday, and he brought her pancakes in bed when she still hadn't got up by midday. The telling thing was she didn't even have hangovers any more; she just needed to sleep. He asked what it was she was trying to forget, or cover up, but she just said she wanted to have a good time. She insisted she wasn't unhappy. But George suspected there was more to it.

'Is it me?' he asked, because it was since the wedding that she'd deteriorated.

'Of course not. I love you.'

'Then what is it? People who are happy don't behave like this, Victoria. You're losing your grip. I'm worried.'

He pushed and pushed, until suddenly she broke down and wept all over her breakfast tray.

'I hate myself,' she sobbed. 'I'm not the person I want to be.'

'Come on. You're beautiful. Successful. Popular. Well, when you're not drunk and being rude to people.'

'But I'm a fake. It's a complete act. I'm totally manufactured. All those clothes – they're just a suit of armour. My dressing-up box, so I can pretend to be someone I'm not. A silly little show-off.'

'So what is it you want to be?' George was utterly mystified.

'Someone warm and loving and caring, who doesn't think all this crap is important.'

'But it's not.'

'I can't operate without it.'

'You're crazy.'

'Exactly.'

'No – that's not what I meant. I meant you can be the person you want to be. You're not hard and shallow and superficial, otherwise you wouldn't have told me all those things.'

George looked at her, curled up on the bed, her face pale with misery. He reached out and stroked her hair.

'Do you know what I think?' he asked softly. She shook her head, not looking at him, just staring blankly at the wall. 'I think we should have a baby.'

She sat up suddenly.

'What?'

'You could chill out. Stop all the superwoman stuff. I earn enough for both of us. If you're not spending money on clothes, that is.' He tried to joke. 'I mean, if you really mean what you're saying, and you'd be happy to slob out in leggings—'

Before he could finish his sentence, she dealt him a stinging blow around the head.

'You're taking the piss out of me!' she shouted. 'I wouldn't expect you to understand. I don't want a bloody baby. That's the last thing I want. Don't you see? I'm a useless mother. I've already ruined Mimi's life. Why ruin another?'

'Hang on a minute. You haven't ruined Mimi's life. She's perfectly happy.'

'Only because of you. Not because of anything I've done.'

'I'll be here for the next one.'

She seemed almost possessed as she pressed her face close up to his and screamed at him.

'There isn't going to be a next one!'

George backed away, not realizing he had hit such an incredibly raw nerve. Victoria threw herself back on the bed, sobbing wildly.

'For heaven's sake, Victoria. You're being totally irrational. Let's talk it through.'

He remembered pleading with her. He honestly thought a baby would help. Would stop her senseless pursuit of self-destruction. Would give her something to live for. She'd called him naive.

'It's hell!' she'd screeched. 'Motherhood is absolutely hideous. Why do you think I'm such a mess? I can't stand the responsibility. I can't stand the fact that however Mimi turns out, it's down to me. That she's living proof of all my mistakes.'

'But you love her, don't you?'

'Of course! That's what makes it worse. It would be so much easier if I didn't. No guilt. No regret. No fear. No burden of duty that I keep trying to escape from, but can't, because she's always there. That's why I drink, and get totally out of it, because for five minutes I can be the person I would have been if I'd never had her. And at least now I know that you'll be there to look after her.'

'Bloody hell.' George was appalled.

'You don't understand, do you?'

'I don't know why it has to be so complicated. I don't know why you can't just . . .'

He wanted to say grow up, but he didn't dare.

'Well, there you go. Now you know what a horrible person I really am. And that I'm using you.'

She wiped her nose on her sleeve, staring at him defiantly. He felt rather sick at her admission. Was that all he was to her – some sort of father figure for Mimi who would absolve her of any responsibility? He realized then that having a baby really was the last thing Victoria would want to do. And he had to admit that made him feel sad. He'd become increasingly attracted to the idea of fatherhood lately. He'd thought about it, had even decided which room in the house would make the best nursery. Well, after today, that was obviously one fantasy that wasn't going to come true. He couldn't trust Victoria, for a start. She was so fragile, so vulnerable, so volatile. He didn't have the strength or the wisdom to withstand all the fury inside her. She needed breaking, like a wild horse, and maybe he wasn't the man to do it. He wouldn't mention the baby subject again. All he hoped was that having broached the matter of her drinking, and brought it all out into the open, she might take a step back and think about it.

If anything, she became even worse. Impulsive, impetuous. Her clothes became wilder: her skirts shorter, her heels higher, the fashion more extreme. George became increasingly worried. He noticed a slight tremor of her hand as she poured milk into her morning coffee, as if what she really wanted was a slug of vodka.

Mimi, meanwhile, had undergone a metamorphosis from a plump, sweet-faced twelve-year-old to a rangy nymphet. And although the two of them still got on like a house on fire, George found the fact that she was growing up so quickly very disconcerting. The girls at her school were a precocious bunch, mostly with wealthy parents who didn't seem to worry what they got up to as long as it didn't interfere with their own social lives. They had large disposable incomes and few rules. George didn't feel comfortable with their topics of conversation, their taste in music or their dress sense – Mimi's attire had become more and more outlandish; she dressed somewhere between a ragamuffin and a streetwalker. Victoria didn't seem perturbed.

'She's just looking for an identity. She won't be dressing like that when she's twenty-seven. Just go with it.'

George, realizing how important identity was to Victoria,

didn't feel equipped to argue. But he really couldn't cope with Victoria's passive acceptance, indeed almost encouragement, of certain aspects of Mimi's behaviour. It seemed to be the norm for girls of her age to go out to clubs and parties, and drink and smoke. Although Mimi remained sweet-natured and happy to hold a conversation with him, unlike a lot of her friends, who were incapable of stringing two words together, George disapproved strongly of her lifestyle.

Victoria shrugged it off.

'It's up to her.'

'She should be warned of the dangers.'

'She knows the dangers. She's not stupid.'

'How long is her rein, Victoria? Would you let her sleep with somebody? Take drugs?'

Victoria looked at him as if he was mad.

'You don't seriously think she's *not* going to do those things, do you?'

'I think she needs some guidance. But I'm not sure it's my place to give it to her.'

'Feel free.'

George awkwardly tried to tackle several of the subjects with Mimi, who patted his hand and told him she knew exactly what she was doing. Which he didn't find in the least bit reassuring.

The crunch came on Mimi's birthday. George had booked a table for her and three friends in their favourite restaurant, which basically served burgers and pizzas but in a slick environment, all white leather and glass with gorgeous young waiters who indulged their every whim. Mimi had insisted that she wanted George and Victoria to come to her meal as well – unusual in itself, as all her friends seemed to despise their parents and spent as little time in their proximity as possible. But George and Victoria, it seemed, were cool.

That evening, Victoria outshone Mimi and her friends and looked no older than they did. Her outfit was shorter, tighter and more outrageous. George thought he might once have felt pride, but now he felt uncomfortable. It felt rather like a wedding guest upstaging the bride. He watched as Victoria slugged down three Cosmopolitans in quick succession, then became more and more animated, giggling with the girls and flirting with the waiters, who were falling over themselves to serve her.

Despite George's discomfort at Victoria's behaviour, he told himself to chill out and enjoy the evening.

The *pièce de résistance* was going to be the birthday cake. George had been in and arranged it with the manager the day before. Just as it was due to arrive, on a given signal, Victoria upstaged it by producing tickets for the opening night of a new club. There were shrieks and squeals of excitement.

'Uber-cool!' shrieked Yasmin.

'The others are going to be so sick on Monday!' crowed Leyla.

'Your mum rocks,' Joo announced to Mimi.

'We need to leave *now*,' Victoria announced. 'If we're not there by eleven, they won't let us in.'

'Hang on,' said George. 'Mimi's cake . . .'

Victoria waved a dismissive hand.

'Cake?' she snorted. 'These tickets are like gold dust. Get them to put it in a doggy bag.'

She swept out, followed by her phalanx of followers, just as the manager appeared with a tower of chocolate brownies interspersed with balls of ice cream, scattered with silver sugared almonds, sparklers and candles. George sat alone at the table and stared at it.

'I'm still going to have to charge you for it,' said the manager.

'I'm sure you are,' said George drily. 'Give it to another table, with my compliments.'

He paid the bill and went home.

At two o'clock that morning, Mimi called him in a panic.

'George – I don't know what to do. Yasmin's throwing up in the toilets, Leyla's got her hands down some guy's trousers and I can't find Joo anywhere.'

'Where's your mum?'

There was a small silence.

'Um – I haven't seen her for a while either.'

'I'll come and get you.'

Twenty minutes later, George waded his way into the club, having threatened the bouncers that they had let a group of underage girls in and if the place wanted to keep its licence longer than their opening night they had better let him in. It took him half an hour to round up Mimi's friends, who were in varying states of inebriation and undress. Mimi was tear-stained and exhausted.

'I'm sorry, George,' she kept repeating. 'I didn't really want to come in the first place.'

'You didn't get much choice,' replied George grimly. 'Where *is* your mother?'

There was an awkward silence.

'I think she's in the VIP area,' Yasmin finally ventured.

George had another terrible battle trying to get past a bouncer standing with his arms crossed in front of a red rope, but eventually found that a twenty-pound note did the trick. The VIP area was crammed with Bath's most influential faces; faces he'd been doing his best to avoid in recent months. He kept his head low. Eventually, in a dark corner, he found Victoria straddling the lap of a blond man in leather trousers. He stood over them for a moment before Victoria looked up.

'Darling,' she cooed, not a trace of guilt on her face. George could tell by her eyes she was totally bombed. 'This is Nick. Nick owns a share of this gorgeous, gorgeous place.'

'Lucky Nick.' George managed a glimmer of a smile and held out his hand. 'George Chandler.'

'Right.' Nick held out one hand for George to shake, and caressed Victoria's thigh with the other.

'Victoria's husband,' George added helpfully.

George steered Victoria out of the club and into the night air, where the girls were waiting, pale-faced and rather subdued, and virtually shoved her into the waiting cab. Mimi clutched at his sleeve.

'I'm sorry.'

'Hey, it wasn't your fault.' He hugged her. 'I'm just sorry your birthday's been spoilt.'

'The meal was great. Thanks.'

He held Mimi tight, realizing that this was probably as close as he was ever going to get to having a daughter. He must have been mad to suggest having a baby to Victoria. For a moment he felt his throat tighten, and he swallowed hard. It was weird. He'd never really seen himself as a family man, but now it had become something unobtainable he suddenly wanted it very much indeed.

The next morning George stood over Victoria as she drifted into consciousness. He'd slept in the spare room, he was so livid with her. He couldn't have stood her comatose body next to his, her total oblivion.

'I'm only going to say this once.' He could barely control his voice, it was shaking with so much rage. 'You are totally irresponsible. I don't know what you were on last night, but you can cut it out if you're going to stay under this roof a minute longer. You were in charge of those girls last night, but it didn't occur to you to keep an eye on them for a second. In fact, if it wasn't for Mimi . . .' He trailed off as he realized Victoria had drifted off to sleep again. Enraged, he pulled a sheaf of lilies out of a nearby vase and threw the water over her lifeless form. She sat up soon enough, spluttering.

'Bloody hell, George.'

'Your fifteen-year-old daughter's got more common sense

than you have. And don't ever, ever humiliate me like that again.'

Victoria blinked at him, her hair hanging in rat's tails round her face.

'For God's sake, George. Get a grip. When did you have such a sense of humour failure?'

'When I found my wife with her legs wrapped round another man's waist?'

'We were talking business.'

'There was only one business you looked like you were doing, darling. And to be honest, you're getting a bit long in the tooth.'

He knew that would hurt. Any dig about looking her age would gnaw at Victoria for days. It was the only way he knew how to get at her. And he was right. As he left the room, he heard the empty lily vase smash against the wall behind him.

When he discovered her affair with Nick Taverner less than a month later, he didn't put up a fight. Maybe that was cowardly and gutless – what kind of a man didn't fight for the woman he loved? But he was battle-weary.

He had, however, asked her why.

'Because he doesn't nag me,' said Victoria simply.

There was a small pause while George took this in.

'Yet,' he replied. But he didn't try and dissuade her.

He wasn't surprised. Nick Taverner was older than him – forty-something – but devilishly good-looking in a hair-dresserish sort of way. He had fingers in more pies than Mr Kipling and a dreadful reputation as a womanizer. Quite the opposite of George. Nick Taverner, whenever he met him, made him feel like a square. A plodder.

It wasn't Victoria leaving him that had broken his heart. It had been broken long before, when he'd realized they could never be the family unit he longed for. He was left with a dull, empty ache, and a longing for what might have been if he'd had the courage to face her full on. But then, would a tamed

Victoria have been what he wanted? Had he broken her spirit, the appeal might have gone.

He watched as Victoria and Mimi drove off like Thelma and Louise in her open-topped BMW, then spent the whole weekend scrubbing the house bare of any evidence of either of them. He took down the pretty Jane Churchill curtains in the bedroom, replaced them with a dark wood Venetian blind, and bought a new set of bedlinen in a sober masculine stripe. He repainted Mimi's bedroom, brushing over the pearlescent lilac that he'd chosen with her a few months before with a deep red, and lined the walls with bookshelves. He threw out any vestiges of femininity from the bathroom, bundled up cushions and throws and vases and shoved them in the attic, chucked out all their magazines. Until the house was austere. Clean lines. Masculine. They didn't need him. And he didn't need them.

Then he phoned Justin and they went on a lads' weekend to Barcelona, where they went to a Stones gig and got absolutely hammered . . .

'And I haven't seen them since.' George came to the end of his tale and looked bleakly out to sea, unable to meet Lisa's eye. 'Until this afternoon. And that's the honest truth.'

Lisa detected a change in George's tone of voice. It sounded tight, almost strangled, and she suspected he was trying not to cry.

'Do you sort of understand?' he managed to ask.

Understand? It was George who couldn't possibly understand. Lisa had guarded herself against this sort of eventuality for so long. She'd kept men at arm's length, pushed them away when they got too close, protected her independence fiercely even though it was lonely at times, bloody lonely. And it was all so that she didn't have to feel that feeling again. That wave of absolute desolation, when her veins had been flooded with icy cold water, as if she had been walking a tightrope and suddenly noticed the safety net had been removed. She could remember it now so clearly. She could even smell the room, the reek of sex and Andrea's perfume. That gut-wrenching moment when she realized that the one man who she could trust and rely on, who would always be there, as solid as a rock, had betrayed her. In that instant, the whole essence of her father had crumbled.

And here it was again. She'd trusted George. She'd allowed him to get too close. Not wittingly. It had crept up on her. Because after years of stalwart, self-imposed isolation, it had been nice to share things with someone, and not feel as if you were entirely responsible for the repercussions of every single decision you made. And by allowing herself to relax, she'd laid a trap for herself. She'd gradually been seduced into a situation that went against everything she had tried to protect herself from. And now, she was paying the price. The man she had come to . . . well, yes, she supposed she could say love . . . was not what he seemed. He'd been keeping a dark, murky secret when she'd trusted him implicitly. He had deceived her, and who knows how long he would have carried on deceiving her if he hadn't been caught out? How could she have been so stupid? Hadn't she learnt that the only person in the world she could trust was herself? She shivered with the realization.

George touched her gently.

'Lisa?'

She shrugged him off. There was no point in having a tantrum about it. If she wailed and gnashed her teeth, that would prove she cared. The last thing she wanted to show was that she was vulnerable. She had to be strong, like before. She'd picked herself up that time, walked away and started again. Lisa set her shoulders square, determined to keep her dignity, and mentally ran through her options.

This time around it was a little more complicated. She couldn't just walk out without a backward glance, as her instinct told her. There was too much at stake. Ever practical, Lisa pinpointed the most important thing was to get the hotel up and running. They needed to start pulling in some revenue as quickly as possible. Otherwise they were all sunk. They had, after all, been spending money like water over the past couple of weeks. They could hardly call a halt to the refurbishment. They needed to start recouping their investment and quick. Once they were in profit, then she could decide what to do. She wasn't going to bail out now.

She looked at George. She had to be businesslike about this. There was no time for histrionics.

'Of course they can stay. As long as they don't mind helping out,' she said briskly. 'We could do with some extra pairs of hands. And we've got plenty of bedrooms. As long as they're out by the opening.' She stood up before she delivered the next blow. 'I'll go and move my things to another room.'

He looked startled, jumping to his feet. He put a hand on her arm as she turned to make her way back up the beach.

'You're not going to let this come between us?'

Lisa tossed back her hair impatiently.

'For God's sake, George. It's a pretty big one, not telling someone you're married. On a scale of one to ten for shit behaviour, it's about an eleven. Probably worse than having an affair. It's inexcusable.'

She set her mouth in a hard line and stared at him. She had to remain strong, impassive, immoveable – just as she had with her father that afternoon. Otherwise she would go to pieces.

He took a deep breath.

'Lisa, I am deeply, deeply ashamed. And horribly wrong. But after Victoria . . . well, I didn't think I'd want anything to do with another woman again. I didn't see the point in laying myself open to get hurt. But then you came along. Suddenly, it was worth the risk. But instead of hurting myself, I've ended up hurting you. Of course, now I can see how selfish it was. But at the time, it was just a defence mechanism . . .' He swallowed hard, passing a hand under his eyes and blinking. 'I made a mistake. I didn't set out to deceive you. It just . . . happened. Do you understand at all?'

Lisa was silent for a moment. He was almost voicing her own philosophy, parroting her own mantra back at her. She hesitated. Maybe she was being unfair? She didn't have the monopoly on betrayal, after all. Had the shock of George's revelation robbed her of her humanity? Just as her father's had? She had felt almost robotic at times, in her attempts to shut down her emotions and protect herself. Just for a moment, she allowed herself a second in George's shoes, and it dawned on her that maybe he deserved a fair hearing.

'I . . . suppose so.' She was hesitant, reluctant to capitulate when she had felt so wronged.

'I know I'm guilty. I know I was deluded, misguided, a total fucking ostrich. But that's the only way I could keep her out of our lives. To me Victoria is like Pandora's box. The minute I acknowledged her existence, I was afraid of what might be unleashed.' He rolled his eyes self-deprecatingly. 'I know that sounds melodramatic, but in my head she's like some terrible Greek legend. The only way I could cope was by pretending to myself she'd never happened.'

'And now she's here . . . you want her to stay?'

'No! I just want to see the back of her. But I know if I don't help her . . .' George was struggling to explain. 'Now she's resurrected herself, I've got to kill her off once and for all. So she no longer has any power over me. I've got to sort out the practicalities. And I've got to do it face to face. I don't trust her. If I send her packing, she's capable of all sorts of tricks. And, of course, there's Mimi . . .'

He looked anguished.

'I do really care about Mimi. And I'm not sure Victoria does. I mean, I'm sure she loves her, but she's more than capable of using her as a weapon. And that's not fair. She's only a kid, and she hasn't had it easy. If I can sort this out . . . amicably . . .' George grimaced, knowing that this was optimistic. 'Well, maybe we can make the best of it. Otherwise, she's won. She's strolled back into my life and blown it apart. Again. Please don't let her do that.'

He went to put his arms around Lisa. She immediately went rigid, but he squeezed her to him.

'I don't want to carry on unless I've got you right beside me. There's no point otherwise. That place is about us, Lisa. Look at it.'

He pointed back up the cliff.

'We've taken the risk. We're going to make it a success. You and me. With a bit of help from Justin, of course, but we both know he's just playing at it. But that place is our bloody dream. We've given up everything for it. And it's nearly within reach. We're so close. Don't let Victoria take it away from us.'

Despite herself, Lisa allowed herself to relax and put her head on his shoulder. George was right. They'd come so far. Was she really going to let her stubborn pride get in the way of their success? Because who'd be the winner then?

'Are you with me?' he whispered, ruffling his hand through her curls.

'Yes,' she whispered back, not sure if the taste of salt on her lips was the sea air or their mingled tears.

Mimi was a well-travelled child on paper. She had plenty of exotic stamps on her passport, for Victoria was keen on long-haul holiday destinations. But she had never realized that such a paradise existed on the shores of the very country she lived in. She'd always thought the English seaside was naff – cold and cloudy, with stony beaches and ugly, mottled people pouring tea out of thermos flasks. But no – here the sun was shining in an azure blue sky, the velvety green cliffs of the coastline were standing out in stark relief over a shining sea that would put the Med to shame. The sands were as golden as any she had seen on her travels. All her senses were assaulted. Shouts of delight and the screams of seagulls floated through the air from the beach, jumbled beats oozed from the shop-fronts, the smell of ozone mingled with the mouth-watering scent of frying chips from a nearby van. Everyone was smiling in the sun, going about their business at their own pace. Children marched out of shops triumphantly with buckets and spades and fishing nets, awkward in their new flip-flops. Parents joined hands when they hadn't done so in years, smiling indulgently. Babies licked their first ice creams from the confines of their chariots. Young lovers applied sun cream to each other, languorously exploring skin that had not been touched for weeks in the rat race of normal everyday life. Two boys shot out of a door in front of her, each clutching a surfboard, and raced down the street towards the sea. She watched after them, admiring the breadth of their shoulders, the slenderness of their waists, their skin the colour of runny honey.

Mimi soon realized as she walked through the few little streets that made up the village that she was totally inappropriately dressed. It hadn't been particularly warm when they left Bath that morning, and now she felt ridiculously trussed up in the heat of the early afternoon sun. People were looking at her askance as they walked past in next to nothing. She shrugged off her blazer but she still felt overdressed in a kilt and long boots.

She wandered into a little boutique that was crammed with flowery print surfer-chick dresses and racks of beaded jewellery. Acid jazz trickled out of the speakers as she flipped through the racks, deciding on her costume. Clothes were very important to Mimi: how could they not be, with Victoria for a mum? But to Mimi it wasn't about labels and how much you spent, it was about putting a look together for as little as possible, and not being the same as everyone else. Yet strangely, now she was here, she wanted to look exactly like all the other teenagers who were wandering the streets – carefree, sun-kissed, casual.

She chose a crocheted halter-neck top, a blue sarong and a pair of flip-flops embroidered with shells, then took them into the changing room. She ruffled her hair, trying to free it from the spray that had held it in shape earlier. She looked in the mirror and sighed. She looked like Malibu Barbie meets the Queen of the Dead. She had a long way to go before she looked like a beach babe. The black hair had to go. And she needed half a gallon of fake tan. But it was a start.

She went over to the till, holding her old clothes.

'You want to wear all that now?'

She looked up into a pair of aquamarine eyes.

'If that's OK.'

The assistant grinned at her.

'You were kind of overdressed for the beach.'

'Just a bit.'

'I'll cut the labels off for you.' He held up a pair of scissors. 'Come here.'

Mimi stood still obediently as he snipped off the price tags, surreptitiously sneaking glances at him. He was wearing combat shorts and skater shoes with bright green laces. His hair was dirty blond, shoulder length, the ringlets slightly matted from the sea salt that had been allowed to dry on it. Mimi felt a sudden urge to run her fingers through it. At last he had finished and Mimi fished in her blazer for her purse.

'Are you here on holiday?'

'Not exactly.' She pulled out a few crumpled notes left over from her birthday money. 'I've come to visit my stepdad.'

'Come down later. There's a band on at the Old Boat-house.'

'Are they good?'

'Just a second-rate cover band, but who gives? We have a laugh.'

He smiled as he slid the clothes she'd been wearing into a carrier bag, shook it out and handed it to her. Mimi noticed that the badge on his shirt said he was called Matt. Her tummy gave a little flip as their fingers touched, hers so pale, his golden brown.

'See you later, maybe.'

'Maybe . . .' Mimi managed a smile, and turned to walk out of the shop.

That was amazing, she thought. He'd been so friendly. But at the same time she didn't feel like she'd been hit on. The guys she knew in Bath were either only interested in one thing, or cut you dead. On the whole they were public school twerps who tried to prove they were richer and cooler than everyone else by driving fast in the hot hatches their parents had misguidedly bought them in order to relieve themselves of the endless fetching and carrying. They spoke in mockney accents and pretended to take lots of drugs. Mimi found them less than fascinating. In five minutes in Mariscombe, she had seen many Adonis-like creatures whom she could barely tear her eyes away from – not plastic action men, but rippling, tawny-haired creatures with smiling eyes and faded shorts; living breathing sources of fascination she longed to befriend. If not more. Mimi had preserved her virginity long past her friends. There was no one in Bath she deemed worthy of the honour of taking it. No one made her pulse race or her breath short. Mariscombe was a different story. With a sigh, she turned to walk back up the hill, wondering what had happened between her mother and George.

She'd been gutted when her mother had left George to go and live with Nick, although she hadn't shown it. She'd learned long ago that it was always easier to go along with Victoria's plans. But in retrospect, if she had realized how awful it was going to be, she would have put up a fight. She'd missed George dreadfully. He'd always been there – and not just as someone to drive her around or give her money. He'd genuinely taken an interest in her, and Mimi had quickly come to miss that attention, the camaraderie between them.

Nick, by contrast, had been utterly hideous. He'd made it very obvious from the start that she was an interloper. That her very presence in the house inhibited him and made him feel old. She'd come to enjoy pointing up his age, turning up her music deliberately, even though she didn't particularly want it on loud, because asking her to turn it down made him look like an old fart. Whereas George had made a point of including her in their daily life, Nick deliberately excluded her. He made her take the bus to school while George had been happy to drive her – in fact, he'd insisted on it. Her exclusion was disguised as freedom, of course, because Nick was cunning. He even put a fridge in her annexe so she could have her own food, on the pretext that he thought she would enjoy having her independence. But she didn't want independence. The time she had used to love best was when she and George made spaghetti bolognese together, ready for Victoria when she came home from work. And for all her mother's faults, those times had been really special. Mimi always made the garlic bread and the salad while George did the sauce, then they had thrown a piece of spaghetti at the fridge to see if it was cooked – a ridiculous ritual they always went through even though it was really easier just to bite it and see, but it never failed to amuse them.

Nick was not the type to throw spaghetti at the fridge.

Not that it mattered now. Nick was out of their lives for good. Mimi had made sure of that. There had been a few hairy moments afterwards, of course. Especially when she had realized it wasn't going to be so easy to turn back up on George's doorstep. Even more so when it became clear that they were in dire financial straits – Nick's idea of revenge was to cut them off completely, and a very effective job he had done too. But anything was better than the pair of them being in his clutches, even if they were now penniless.

It had taken Mimi several days to find out where George had gone, but eventually she had winkled it out of his secretary at work. Mimi had great guile when she wanted to use it. Her acting skills were second to none. It had then taken her several weeks to persuade Victoria that they should throw themselves on George's mercy. She was actually surprised that her mother not only had pride but also seemed ashamed of how she had treated George. Only when the cashpoint had flashed at her 'refer to bank' had she finally capitulated.

Mimi was utterly convinced George would come through

for them. She knew he adored her mother. The look in his eyes when he gazed at her was unforgettable. The pain in his eyes when she'd told him she was leaving was horrific. Mimi hadn't seen such depth of emotion in anyone before or since. Certainly not Nick. The only emotions she'd seen in him were lust and greed. Flesh and money did it for him. And now he'd taken Victoria for everything she'd got and proved that his brain was divided between his wallet and his trousers, he was history. Mimi was certain George would be their salvation.

There was, of course, one small obstacle. The girl with the paintbrush. Even in her scruffy decorating clothes, Mimi could see that she was quite stunning. Whoever she was, she was the complete antithesis of Victoria – curvaceous, bubbly and down to earth, as opposed to slender, cool and detached. She'd seemed a bit common, too – Mimi wasn't a snob, but she couldn't help noticing the girl had a regional accent. But all these things were good, because it meant that George had gone for the complete opposite this time. Which meant he was avoiding anything that reminded him of Victoria. Which meant he was still in love with her.

Mimi trudged up the hill and felt the sweat start to trickle down her back. George would have Victoria back in a flash, she was certain. And if he needed a little gentle manipulation, then she was the girl to do it. George had always been putty in her hands. Not that she'd ever, ever used him. She loved him too much for that. But for his own good, she was prepared to put the pressure on.

When George and Lisa got back from the beach, he found Victoria sunning herself in the garden.

'You can stay for two weeks,' he told her. He and Lisa had decided it was best if there was a time limit. 'But no funny business.'

'Funny business?' She looked rather put out.

'You know exactly what I mean.'

'I don't. Not really. But I promise I'll behave. And I'll do everything I can to help. Who've you got doing your PR?'

'No one. We're doing everything ourselves.'

'Well, I'll do it for you. I'll get all the travel journalists down. And the magazine editors—'

She was pacing up and down excitedly.

'Stop.' George put up his hand before she got carried away. 'You know we're on a tight budget.'

'But you are having a launch party?'

'No.'

'For heaven's sake, you've *got* to. You've got to stake your claim. Make a splash. You can't expect people to know about you if you don't tell them.'

As George opened his mouth to protest she put up her hand, mirroring his actions of a moment before.

'Stop. I know exactly what you're going to say. You can't afford it. But you can't afford not to. You only get one bite of the cherry. And it needn't cost a fortune. I promise you, with this setting I don't need a huge budget.'

'Victoria, there isn't a budget at all.'

'Listen, for the sake of a couple of thousand pounds I'll have them queuing round the block to get in. What else are you going to do? Send out a manky little press release that will go straight in the bin? For heaven's sake, George. You're spending a fortune on this place. It's a false economy not to publicize it, and you know it.'

George sighed. He knew she was right.

Ten minutes later he went to find Lisa. To tell her that Mimi and Victoria were staying. And that they were going to have to find the money for a launch party, the one thing they'd all agreed they didn't want to bother with. As he walked through the hallway, he saw a tall, rangy figure with a mop of black hair walking through the door.

'Mimi?'

Her funny little face creased into a smile and his heart buckled. He held out his arms and she rushed to hug him.

'George. It's so good to see you.'

For some reason, feeling his arms around her made her want to burst into tears. So she did.

'Hey, it's OK.' He rubbed her back.

'It's been so awful.' Her voice was muffled. 'He was such a bastard to her, George.'

'I know. I got the gist.'

Mimi looked up at him, her face tear-stained.

'Did she tell you he was hitting her?'

George looked shocked.

'No. She just told me . . . well, about your friend.'

'I didn't think she would. She never told me, either. But I heard him. It was always when they'd been drinking, but that's no excuse, is it? I know Mum can be awful, but he could have really hurt her.'

Mimi looked at him solemnly. George felt sick. He knew how infuriating Victoria was. Many, many times he'd suppressed the urge to grab her by the arms and shake her. But he'd never laid a finger on her, no matter how much she'd goaded him. Obviously Nick Taverner didn't have his self-control.

He put his arm around Mimi and squeezed her.

'It's OK,' he said softly. 'You don't have to go back.'

'But where will we go?'

'We'll sort something out.'

What, George couldn't imagine. But he couldn't let Mimi down. He suspected that he represented the only male stability she'd ever had in her life, this strange little girl with no father, whose own grandparents had rejected her, although George often suspected that this was perhaps Victoria's fault rather than theirs.

He smiled down at her, pulling the fringe of her sarong.

'What's all this, anyway? Have you turned into a surfer chick?'

'I felt like a total dork in what I was wearing. I just spent the last of my birthday money.'

George felt a pang of guilt. He hadn't sent Mimi a card or a present, which of course he should have done. She didn't deserve to be cut off just because of Victoria's behaviour. He decided it would be crass to start pulling cash out of his pocket now.

'Nobody bothers too much about clothes down here. It's very laid-back.'

'It's fantastic,' said Mimi softly, her eyes shining. 'Are you going to let us stay?'

'Just for a couple of weeks, while you get things sorted.' George ruffled her hair.

He looked up to see Justin standing in the doorway looking thunderous.

'What the fuck,' he demanded, 'is Victoria doing here? Please, somebody tell me I'm seeing things.'

Later that evening, George, Lisa and Justin held a council of war.

'I can't kick them out,' said George. 'Victoria's bleating on about alimony and settlements. I've got to keep her sweet.'

Justin snorted.

'No, you haven't. What does she mean, alimony? She contributed nothing to your household in all the time she was there. She was the one who left you, if you remember. You owe her nothing, George.'

George sighed.

'No, but there's Mimi to think of.'

Justin pointed an admonishing finger.

'You're not actually her father. You're not responsible for her. Anyway, she's big enough to look after herself. She must be eighteen by now.'

'No, she's not. She's seventeen. And she's the innocent party in all of this.'

Justin raised an eyebrow.

'Haven't you heard the phrase like mother, like daughter? You're a fool, George.'

'Justin, for God's sake, shut up,' said Lisa finally. 'If I don't mind them staying then I don't see why you should.'

Justin scowled and looked out of the window. George tapped his pen on a pad of paper.

'I've told them two weeks, max. I've told Victoria to get a decent lawyer to sort out her business affairs. Nick Taverner's completely ripped her off.'

'Good for him.'

'Leave it out, Justin,' George snapped. 'He's a complete tosser. Victoria caught him groping one of Mimi's friends in the hot tub.'

Justin rolled his eyes.

'Just be careful, George,' he sighed. 'And if you want a decent lawyer for yourself, just say the word.'

Lisa stretched and yawned.

'Can we stop wasting time and get on with more important things, please?' she asked. 'The carpenters are arriving to-morrow to fit out the bedrooms, we start interviewing staff on Monday and we need to start pinning down suppliers. Because in case you've forgotten, we've got precisely four weeks before we're due to open . . .'

Later, when Lisa had gone off to have a shower and wash the day's dust out of her hair, Justin cornered George again.

'You're my mate. In fact, I'd go so far as to say I'm your best mate. I'm not going to go on about the fact that I feel a bit shafted.'

'Why's that?'

'Because if I'd known you were still married to that witch I'd never have gone into business with you. There's nothing that woman isn't capable of.'

'I know you never liked her, but—'

'Look – I'm not boasting, but I'm a wealthy guy. I've got a built-in gold-digger radar and right now it's sending off major distress signals on your behalf—'

'Please, Justin. I'm in total control.'

'Promise me. If you get one moment of weakness . . . if she starts playing mind games with you—'

'She won't get a chance!'

George was adamant. Justin put a hand on his shoulder.

'Just keep your guard up. That's all I'm saying.'

'Hey – with you around to protect me, she's not going to get anywhere near me. You're like a bloody Rottweiler,' George joked.

'I need to be,' said Justin darkly. He hadn't fallen for that demure, vulnerable act, not for a moment.

When Mimi tried to persuade Victoria to come down with her to the Old Boathouse later that evening, she nearly bit her head off.

'For heaven's sake, Mimi. You know I'm trying not to drink.'

Mimi looked nonplussed.

'You don't have to drink. Have Coke. Or water.'

Victoria looked at her witheringly.

'You really have no idea, do you?'

'No,' said Mimi. 'Can't we just go and watch the band?'

Victoria threw herself on to the bed.

'Don't you go putting me under pressure as well!'

'Me? As well as who?' Mimi was genuinely bewildered. When you took everything into consideration, everyone had been rather good to Victoria. But her mother seemed more stressed than ever. She was lying face down, her head buried in a pillow.

'I don't know!' Her voice was muffled. 'Just go and enjoy yourself, will you? While you still can.'

'Whatever.' Mimi hated the expression. It seemed the ultimate in teenage indifference, but at that moment it seemed the most appropriate comment.

As soon as Mimi had gone, Victoria lay staring at the ceiling. Today had been absolute torture for her. Deep down, she'd been hoping for some sort of epic rapprochement. She'd convinced herself that George would melt on seeing her; that he would be overjoyed and would ooze forgiveness. But the look on his face had said otherwise. His expression had been one of . . . well, it could only be described as distaste. Certainly not delight. And, like Scarlett O'Hara on realizing she no longer had any hold over Rhett Butler, Victoria was shaken to find that her charms had lost their power.

She'd watched George touch Lisa, smile at her, and had felt bitter envy. She longed for his embrace, his reassurance, his solidity. But she had no entitlement. Despite the piece of paper that bound them together in the eyes of the law, Victoria knew she had blown it ages ago, and now she wept bitter tears of regret, cursing her weakness, her selfishness, her lack of judgement. Her inability to recognize the love of a good man when it was staring her in the face . . .

Mimi was a bit nervous going into the Old Boathouse on her own. For a start, she wasn't sure if she was wearing the right thing. She was never going to look like the rest of the girls she'd seen parading around Mariscombe, so she decided to cultivate her own beach-punk style. She'd fished out her oldest, most patched denim skirt, teemed it with the halter-neck she'd bought earlier that day, pinched a pair of Victoria's towering rope-soled espadrilles, then added a pair of fishnet tights that she cut off just below the knee, and strung several strings of love beads round her neck.

She pushed open the door and was hit by the heat of bodies and the babble of chatter. She elbowed her way to the bar and ordered a San Miguel. After about five minutes, she finally spotted Matt. He bounded over and gave her a hug.

'Hey. You made it.'

'Yeah.'

'Cool. Come and meet the guys.'

He dragged her over to a crowd of people sitting by the jukebox. They were all incredibly friendly. By the time the band came on Mimi had been invited to two more parties and a beach barbecue over the weekend. She was amazed. This was so different from an evening out in Bath. That would entail two hours of fierce debate while they all decided where to go. Then when the destination was pinned down there would be at least an hour while everyone looked each other up and down and slagged off each other's outfits, mixed with sporadic texting to change arrangements. Then suddenly it would become a drinking marathon and by ten o'clock all her friends would be legless. Before long they would be fighting, crying or getting off with someone they hated. Two hours later would come the military campaign to get everyone home: phoning the most malleable parent, scraping money together for a cab or cadging a lift off someone. But not before someone was sick or had passed out. That wasn't going to happen here. Firstly, because there wasn't a great choice of destination – this, it seemed, was where everyone hung out. And they weren't on a mission to get drunk. Sure, they had a few beers, but they seemed to be able to stop before they fell apart. Mimi suddenly realized how much she had actually hated her social life. She'd never really felt part of the gang. She doubted if any of her friends had ever felt they belonged, because the whole point was to make everyone feel alienated.

Here, however, everyone seemed intent on making her feel welcome. During the band, Matt came over and rested an arm on her shoulder. Not in a lecherous way, just as if they'd been mates for ages. She turned to smile at him and he grinned back.

'Great band.'

Mimi nodded.

'How long are you staying?'

Mimi didn't answer straightaway.

'Who knows?' she answered. 'Maybe for ever?'

From the other side of the bar, Justin watched Mimi mingle with a sinking heart. That was the last thing he needed, Mimi getting her feet under the table in Mariscombe and deciding she wanted to stay. For in some ways, she was more of a threat than her mother. Justin knew George had a soft spot for the girl, and if he was handling Victoria with kid gloves it was because he was concerned for Mimi. And even Justin had to admit she was a nice kid. Whoever her father was, he must have been a decent bloke, because Mimi certainly didn't get her equable nature from her mother.

Justin was determined not to let Victoria mess things up for George and Lisa. He didn't care about himself, but he knew The Rocks was vital for the two of them. And Lisa was good for George. He was his old self again around her, not the superficial twat he'd become when he'd got married. He looked around the bar – Mariscombe definitely wasn't the sort of place you could pick up a contract killer, he thought gloomily.

Justin sighed, took his change from the barman and picked up the bottle of wine and two glasses he'd ordered. He made his way back over to the window seat and looked down into a pair of laughing eyes.

'Hi,' he smiled, and immediately felt better. Maybe he'd do better minding his own business.

When George crawled into bed beside her later that night, Lisa pretended to be asleep. She didn't want to discuss the day's events, because she still wasn't sure how she felt. She knew if they made love, which they would normally do, that it would somehow cement her forgiveness, and she didn't quite feel ready for that. It wasn't that she wanted to punish him by depriving him of her body. But sex often made her feel vulnerable and she didn't trust herself not to have some sort of post-coital breakdown, which would show George exactly how hurt she felt.

Next to her, George listened to Lisa's breathing and wondered if she really was asleep. He still wasn't quite sure where he stood. Lisa might have forgiven him verbally, she might have accepted Victoria's presence under their roof, but there had been a steely look in her eye all evening that he hadn't seen before. He knew Lisa was a tough cookie and he was still wary of reprisals. And he knew enough about women to know that forgiveness wasn't cut and dried, that there might be recriminations and barbed remarks for some time to come. He needn't think he'd got away with it.

To take his mind off his predicament, he started running through the lists of things he needed to achieve in the coming week, the people he needed to phone: building control, the printers, ordering yet another skip, the girl who was doing the curtains. But sleep wouldn't come. And pervading his thoughts was a persistent image that he desperately tried to shake out of his head. The image of Victoria lying in bed only a few rooms away. She would be naked, because she always was, even in the depths of winter. George gritted his teeth, trying to think of anything but the slender limbs he remembered so well, but it was impossible. Even as he lay there, he thought he could smell her scent. She was invading him, his mind and his senses. She was in his thoughts, in the very pores of his skin. He'd forgotten the power she had over him. Two years of total abstinence might never have happened.

He should have sent her packing. It wasn't the fear of what she might do that had made him succumb to her pleas, no matter what he had told Lisa and Justin. It was because once he had seen her, he couldn't resist. He was crazy. He was torturing himself. It was like an alcoholic pouring a drink and leaving it on the table all day.

Perhaps making love to Lisa would help get Victoria out of his system. He debated sliding an exploratory hand over her curves. Usually he wouldn't hesitate: Lisa was always happy to be roused from her slumber. She wasn't the type to bat away nocturnal advances. He stroked the curve of her belly and kissed her shoulder, breathing in the tang of her shower gel, inhaling it deeply. In her semi-conscious state she pressed herself against him in a gesture of encouragement.

'I love you,' said George later, burying his face in Lisa's curls, but she didn't reply. Her breathing told him she was asleep again. He wasn't even sure she'd woken properly. He lay back on the pillows as his beating heart subsided to its normal rate.

Lisa was gorgeous and he did love her. It was just his mind playing tricks. By the time he got up tomorrow he would be in total control.

Nine

Bruno had decided that one of the few members of his staff who had a modicum of conscientiousness was the little chambermaid, Molly, who sometimes doubled up as a waitress. He'd watched her this morning at breakfast service. She kept her eyes open all the time, clearing plates away as soon as they were empty, bringing fresh tea and coffee, replenishing toast. She greeted the guests with a smile. She constantly tidied the table where the fruit juices and cereals were laid out, mopping up spills and topping up the jugs. The other waitresses stood around gossiping or looking at their fingernails.

And as a chambermaid, she was meticulous too. Bruno slipped into the rooms to inspect them after they had been changed. Molly's rooms were always pristine. Hospital corners to the beds, pillows beautifully plumped, mirrors gleaming. Somehow her rooms smelled sweeter.

He cornered her in an upstairs corridor. She seemed to be on her guard, keeping her trolley between them as if for protection. He knew she was from Tawcombe. Girls from Tawcombe often seemed to be on their back foot, as if someone was likely to discover that they didn't belong in Mariscombe and send them packing. They were a bit chippy. But then, thought Bruno, he'd be chippy if he'd drawn the short straw – it never ceased to amaze him that two places, one heaven, one hell, could be separated by only a couple of miles.

'I wondered if you'd like to be considered for the housekeeper's job?' Bruno asked her, and she stared back at him.

'I've watched you. You do a good job. Yours are the sort of standards I'm looking for.'

She shook her head.

'I don't think I can take it on.' Her voice was soft, slightly husky. 'I can't put any extra hours in.'

'It wouldn't entail much more.'

But she couldn't be persuaded. She seemed in a hurry to get away from him. Bruno wondered what it was that was holding her back. Perhaps she had another job elsewhere that she didn't want him to know about. He knew there were plenty of people around here who held down two or three jobs during the summer. They had to make hay while the sun shone, grafting during the high season to make up for the leaner winter months when they might not be able to earn anything at all.

'We'd make it worth your while, Molly. You'd have a proper salary. And if you wanted to live in, you could.'

'Thanks, but I don't think so.'

Bruno frowned.

'Why don't you think about it? And if there's anything I can do to make it possible for you . . .'

'Sorry. But thanks for asking.'

She practically ran down the corridor. Bruno sighed. It was bloody frustrating, but if she didn't want to better herself there was nothing he could do about it. Some people were happy with their station in life, he supposed. The last thing he wanted to do was force her into it.

On the bus on the way home that afternoon, Molly's mind was whirring. She rested her cheek against the cool of the windowpane, thinking about the conversation she'd had with Bruno. There was absolutely no way she could take the house-keeper's job on, so she might as well stop torturing herself. She chewed her lip. Life just wasn't fair. It would be amazing to have a proper job. Almost a career. Caragh had started off as housekeeper, and look at her now. But it wasn't possible, so there was no point in thinking about it. Nevertheless, Molly ran through various possibilities in her mind, trying to find a solution. It was so frustrating . . .

She sat up, feeling slightly sick, as the bus lurched off the roundabout and down the main road into Tawcombe. It was ridiculously narrow, lined with dilapidated Victorian terraces that had once seen better days. Occasionally the bus had to pull up on to the pavement, if it met another large vehicle coming the other way. It swung past the scrap of beach in the centre of town smothered in shingle and empty tin cans and drying seaweed, then rumbled past the small harbour that not even the most euphemistic of tourist guides could describe as picturesque. There was an overriding sense of desolation in Tawcombe. There was no hope of a renaissance like there had been in nearby Ilfracombe, several miles up the coast. Tawcombe kept the dregs, after all, and they had no pride in their surroundings, no incentive to better themselves.

Molly sighed. Once you were amongst the dregs, it seemed there was no way out. Even if someone threw you a lifeline, you couldn't grab it. The bus bowled into the bus station, the doors opening with a malevolent hiss. Thankful that the journey had come to an end, Molly ran down the steps without bothering to thank the driver – he was a miserable bastard, always picking his nose – and headed out of the station, hurrying along the street.

Why did people think that living by the seaside was so idyllic? Tawcombe was a dump, rife with drugs and no-hopers, thirteen-year-old girls pushing prams and smoking fags, post-natal bellies hanging out over the top of their hipsters. Foulmouthed, shaven-headed youths lolled on the steps by the harbour, watched by fat old men with greasy trousers who fondled themselves indiscreetly, their only hope the three fifteen at Chepstow. The streets were littered with fish and chip wrappers, untaxed cars, empty beer cans. The evening pavements were peppered with chewing gum and splats of sick, pecked at by undiscriminating seagulls and studded with undigested rice from the myriad takeaways that lined the harbour front. There were boarded-up windows, jacked-up motors. The air smelt stale.

Molly turned the corner into Uffculme Row. Three doors along she could see the steps outside the house she lived in. And sitting on the third step up, a figure. As she approached, the woman looked at her. Her skin was dull, her hair straggling, with three-inch grey roots that transformed into faded, washed-out black. Her fingers were crammed with sovereign rings, the nails bitten ragged, the skin chapped. She wore flared tracksuit bottoms, shiny blue acrylic with a white stripe down the side, and a grey sweatshirt. There was a thick gold necklace round her neck, hung with crosses, horse heads, a St Christopher and a shamrock, showing sentimentality for the country of her origin that she'd never actually visited.

'Hello, Molly.' Ten years in this county and the Scouse accent was as strong as ever.

'Where is he?'

'Fast asleep. I just came down for a fag.' Her eyes looked accusingly. 'As I'm not allowed to smoke in the flat.'

'No, you're not.'

Molly pounded up the steps without a backward glance and opened the door, recoiling in disgust at the smell – cat pee and stale rubbish, courtesy of a full bin bag dumped at the bottom of the stairs. There was a huge pile of unopened post – junk mail and free newspapers. She could feel the thud of drum and bass from the basement. She ran up the stairs, careful not to trip over the worn carpet, and pushed open the door to her flat.

Alfie was in the playpen. His cheeks were flushed and tear-stained; his hair damp with sweat. He'd obviously sobbed himself to sleep, his little fist clutched round his favourite bear. Molly bent down and picked him up, cradling him in her arms, feeling the warmth of her love suffusing her. It was as sweet and comforting as a shot of morphine as it swept through her veins, easing her anxiety if only for a moment.

This precious moment was all that mattered. She gazed down at the little boy.

Already, he looked so like him. As she traced her fingers over Alfie's eyebrows, so pronounced in his little face, and brushed his silky dark hair, the memories came flooding back. Those cheeks, those lips, the eyes that had smiled at her, burned through her . . .

Molly placed the sleeping baby in his cot and turned away. There was no point in torturing herself. But sometimes she couldn't help it. Wondering what might have been, if the three of them had been a family. What life would have been like; whether Alfie would have had a brother or a sister. Whether they would have had a wedding. For a second she caught a glimpse of herself at an imaginary altar, lifting her cream lace veil to look at her groom—

Why did she do this to herself? She thought she'd taught herself not to daydream. Joe was dead, and he wasn't ever coming back.

Five minutes later, reeking of recently smoked cigarettes with a hint of Diamond White underneath, her mother stomped into the room.

'I don't suppose it was pay day?'

'No.'

'You've no spare cash?'

Molly stared at her mother.

'Of course I haven't.'

'I must have saved you a few quid today.'

'You're not seriously expecting me to pay you? For looking after your own grandson?'

Teresa Mahoney looked petulant and sulky. Molly felt her throat constrict with disappointment. Why did her mother always have to let her down? For one wild moment on her way home on the bus, she had wondered whether, if today had gone well, her mother might help her out more so she could take on the housekeeper's job. But she wasn't going to mention it now, absolutely no way. She wasn't going to be beholden to her own mother.

Teresa was glaring at her, hands on hips.

'Fine. If you just want to use me. That's typical of you.'

She was on the attack, spoiling for a fight. Molly got up to put the kettle on. Her mother persisted.

'I could have been working down the old people's home today, earning proper money, instead of running round after you.'

'Forget it, Mum. I won't ask you again.'

'Some thanks would be nice.'

'Thank you.' Molly gritted her teeth.

'You're an ungrateful little bitch, aren't you? I didn't bring you up to use people the way you do.'

Molly concentrated hard on filling the kettle. She had to bite her tongue when her mother went off on one of her tirades. They were always totally unfounded. Molly didn't use people. Ever. It was one of her golden rules, having been mercilessly exploited throughout her childhood. She knew what it was like to be taken for granted.

Ten

They'd started off life in her mother's native Liverpool, she and her four brothers and sisters. Molly was the second oldest. She'd never been quite sure which of them had the same father, if any, for the men came and went in their mother's life more frequently than she changed her sheets. It was no real secret what her mum did to supplement her income. Molly sometimes wondered if her own father had been a client or a lover, and clung to the hope it had been the latter, for her mother had been beautiful once. She'd seen the photos of the glamorous girl with the lustrous long black locks and flashing eyes: Catherine Zeta Jones, she'd reminded her of. There was no evidence of that now. Over the years the curves collapsed into mounds of sagging flesh, the cheekbones disappeared under jowls, and Teresa's clientele changed from the discerning to the desperate, paying for Teresa's willingness to be degraded rather than her looks.

Life for Molly and her siblings was tough. The only thing they were ever sure of was that there would be no tea, no clean clothes for the next day. It had been down to Molly to scrat around for something for them to eat, then strip off their shirts and blouses and put them in the kitchen sink with a squirt of washing-up liquid, then hang them in front of the gas fire to dry for the morning. She cut her brothers' hair with the kitchen scissors and dragged the nit comb through all of their curls, including her own. No one was going to accuse the Mahoneys of not being clean while she was in charge.

When Molly was nine, there was a glimmer of hope. Her

mother had a boyfriend, a proper boyfriend called Jeff who drove lorries, and although he took no notice of the children he seemed to like Teresa. Well enough for them both to decide to move to Devon, where he came from. Molly remembered the excitement as she and her older sister Siobhan climbed into the cab for the journey down and the rest of the kids scrambled into the back of Jeff's lorry. As they trundled down the motorway, Molly allowed herself to daydream about what was waiting for them at the other end. Jeff had organized them somewhere to live, apparently. Molly imagined a pretty little house overlooking the shore, and a life filled with seashells and sandcastles and rock pools. It was all going to be so different. Nothing bad happened at the seaside, surely?

She couldn't have been more wrong. The dreary, grey patch of water they could glimpse from the flat in Tawcombe was more depressing than anything Molly had ever seen. And two weeks later Jeff and Teresa had a terrible, terrible fight. Jeff left her mother with nothing to show for it but two black eyes. And now, instead of struggling in Liverpool, where they'd had a support network and understood the rules, they had to find their feet in a new town. Teresa wouldn't go back, because she didn't want to lose face. She'd boasted to everyone that she was going to have a better life, crowing that she was getting out of the slum and away from the scum. No one would show her an ounce of sympathy if she went crawling back with her tail between her legs. So they had to make a go of it.

It was a struggle. Sometimes her mum had money, though Molly never liked to think why. But at least then they could have a feast. They'd be down to the pub on the harbour front for Sunday lunch. But Molly couldn't eat it. The greasy beef would stick in her throat, and she'd look around the men laughing at the bar, wondering which of them she had to thank for her meal. The others were happy enough to scoff it down, slurping their bottles of Coke through straws, begging for ice cream, and Molly made sure they had their fill, for it might be a week or two before any of them saw a vegetable again.

She was twelve before she discovered that the haven she'd dreamed of was only a bus ride away. There was a school trip to Mariscombe, and as the coach turned the corner and Molly saw the sparkling sea and golden beach, she recognized it as the place she'd dreamed of, the place she'd thought she was coming to when they'd left Liverpool. There and then she vowed she would escape here as soon as she could.

When she was fifteen, she managed to get herself a summer job at the Mariscombe Holiday Park, a magnificent site perched on the cliffs overlooking the sea. It was down to a crack team to clean out the static caravans, scrub the shower blocks and bring all the amenities up to scratch. For Molly it was paradise. Even if cleaning up after people who didn't seem to care what state they left the place in was hard and unsavoury work, it was fantastic fun being on the site and being part of the team who kept it together. After the changeover was complete and the new incumbents were settled, the staff would all flock to the beach for the evening. Molly was afraid of the water itself – the waves were disconcertingly high – but she was happy to sit on the sand drinking beer. Sometimes there'd be a barbecue, or someone would go and buy a dozen wraps of chips, and they would party until the sun went down, the boys showing off their skills in the surf, the girls showing off their tans. Often she didn't go home. There was always someone's place to crash in, or occasionally if it was hot they would crash on the dunes. Molly was happy. She'd found somewhere she fitted in, where the balance between hard work and hard partying was just right. She longed for the day when she could leave school and come and get something more permanent, escaping her mother's foul tongue and evil temper for ever. Her younger brothers and sisters would have to fend for themselves. She no longer had any control over them anyway – Kieran was a glue-sniffing little oik at eleven and Macy had been caught shoplifting twice already. They didn't thank her for trying to impose routine and discipline, so Molly didn't see why she should waste her life any longer.

The first time she came into contact with Joe Thorne she was carrying her mop and bucket and her box full of cleaning agents across the site, dressed in the ugly green uniform all the support staff wore. He was just coming out of the caravan she was heading for. He paused as he came down the steps. For a moment he seemed confused as he gazed at her, seemingly lost for words. He reached out a hand to touch her arm, as if to convince himself she was real. Molly looked at it, transfixed, then looked back at him, unable to think of a word to say. Then suddenly he recovered his composure and took his hand away, smiling.

'Just doing a bit of maintenance.'

He winked, jumped off the last two steps and strolled off across the grass, whistling. Molly breathed in the scent of him and felt quite giddy. She was surprised. She was usually quite immune to the charms of the opposite sex. She could withstand any overture stony-faced. Her mother's lifetime of degradation at the hands of men meant Molly was in no hurry to rush into anything. Usually if someone had touched her like that, uninvited, she would have shaken them off, given them a sharp word. But in that fleeting exchange Joe had made her feel quite woozy – his eyes had looked straight into hers for one moment, and she felt as if he'd looked right into the core of her. She wondered what it was he had thought, what he had registered, for something had definitely passed between them. Molly wasn't fanciful, and she'd discovered a long time ago that daydreaming and romanticizing often led to disappointment, so she was surprised to find her heart thumping as she watched him disappear. Was this, she wondered, love at first sight?

Molly knew she was pretty. She was petite, with a perfect heart-shaped face and indigo-blue eyes, and dark hair that sprang in thick waves back from her forehead. But in her shapeless uniform, with her hair scraped back in a scrunchie, she doubted he'd seen any potential. Telling herself to get real, Molly climbed up the steps and into the caravan, bumping straight into a young girl who was hastily adjusting her clothing.

'Shit. I've got to go. My mum and dad are leaving any minute.'

The girl pushed rudely past Molly, who stood aside in bemusement. The encounter told her to harden her heart. Joe probably pulled that trick on all the girls, to make them think they were in with a chance. Looked at them as if they'd stepped straight out of his dreams, then rushed off leaving them in confusion. No, Molly told herself sternly. She wasn't going to be fooled.

As she started cleaning out the mess in the caravan, she reminded herself of everything she'd heard about him. Joe's reputation as a wild boy went before him. His parents owned the site and he was supposed to help out with the running of it, but no one was quite sure what he did – as little as possible, it was generally agreed, but somehow he got away with it and didn't create resentment. All the other girls who worked on the campsite sighed, but knew they weren't in with a chance. Although he was a dreadful flirt and a tease, and had wandering hands, everyone knew there was no point wasting your time in losing your heart because, at the end of the day, Joe was spoken for.

Joe's girlfriend was Tamara Taylor, a honeyed, athletic goddess with golden hair tumbling over her shoulders, a girl who would never have to clean out a toilet in her life. Her father was loaded. He owned a frozen-food factory on the outskirts of Tawcombe, which supplied nearly every pub, hotel and restaurant in North Devon with chips, peas and chicken nuggets. It was rumoured that Cliff Taylor loathed Joe with a vengeance, and considered him a good-for-nothing, free-loading, time-wasting little shit. But as every father knows, to disapprove of a daughter's boyfriend is to render him even more attractive, so Cliff was biding his time, confident that Joe would show his true colours eventually and Tamara would come to her senses, seeing him for the bit of rough he was. And in the meantime Joe played fast and loose whenever he pleased, returning to Tamara as if butter wouldn't melt. Molly decided that she had just been a pawn in one of his games. She was not going to be one of his victims, she decided as she squirted thick bleach all over the kitchen worktops. No way.

Two days later, Molly was standing at the bus stop when a car pulled up. She could hear Eminem pounding through the speakers. The passenger window wound down and she peered in. It was Joe.

'Get in, then.'

'Where are you going?'

'Do you care?'

She tipped her head to one side and smiled at him.

'I'm on my way home.'

'I know. Seventeen Uffculme Row, Tawcombe.' Molly felt a delicious shiver trickle its way down her spine as he surveyed her seriously. 'I looked up your details in the office.'

Instinctively, she stepped back from the car, reminding herself that she wasn't going to be toyed with. Nevertheless, she felt disconcerted that she had made an impression on him. Even if he was playing with her for his own amusement, he'd been in her thoughts. She felt a tingling excitement pool in the pit of her stomach. Desperately she looked down the road, praying that the bus was coming. She couldn't cope with this, not for a moment longer . . .

'For heaven's sake, get in. It's going to piss with rain any minute and the bus is always late. You'll be soaked.'

As if on cue, fat raindrops began to fall. Molly hesitated. Joe tapped his fingers on the steering wheel.

'I'm not going till you get in.'

Even though every grain of sense in her screamed not to, she got in. As she shut the door, the smell of him hit her nostrils and her pulse seemed to treble. The scent was magical, intoxicating, and her head swam.

'I'm off to Tawcombe to see a man about a dog,' Joe explained as he accelerated up the hill, casting a glance at his watch. 'Not till six, though. Do you fancy a drink?'

'I've got to get home,' said Molly, knowing she sounded prim.

'What for? *Home and Away?*'

'I've got to cook my brothers' and sisters' tea.' This was an outright lie. Molly hadn't cooked for them for weeks. None of them were ever home; they roamed the streets like waifs and strays. She'd given up on the lot of them.

Joe pulled up outside the Lamb. He switched off the engine and turned to look at her, gazing at her solemnly. Molly thought she was going to pass out under his scrutiny. She scrabbled for the door handle, but he put out a hand to stop her.

'Come and have a drink. Just a quick one. Surely you can take half an hour off?' He reached up and ran a finger lightly under one of her eyes. 'You look tired. You could do with a break.'

Later, Molly looked back and knew that had been the split second that was to change her life for ever. If she'd just said no, things would have been so different. For all of them . . .

Molly had felt awkward going into the Lamb with him. It was one of the worst dives in town, one she wouldn't dream of going into usually, and there could only be one reason for Joe wanting to go in there. But after ten minutes she was completely unaware of her surroundings. The two of them totally clicked. Joe fired questions at her and she answered. Some of them were logical and some crazy. And after two Smirnoff Ices she had the nerve to fire his questions back at him, and found he was disarmingly honest.

At eight o'clock, she reluctantly got to her feet.

'I'd better go.'

He stood up and walked her to the door. She lifted her hand in a gesture of farewell. He responded by crooking an arm round her neck and pulling her to him in a rough gesture of fondness.

'Come here, you.'

She looked up at him, laughing. Then he pulled her in a little tighter and rocked her. She put a hand on his waist to steady herself and, suddenly, she was in his arms. They stood very still together for a moment, their foreheads touching. She breathed very deeply to calm herself as he ran his fingers through her hair, either side of her face, cradling her head gently.

'Molly . . .' he whispered her name.

Terrified and confused, she pulled away from him. No one had ever made her feel like that, not even in her dreams, and she was petrified. Because she couldn't control her feelings. And because she'd heard all the stories, time and time again. She wasn't going to be another scalp on his belt. She wasn't . . .

'I've got to go,' she said, and ran out of the pub without looking back.

It took Joe two weeks to wear her down. And during that two weeks he occupied her every waking moment and her every sleeping dream, as she veered between wild fantasies and stern lectures to herself. No way could he be really interested in her, a little scrubber from the backstreets of Tawcombe. Was she just a challenge he couldn't resist? It was obviously a point of honour. He was an arrogant little shit, she told herself, who didn't like thinking somebody could resist him.

But the truth was, she couldn't. He finally ran her to ground, one glorious evening when she'd decided to take the coast path back from work. By going that way she could cut across to a bus stop further along than the one she usually caught, avoiding the protracted detour the bus took through various villages. She was all alone on the top of the cliffs, treading her way carefully along the narrow, treacherous path that only the most intrepid of tourists followed.

She turned a corner and saw him sitting on a bench, staring out to sea. Looking back, of course, she realized it was no coincidence. He turned and gave her a slow, lazy smile.

'Molly . . .' he said.

'I'm just on my way home.' She could feel her cheeks flush pink.

He nodded down the cliff, to the rocks at the bottom. He put a finger to his lips to tell her to be quiet as he beckoned her over.

'You're just in time.'

'For what?'

She came and sat next to him. He pulled her close, then pointed. Amidst the rocks at the bottom of the cliff, bobbing about in the blue water, were three sleek black heads. Molly smiled in delight.

'Seals!'

Joe nodded, unable to take his eyes away.

'I come down here every night to watch them. Do you want to go further down, get a better look?'

He pointed to a tiny narrow path on the cliff's edge, only inches wide and almost vertical. Molly nodded.

'OK.'

As they scrambled down the cliff, Molly's heart was in her mouth. It was a long way down and the rocks below looked unforgiving, but eventually, after much scrambling, the path gave out on to a grassy platform, about ten metres square.

'No one ever comes down here. It's the perfect viewing point.'

They lay on the warm ground and watched the seals frolicking in the water. After a few minutes Molly realized that Joe wasn't paying them attention any longer; he was staring at her.

'What?' she asked, slightly defensive.

'You,' he answered simply. 'I can't stop thinking about you.'

Molly felt her stomach do a slow somersault. She should have laughed him off; rolled her eyes and told him to sling his hook. But she was transfixed. She couldn't tear her gaze from his, and as he leaned over to kiss her, she pulled him towards her greedily, longing for his touch, and it was every feeling she had imagined.

Molly had attached no great sentimental value to her virginity. No one did in her world. She'd got rid of it neatly when she was fourteen, to an old boyfriend of her sister's, to see what all the fuss was about, and she'd been neither impressed nor traumatized by the experience. She'd had the odd encounter since, but nothing memorable. Now, however, she was suddenly flooded with a feeling that told her she had missed the point somewhere along the line. She wanted him to touch her everywhere. She flung her clothes off with a feverish urgency, oblivious to the fact that they were in broad daylight. Nothing else mattered but being possessed by him.

Afterwards, they lay in each other's arms for a moment, breathless, panting. Joe rolled over on to his back, wiping his hand across his forehead, and closed his eyes with what seemed to be a sigh of satisfaction. As her heart began to slow down to its normal pace and the feelings that had flooded her slowly ebbed away, Molly panicked. What the hell had she done? How many other girls had Joe lured down here, with his Disneyesque tableau? Did the seals know that they were part of his mating ritual, his seduction technique? Were they trained to perform for his victim's delight, knocking them off their guard? She scrambled to her feet, pulling her clothes back on. Joe had made his conquest. He'd proven himself irresistible. And she'd proven herself weak. She looked at him, at his chest rising and falling, oblivious to her torment. He seemed to be fast asleep.

Her legs were trembling, weak from the climb down and the emotion, as she scrambled as fast as she could back up the rocks. For some reason she found she was crying. It wasn't fair. She'd laid herself completely open, stripped herself naked both literally and metaphorically. He'd taken her, taken the very core of her. And now he'd got what he wanted, now he'd gratified himself and satisfied himself, that would be it, she knew. Tomorrow night he'd be outside the Jolly Roger with Tamara, dropping kisses on to her bronzed shoulders, running his thumb along her back . . .

'Molly!' His hand was on her shoulder. He'd followed her up. 'Where the hell are you going?'

'Home . . .' she managed through her tears.

'Why?' He grabbed her by both elbows and looked at her, bewildered.

'You've got what you wanted.'

'No!' He looked into her eyes, genuinely flummoxed. 'You don't understand. I want you.'

She was panting with the exertion, too exhausted to run.

'You want me? Why?'

'Because . . . you make me feel like me.'

She frowned.

'What do you mean?'

'I can be myself with you. You don't expect things from me. And you don't disapprove.'

'Disapprove? What of?'

Joe shrugged.

'You know my reputation.'

'Yes,' said Molly meaningfully. 'What about Tamara?'

Joe sighed.

'I'll have to tell her.'

'Tell her what?'

'About us.'

Molly frowned. 'It's a bit soon, isn't it? I can't remember agreeing that there is an *us* . . .'

He grabbed her by both arms.

'Come on, Molly. You've got to admit that was special. That wasn't just a quick leg-over. Was it?'

'I suppose not . . .'

'We can't just walk away from this.'

'I'm not going to be your bit on the side, Joe.'

'No. You're not. I'm going to have to finish with her. But Molly . . .'

'What?' Molly narrowed her eyes suspiciously.

'I can't do it yet.' Joe lit a roll-up. 'My dad's in the middle of a deal with her dad. They want to open a restaurant on the site. Tamara's dad's going to put up the cash. And he's on the council, so he's going to make sure they get planning permission. But if I dump Tamara . . .'

He trailed off, drawing hard on his cigarette.

'He'll pull out?' said Molly. She wasn't dim.

Joe nodded.

'I can't risk this deal falling through because of me. It would just prove everything that my parents have ever thought. That I'm a loser.'

'I understand . . .' Molly looked crestfallen.

'It doesn't mean I don't love you. But I'm going to have to be careful. I'm going to have to choose the right time to tell her. The council meeting's at the end of this month. Once they've got permission, the deal will go through. Then I can get rid of her. You've got to trust me, Moll. Will you wait?'

Molly managed a nod. She felt like a snow globe that had been picked up and shaken, her tummy filled with particles of shimmering glitter. Of course she'd wait for him. Until the end of time, if necessary. You didn't pass up the chance to feel like this again for the rest of your life.

For the next four weeks, they carried on an intense, clandestine affair. Sometimes they didn't make love. Sometimes they met in an out-of-the-way pub and held hands, fingers entwined, palms pressed close together. Sometimes they went to an empty caravan on the site and played house – making tea and watching videos wrapped in each other's arms. Molly never nagged him about Tamara. That wasn't her style. And in a way, she preferred it like this. She knew if their relationship was out in the open, the dynamics would change. They would have to take other people into consideration. There would be pressures. By keeping it secret, they kept it on their terms. If only, thought Molly, it could stay like that for ever . . .

'Let's run away, Moll.' Some weeks later, they were lying on the grass on the very spot they'd first made love.

'Where to?'

'Dunno. Ireland, maybe? Somewhere wild and beautiful where you can be you and I can be me and we can have beautiful children and not put them under any pressure. Just take them fishing and to the fair and buy them fat ponies and live in a little cottage. I'll play the guitar and you can bake bread—'

'That's sexist!' murmured Molly, running her hand over the smooth skin on his stomach.

'OK. I'll bake the bread and you can play the guitar. I don't mind, as long as we can be left just to get on with our lives.'

She wondered what pressure it was that he felt. To her, he seemed to have an ideal existence. Security, the freedom to do what he liked, parents who seemed to dote on him, despite what he claimed. Why on earth would you want to run away from that? He should try being brought up in a scummy flat in Tawcombe with a mother who didn't give a shit and a father he'd never even seen.

'What have you got to worry about?' she demanded.

'Everyone thinks I'm a loser. A waste of space . . .'

Molly looked surprised.

'Like who?'

'Everyone. My parents. Well, not so much my mum. But my dad. And my older brother. They seem to think I should be more responsible. That I should be wheeling and dealing. Putting on a suit, driving a posh car. But that's not me. I don't really give a toss about money.'

'Try not having any,' said Molly. 'You might change your tune. Not having any money sucks.'

Joe eyed her thoughtfully.

'You think the same, then? You think I should get myself a proper job? A career?'

'I didn't say that,' Molly replied. 'But I don't think you realize how lucky you are.'

Joe looked bleakly out to sea.

'That's what everyone keeps saying. But I don't think they realize how difficult it is. Not living up to everyone's expectations. I just want to have a *life*.' He spat the last word out vehemently. 'I just want to enjoy myself while I can.'

Molly was shocked at the expression in his eyes. It was as if a light had gone out. The devil-may-care Joe had disappeared. She slid her arms round his waist, anxious to reassure him.

'There's nothing wrong with that.'

'Exactly.' He picked up a strand of her hair and wound it through his fingers. 'You understand. That's why I want us to run away together . . .'

Molly rolled into his embrace. To lie in his arms while he dreamed of a future with her was heaven, to be part of his fantasy filled her with a golden joy she couldn't describe. And now he was kissing her, gentle, wonderful kisses, and then he was making love to her . . . proper *love*making, not screwing her, or shagging her, or getting his leg over, but engaging her in something that left her wordless and weeping and him mute with wonder. And thank goodness it seemed to dispel his black mood. His gloom had frightened her, because she wasn't sure how to deal with it. Something she didn't understand weighed heavy upon him.

Now he was looking down at her.

'I've never felt like this before about anyone. You make me feel safe and happy. You make me want to . . . just be with you. You don't put me under pressure. You don't make demands on me. You don't . . . expect anything.'

Molly shook her head, puzzled.

'Expect anything? Like what?'

'I can't explain. You don't expect me to toe the line. Be responsible. Play the game.' He stroked her face. 'It's all bollocks. Because all I really care about is you. I love you, Molly.'

She'd never expected to be loved, especially not by some-one like Joe. Suddenly it gave her a new perspective. And courage – the courage to go back on a decision she'd made two days before. She'd meant to keep it a secret, deal with it in the only way she knew how. But if what he was saying was true . . .

'Do you really?' She had to be sure.

He nodded.

'I wouldn't just say it. In fact, I've never said it before. Not to anyone. But I'm going to say it again. I love you.'

'Me too,' murmured Molly, melting at his touch. 'I love you too.'

He hugged her tightly.

'Where shall we go, Moll? What shall we do?'

'Joe . . .' Her nerve was going to fail her. She had to tell him.

He looked at her anxiously.

'What? What is it? Don't you want us to be together?'

She nodded, biting her lip. They'd tried to be careful, but just once or twice, she knew, passion had overtaken them, and crossing fingers had never been a reliable contraceptive.

'I'm pregnant.'

His face was expressionless. She was filled with dread while she waited for his reaction. He was going to panic. He was going to totally freak. But then he smiled, his face filled with a joy that lifted her heart.

'There you go, Molly. You see? We're meant to be to-gether.' He held her tight, rocking her from side to side. 'I'm going to tell Tamara it's over. Then I'll tell my parents.'

'Are you sure? You don't think it's too soon?'

'Too soon?' He shook his head. 'Too soon? If anything, we've left it rather late. I should have told them weeks ago.' He gave her a squeeze. 'You know what? My mum is going to be so thrilled. She loves babies. She's always complaining because Bruno hasn't got married yet. She's desperate for a grandchild.' He gave her another hug. 'Just for once, maybe

I'll get one up on Bruno by giving my parents what they really want.'

Molly wasn't so sure that what Mr and Mrs Thorne were after was an illegitimate grandchild via a skivvy from the campsite, but she didn't say anything. She was so relieved that Joe appeared to be thrilled by her news; ever since she'd twigged that she was pregnant she'd been worried that would be the end of them, and that she would have to do the unthinkable. Her heart soared. She was having Joe's baby, and he loved her.

The next day, Molly felt in a strange mood. Excited, elated and exhausted. The hormones of pregnancy were kicking in, sapping her strength. She just wanted to see Joe, to feel his arms around her, and for him to tell her it was all going to be OK. Even though she kept telling herself that of course it was. They loved each other, didn't they? And she knew how to look after babies; she'd done enough childminding in her time, for neighbours. They just needed to sort out the practicalities. And bring it all out into the open . . .

She looked at her watch as a wave of nausea washed over her. She often felt like this in the middle of the day. She decided to take the afternoon off sick. She'd never done it before, after all. And she just wanted to sleep. If she went to bed for the afternoon, she would be fresh for seeing Joe later. He was seeing Tamara at lunchtime to tell her it was over. She felt a prickling of guilt, for Tamara was the innocent party in all of this, and Molly hoped she wouldn't be too devastated. Quickly, she reassured herself that there would be any number of people queuing up to replace Joe: Tamara was beautiful and rich. Girls like Tamara had the pick of the bunch.

She decided to go and tell the site manageress she had to go home.

'You look rough,' agreed Maureen. 'I hope it's not a bug. I don't need anyone else going off sick.'

'I expect it's just a twenty-four-hour thing,' said Molly. She didn't feel guilty about skiving off; she really did feel ill.

It was so boiling hot and sticky, she decided she would take a taxi. She didn't trust herself not to throw up on the bus. She walked down the hill into Mariscombe to get a cab; there were always a few waiting by the main parade of shops. She passed the terrace of the Jolly Roger, then stopped in her tracks.

Joe was holding court at a table. Joe, laughing, looking gorgeous in his cut-off jeans and no shirt, his hair held back with a bandana, waving a bottle of beer as he told a story. And beside him, Tamara. Tamara, shimmering, golden, in a tiny pink skirt and halter-neck, gazing up at him in adoration. As he came to the punchline, there were guffaws of laughter and Joe sat down, sliding his arm around Tamara, turning his head to kiss her. Silhouetted against the blue of the sky, they looked like a king and queen surrounded by their courtiers.

Molly sat down heavily on a nearby bench. How the hell could she have been so stupid? All that bullshit, he hadn't meant a word of it. And suddenly she saw the truth. How could he possibly be interested in her, when his future lay with the golden girl whose wealth would make sure he never had to lift a finger? A life with Molly would mean drudgery. A baby would be a millstone. Joe would be trapped; more trapped than he was already. He must have realized that. Something had brought him to his senses. Of course he wasn't going to finish with Tamara. He'd have to be crazy. She wondered how he was planning to get rid of her. Looking at him now, it wasn't playing on his conscience. Well, it didn't matter. She was going to save him the bother . . .

She was ready for him early that evening as he came into the Lamb. She was waiting at their usual table. He was wearing faded jeans and a pale blue shirt with the sleeves rolled up. He gave her a smile and went to hug her, but she recoiled, staring back at him stony-faced.

'What's the matter?' he asked, concerned. 'Are you OK? Is it the baby?'

'You don't have to worry about the baby,' she replied coolly.

He looked at her suspiciously as he sat down.

'Of course I do.'

She gave him a tight smile.

'Well, don't. I had an abortion this afternoon.'

She was surprised to see the speed at which the colour drained from his face.

'You can't have done.'

'I did. I booked it in last week. You're in and out in two hours. It's just like having a tooth out.'

Joe had gone as white as a sheet.

'You got rid of our baby?' he whispered.

'I'd have thought you'd be pleased.' Molly kept her tone brisk, businesslike. 'It leaves you free to do whatever you want with Tamara.' She looked away, because if she looked at him she might cry. 'I saw you with her at lunchtime. In the Jolly Roger. She didn't look *too* upset that you'd dumped her.'

'Molly, today wasn't the right time . . .' Joe trailed off, knowing full well he couldn't defend himself. 'She'd had a row with her dad. She wouldn't have been able to handle it. I've got to wait for the right time.'

'So you keep saying,' said Molly, standing up. 'Anyway, now you don't have to worry.'

But Joe didn't seem to be listening.

'I can't believe you did that. Without asking me.'

'What was I supposed to do, Joe? I'm sixteen years old. I can't bring up a baby on my own. And we're not going to play happy families. After all, you've said it yourself often enough. You don't want any responsibility. You just want a life. So have a good one.'

And with that, she walked out of the pub.

*

She lay in bed that night unable to sleep. Half of her wanted to get up and rush to him, tell him it wasn't true. But she was incredibly tired. She could barely lift her head off the pillow. And she wasn't going to let him off that easily. He had to suffer for at least one night. It was the only way she could make him realize how badly he could make others feel. And now she'd seen his reaction, his horror, his remorse, she knew she had him. When he found out their baby was still alive, she thought, he would be overjoyed. They could start to make plans.

The next morning, she got up filled with expectation. She'd go to work, get her shift out of the way and then go and find Joe. She wasn't sure how she was going to explain herself yet, but no doubt he would be so relieved that she wouldn't need an excuse. Maybe it had been rather a drastic thing to do, but Molly reasoned that Joe needed bringing to his senses.

As soon as she arrived at work, she sensed that something had happened. Everywhere seemed unnaturally quiet. She went over to the site office. Maureen looked up, her face rather grim.

'What's happened?'

'It's Joe Thorne. He drove his brother's Porsche off Mariscombe Point last night.'

Molly held on to the door frame, her knuckles white.

'What?'

'No one knows why. They think he was drunk.' She gave a sharp bark that masqueraded as a laugh. 'Well, that goes without saying with Joe. They found the wreck this morning.'

Black specks danced on the edge of Molly's vision. She wasn't quite sure what Maureen meant.

'Was . . . he in it? In the car, I mean?'

Maureen looked puzzled.

'Yeah.'

'Is he dead?'

'What do you think? It's fifty feet down on to rocks.'

There was a rushing sound in Molly's head and everything seemed to swim in front of her. Maureen looked at her.

'I think you should still be off sick. You look awful.'

'Yes,' said Molly. 'I need to go home. Right now.'

'Go,' said Maureen. 'It's going to be chaos as it is, without a sick bug.'

'Was it an accident?'

'Nobody knows,' said Maureen. 'But knowing Joe he was three sheets to the wind. Apparently he'd been in the pub all night. The police will get to the bottom of it, no doubt . . .'

Molly lay down on the back seat of the cab on the way home, holding her tummy, her eyes tight shut, wishing and wishing that any moment she would wake up and realize this was some awful nightmare her guilt-ridden mind had dreamed up.

Joe was dead. Joe was dead. And the last thing she'd told him was that she had killed their baby . . .

All she could think was that she had to keep her head down. If anyone found out about her affair, about the baby, then they would know she was to blame. That because of what she'd told him, Joe had driven himself over that cliff. Over and over again she convinced herself that she hadn't been wrong to tell him what she did. Seeing him on the terrace that afternoon with Tamara had been justification enough. He'd had no intention of being faithful to her. But Molly didn't want the truth to come out in public. She knew, because of what she was, and because of the calibre of people she would be up against, that somehow she would be held accountable. There would be no sympathy for the little strumpet who had brought on Joe's demise.

Molly knew she had to steel herself. There would be no one at all with whom she could share her plight. But she'd been brought up tough. The Mahoneys didn't waste time on guilt and sentiment. They'd been taught to be self-reliant. For two days she stayed locked in the house, coming to terms with her situation. For once she was glad that her family were so self-absorbed and disinterested, for they showed no concern. She gave them the same excuse she'd given Maureen, that she had a bug, and to a man they grimaced.

'Ugh,' said Siobhan. 'Do you have to bring your germs back here? I'll kill you if I get it.'

Her mother was equally unsympathetic. But at least they kept out of her way in their eagerness to avoid contagion. She lay on the sofa for two days, unable to cry, drifting in and out of a troubled sleep, paralysed with terror and uncertainty. On the third day she dragged herself into the bathroom, had a long shower and got dressed in her uniform. She had to face her colleagues. She went back to work, knowing that she would have to teach herself not to flinch at the mention of Joe's name. Of course, gossip was rife. The word was he'd driven over the edge after a huge row with his brother in the afternoon. Molly felt relieved that there was an apparent explanation, that the police weren't hunting high and low for a motive for his suicide. They were satisfied that it had been a gesture of drunken defiance; Joe's way of putting two fingers up to the family who thought he was worthless.

She agonized over whether to go to the funeral. Of course, all the staff from the campsite were going. Practically the whole of Mariscombe was going, so her actual presence there wouldn't be questioned. She just wasn't sure whether she would be able to keep her composure. She'd never been to a funeral before. In the end, she decided she would.

The little church was packed. Molly just managed to squeeze into a space at the back, but the congregation spilled out of the doors and into the churchyard, where the service was relayed on a set of speakers specially set up for the occasion. Some had dressed smartly and traditionally, some came in their work clothes, others just came as they were, as they'd always been with Joe, as they wanted him to remember them and wanted to remember him. Molly wore her uniform. She didn't want to attract any attention. Anyway, what the hell did you wear to the funeral of the father of your unborn child?

At the front of the church, flanked by her parents, was Tamara. She'd chosen to wear white, a long white linen dress with a ruffled skirt that fell nearly to the ground, and her ash-blond hair tied back. She looked, Molly decided, almost like a bride waiting to take her place at the altar, except her face was drawn beneath her tan, her lips pressed together, her nails digging into her palms. Molly felt no resentment. Tamara didn't know that Joe had cheated on her and Molly certainly wasn't going to tell her. That would be too cheap, too cruel. It was Molly who'd been stitched up, Molly who'd been taken for a ride and fed false promises. She could see Tamara had no idea; that her grief was genuine and not tainted by the knowledge that Joe had been tupping a little nothing from Tawcombe on the side. It was Molly's secret, one that she'd take with her to her own grave.

And then a couple walked up the aisle, taking painfully slow steps. The woman looked steadfastly ahead, not daring to look to the left or the right at the sympathetic smiles and pitying glances of the congregation. The man held tightly on to her elbow, whether for his or her support it was difficult to tell. They stepped into the pew at the very front amidst a dreadful, respectful silence that was punctuated by the odd cough.

Joe's parents. Her baby's grandparents.

Finally, a man with thick, black curls and broad shoulders stepped into the church, the heels of his shoes ringing out on the stone floor. Bruno, Joe's brother. Molly wondered what the rumoured row had been about. Joe had been bitter about Bruno whenever he mentioned him. He had been everything Joe wasn't: wealthy, successful, capable, responsible. Someone his parents could be proud of . . . But Molly had got the impression that Joe secretly looked up to Bruno, that he didn't actually dislike him, despite the fact that the sun shone out of his proverbial.

Molly watched Bruno carefully from her seat at the end of

the aisle. Although Bruno was older than Joe, and stockier, she could see the resemblance in their bone structure, the dark eyebrows, the dimple in the chin, and it made her heart hammer in her chest. He was wearing an immaculate grey suit, his expression grim as his eyes met the vicar's and he gave an almost imperceptible nod. They were ready.

Molly gripped on to the back of the pew in front of her throughout the service, clenching her teeth to stop herself from crying. As the service ended and the congregation turned to leave, the PA blasted out 'No Woman, No Cry' by Bob Marley, the poignant organ chords and the hypnotic reggae beat filling the tiny church, bringing tears to the eyes of those who had so far managed to remain composed. Molly bit down hard on her lip. She remembered Joe playing this in his car so loud the bass blasted through her body, earning him glares of disapproval as he drove through the streets of Mariscombe.

She didn't have the luxury of being able to shed tears. Somehow they hadn't come, because the emotions she felt were battling for supremacy and it wasn't grief that had won. It was trailing in third place behind guilt and anger. Joe had played fast and loose with her heart, and she'd tried to punish him, fighting back with the only weapon she had. Except it had backfired and she had misjudged him. Those dark moments she'd witnessed, those black moods, his apparent self-loathing and need to escape obviously went deeper than she had realized. It was Molly who had tipped him over the edge.

She shuffled outside with the rest of the congregation. The burial was to be family only.

But I am family! Molly wanted to cry out. *I'm carrying his child. Your grandchild!*

She stood amidst the throngs on the pavement, as people stood in little clusters, not knowing where to go next. People who hadn't seen each other during the service hugged word-lessly. The young ones started to trail down the hill on their way to the Jolly Roger, where an unofficial wake was going to be held. Molly stood, rooted to the spot, not knowing which way to turn. She couldn't go and mourn Joe with her colleagues; she couldn't sit there amongst them as they sang out his favourite songs and drank to his memory.

She'd got through the service with a determined stoicism, not allowing herself to crumble, for she knew if she made a spectacle of herself that her cover would be blown and her life would never be the same, that she wouldn't be in control of her own destiny. Besides, his parents and brother had carried themselves with such dignity. As had Tamara – Molly didn't hold anything against the girl. It certainly wasn't Tamara's fault that Joe had been a two-timer. And for all she knew there had been countless other girls at the funeral nursing a broken heart.

But no matter how many times she told herself that Joe was rotten to the core, that he was feckless and a coward, she couldn't forget the feelings he had awakened in her. Over and over again she relived the closeness they had shared, his wonder. As she watched the crowds disperse and the now empty hearse pull away and make its way back down the hill, she felt a crystal clarity descend on her. All the turmoil of the past few days and nights fell away. She couldn't get rid of their baby now. It was the only connection Joe had with the world. His legacy. A living reminder of the love she had felt. Even though he had treated her abominably, she would never forget the feeling of being in his arms, the way he looked at her when they made love, the way he suddenly gazed at her and ran his hands through her hair and kissed her, as if she was his reason for living.

Her family didn't ask too many questions when her condition became apparent. She said the father was someone who'd been to stay on the site and they'd accepted that without demur. Casual sex followed by pregnancy was far from unusual in the circles they moved in, after all, though her mother told her she was mad not to get rid of it.

'Don't make the same mistake I did,' she said darkly. 'It'll ruin your life.'

Thanks, thought Molly wryly, even though she'd never been under any illusion that her mother was grateful for her offspring.

Siobhan's only comment was that now she'd get her own flat. Which she did, but not a council flat. That wasn't Molly's style. She went and found a place of her own. She'd saved up quite a lot of money from her job, enough to pay a deposit and a few months' rent, and there was plenty of accommodation in Tawcombe. No one was queuing up to live there, after all. The place she got was just a room in a Victorian house in a seedy row of terraces near the harbour. It was shabby, but it was her own, and she had one of the large rooms at the front of the house – the kitchen and bathroom were shared, but at least she had a sink so she could make a cup of tea.

Nobody at work noticed, for her pregnancy barely showed in the first few months and the uniform was capacious enough to hide any suspicious bulges. She stayed on until the end of October, until the campsite closed for the winter, then she got a job at the supermarket in Tawcombe until two weeks before her due date, squeezing her bump behind the till.

The day she gave birth she was in hospital on her own. The midwives were kind. They didn't ask any questions or make her feel like a freak. Perhaps they were used to single girls who had been abandoned by their impregnators. The baby was a boy, which she'd known it would be. She called him Alfie, because she and Joe had watched a pirate DVD of the movie one afternoon in one of the caravans, and he had laughed and said he'd have played the part way better than Jude Law. And Molly had agreed with him. She was sure that was the afternoon she'd caught, because she'd been so happy.

They put her in a bed right at the end of the ward, so she wasn't at the mercy of prying eyes, and didn't have to watch all the proud fathers cradling their newborns. They kept the curtains drawn around her. It was a strange new world, with its strip lighting and regular deliveries of food on a tray. The only thing she could bear to pass her lips was the orange juice that came in a ridged plastic glass with a foil top: it was impossible to get it off without spilling half.

'I want to get out of here,' she said to the nurse.

'I'd stay here for a few days, love. Get some rest, if you can.'

But Molly couldn't wait to escape.

The only consolation was she could get straight back into her jeans. She'd barely put on any weight. It was all Alfie and water. Her skin just felt slightly loose on her tummy, but it all squodged in when she zipped herself up.

'Look at you,' said the nurse in envy. 'You're teeny tiny. How are you getting home?'

'Taxi.'

The nurse frowned.

'You haven't got a baby seat.'

'No point,' said Molly. 'I won't be going in a car again after this.'

'I'm not supposed to let you out without a proper baby seat.'

Molly looked at her impassively.

'Well, I'm not staying here any longer.'

The nurse's face screwed up in concern.

'Are you going to be all right, love?'

Molly shrugged. She wished she'd been given one of the hard-nosed nurses who didn't seem to have an ounce of sympathy – Molly couldn't understand why they'd chosen a supposedly caring profession. Care didn't seem to come into it. But the girl looking after her was going to make her cry if she didn't stop being nice. Because Molly knew the niceness was going to end here.

It had been incredibly tough. But she wasn't the only one doing it, as she found out when she went to the post-natal drop-in classes. There were girls younger than her, girls who were on their second or third, though Molly found she had

226

little in common with them; all they wanted to do was smoke and gossip. But she soon struck up a friendship with an older mum called Skyla. Skyla was ten years older than her, with three kids, and was the most laid-back person Molly had ever met. She was a bit of a hippy, with pink dreadlocks and rainbow-coloured dresses and a pierced eyebrow, but her calm aura was infectious, and she imbued Molly with the strength to cope, giving her endless tips on how to help Alfie settle and how to manage him. Nothing seemed to faze her, and more than anything she clearly adored her children, which was more than Molly could say for any of the other girls she'd met. Skyla had a tiny fisherman's cottage, painted in bright colours with murals all over the walls, and the kids all slept in a jumble on a big mattress on the floor of her bedroom. And Skyla always seemed to have time for them; she was always doing finger painting or baking flapjacks or building an ant farm, and all the while the baby was plugged into her breast. Molly loved it there and spent more time with Skyla than she did in her own home. One day, she promised herself, she would have a little place like this, a place that smelt of cinnamon and scented candles and was filled with the sound of laughter and music – no television. It was a haven, a place of safety, away from the harsh reality of her grimy flat and her self-centred family who'd never shown her a fraction of the affection she got from Skyla. She, meanwhile, had fallen head over heels with her little boy. She could gaze at him for hours, his tiny hand clamped around one of her fingers, unable to decide which bit of him she loved best – his cupid bow lips, his pronounced eyebrows, his shell-like ears, the dark down on top of his head. Sometimes it all closed in on her and she wanted to break down. He deserved so much better than what she had to offer him. But she had to remain tough. There was, after all, no alternative.

By the time Alfie was six months old, Molly knew she had to find work. She couldn't survive on the paltry sum they were supposed to get by on. She struck a deal with Skyla – Molly would look after her kids while she did her aromatherapy massages at the healing centre, and Skyla would look after Alfie in return while Molly went to work.

Despite herself, she was drawn back to Mariscombe, taking a job as chambermaid at the Mariscombe Hotel. She got at least another pound an hour than she would in any of the tawdry hotels or guesthouses in Tawcombe, and she reasoned that at least she had pleasant surroundings to work in. And in a funny way it made her feel closer to Joe. She knew the hotel was owned by his brother and to her there seemed to be a certain justice that the Thornes were indirectly contributing to the upbringing of the baby they didn't know existed.

For just over a year, she had managed. It was exhausting, for when she wasn't working she was looking after Skyla's kids, who were a wild but loving bunch. But the extra money meant she could buy things for Alfie she wouldn't have been able to afford otherwise, and make their lives a little more comfortable. And she enjoyed her work. Just as there had been at the campsite, there was a sense of camaraderie amongst the staff at the hotel. And although she never socialized with them, for she always had to rush back home, it was fun eating chocolate biscuits in the staffroom and listening to the torrid details of their private lives. They teased her for not coming out. They thought she was having an affair with a married man, and she let them. It was far easier than hinting at the truth. Not that anyone would work it out now. Joe had been dead for nearly two years; he had become a memory, almost a legend. But Molly wasn't going to risk anyone putting two and two together.

She'd been careless, only a few weeks ago. It had been a beautiful spring day, and she was in charge of Sklya's mob for the whole afternoon. She decided on impulse to take them to the beach. Why should Alfie be deprived of its pleasures, just because of his murky history – a history that was hardly his fault? She made a mound of egg sandwiches and piled them all on to the bus with their various buckets, spades, balls and swimming costumes. Alfie was in seventh heaven, digging concertedly as if for victory and splashing about at the edge of the water. When the inevitable happened and a gang of staff from the hotel spotted her, Molly's heart clattered in her chest as she smoothly told them she was looking after a friend's children. When Alfie pottered up, chanting 'Mu-mu-mu', she scooped him up, laughing.

'Molly!' she instructed. 'Say Molly. Molly Molly Molly.'

It was only Hannah who looked at her strangely. Of everyone who worked at the hotel, she liked Hannah best. Hannah had confided in her, about wanting a nose job, and Molly sometimes felt guilty that she wasn't being honest with her in return. Did Hannah suspect something? Hastily, she herded all the children together and gathered up their stuff, ready for the journey home. She couldn't be sure one of them wouldn't give something away.

Later, as the bus wound its way through the lanes back to Tawcombe, she determined not to go to the beach again with Alfie. She wasn't sure why she'd risked it. But she'd felt drawn there, somehow. She resented being in exile, even if it was a self-imposed exile. But lately she'd felt as if Alfie deserved if not his birthright then at least the pleasure of the surroundings in which he'd been conceived. More and more she hated the fact that he was being brought up in Tawcombe, that his little world consisted of seedy flats and dreary corner shops, apart from the haven of Skyla's cottage.

Now even that had been taken away from him. Skyla had told her last week that she was going off round the country over the summer, doing her massage at the alternative festivals, so she wouldn't be there to help her out. She'd been very sorry; she'd even tried to persuade Molly to come too, but Molly didn't have the confidence to up sticks and essentially camp for the next three months. And she couldn't earn a living at a festival – what did she have to offer a load of spaced-out hippies? She had to stay put.

And she was becoming more and more alienated from her

family. Her mother was hard and selfish. Her sister Siobhan was a little more sympathetic, but she had fallen in with a bad crowd, all drink and drugs and motorbikes, which meant Molly didn't trust her. But she had to rely on their help to keep her job going. It was coming up to peak season; if she started missing shifts at the hotel she knew she would be out on her ear.

And now Bruno was back, which for some reason was making her twitchy. After all, he didn't know her from Adam. For one second that morning, when he'd offered her the job, Molly had been tempted to confide in him. There was something about him that she instinctively trusted. She was tired, so tired, and Alfie didn't have the life she wanted for him. Far from it. But she knew if she opened her mouth all hell would break loose. There would be any number of denials and accusations. And anyway, how would she prove that Joe was the father? They would think she was pulling a fast one, trying to get money out of them.

For the first time in her life, Molly was starting to realize the starkness of her plight. Bruno's job offer that morning had only served to heighten it. There was no way out for her and Alfie. No way out at all.

Eleven

Lisa was used to the wiles of women. Hysteria, bitchiness, neuroses and jealousy had competed with each other for supremacy in the world she had, until recently, moved in, and in general she was immune to them. Promotion work inevitably invited comparison, but somehow Lisa always managed to smooth out any rivalries she came across on the circuit. She was too down to earth to get involved in petty arguments.

So Lisa was surprised to find that she had a deep-rooted dislike combined with an instinctive mistrust of Victoria. It had nothing to do with the fact that she was George's wife. It was the way she carried herself, the look she had in her eye, the way she courted attention. Everything was considered; everything was done for effect, from the way she crossed her legs to the way she pushed her hair back from her eyes to the languid way she spoke, as if she could barely be bothered to communicate. Lisa was observant and she sensed that every one of Victoria's moves was carefully planned and rehearsed. There was nothing spontaneous about her behaviour. Which, despite all George's reassurances that he was immune, made Lisa very cautious indeed.

Besides which, she made Lisa feel very self-conscious about her own shortcomings. Lisa had never been neurotic about her weight, but next to Victoria she felt cumbersome rather than curvaceous. And every time she spoke she was conscious of her bumpkin accent. She felt certain she'd heard Victoria mock her, muttering 'ooh-aar' behind her back, though she couldn't prove it. To top it all, Victoria's achingly hip designer wardrobe made her feel a total frump.

Lisa wasn't used to feeling insecure. She told herself to get a grip as she got out of bed a couple of days after Victoria's arrival. Resisting the urge to shower, wash her hair and put on full make-up, she defiantly pulled on her scruffy old tracksuit to go down to the village for bread and croissants, tying her curls in a loose ponytail and plonking a baseball cap on top of her head. She wasn't going to pretend for anyone.

Ten minutes later, as she pushed open the door to the bakery, the delicious scent of yeasty, warm bread enveloped her and her mouth watered. She joined the queue, scanned the counter anxiously and was relieved to see there was one almond croissant left: this had become her morning treat over the past week.

Then she watched in horror as the woman behind the counter picked up the object of her desire with a pair of tongs and slid it into a paper bag.

'I'm sorry, love.' She smiled sympathetically at Lisa as she handed it to the customer in front. 'Last one. You should get me to put one aside for you. We only ever do half a dozen.'

'Never mind,' said Lisa bravely.

The man turned and Lisa found a pair of dark grey eyes looking into hers.

'Never let it be said that I've deprived a girl of her breakfast.' His voice was deep; from two paces away Lisa could feel it resonate through her body. He held the bag out to her solemnly.

'Please – don't worry.' Lisa held up her hand to reject his offer, smiling awkwardly. 'I'm sure I don't need the calories.'

The man ran his gaze over her, as if to appraise her body mass index. She in turn took in his black curls, his broad shoulders, his thick brows. He was dressed in khaki chinos and a rumpled white linen shirt. Then he smiled and it was like the sun coming out over the sea on a cloudy day.

'I insist,' he pronounced. 'I'll have a *pain au chocolat* instead.'

Lisa took the bag reluctantly.

'Thank you.'

The assistant duly served him with a replacement *pain au chocolat* and as he left the bakery with his purchase he gave Lisa the faintest wink, leaving behind nothing but a lingering trace of cologne that cut through the smell of fresh bread.

'Gorgeous, isn't he?' sighed the woman behind the counter. 'He could knead my dough any day.'

'Lovely,' agreed Lisa, slightly flustered by the encounter. 'Um, I'd better have six croissants as well. For the others.'

'Bigger than your usual order, isn't it?'

'Oh yes,' said Lisa meaningfully. 'We seem to have quite a houseful all of a sudden.'

As she walked back up the hill, she mused that there was nothing like an act of chivalry to brighten one's day. She wondered who the man was, whether he was local or just passing through. He certainly stood out; he wasn't particularly tall, but he had a certain presence. Usually, if someone winked at her, she felt slightly repelled, but somehow from him it had been perfectly acceptable behaviour, not lecherous or overly familiar.

Whoever he was, the encounter had certainly boosted her confidence, and she felt more than ready for Victoria and her skinny little arse.

Bruno walked back through the hotel car park, wiping pastry crumbs from his lips and feeling a curious desire to break into a whistle. It was funny, he thought, how he could be oblivious to the legions of attractive women who sauntered scantily clad through Mariscombe every day, then suddenly have his eye caught by someone out of the blue. The girl in the bakery had been undeniably pretty, but there was more to her than mere good looks – she had something that set her apart. A twinkle in her eye, a ready smile . . . Bruno wasn't sure what it was, exactly. But the encounter had definitely lightened his mood.

He went through the revolving door and into reception,

where a team of workmen were painstakingly renovating the gloomy panelled woodwork as unobtrusively as possible. Hannah was behind the desk, busy printing out the next day's arrivals. She was his next target. And to be honest, once he'd finished with her that was about it. Apart from Frank, Molly and Hannah, the rest of the staff were total slackers. But he reminded himself that he had to be positive.

'Hannah,' he said. 'I want to talk to you about something. Come into my office.'

Hannah was his protégée. Bruno thought she was probably management material, but not yet. She didn't have enough experience. He did, however, have another plan which would make the most of her talents. Something he thought she would enjoy . . .

'Wedding coordinator?'

Hannah gawped at Bruno, completely baffled. He spread some sheets of paper out in front of her, statistics and articles he'd garnered from magazines and from the Internet.

'The average spend on a wedding these days is more then twenty grand, apparently,' he explained. 'I think we deserve a slice of that. We've got the location, we've got the facilities. I've applied for a licence to hold ceremonies here already – I'm told there's no reason why we shouldn't get one.'

'Wow.' Hannah looked impressed. 'That's such a great idea. I don't know why someone didn't think of it before.'

'Perhaps because it might involve hard work?' replied Bruno drily. 'I think the whole philosophy of this place has been to get away with as little effort as possible.'

'You're so right,' she agreed.

'I want you to start working out some packages and put a brochure together. Obviously getting the price right is key. But we can do different levels. From a simple beach barbie wedding right through to getting a helicopter for the happy couple to go away in.' He laid out some brochures on the table. 'Here's some examples I got from other hotels with similar facilities to ours. Use these as a guide. And I suggest you get together with Frank.'

'What?' He saw her blush red almost instantaneously.

'Talk through menus with him. And table plans. Decide how many guests we can accommodate comfortably. Maybe we could supplement the space with a marquee – we could easily put one on the lawns beyond the terrace.'

Hannah managed to recover herself. She nodded.

'Maybe we could do hen and stag packages too. Not tacky ones . . .' she added hastily. 'Surf and spa weekends. For the boys and girls together.'

'Nice one.' Bruno was pleased. He'd instinctively thought Hannah was the girl for the job, and it seemed he was right. 'I can't pay you any extra for this straightaway. But you'll get a generous commission on any weddings that get booked. So the sooner you can get it up and running, the better.'

When she got back to The Rocks, Lisa found George in the kitchen with Victoria, who was wearing a U2 tour T-shirt and not a lot else.

'Bloody hell! I wondered where that had gone!' George was saying, clearly delighted to see this treasured possession again.

'It got muddled up with my stuff when I left.' Victoria smiled. 'I use it to sleep in, when decency is called for.'

As it only just covered her bottom, Lisa didn't think it counted as decent, but she wasn't going to say anything. To her, it just symbolized Victoria's desperation for point-scoring. If she thought her reminders of their past life together were subtle, she was wrong. To Lisa, they were the signs of a desperate woman.

George, meanwhile, did his absolute very best not to peep under the grey marl to see what sort of knickers Victoria had on. She spent more on lingerie than most women's annual clothing budget. He made his way determinedly over to the cafetière.

'So what are your moves today?' he enquired. 'Obviously we've got rather a lot to be getting on with . . .'

'Oh, quite. I shan't get in your way. I . . . need to sort out a lawyer, I guess. And maybe . . . legal aid?'

George looked at her quizzically.

'Legal aid?'

'I keep telling you. I haven't got a bean.'

'Victoria, I don't think people who drive BMW soft tops actually qualify.'

'But I need my car.'

'You need *a* car. Not that car.' George carefully measured out four spoons of freshly ground coffee beans. 'My first suggestion would be to trade that thing in for something sensible. Like a Ford Focus.'

Victoria looked appalled.

'You're winding me up.'

'You said you need cash. That car's worth over twenty thousand. You could get a decent runaround for five. Which would leave you fifteen to get a deposit on a flat. Or whatever.'

Victoria stuck out her bottom lip.

'I'm no good at doing deals. I'll probably get majorly ripped off.'

George rolled his eyes at this blatant nonsense.

'It's perfectly simple. Just go online, see what price they're getting, then stick an advert in. The sun's out – they'll be queuing round the block.'

Victoria was quiet.

'Can I borrow your computer?' she asked finally.

George sighed.

'Yes. But you're not hogging it all morning. I've got work to do.'

Victoria kissed him.

'You're a poppet. I don't know what I'd do without you.'

George smiled a mirthless smile in return.

'Tell Mimi if she wants a job there are plenty of things I could find her to do.'

'Oh, I think she's already fixed herself up with something,' Victoria said airily, lobbing tea bags into a brace of mugs.

George frowned.

'What?'

'She met some people in the Old Boathouse. She's helping out a girl who's got a stall down by the beach. They do hair-braiding and henna tattoos and stuff. She's thrilled to bits.'

'Oh.'

'I'm just going to take her up a cup of tea. And can I pinch one of these croissants?' Victoria helped herself from the paper bag on the side before anyone could answer. 'Oh, yum. Still hot. Any raspberry jam?'

Lisa gritted her teeth and produced a pot of strawberry conserve.

'Only strawberry, I'm afraid,' she said sweetly. 'But do help yourself.'

Lisa had decided that her best policy was to hold her tongue and not interfere. If George wanted to help Victoria, so much the better. Perhaps she would sort out her affairs and be on her way.

'I've got the woman coming to measure up for curtains today,' Lisa reminded George. 'And we need to be totally sure what we're going for if they're going to be done in time.'

'Curtains?' Victoria seemed to perk up considerably. 'What are you having? Can I have a look?'

'No,' said George, very definitely. If Victoria started to interfere, it would get too complicated. And the budget would soar sky-high. 'We're going for cream linen tab tops.'

Victoria put her head to one side. Lisa clenched her jaw as she awaited the verdict.

'Classic but safe,' she finally decreed. 'Any trimmings? VV Rouleaux do a fabulous ribbon trimmed with shells.'

George plunged the cafetière too hard. Hot coffee spurted everywhere. What really annoyed him was he'd seen the ribbon she meant himself, in last month's *House & Garden*. Of course it would be perfect, but as a single metre cost more than the actual fabric, it was out of the question. He was already finding it frustrating that he couldn't have exactly what he wanted, but he knew that it was vital for them to stick to their budget. The last thing he needed was Victoria sticking her oar in.

'Victoria, please don't interfere. You know what they say. Too many cooks,' said Lisa firmly. 'We're keeping everything simple. We can always add on later if we want to. But for the time being we can't afford to make any expensive mistakes.'

Victoria gazed at her. George swallowed nervously.

'In which case, don't listen to me,' she replied eventually. 'All the mistakes I've ever made have been very expensive.'

She picked up her two mugs of tea and left the room.

Lisa looked at George, who smiled ruefully.

'With any luck she'll be gone by the end of the week. If no one pays her any attention, she'll soon get bored.'

He walked over and handed her a cup of coffee, giving her a conciliatory kiss on the cheek.

'You have forgiven me, haven't you?'

Lisa tossed back her curls.

'What's to forgive? I can see perfectly well why you wanted to forget her,' she replied archly.

George winced. The truth of it was, you couldn't get two people more different than Victoria and Lisa. They were poles apart. Which was why he loved Lisa so much.

'I love you, you know. I'd never do anything to hurt you,' he told her.

'I know,' Lisa sighed, curling an arm round his waist. George pulled her to him, burying his face in her neck, nuzzling her. To his huge relief, she seemed to melt at his touch. That was the wonderful thing about Lisa. She didn't bear grudges.

'Sorry,' said Victoria, as they sprang apart. 'I forgot to ask. Does anyone know if there's a decent hairdresser round here?'

*

Later that afternoon, Caragh barged into Frank's room and was disgruntled to find him and Hannah huddled over a mountain of brochures and recipes and wedding magazines.

'What the hell are you doing?' she demanded.

'Working out a wedding package,' Frank replied. 'Hannah's been made wedding coordinator.'

As Caragh took in this information, Hannah trembled. She had a feeling Bruno hadn't told her about this new development, and if there was one thing Caragh hated it was being left out. Just as she feared, Caragh gazed at her scornfully.

'What do you know about weddings?' she demanded. 'It's not like anyone's ever going to ask you to marry them.'

Hannah looked aghast and ran out of the room.

'You bitch,' said Frank.

Caragh flopped on to his bed.

'Come here,' she ordered.

'No way,' he replied, and went to find Hannah. He found her sobbing in the kitchen.

'She's right,' she sobbed. 'I'm bloody hideous.'

'Hey,' soothed Frank. 'No, you're not. You're not. I think you're . . .'

'What?' demanded Hannah, her face blotchy and streaked with tears.

'Come here,' said Frank, pulling her into his arms. To his surprise, she pushed him away.

'Oh no,' she said vehemently. 'That's the ultimate bloody insult. A sympathy snog. That's the last thing in the world I want.'

Frank slunk back to his room. He felt a bit confused. There had been a moment there when he genuinely wanted to kiss Hannah, but was it just out of sympathy, he wondered? With the best will in the world, even with beer goggles on, you couldn't call her attractive, and he wasn't going to lie to her. But there was something about her. Her honesty, her kindness.

The way she encouraged him and supported him. Was she more than just a friend? How did he feel about her?

He went back into his room. Caragh was still lying on the bed.

'Haven't you gone yet?' he snarled, then realized with a shock that she had her hands down her knickers.

'I decided if you weren't going to do anything about it, I'd do it myself,' she breathed. 'And to be honest, I think I'm doing quite a good job. Maybe I don't need you after all.'

Frank hated himself for it, but he couldn't tear his eyes away.

At tea time, Lisa found George and Victoria standing in the hallway with a paint chart, brows furrowed.

'I think you're making a huge mistake,' said Victoria. 'It's far, far, far too cold. You need something with warmth.'

'What's the matter?' asked Lisa.

'We're trying to pin down a colour.' George held the chart up, scrutinizing it with eyes narrowed.

'I thought we'd agreed white?'

'Yes, but *which* white?'

'White's white, isn't it?'

George and Victoria stared at her.

'*God*, no.'

'Oh.'

Victoria started stalking around the reception area, waving her hands.

'You've got to remember that the light here is going to be changing constantly. So you need something that works in bright sunshine and gloomy, horrible winter. And you want soft, not stark. This isn't the Med. You simply can't get away with Brilliant White.'

Lisa's eyes turned to the stack of paint pots that the decorators had lined up ready to start the next day. Each one was marked Brilliant White.

'Me, I'd go for Farrow and Ball's Slipper Satin,' Victoria

pronounced. 'It's a darling colour. Terribly forgiving. And it goes with everything.'

Lisa suddenly found she was trying desperately hard not to laugh. How could a paint colour be darling? Or forgiving? And surely the whole point of white was that it went with everything?

'Estate emulsion on the walls,' Victoria continued. 'And dead flat oil on the woodwork. The key to it all is matt. Matt matt matt.'

'I see,' said Lisa, who didn't have a clue what she was on about.

George was walking round with the chart, holding up a tiny square against the walls, the windows, the woodwork, squinting anxiously.

'Victoria's right, you know.'

'It's going to cost us a fortune,' objected Lisa.

'Better to make the investment now than to make an expensive mistake.'

'Oh well,' said Lisa. 'You know best. What do I know?'

George looked pained.

'Don't be upset. Victoria happens to be good at this sort of thing, and she is right. It's my fault, I should have thought about it more carefully.'

Lisa cleared her throat and spoke quietly.

'Is she going to interfere with everything we've already decided?' she asked. 'Or is she going to crack on with sorting her own life out?'

George blinked.

'Point taken,' he replied. 'I'll have a quiet word.'

By the middle of the week the decorators had begun their task, arriving with masks and spray-guns, and soon the air was filled with the smell of fresh paint. The transformation was remarkable. As the walls and woodwork turned white, the house suddenly became suffused with light and the rooms seemed twice the size. And despite herself, Lisa suspected that

Victoria had been right – the colour she'd picked did have a softness and subtlety when you looked closely. Not that she was going to admit it.

Thankfully, however, whatever George had said to Victoria seemed to have hit home, and she was keeping a low profile. She and Mimi had one of the rooms on the top floor and they came and went with the minimum of interruption, apart from a minor kerfuffle when someone came to take Victoria's beloved car away, though she soon perked up when she looked at the cheque. Meanwhile, she was hard at work designing everything from the logo to the brochures and had any number of contacts she was happy to exploit on their behalf. She made a huge effort to be deferential towards Lisa, asking for her opinion and her approval. Lisa began to worry about Victoria's bill.

'It's OK,' George assured her. 'She feels so guilty about landing on us that she's insisted we don't pay.'

'But she's broke,' Lisa protested, wondering for a moment why she was suddenly on Victoria's side.

'Let her get on with it,' George advised. 'You don't normally get something for nothing out of her.'

'Too right,' said Justin darkly, who was still twitchy about Victoria's presence. Lisa was growing very fond of Justin, who was helpful in his own inimitable way, very supportive of her and very protective. While he was around she felt she had an ally. And he had some crazy ideas that would give The Rocks the edge it needed. Like turning one of the downstairs utility rooms into a wet room, with an adjoining area for storing surfboards and wetsuits.

'Element of self-interest there, don't you think?' asked George, for Justin had thrown himself into the surfer's life-style, taking any opportunity to sneak off to ride the waves.

'No point in owning a hotel if you can't take advantage of the facilities,' retorted Justin, pushing back his hair that was already bleached white from the salt and the sun.

Meanwhile, six free-standing, copper-coated baths arrived

and sat in the hallway, waiting for the carpenters to build platforms for them to be mounted on to in order to take advantage of the views. George was adamant that luxury bathrooms were the key to a successful hotel, and so they were sacrificing two of the smaller bedrooms so each room could have its own en suite.

The decision-making was endless. The office was a mound of brochures – from doorknobs to glassware to bedlinen to lighting. George was in seventh heaven. This was what he loved best. The finishing touches. Lisa laughed at him agonizing.over the detail.

'Do we go for a pewter or a polished nickel finish? And do we go for knobs or levers?' he wondered.

'You choose!' she insisted. 'I haven't a clue. You know me. I really can't get excited about what doorknobs to have.'

George looked at the brochure and sighed.

'Starfish handles on the bathroom doors,' he finally pronounced. 'And the rope-effect levers on the bedrooms.'

Lisa privately thought that plain round knobs would be perfectly adequate, but she suspected that wasn't the right thing to say. And she knew that it was her inability to understand the importance of the right doorknob that made her so different from Victoria. She had to admit that George's obsession with the minutiae of the hotel was starting to get to her. He insisted that it was all in the planning; that of course the finish on the knives and forks should be considered, as closely as the table linen and the lighting and the glasses.

'Trust me, people notice these things,' he told her. 'It's what will make us stand out from an ordinary hotel.'

'But I thought we were keeping things simple.'

George sighed.

'Which is why everything has to be exactly right.'

'Oh,' said Lisa, as if that made everything clear, though it didn't.

*

It was at the beginning of the following week that things started to go wrong. Lisa felt like tearing her hair out.

'Where's the man from the council?' she demanded. 'He was supposed to come and inspect our fire doors this morning and give us our certificate.'

Although they weren't doing any major structural work, there were still plenty of rules and regulations to follow, and Lisa was finding it frustrating that they couldn't begin one job until they'd finished another. When she phoned the man from the council he insisted that they'd called and postponed his visit themselves.

'Rubbish!' Lisa snapped at him. 'It's typical of you bureaucratic types to pass the buck. I want you here by midday.'

George cringed. You didn't talk to people from the council like that, not if you wanted the right pieces of paper at the right time. But miraculously it worked.

'You don't take any crap, do you?' he said admiringly.

'No, I don't.' Lisa put a defiant tick on the enormous whiteboard George had put up in the office. It was a meticulous timetable of all the jobs that needed doing in consecutive order, detailing contacts, reference numbers, telephone numbers, delivery dates. That way everyone knew what was going on and no one could claim ignorance. George had learned the hard way that communication was the key.

By Thursday, Lisa sat at the desk in the office for a moment and put her head in her hands. The wrong tiles had turned up for the bathrooms. It was like a television makeover show gone horribly wrong. This was the fifth disaster in as many days, and somehow she suspected there was a gremlin at work. She knew that in this day and age people often made mistakes, that orders got cocked up, that tradespeople were over-committed and played clients off against each other, as did bureaucrats. But there had been a suspicious number of glitches.

George was irritatingly phlegmatic about it.

'Listen, this is all perfectly normal,' he said calmly. 'In fact, I'd be worried if something didn't go wrong.'

'Someone doesn't want us to succeed,' Lisa insisted.

'You're being paranoid. In my experience, things are going swimmingly. There've been no real nightmares.'

At that moment, Victoria came in with the final artwork for the logo.

As she and George bent their heads over the desk, Lisa surveyed her thoughtfully. Could Victoria be at the bottom of all this? Deliberately putting Lisa under stress, in order to put her relationship with George under pressure? There were still times when George deferred to Victoria over some detail, and Lisa tried not to feel threatened. After all, if she couldn't express an interest it wasn't surprising he went elsewhere for a second opinion, and he obviously respected Victoria's.

Was she, as George had implied, being paranoid?

'Lisa? What do you think?'

George was giving her a rather reprimanding look over the top of Victoria's head, as if to chide her for not paying attention.

'Sorry, I was miles away.' Lisa came over to the table to admire the handiwork, and had to admit it was stunning. 'It's gorgeous, Victoria.'

George held the paper up to the light to examine it more closely. 'Maybe we could have it etched on to the wine glasses? What do you think?'

Bloody waste of money, thought Lisa, but she was pretty sure that was the wrong thing to say.

'Lisa, you look exhausted.' Victoria was peering at her, concerned. You look really stressed. I think you've been over-doing it. George, you've been working her too hard.'

Lisa felt uncomfortable under their scrutiny. What did Victoria mean, she looked exhausted? Was that Victoria-speak for rough-as-a-badger's-arse? She knew she was hot and sweaty and she hadn't washed her hair that morning as it took so long to dry. And she had a stained sweatshirt and filthy jeans on. Victoria, conversely, was in a pale blue linen dress and sneakers, looking cool and *soignée*.

'There's a fab beauty salon in Bamford,' pronounced Victoria decisively. 'George, book her in for a massage. She can't go on burning the candle at both ends. She'll drop dead with exhaustion.'

Lisa wiped her forehead with the back of her hand, feeling rather like a little girl being scrutinized by her anxious parents.

'I'm fine,' she insisted.

'No,' said Victoria. 'I know what George is like. He doesn't realize us girls need pampering. I'll book you in myself.'

She flipped open her mobile and scrolled through her address book. Lisa watched her suspiciously. Was that the very phone she'd used to create havoc, cancelling appointments and changing orders? And was this now a double bluff, feigning concern, chastising George for his negligence in order to put Lisa off the scent?

She decided not to protest. Perhaps she was being neurotic. She didn't even have Justin to reassure her, as he'd disappeared for a few days on business. For a moment she felt very alone. George had as good as told her to stop fussing.

'It'll all happen,' he said.

'Yes,' Lisa replied. 'It'll all happen because I'm making it happen.'

Not, she wanted to add, dithering about doorknobs.

The next day, Charlie the plasterer didn't turn up to make good the bathroom walls where the old suites had been ripped out. Which meant the plumber couldn't go in and fit the baths, which meant the tiler couldn't do the walls and the floors. Lisa thought she might scream. When she'd called Charlie to give him an earful, he'd protested that someone had told him that the tiling and the plumbing were being done first and he was to wait till next week.

'Rubbish! Who told you that?'

'I can't remember.'

'How convenient,' Lisa retorted drily. 'I want you back here now.'

'I'm on another job,' he protested. 'Down at the Mariscombe Hotel. I can't just walk off.'

'Why not?' asked Lisa. 'You've walked off my job.'

She slammed the phone down, knowing there was no point in arguing. She was so incensed, she decided to walk over to the Mariscombe Arms for a drink to calm herself down. Leonard, as ever, provided her with a sympathetic ear as she ranted.

'Don't listen to Charlie's excuses,' he advised. 'He's gone down to the Mariscombe Hotel because when Bruno says jump, everyone jumps.'

'That's totally unfair. He can't operate like that.'

'Try telling him that.'

'I will.' Lisa tilted her chin up defiantly.

Leonard laughed.

'Good for you, girl. You'll be the first person in Mariscombe to stand up to him. Bruno Thorne's got everyone on a string.'

'Not me, he hasn't.' Lisa almost snatched the spritzer Leonard had made her out of his hand and gulped thirstily.

'I wouldn't be surprised if it's him who's been putting a spanner in the works all along.'

Lisa's eyes grew large over the top of her glass.

'Do you think so?'

'Typical Thorne behaviour. Big fish, small pond. Stamp out the opposition.'

'But The Rocks is tiny compared to his place. We're no competition, surely?'

'Ah, yes, but he wanted to buy it, remember? And he's not a good loser.' Leonard crossed his arms self-importantly. 'I should know. He wanted to buy this place but I beat him to it. He made me suffer for it, I can tell you. I couldn't get a builder to give me a quote. I couldn't get any staff. I had to bring in people from outside in the end.'

Lisa thought back over all the petty incidents of the past week. Bruno probably knew all the suppliers in the area. It wouldn't take much for him to have a quiet word in the odd ear. If he considered himself top dog, he probably would take pleasure in sabotaging their efforts.

'Bastard!' she spat.

Leonard blinked.

'Don't shoot the messenger.'

Lisa laughed, despite herself.

'Not you. Bruno Thorne.'

She slammed her glass down on the counter. Leonard picked it up.

'Top up?'

'No thanks.' Lisa slid off her seat. 'If I have another drink I'll probably end up punching him.'

'It's no less than he deserves,' opined Leonard, watching in ill-disguised admiration as Lisa marched out of the pub, her curls streaming behind her.

The receptionist at the Mariscombe Hotel looked alarmed when Lisa demanded to see Bruno.

'He's not here,' she stammered. 'I think he's working from home this morning. Shall I tell him who called?'

'I'll go and see him at home.'

'He did say he didn't want to be disturbed.'

'Tough.'

Lisa marched back out of the reception area and through the revolving door. Hannah wondered if she should phone ahead and warn Bruno that there was a wild-eyed creature on the warpath heading in his direction. But then the phone started ringing and by the time she had dealt with the enquiry there was a queue of people at the reception desk waiting to check out. And by the time she'd dealt with that she had forgotten all about the interruption, because she was too busy daydreaming about the letter she'd received that morning.

She had an appointment! They'd booked a bed for her in

two weeks' time. And she'd managed to book a fortnight's holiday to coincide. She'd been lucky to get leave, but because it was just before the high season she'd managed to wangle it with Bruno, who noticed from her records that she hadn't had any time off since Christmas and had scolded her gently. But she'd been saving it up deliberately, because it would take that long to convalesce. She didn't suppose Bruno would take kindly to a receptionist who looked as if she'd done two rounds with Mike Tyson.

And now the operation was imminent, she couldn't believe it. She'd been to see the consultant on her last day off, and it had been quite surreal, looking through his before and after portfolio, discussing possible sizes and shapes with him. He'd even done a computer-generated reconstruction of what she might look like, and she'd been thrilled with the images.

'If you're nervous about anything, just give my secretary a ring,' he had said. But Hannah wasn't nervous at all. Unfeasibly excited, perhaps. But not scared. After all, this operation was going to change her life!

Lisa knew exactly where Bruno lived, because Leonard had pointed his house out to her from the window of the Mariscombe Arms one evening, and she had admired it ever since. It was typical of him, she decided, to buy the most expensive house in the village. It was set in a secluded location halfway along the beach, a square, flat-roofed Art Deco jewel with a curved frontage overlooking the sea, with panoramic views. It had to be worth a couple of million.

It was so secluded, in fact, that there wasn't even a proper road leading to it; just a rough track that meandered parallel with the dunes, bordered with bracken and fuchsia hedges. Chiffchaffs and stonechats skittered across the path in front of her and jewel-bright butterflies wove their way in and out of the undergrowth.

It was a great deal further than Lisa had anticipated. By the time she arrived at his front door, the new flip-flops she had bought in the surf shop two days ago had rubbed the space in between her toes red raw and she had worked herself into a fury. Who did Bruno Thorne think he was? Lisa could exactly imagine what he was like – she'd met his type often enough in her job. Loud, flashy, jumped-up men who expected everyone to jump to attention when they clicked their fingers. She could already imagine his oversized Rolex; probably a thick gold chain round his neck too; designer sunglasses. Awash with expensive aftershave. Well, he'd better watch out. She knew exactly how to deal with his species and she didn't take any prisoners.

She lifted the heavy knocker on the front door and rapped assertively, squaring her shoulders, ready to look him in the eye. She waited a few moments and was about to knock again when the door opened.

She wasn't remotely prepared for what she saw. Bruno Thorne was wearing a dusty-blue polo shirt and baggy shorts, his feet bare. His black curly hair was unkempt and he clearly hadn't shaved yet that morning: there was a smattering of blue-black stubble over his jawline. He held a mug of coffee in his right hand.

It was the man from the bakery.

'Hello,' he said uncertainly, his face a picture of bemused puzzlement. 'We've met, haven't we?'

Lisa faltered, but only for a second. She didn't care if he'd given her the last almond croissant. She had a bone to pick.

'Yes,' she snapped. 'I'm Lisa Jones. And you've pinched my plasterer.'

Bruno's eyebrows, thick and dark, shot skywards.

'Have I?'

'Don't pretend you know nothing about it.' Lisa wasn't going to give him an inch. 'It's out of order. You might think you can own everyone just by waving your chequebook, but you're wrong. I'll fight you every inch of the way, if that's the way you want to play it—'

'Hey, hey, hey – slow down a minute.' Bruno put his hand

up to stop her tirade. To her annoyance, he was grinning. 'Do you want to stop and tell me exactly what it is you're on about?'

'Don't patronize me!' Lisa shook back her hair.

'I didn't mean to patronize you at all. Why don't you come in?'

His tone was light and he seemed totally unruffled by her accusations as he opened the door wider and waved his cup to usher her in. Disconcerted, Lisa hesitated. She'd been braced for immediate battle, not a disarming invitation.

'OK,' she agreed, and followed him through a light, airy hallway with an open-tread staircase. He opened another door and stood to one side to let her past.

'Go on through.'

As she passed him, she caught the faintest trace of his cologne again. Lime? Basil? Bergamot? Something so subtle and delicious she wanted to breathe it in again.

The next moment her breath was taken away entirely. The room she was in was at least thirty-foot square. The curved outside wall was made entirely of folding glass doors leading out on to a veranda, while the others were painted in a very pale eau de nil that seemed to be a reflection of the water outside. In the centre of the room, facing out to sea, was a three-sided arrangement of sofas in cream suede surrounding a chunky driftwood coffee table. On the wall behind were three large canvasses, each about six-foot square, of brightly coloured abstracts – one was deep purple, one deep pink and one deep red. Tucked away in a corner was a baby grand piano – the very fact that it seemed small indicated just how large the room was. There was a large inglenook fireplace on the far wall, flanked on one side by a pile of neatly stacked logs that reached the ceiling; the other side was lined with shelves on which were ranged a vast selection of books, from thick, glossy tomes on art right down to a selection of battered airport paperbacks. A worn zebra-skin rug was slung in front of the fireplace and lounging on it was an enormous golden dog whose ears twitched as Lisa looked around her in amazement.

It was the room of someone who knew exactly what he wanted but had nothing to prove. Entirely the opposite of what she had expected.

Bruno indicated the central sofa and she sat down squarely, rather wrong-footed by her environment. It was so stylish, so utterly right. She felt the suede of the seat underneath her: it was incredibly soft and inviting. How divine to flop down on to it, put your feet up and just watch the sea . . .

Bruno sat down on the adjacent sofa, throwing his arms behind his head and stretching his legs out in front of him.

'Now, do you want to tell me exactly what this is all about?'

Lisa was determined to stand her ground. She might have been temporarily fazed, but she wasn't going to let it unnerve her. Bruno might have immaculate taste, but that didn't mean he wasn't capable of playing dirty.

'I don't know what your game is, but I've just come to say that we're not giving up, so you might as well.'

The side of his mouth turned up in a smile.

'Game? I'm afraid I don't have much time for games these days.'

'Mysterious objections to what we're doing? The man from the council being bloody-minded and moving the goalposts? The electricity board not turning up when they say they will? The plasterer letting us down and mysteriously turning up at your place?'

Bruno ruffled his curls in bemusement.

'Sounds like everyday life in North Devon to me.'

'We know you wanted The Rocks and you didn't get it.'

'I can assure you if I'd wanted it that much, it would be mine by now. But it wasn't worth what you were prepared to pay for it.'

Lisa felt a small prickle of unease, but she was determined not to be put off.

'I saw the plasterer working at your hotel. You pulled him off our job. You've put our schedule out completely.'

Bruno rubbed his jaw as he considered what she was saying.

'Charlie probably came to me because he knows I pay. There's a lot of new people in town who don't, and the local labour's had their fingers burned more than once. I'm sorry, but it's not my fault if he's passed you over.'

'Someone actually called to tell him not to come to us.'

'Well, it wasn't me. I promise you.'

Lisa looked down at the floor. There was something in Bruno's stance that told her he was telling the truth. A small nagging doubt in the corner of her mind spread into a larger one. Had she got the wrong man? He certainly seemed too cool for petty phone calls; she couldn't imagine him bothering.

She cleared her throat and tried to find her voice.

'Maybe there's been a . . . misunderstanding.'

'Maybe you should do your homework before you start making accusations. I could probably sue you for slander.'

Lisa tried to swallow down her panic, thinking that she'd made an utter fool of herself. For an awful moment, she thought she was going to cry. She put her head in her hands, desperately pushing back the tears, realizing she'd completely overreacted, that she'd been so overwrought by recent events. And now the most powerful man in Mariscombe was threatening to take her to court—

'Hey – it's OK. I'm only joking.'

Bruno was standing over her, looking anxious. She could smell his cologne again. Mandarins? No, something more peppery. Whatever it was, it was making her head swim.

'Look, I'm just about to have some lunch. Why don't you join me? We can talk everything over.'

Ten minutes later, Lisa found herself sitting at a table on the wooden veranda overlooking the sea. Bruno brought out a big white plate on which was perched a thick wedge of oozing, creamy Brie, a chorizo sausage and a mound of gleaming black olives.

'Help yourself,' he instructed, then disappeared back inside only to emerge with a French stick, a bottle and two glasses. He poured her a glass of wine so cold that condensation instantly coated the outside of the flute. The glass was heavy, with an elongated stem, and Lisa clutched it tightly. The liquid inside sparkled pinky gold.

'Prosecco,' he informed her. 'It's the only thing to drink at lunchtime. It's so light, it won't give you a thick head or make you want to fall asleep.'

Lisa sipped it appreciatively. It was sweet, redolent of peaches. And despite his reassurance that it was barely alcoholic, it made her feel slightly giddy. As if the bubbles were in her head. A not unpleasant sensation. Then she remembered she'd already had a drink, at the Mariscombe Arms. She'd better be careful. She didn't want to make a bigger fool of herself than she already had.

'This house is . . . stunning,' she ventured, realizing her words were insufficient.

'What were you expecting?' he grinned. 'Some sort of hideous shag-palace? White carpets and mirrored ceilings? A revolving bed?'

'No!'

'Don't worry. I know my reputation round here. I'm a diamond geezer with more money than sense.'

'Perhaps you shouldn't turn up in a helicopter, then.' Lisa knew she sounded impertinent, but it annoyed her when people moaned about their reputations when they clearly courted them.

Bruno didn't seem ruffled, however.

'Not mine, I can assure you. I've got a friend with a place down in Cornwall and he sometimes offers me a lift from London when he's going down. Saves me a tedious four-hour drive.'

Lisa took another sip. She knew she should apologize and

the effect the wine was having made her realize she needed to do it sooner rather than later.

'I'm so sorry I flew off the handle earlier.' She lowered her lashes bashfully. 'It's been a stressful couple of weeks for more reasons than I can go into.'

She wasn't going to mention ex-wives and stepchildren jumping out of the woodwork. It sounded preposterous. And, anyway, it was none of his business.

'Don't worry.' He flashed a sympathetic smile. 'I know how frustrating life can be down here when you're trying to get things done.'

'People were very quick to point the finger at you.'

Bruno's eyebrows went up again.

'Don't tell me. Leonard Carrington.'

Lisa looked at him in amazement.

'How on earth did you know?'

Bruno sliced himself a chunk of Brie while he considered his reply.

'Leonard can never resist the chance to have a pop at me. He wanted to buy this place and I pipped him at the post. He's never forgiven me.'

Lisa's mouth dropped open in outrage.

'But he said *you* wanted to buy the Mariscombe Arms, and that you tried to sabotage *him* when he ended up buying it.'

'Hasn't he stopped bleating about that? Yes, I was going to buy it, but I pulled out because I thought I was overstretching myself at the time. He was just pissed off because I bumped the price up. I certainly didn't sabotage him. He did that very successfully for himself. No one wanted to go near him because he always expects something for nothing.' His eyes creased up as he twinkled at her. 'Unless there's a pretty girl involved, and then he's more than generous.'

'Bloody hell!'

'Leonard is a lecherous old fruit with an overactive imagination and not enough to do. You don't want to believe a word he says.' He paused for a moment. 'And I don't suppose he told you he was after The Rocks as well as you?'

'No!' Lisa's eyes crackled and snapped with indignation.

Bruno couldn't help laughing. 'He tried desperately to do a cash deal with the woman who owned it. But she wasn't having any of it.'

'Mrs Websdale?' Lisa mulled over this new development. 'According to Leonard, they were . . . well . . .'

She didn't like to elaborate on Leonard's claim, as even now the idea seemed preposterous. Bruno said it for her, with yet another mischievous twitch of his eyebrow.

'Lovers? In his dreams, maybe. Like I said, Leonard sometimes finds it hard to separate fantasy from reality.'

He leaned across the table to fill up her glass. His forearm was muscular; the watch on his wrist slender, Swiss and far from the chunky gold timepiece she had anticipated. Lisa pushed a few tendrils of hair back from her forehead. The heat, the wine and the realization that she had been more than hasty in her actions were making her feel flustered.

'I feel such a fool.'

'It's a hotbed, Mariscombe, I'm telling you. It might look like paradise, but scratch the surface . . .' He made a throat-cutting motion with a tanned forefinger. 'We don't have to be at each other's throats, though. Personally I'm delighted by what you're doing. A boutique hotel is just what Mariscombe needs to boost its image. And we all get the benefit from any good publicity. It's not in my interests to wish you any harm. Why don't we bury the hatchet and be done with it?'

Lisa nodded her head eagerly.

'I think I'm guilty of listening to too much gossip.'

'There's certainly plenty of that round here.' His expression was wry. 'There's nothing the locals like better than winding up newcomers. It's practically a spectator sport. It's infuriating, but you get used to it.'

'It's not quite what I expected, I must admit.'

'When I was eighteen I couldn't wait to get out of here. I

couldn't stand the village mentality – everybody knowing everything about you from your inside leg measurement to who you had your first snog with. But something drew me back. It does have a certain charm.'

Lisa indicated the view. The early afternoon sun had turned the sea into a verdigris millpond with only the faintest trace of movement at its very edge. The sand burned almost white in the heat.

'There's that for a start.'

'Yeah.' Bruno looked across the water thoughtfully. 'I guess there's a period in your life when you need the bright lights and a bit of a buzz. But then it all begins to pall.'

'You're glad you came back, then?'

There was a small pause.

'It was . . . time.'

Lisa, remembering the other bits of village gossip she had absorbed, sensed she had strayed on to sensitive territory. Bruno turned to her with a smile that was rather fixed.

'Anyway, tell me about The Rocks. Have you got rid of those awful quilted headboards?'

Lisa laughed.

'Don't worry. They were virtually the first thing to go. We've filled about seventeen skips. Dear Mrs Websdale – she was so proud of what she'd done. She'd be horrified if she knew we'd gutted the place.'

She went on to describe the changes they were making. And as she spoke, she couldn't help mobbing herself up, pointing up the difference between herself and George.

'You probably know this,' she leaned forward, her eyes shining with mischief, 'but there's more than one type of white paint. At least twenty-seven, apparently. And it matters which one you choose.'

Bruno laughed. Lisa saw his teeth were very white. Porcelain white, she decided.

'Paint snobs,' he agreed. 'They're like champagne snobs. Go to pieces in a blind tasting. Can't tell the difference between vintage Krug and a ten-quid bottle from the super-market. Same with colour – most people couldn't tell trade gloss from Farrow and Ball eggshell in a line-up.'

Lisa felt comforted by his words. Assuming he was being genuine, of course. She was fairly sure the paint on his walls wasn't DIY-store emulsion. She felt a tiny bit guilty that she'd looked to Bruno for reassurance, but sometimes over the past week or so she'd felt alienated, a bit of a bumpkin, and it was nice to be told she wasn't necessarily wrong.

'Anyway,' she went on, 'assuming we don't have any more cock-ups, we open in just under three weeks.'

'It sounds wonderful. I'm very envious. It's exactly what I'd like to be doing.'

For one awful moment, Lisa wondered if she'd said too much. Had she given away all their secrets? Was Bruno going to pinch all their ideas, run off and do exactly the same thing at the Mariscombe Hotel? She shouldn't have had that second glass of wine – alcohol always made her tongue loose. Then she told herself not to be silly. Bruno had a mind of his own. He didn't need to copy anyone else, that was evident.

'I'll send Charlie back over to you tomorrow,' he was saying. 'My job can wait. Mine's more of a long-term project.'

'You're very kind. Thank you. And I better get back. Everyone will be wondering where I am.'

Lisa stood up and put out her hand for him to shake.

'That's rather formal,' he said, leaning forward and brushing his cheek against hers. 'It was nice to meet you, Miss Jones.'

Lisa swallowed as she felt his stubble graze her skin. 'Lisa, please,' she said weakly.

'Lisa.'

He was so close she felt his voice inside her as he spoke her name. She took in a shaky breath. 'It was nice to meet you too.'

'Bruno.'

'Bruno.' As if she didn't know.

They exchanged a smile. His eyes were slate grey, thought Lisa. The colour of the sea when the sun went in.

'Listen, we'll be having a launch party. I'd love you to come. I'll send you an invitation.'

'Sounds fantastic. I can't wait to see what you've done. And in the meantime if you have any more problems, give me a call. I can't promise any miracles, but I might be able to help. I might as well try to live up to my reputation as a puller of strings.'

For a fleeting moment, Lisa wondered if this was a cover-up job, then told herself not to be ridiculous. The man she'd just met hadn't got where he was by treading on other people's toes. He didn't need to sink to those levels. Bloody Leonard. She was going to kill him when she next saw him.

She ran lightly down the steps to the edge of the dunes below, then turned to wave before setting off down the beach. Bruno had told her it was far quicker to go that way than back along his drive and at least she could take her flip-flops off to walk along the sand. Her feet were killing her; she'd have to stop off in the village for some plasters.

As she walked back along the water's edge to The Rocks, she considered her new acquaintance. Bruno had been a million miles from what she'd expected. The image she'd conjured up in her mind was of a flash, self-satisfied, self-made tycoon. She'd been certain she was going to loathe him on sight.

But the man she had just met was so laid-back he'd almost fallen over. And utterly charming to boot. In fact, Lisa was rather cross with herself. She'd been almost putty in his hands by the time they had finished lunch. She didn't usually allow herself to be sweet-talked like that. Was the sea air making her soft? She'd asked Bruno Thorne to the launch party, for heaven's sake! Their biggest rival – what was she thinking of? Never mind – she didn't have to send him an invitation. And he was unlikely to turn up without one.

Satisfied that she would be able to harden her heart

to Bruno's charms in future, Lisa paddled in the frill of foam that lapped upon the sand as the sea inched its way inwards, wincing as the salty water soaked itself into the blisters between her toes.

From his vantage point on the veranda, Bruno watched Lisa's figure becoming smaller and smaller as she made her way back along the beach, utterly intrigued. She was such a beguiling mixture of tough and naive. She'd gone in with all guns blazing, but by the end of the meal she was butter-soft and had opened up far more than she probably should have.

Bruno wondered exactly what the set-up was at The Rocks. She'd talked about partners, but whether they were business partners, or if one of them was something more, he couldn't tell. There was one person who'd be able to give him the low-down. Bloody Leonard. The mouth of Mariscombe. But Bruno certainly wasn't going to go and ask him. If he showed so much as a flicker of interest, Leonard would have them *in flagrante delicto* by the end of the week.

Besides, thought Bruno, he had plenty on his plate sorting out the hotel. The revamp at The Rocks was going to set a new standard and he didn't want to be too far behind. At least now he knew what he was up against.

Mimi sat back in her seat gingerly. She'd already found a wad of chewing gum under one table and had to move. She'd got no idea a train could stink so much: of other people's sweat and stale smoke and cheap perfume. She got out her magazine and began to flip through it idly, but although she was looking at the pictures she wasn't really seeing them. Her mind was working overtime.

It was a very peculiar thing, being a teenager. Grown-ups spent so much time worrying about whether you were going to take drugs or sleep around that they never suspected you could be up to something really evil. It had been easy for her to slip into George's office while no one was looking, check up on the appointments on the noticeboard then cancel a couple of key arrangements and alter a couple of orders in order to cause chaos.

And now she was embarking on the final part of her plan.

She'd got Yasmin to do some photos, with Leyla's help. Yasmin had, after all, once been approached by a scout from a model agency, at Paddington Station. She'd laughed in the scout's face, telling her modelling was for divs: she was going to do Law at Cambridge. Yasmin was fiercely bright as well as ravishingly beautiful, a fact which Mimi, being neither, thought was rather unfair. But she didn't hold it against her friend, because Yasmin always came through for her. She'd taken on this latest task with huge enthusiasm, relishing the challenge, plundering her wardrobe for fishnet and feathers and leopard-skin and leather, dressing herself up and pouting provocatively for the camera wielded by Leyla. They'd emailed the results to Mimi's Hotmail account. Mimi had picked them up from the Internet cafe in Mariscombe, then forwarded them on with a covering letter. It had only been three days before she got the reply she wanted.

And now here she was. She got off the train at Birmingham New Street, pushing her way through the throngs to the taxi rank outside, trying to accustom her nose to the stench of fumes and fast food that now seemed such an unpleasant contrast to the fresh air she had been breathing of late. Mimi had always assumed she would be a city girl for the rest of her life. Now she couldn't wait to get out. Her hair already felt lank with the filth; her pores were clogging. She could scarcely breathe as she clambered into the back of a cab. She told herself that by late this evening she would have the sea breeze on her face and the taste of salt on her lips again. She was amazed how much she craved it.

She had adapted incredibly quickly to the beach life. It suited her: the casual, easy attitude, the way everyone just went with the flow. There was no competitiveness – they all seemed to be friends on an equal footing, with no pecking order based on looks or cash. And she loved helping Cassie out on her stall. Mimi did the braiding, winding brightly coloured beads into people's hair so they could adopt a different identity during their week's holiday, become someone else. All in all, Mimi felt relaxed for the first time in her life. Usually when she went out she had to brace herself for bitching, squabbling and histrionics. In Mariscombe, everyone was cool.

Especially Matt. Whenever she thought about him, she felt a warm glow in her tummy. He made her feel so . . . what? She wasn't exactly sure. Safe, she finally decided. Safe and comfortable. All the other blokes she'd ever met that she fancied made her feel insecure and anxious, a sensation she hated so much that she positively avoided contact with them. But Matt . . . Being with him was a joy, because she could just be herself, and he didn't judge her on anything. Not her quirky clothes sense, or her family set-up, or her off-the-wall taste in music that didn't seem to coincide with anybody else's. For the first time in her life, she didn't feel like a misfit or a freak. She was just Mimi.

Not that she and Matt were an item. At least, she didn't think so. They spent lots of time together, on the beach after work or in the Old Boathouse in the evening, listening to bands or playing pool. And he often held her hand while they walked somewhere, or draped an arm around her shoulder. But they hadn't kissed. Not yet. And Mimi thought she was grateful for that, because she knew where kisses led, and she wasn't quite ready. Not yet. Though she thought Matt might be the one . . .

By now the cab was gliding past bars and cafes and clubs, then turning into a little side road lined with mock Victorian lamp-posts bedecked with hanging baskets. It pulled up in front of a glass-fronted office. Mimi was surprised. It looked far less seedy than she'd thought. For a moment she wasn't sure about what she was doing. This was a professional set-up that made serious money, not the scruffy office over a betting shop that she had expected. But she'd come this far. She wasn't going to waste a train fare by not trying.

'I've got an appointment with Tony,' she informed the receptionist, trying not to feel awkward in the presence of her perfect white-blond hair and full red lips. She sat down to wait on a white leather sofa, flipping through a copy of *Vogue*, desperately trying to ignore the fact that her stomach was churning with nerves.

'Miranda Snow?' She looked up, to see a man wearing a black suit with a white T-shirt underneath. His silver hair was cropped short and when he smiled she saw he had a diamond in one of his front teeth. 'Tony Lavazza.'

He held out his hand and she scrambled to her feet. As they shook hands, he ran an appraising gaze up and down her body, frowning.

'You don't look much like your pictures.'

'There's a good reason for that.' Mimi ran her fingers through her hair nervously. 'They're not of me. But I knew you wouldn't see me otherwise.'

Tony scowled.

'Are you messing me about?' he demanded. 'I can't get you work. You haven't got the figure. Or the looks.'

He saw Mimi flinch.

'I know I haven't,' she said angrily. 'I'm not stupid.'

Tony looked uncharacteristically chastened.

'Sorry, love. I don't mean to be cruel, but you won't believe the birds I get in here who think they're God's gift to the camera. You're cute looking, but you're not right for glamour.'

'Let's get things straight. I wouldn't take my top off for you if I was starving.'

'Then what are you doing here?'

'I want to talk to you about Lisa Jones.'

'Lisa?' A dark cloud flitted over his face. 'Has she sent you?'

'No.' Mimi put her head to one side and smiled right at him. 'Far from it. If she thought I was here, she'd be very worried. Very worried indeed.'

She left half an hour later with exactly what she needed. It was a shame. She liked Lisa. She really did. But she had to go. Lisa didn't need George. Not like her mum did.

Victoria was trying so hard. Mimi felt proud of her. She knew she was struggling to control her drinking. She might not actually be a card-carrying alcoholic, but she rarely used to wait for the sun to be over the yardarm before hitting the Oyster Bay big time. Mimi knew she'd cut down to just the occasional glass of wine since she'd arrived at The Rocks, mainly because when she got drunk she lost the plot and alienated people. She also knew Victoria was working her socks off to pay George back for his kindness, putting more effort into the design of their brochures and menus, their logo, their overall corporate image, than she'd ever done with any other client.

And she knew how much it hurt Victoria to see George and Lisa together. She knew because she'd heard her sobbing into her pillow late at night.

'I've been a fool and I've got everything I deserve,' she told Mimi, but Mimi wasn't going to stand by and watch her go under.

Mimi was under no illusions about her mother's short-comings. She knew Victoria was spoilt and manipulative. Not to mention vain and utterly crap with money. Yes, she had any number of faults. But Mimi loved her mother and was fiercely protective of her. She might be the first to criticize her, but she wouldn't stand by and let anyone else run her down. And she was shocked to see how little fight Victoria had left in her. She'd lost all her confidence. She was, Mimi sensed, petrified of a future without money, without a roof over their heads. Without a man.

Victoria hadn't had things as easy as people might think. Bringing up a child on your own was tough and Mimi recognized that it had been a struggle. Especially as Victoria's own parents had turned their back on her, to all intents and purposes. They might not have actually seen her starve, but they didn't give her the support she needed. They certainly hadn't given her any affection. Mimi remembered her grandmother's occasional visits – 'guilt trips', Victoria had dubbed them – and recalled a brisk, angular woman sweeping in and out of the house without so much as a kiss or a hug for her own granddaughter. Not even a packet of Dolly Mixtures. Would that have hurt?

Mimi still found it hard to believe they could have been so cruel, that they held their snobbish values over their own daughter's well-being, that their sniffy disapproval came before what should surely have been unconditional love. Now she was older, now she could make a mature assessment of their circumstances, Mimi was determined that Victoria shouldn't be short-changed. Yes, she'd made mistakes – didn't everyone? – but she shouldn't be crucified for them. She needed love and support as much as the next person.

At first, after Nick had cut them off and before she had found George again, Mimi had wondered whether her real father, her biological dad, might be the one to save them. Maybe it was time for him to cough up, face up to the responsibility he hadn't even known existed for seventeen years. After all, reasoned Mimi, if he had a bit of money lying about going begging, they could certainly use it. He'd got away with a good seventeen years of child maintenance, hadn't he? Perhaps it was payback time.

Victoria had always been fairly open about who her dad had been. In the past Mimi had sensed that to declare any real interest in him might have caused ructions, so she'd never bothered to find out very much about him. But once she'd decided that he could be the answer to their problems, she'd pieced together the few scraps of information she had and had tracked him down quite easily to an address on the outskirts of Bath. Which was a relief – after all, he could in theory have been anywhere in the world.

The house was tiny, terraced, rather run down but quite

pretty, with a white front door and big pots filled with geraniums that gave it a continental feel. There was a sign outside advertising furniture restoration and French polishing. By peering along the alley that led down the side of the house, Mimi could see evidence of some sort of ramshackle workshop in the back garden. She felt a small prick of disappointment. Somehow she didn't think she had stumbled across a potential gold mine. The hunky school handyman who had fathered her hadn't gone on to make his fortune, as she had sometimes fantasised. He wasn't going to reappear in their lives, conveniently unattached and miraculously wealthy, only for him and Victoria to fall into each other's arms. He wasn't going to hug the daughter he'd never known he had, and whisk the pair of them off to his small but tasteful manor house to live happily ever after.

Mimi was still curious, nevertheless. While she was there, she might as well catch a glimpse of the man whose genes she shared. She waited nearly two hours before he finally emerged, in a baggy T-shirt and khaki shorts, a well-built man with shaggy hair and a beard. Definitely attractive, in an alternative, artisan way. She could see an earring and he was smoking a roll-up. She peered at him for signs of any resemblance to herself and thought that perhaps that was where she had got her slightly crooked nose and her full lips. Moments later a woman with long hennaed hair followed him, in a turquoise batik skirt. They got into a transit van and drove off, the exhaust spluttering and the engine protesting. No, thought Mimi, thinking of her mother's penchant for sports cars. This was definitely not her route out.

She hadn't felt particularly strongly about the man she'd seen. He'd looked quite handsome, but she couldn't imagine what he could bring to their lives. He'd have to restore a lot of furniture to keep Victoria in the style to which she was accustomed. Besides, he looked to have a life of his own. She wasn't going to go knocking on his door. It wasn't as if he'd rejected her, after all. He'd never known she existed. Mimi had told herself, before she went to look for him, that she would go with her instinct. If she felt compelled to meet him, then she would. But when she looked at him, she felt nothing. As she'd taken the bus back through Bath that afternoon to the horrible hotel they were still staying in, she'd finally decided that there was only one person who could get them out of this mess. Only one person who had ever provided them with love and security and laughter and a home. And no way was Mimi going to let George slip through her fingers again.

Now, she'd managed to get them as far as The Rocks. All she had to do was her cuckoo act. She had to budge Lisa out of the nest. Mimi was a thoroughly resourceful creature. She'd worked out that Lisa must have secrets, because everybody did, and she watched and listened carefully for clues. Before long, she heard Lisa regaling people with the story of how she and George ended up buying The Rocks. Lisa told a good story: she exaggerated stripping off at the motor show until everyone had tears in their eyes from laughing.

'My agent wasn't best pleased, I can tell you,' she finished off. 'In fact, I think I was the first person ever to tell Tony Lavazza to stick it. But I've never regretted it. Not for a second.'

It hadn't taken Mimi long to track down Lisa's agent. She'd used Yasmin to bait him. And just as she surmised, Tony was eager for revenge, as the photographs in the bottom of her rucksack proved.

Twelve

Hannah was very worried about Molly. She'd missed two shifts in the last week, claiming illness. And she did indeed look pale, but Hannah suspected there was more to it than just a summer cold. Molly seemed jumpy and agitated. She shot off home after work like a scalded cat. And while she was at work she was withdrawn. She seemed to keep herself to herself. Whereas once she would have joined in the gossip over a coffee, now she carried on working without a break. Molly had always had a ready smile; she had warmth. Everyone liked her. But now, a light inside her had gone out.

Hannah decided that it was up to her to do something about it. So she cornered Molly one morning, in the bedroom she was cleaning.

'Moll, if there was something the matter, you would tell me?'

Hannah put her hands on the younger girl's shoulders, forcing her to meet her gaze. Molly looked back at her, wide-eyed.

'Course.'

'You seem . . . well, you don't seem happy.'

Molly shrugged. Hannah noticed that she was incredibly thin, her collarbones jutting out of her uniform. And her face was milky white, with purplish-blue shadows under her eyes.

'I'm fine.'

'Bruno told me you didn't want the housekeeper's job.'

Molly looked at her sharply.

'So?'

'I think you'd be good at it.'

'I don't want the responsibility.'

'It's not that big a deal, counting sheets.'

'Yes, it is.' Molly was sharp. 'Anyway, I might be leaving.'

'Why? Where are you going?'

'I dunno.'

'You like it here.' Hannah frowned, puzzled by what Molly was saying. 'Don't you?'

Molly was silent for a moment, then shut her eyes. Hannah suspected she was trying not to cry.

'Yes, I like it here,' she said wearily. 'But . . . I might have to move. That's all. Family stuff.'

Hannah hugged her, instinctively sensing that the girl was struggling inwardly.

'You know you can talk to me. If you want to.'

Molly managed a smile.

'Thanks.' She wriggled out of Hannah's arms and made for her trolley, fishing around amongst the cleaning agents for the window cleaner. 'I'd better get the mirrors done. I don't know why people have to touch them with their mucky fingers, but they always do.'

She smiled brightly at Hannah, making it clear the conversation was over, then squirted the bedroom mirror liberally with Windolene.

As soon as Hannah left the room, Molly blinked back the tears she had been trying to hide, wishing fervently that Hannah hadn't been so nice. She could always cope when people were horrible, but when they were understanding, when they acted as if they might care for her . . . There was a moment back then when she'd thought she was going to lose it.

The strain of the past couple of weeks had almost been more than she could bear, trying to arrange for someone to look after Alfie now Skyla had gone. Her mother seemed to enjoy tormenting her, turning up to look after him late so that she had to kill herself running for the bus, or not letting her know if she would be able to cover until the very last minute.

Molly knew she would never do anything to hurt the little boy – Teresa might be a selfish cow, but she wasn't a total monster. But her nerves were shredded by the uncertainty of her existence. When her mother couldn't cover, Siobhan, her sister, was usually happy to step in, but Molly didn't trust Siobhan's boyfriend Zen one bit. If she knew the two of them were looking after him, she made sure she took all her cash with her to work. Zen was a drug user, a heavy drug user to boot, and Molly knew his type had no qualms about who they pinched money from. And again, although she was certain Siobhan wouldn't let Alfie come to any harm, she felt uncomfortable with the arrangement.

Without reliable back-up, there was no way she could take on the housekeeper's job. Bloody Joe. Why did he have to go and abandon her and Alfie like that? Even if they hadn't turned out to be the love story of all time, then at least they could have shared the responsibility a little bit. And there would have been more money.

Molly sighed as she pulled back the eiderdown from the recently vacated bed, then stripped the sheets and stuffed them in the dirty linen bag. The memory didn't haunt her very often, for she'd trained herself very well indeed to shut it out, but when it came back it hit her hard.

And she had no one to blame but herself.

Hannah was heading back down the corridor when she walked smack bang into Caragh.

'The last time I looked, the reception desk wasn't on the third floor,' she said accusingly.

Hannah pulled herself up to her full height, which meant she was head and shoulders above Caragh.

'I was just delivering a message to a guest,' she retaliated.

Caragh raised a corner of her mouth into a smirk.

'You're quite sure you weren't . . . consorting with a guest?'

Hannah looked shocked.

'Of course not.'

'No. Of course not,' mused Caragh, her voice at its lowest and most dangerous. 'After all, they'd need to be pretty desperate.'

Hannah stood stock-still, rigid with shock. How on earth could anyone be so cruel? What kind of kick did Caragh get from taunting her about her looks? It wasn't as if Hannah was any sort of threat. No one in a million years would choose her over Caragh, with her creamy skin and her glossy auburn bob. But she didn't have to crow about it.

'You take that back!'

The pair of them wheeled round to see Molly in the middle of the corridor, her eyes blazing.

'Hannah's worth a million of you, you stuck-up ginger cow.'

Hannah's hand flew to her mouth. Caragh breathed in deeply, her nostrils quivering with suppressed rage, and looked down at Molly witheringly.

'I beg your pardon?'

'Don't bother doing the snooty manageress bit with me. You're nothing but a jumped-up slut.'

'And you're fired.'

'I don't think so,' Molly shot back. 'Fire me and Bruno finds out about every single fiddle and every single scam you've been operating here.'

'You'd have to prove it first,' said Caragh.

'Trust me – I know where all the bodies are buried.' Molly smiled sweetly. 'I promise you I've got more than enough evidence. Now I want you to apologize to Hannah.'

Caragh looked mutinous.

'No way!' she declared.

Molly stared at her implacably.

'Cash deals with guests?' she asked. 'You forget that the rooms still have to be cleaned, even if the bookings haven't been through the register. I've kept a note.'

An angry red flush was creeping its way up Caragh's neck. She took a step forward and for a moment Hannah thought she was going to hit Molly. But Molly just folded her arms and took a step forward too. Caragh looked her up and down, before turning to Hannah.

'Hannah, I'm so sorry. Please forgive me,' she said, in such sugared tones it was impossible to believe she wasn't genuine. 'It's the wrong time of the month and I've got an awful lot on my plate. I really didn't mean to hurt your feelings.'

'That's OK,' mumbled Hannah.

'I'm sure the guests would be queuing up to sleep with you, if they thought they were in with a chance,' she added insincerely, before turning on her heel and striding off down the corridor, leaving a trail of Chanel in her wake. Hannah turned to Molly, incredulous.

'You were amazing.'

Molly's eyes were hard.

'I haven't finished with her yet.'

Hannah recoiled slightly, shocked at this side of Molly's character.

'You're a bit of a tough nut on the quiet, aren't you?' she said admiringly.

Molly gave a grim smile.

'You don't know the half of it,' she answered gruffly. She pushed her trolley away from Hannah down the corridor, and Hannah knew somehow from the set of her shoulders not to go after her.

Later that afternoon, Caragh was lying naked on Frank's bed. He was pulling his jacket on, getting ready for the evening shift. He should be in the kitchen now, supervising the prep. But she had swooped in on him an hour ago, all fired up, making demands.

He glanced over at her as he did up his buttons. She was stroking her breasts dreamily and unbelievably he felt himself stir again. He wouldn't have thought it possible.

'We rule this place, Frank,' she said to him. 'This is our kingdom. We should have things exactly as we want them.

Your man Bruno is going to get bored any minute. He'll be back to the big smoke once the last of the sun has gone, you mark my words. That's when we'll take over, you and me.'

He didn't have the courage to contradict her. He hated himself for his gutlessness, because he knew what was holding him back. He'd known at the time it was wrong. Taking a bung from a supplier – being invoiced for prime organic free-range meat when what he was supplied with was perfectly ordinary, and splitting the difference with the rep. It had been Caragh who talked him into it, who told him it was chef's perks, regular practice, and if he didn't do it then he was a fool. Now he'd supped with the devil. If he ever got arsy with her, or objected to anything she was doing, she reminded him of what he'd done.

He thought longingly of the advert he'd seen in the local paper. The new hotel that was opening on the other side of the bay was looking for a chef and he knew instinctively it was just the career move he was looking for. Somewhere he could really stamp his own signature, be creative and make a name for himself. Not that he didn't appreciate the opportunities Bruno had given him, but the Mariscombe Hotel was never going to be on the foodie map. He belonged somewhere like The Rocks, a hip hotel that was aspiring to great things and was gastronomically adventurous, but was small enough for him to be able to cut his teeth.

If he hadn't been so weak and gullible, he would have had the freedom to do exactly as he wanted. He tucked his red curls under his chef's hat, sighing inwardly. He was manacled to the crazy Caragh. He was well and truly trapped.

Caragh waited until Frank had got dressed in his chef's whites and gone off to the kitchen. Then she rolled off the bed, pulled her clothes back on and tiptoed out of his room and down the corridor until she found the door she was looking for. She took her pass keys out of her pocket and swiftly undid the lock.

She looked around the room in scornful distaste. The cuddly elephant on the pillow, the Robert Pattinson calendar, the pitiful collection of cosmetics on the dressing table. Carefully, she pulled open the drawers and started searching. Before long, she found a sheaf of bank statements and a building society book, which made interesting reading. But not interesting enough. She shoved them back and carried on looking.

In the next drawer down she found something that made her grin from ear to ear. A prospectus. A prospectus for a private hospital. And with it, a letter.

Dear Miss Baldwin

We are delighted to confirm that a bed has been reserved for you on the above dates . . .

Blah blah blah. She didn't need to read much more. She took out her mobile, programmed in the number at the top of the letter, then stuffed everything back in the drawer and left the room exactly as she'd found it.

Ten minutes later she was in the privacy of her own room at the hotel. She pulled out her phone and pushed a button.

'Is that Mr Burrough's secretary?' she asked. 'It's Hannah Baldwin here. I'm awfully sorry, but I've been thinking about it long and hard. I don't want to go through with the operation. I've come to the conclusion that it's the nose God gave me and I'm just going to have to live with it. It just doesn't seem right to tamper with nature somehow . . . So I'd like to cancel.'

Afterwards, Caragh snapped shut her phone in satisfaction. Silly cow, she thought. What difference did the hideous Hannah Baldwin think a mere nose job was going to make?

Thirteen

The next few days saw a mighty heatwave. The lanes around Mariscombe were crawling with camper vans and Porsches, the former looking for somewhere to park, the latter looking for somewhere to stay. There was a national skive as people wilted in the heat and gravitated to the coast for some fresher air.

'If only we'd been ready,' groaned George, working out on his calculator what they could have made.

'But we're not. And there's no way we could have been. So there's no point in worrying about it,' said Lisa.

Victoria printed off a load of leaflets announcing their imminent opening and bribed Mimi to go and stick them under windscreen wipers in the public car park.

'Only Porsches, BMWs, Audis and Mercs,' she instructed. 'Range Rovers if they're private reg. Discoveries if they're less than three years old. *New* Beetles – not the old ones. Minis if they're convertible with leather upholstery. And avoid anything with child seats like the plague—'

'For God's sake, just do the whole lot!' exclaimed George. 'We need all the custom we can get. Personally, I don't mind if they're driving Robin Reliants.'

Lisa picked up the leaflet.

'You're offering fifty per cent off!' she protested. 'We didn't agree that.'

'*A limited number of rooms available at this special price.*' Victoria pointed out the small print patiently. 'And obviously they won't be available if they ring up.'

'That's fraud.'

'No. It's an introductory offer.'

Lisa looked at George, who shrugged.

'Fine,' said Lisa wearily. 'I'm off to the warehouse in Bristol for towels and bedding.'

As Victoria and George opened their mouths, she put up a hand to stop them.

'I know. I know. White, white. And more white. High thread count. Down from Hungarian geese raised on south-facing slopes. Whatever.'

She flashed them a smile, fond but exasperated, as she left the room. Since her conversation with Bruno a few days before, she'd gained in confidence and learned to deal with George and Victoria. Besides, she had to admit that Victoria was mellowing. Once or twice she had actually taken Lisa's side against George. In fact, if the truth was known, Lisa was beginning to warm to her. It was nice to have another woman in the house to giggle with and moan about cellulite. Not that Victoria had any, but she liked to pretend she did. Lisa had basically fallen back on the old adage that if you can't beat them, join them, and it seemed to be working well. Victoria had been incredibly helpful and Mimi was certainly no trouble – they'd barely seen her; she flitted in and out to change her clothes between working down at the beach and going out in the evening.

And, anyway, Lisa told herself, they'd soon be gone. They couldn't stay here after the hotel was actually open, after all. There simply wasn't room.

'Do you really think it's safe to let her choose the duvet covers?' asked Victoria once Lisa had gone. 'She might spot a bargain and come back with something nasty and floral.'

'I don't think so,' said George, but he wasn't confident. He had a dim memory of Lisa's duvet cover in Stratford and it had definitely had flounces. Definitely.

Mimi was looking at them in distaste.

'You two are complete control freaks, do you know that?'

'Yep,' said Victoria happily.

Mimi turned away. Inside she was churning with guilt. Don't bottle out now, she told herself. Mum needs George. Mum needs George. Lisa will have men queuing up to console her. She's a coper. A doer. A manager. It will be a minor blip in her life.

She forced herself to visualize the future that she saw for them, to give her the motivation for what she was about to do. Mum and George at the helm of The Rocks, which would become the hippest hotel in the West Country. Meanwhile, she and Matt would become the hot new couple in town. She could go and do Theatre Studies at the college in Bamford – she'd already looked into it. Or maybe she could open a shop, selling her own label surf clothing. The possibilities were endless.

There was just one small sacrifice to be made in order for this nirvana to be reached. She'd go to the post office this morning, after she'd handed out the leaflets. Mimi pulled on her crocheted sun hat, stuck her feet into her day-glo flip-flops and set off down the hill.

That morning George had set himself the task of oiling the new decking they'd had laid outside the dining room, a particularly smelly and dirty task, but one which had to be done while the weather was dry and it was certainly that. By one o'clock he was drenched with sweat and suspected he might have sunstroke. He decided he'd go and get himself a little bottle of beer and a sandwich.

As he headed back in through the French doors he spotted Victoria curled up on a picnic rug in the shade of a tree, leafing through some papers, a pen tucked behind her left ear. She smiled up at him.

'I was just going to get a bite to eat,' he said. 'Do you fancy something?'

'Lovely. I'm starving.'

He went through the dining room and into the kitchen. The house felt eerily quiet and he was suddenly aware that this was the first time he and Victoria had been properly alone together since her arrival. Lisa was out, Mimi was out, the decorators were off on another job while the bathrooms were being finished. He rummaged in the fridge and found some ham and tomatoes, then quickly assembled a plate of sandwiches. He filled a jug with a couple of bottles of beer and topped it up with lemonade, then put everything on a tray with plates and glasses, adding a bowl of crisps and a couple of rosy apples for good measure. Then he wandered back outside.

'Nothing like an impromptu picnic. Though it's not exactly gourmet, I'm afraid.'

'It's perfect. Come and sit down.' Victoria patted the rug next to her invitingly. 'You look as if you could do with a rest.'

'How are things going, anyway?' asked George as he sat, placing the tray carefully between them.

'You know what?' said Victoria, reaching out for a sandwich. 'I've put on three pounds already since I've been here and I don't care. Normally, I'd be slitting my wrists or checking myself into some clinic to have my jaw wired. But I really couldn't give a toss. It doesn't matter in this place what you look like.'

'I've never seen you look better.'

George was perfectly genuine. Victoria looked softer. Her hair was twisted up into a clip, tendrils falling down round her face. She wore hardly any make-up, and the sun had brought out the freckles dusted across her nose that were usually covered in foundation. She was wearing a turquoise kaftan over a bikini and beaded flip-flops. He ran his eyes along her legs, the smooth, hairless calves, the knees she always complained were knobbly but that he used to love to kiss behind, her thighs with the sprinkling of pale golden hairs that were almost invisible to the naked eye . . .

George tore his eyes away and hastily poured them each a

shandy, waiting for the foam to subside before he passed her a glass.

'Thank you,' she said. 'And . . . thank you for letting us stay.'

George gave a small, non-committal nod.

'I can't believe the change in Mimi,' Victoria went on. 'She's so happy. Vivacious.'

'I know. It suits her down here.'

'She seems to have real friends. Proper friends. And I think there's a boy involved, though she hasn't said as much.' Victoria bit her lip, anguished. 'What am I going to do, Georgie? I know I can't crash at The Rocks for ever. It's not fair on you.'

'What do you want to do?'

'I'd love to stay around here. It's just a question of whether I can earn any money in this area. And I'd have to find somewhere to rent. I can't afford to buy, that's certain. Trouble is, I know the area's gone mad but I don't know if they're ready for PR yet. There's a guy on the beach who teaches surfing – he was talking to me about needing some publicity. And there's a couple of new restaurants opening. But it's not like anyone's got a PR budget . . . And what else do I do?' Victoria looked at him, her green eyes troubled. 'I'd open a shop but I haven't got any capital. Thanks to Nick Taverner.'

A big fat tear rolled down her cheek. George found himself wanting to say all sorts of things, not least that Nick Taverner had ended up with her money because she'd been spectacularly stupid. But she didn't need telling that.

'Hey,' he said softly. 'Don't cry. We'll sort something out.'

He went to wipe away her tear with his thumb. She put out her hand and held him by the forearm. For a moment they stared at each other, then she put her lips to the inside of his wrist. His pulse was beating at an incredible rate. She must be able to feel it. Despite himself he put out his fingers to stroke her face, to cup it in his hand. Her eyes closed, she ran her mouth over his palm, then over the tips of each finger.

He should never have touched her. He knew that. But he just couldn't resist, because the memory had never faded. She was the only woman who had ever made him lose his self-control. It was pure animal instinct that made him pull her to him and kiss her savagely. George, who could always be relied upon to keep his head, was a man bewitched. At that moment, he would have gladly given up everything just to feel her skin against his, her mouth, to run his hands through her hair.

When their lips met, it was incredible. Could he stop here? George wondered wildly. A kiss was excusable. A kiss could be a gesture of fondness, reassurance; he could justify it to himself later, no problem. Just pull away, he told himself. Be strong—

Strong? Who was he trying to kid? No man on earth would be able to resist. He ran his hands up the inside of her chiffon kaftan, recalling each familiar rib with the tips of his fingers, then finally reaching her breasts.

Before he knew it, they were rolling around on the picnic rug like a pair of randy teenagers. And George didn't care. Moments later, she let herself fall on to his chest, so they could feel their hearts pounding together, their sweat mingling.

'Shit.'

'I know,' breathed Victoria. 'That was amazing.'

'I don't mean shit wow,' said George grimly. 'I mean shit I shouldn't have done that.'

'Listen,' she said. 'Don't worry. It never happened. I'm sorry.'

She gave a twisted little smile.

'It's a long time since I've had a shag.'

George didn't reply. It stung him to hear what had just happened referred to as a shag. To him, it had been almost spiritual. It had felt like a real bond, an incredible moment when time was suspended. He told himself not to be so fanciful. Victoria was right – it was just a shag, and shags often tried to masquerade as something deep and meaningful.

He should be grateful Victoria was being so sensible for once. He was amazed that she didn't leap upon his weakness straightaway and start manipulating him. It was a pretty explosive weapon, after all. If she chose to use it, his whole world would be blown apart in an instant.

'So,' he said shakily, re-buttoning his shorts with trembling fingers. 'Where do we go from here?'

Victoria adjusted her clothing, pulling her kaftan back down so she was decent. She lifted her hair from the back of her neck, in a gesture that made his heart hammer even faster. It was still pounding furiously, but now more from panic than the exertion of sex.

'I mean, what do we do?' he gabbled. 'You can't stay at The Rocks much longer, Victoria. It's not fair on any of us.'

'I know.'

She took both of his hands in hers, staring into his eyes with a mixture of fondness and regret.

'I'm just so sorry I blew it. I can't believe I was such a crazy, messed-up bitch and destroyed what we had. You were the only good thing that ever happened to me, George, and I chucked you away like last season's shoes. But that's just me all over, isn't it?' She sighed. 'Do you think I'll ever get another chance? With someone else?'

'I'm sure you will.' George did his best to sound convincing, but at that moment he would gladly have killed anyone who stepped into the frame and tried to win her affections.

'Hey, you,' said Victoria. 'You'd better take a shower.'

She ran a finger down his chest, which was glistening with perspiration. He shivered. Should he say it now? Should he say he'd have her back? Face the music with Lisa? Destroy everything they'd built up? Create total chaos and mayhem? Safe in the knowledge that he would be plunging straight back into a life fraught with danger, insecurity, tantrums and histrionics. Victoria could say what she liked, but George was fairly certain she hadn't changed. Not deep down. But it had to be worth the risk. They'd just proved that. And he'd take control this time. Remind her of the lesson she'd learned.

Luckily for George, at that moment Justin came round the corner, back from his trip.

'What have you two been up to?' he demanded.

'Fucking like snakes,' drawled Victoria. 'This heat always makes me incredibly horny.'

She picked up her paperwork and wandered off. George could barely meet Justin's suspicious gaze as he hastily jumped to his feet and picked up the lunch tray.

'I hope you haven't.'

'Don't be ridiculous. I'm not a fool.'

Justin looked at him coldly.

'You'd better go and have a shower before Lisa gets back. You reek of it.'

'I've been treating the decking!'

'Yeah, right.' Justin looked him up and down with distaste. 'Just get your brain out of your trousers and put it back where it belongs, will you?'

George clutched the sides of the tray for strength. He really did feel peculiar. The morning's exertion, the heat, the shandy, the sex, being nearly caught out . . . his head was swimming. For a moment he thought longingly of a lie-down, but that was out of the question.

He smiled winningly at Justin, hoping to distract him.

'Come and have a look at what's been done while you've been away.'

Later that afternoon, when Justin had admired the transformation that had taken place during his absence, he cornered Victoria as she came out of her room. She was looking deceptively demure, in a white cotton cardigan and linen skirt, a silk camellia tucked behind her ear. Justin wasn't taken in for a moment. He grabbed hold of her hair and pulled her head back, holding her against his chest as if he was taking her hostage.

'I don't know what you think you're playing at, but pack it in now,' he told her.

Victoria smiled.

'You're just jealous.'

'What?'

'I don't know why you don't admit it.'

'Victoria – I don't fancy you if that's what you think.'

'No. Because I'm not your type, am I? After all, I'm the wrong sex.'

Justin gave a bitter bark of laughter.

'You think I'm gay? Just because I don't fancy you? Don't flatter yourself.'

'No, darling. Because you're in love with George.'

The two of them locked gazes, staring into each other's eyes, as if the first to look away would be the one to lose.

'Why else would you buy into this place?' she taunted. 'It was just so you could be near him. And it's why you don't want me around, isn't it? Because you know I drive him insane with lust. Lisa's not a threat. Lisa doesn't get under his skin. Lisa's safe. Plus she doesn't mind having you around, because she's as naive as George is.' She laughed. 'I'm amazed George has never sussed it. Why else have you never had a girlfriend? Only those flaky little bimbos who only hang off your every word because you give them money. And why else do you follow those cute little bands around? And as for the beach here, well – you must be in seventh heaven. All those tanned surfer dudes to drool over.'

She finished her tirade with a brilliant smile of triumph. It was all Justin could do not to put his hands round her throat and throttle her. He gazed back at her coldly.

'For your information, I'm not gay. I'm just not particularly interested in sex. To my mind, it messes everything up. It stops you getting on with the important things in life. Therefore I am not, as you so smugly assume, in love with George. I happen to respect and admire him. He's one of the few people in the world who isn't a total jerk – except when he comes into contact with you. So I will do everything in my power to make sure you are out of his life.'

Victoria gave him a slow hand clap.

'Beautifully spoken.' Her voice was mocking. 'Lucky old George, to inspire such loyalty in his friends. It'll be interesting to see where *his* loyalties lie, I must say.'

Justin watched her sashay back down the corridor, bubbling with hatred, thinking that if he'd had a gun on him at that moment he would quite happily have shot her. In the back as well. That was the thing about Victoria. You couldn't be ambivalent about her. You either loved her or hated her.

As she walked along the corridor, Victoria held her head high, but in reality she was struggling to hold back the tears. Bloody Justin, he always managed to remind her just what a waste of space she was. She should never have done it. She should never have slept with George. It was a cheap trick that underlined just how worthless she was. Anyone could get a man by using their body.

She wanted George to want her for *herself*. For everything they shared in common – their hopes and dreams and ambitions. This week at The Rocks had convinced Victoria just how much they belonged together. If she hadn't been such a selfish, vain, introspective monster, it would be her name at the top of the invitation she'd designed that morning. But now she'd really blown it. By bringing sex into the equation, she'd scuppered all her chances of getting George back. She knew him well enough to know he'd be cursing his weakness. That rather than being drawn towards her, she'd only succeeded in pushing him away.

And, anyway, as long as Lisa was around, why on earth would he want her? Lisa was gorgeous. Lisa was worthy. Lisa was absolutely everything she wasn't and never could be, no matter how hard she tried.

Later that evening, George was lying next to Lisa, listening to her talking but not really hearing the words.

'I really feel on top of everything now,' she was saying. 'I must say there was a moment when I started to panic, but everything's fallen into place. I'm even getting used to having Victoria around – I have to admit she has some really great ideas.'

'Mmm,' replied George non-committally. He couldn't even say her name, in case some ghastly confession came spilling out.

'You're very quiet,' said Lisa, stroking his forehead.

'It's . . . hard work,' George replied. 'Oiling the decking. I've found muscles I didn't know I had.'

'Perhaps you need a massage.'

'That's very kind of you,' mumbled George, feigning exhaustion. 'But I think I might just go to sleep.' He was terrified Lisa might find some sort of evidence; some trace of Victoria on his skin. Even though he'd scrubbed himself nearly raw with Japanese washing grains in the shower.

As Lisa curled an arm round him, he tried to relax, but his mind was racing. He was pretty certain Victoria wouldn't say anything about what had happened. It had been a moment of madness, something they'd had to get out of the way. A quick trip down memory lane to prove they didn't need each other. A kind of carnal closure. That was it, George reassured himself. Nothing more, nothing less.

He just hoped Victoria saw it the same way.

Fourteen

Bruno didn't think he had ever felt so depressed.

Today was his mother's birthday. And even though the sun was shining, bouncing off the water, with a light breeze to ruffle the hair, he would have preferred relentless rain, because the day's perfection made a mockery of the way he was feeling.

Joanie was sitting on her sofa, the rose-pink cashmere sweater he'd bought her clutched in her lap. He'd bought it because it was pretty and soft and luxurious, and he hoped it would prompt her to wear it, even if only out of politeness. He couldn't bear the shapeless grey cardigan and tracksuit trousers she seemed to wear indefinitely. He felt sure it couldn't be the same outfit she wore day in and day out, but it certainly seemed so. Bruno didn't believe in anything as flaky as colour therapy, but he felt strongly that her mood would never lift while she wore such dowdy clothes.

Choosing the card had proved horrendously difficult. He'd avoided anything that referred to 'mother' or 'son'. And anything sickly and sentimental – all those flowery poems wishing happiness would ring hollow. All he wanted was a card saying happy birthday that wasn't vulgar and didn't depict some scene that would rub salt into her wound. Even flowers seemed reminiscent of funeral wreaths. In the end he'd bought one of the Grand Canal in Venice – it was completely irrelevant to anything in her life and couldn't possibly remind her of Joe.

Joe had been good at birthdays. Joe had always deliberately

bought her the biggest, most tasteless card he could find, and it had always made her smile. The last card he'd bought her, just before he died, had been padded and musical, playing 'My Favourite Things' when it opened. His mother had left it on the kitchen dresser ever since. Bruno had picked it up one day to find that the tune had given up the ghost, even though Joe's signature was still inside, and it had made him feel incredibly desolate. He'd wanted to prise the card open, take out its workings, replace the tiny battery so that his mother could hear the tune again. It was, after all, one of the few tangible reminders that Joe had ever thought about anyone but himself. But the card was made in China, it wasn't designed to have its battery replaced. Bruno had put it back on the dresser feeling more powerless than ever to do anything to alleviate his mother's grief.

Today, Bruno had been absolutely determined to get Joanie out of the house. He'd booked a table for lunch at the Admiral Hotel on the estuary just outside Bamford. It wasn't his sort of place, but they had a terrace where you could look out over the water, an excellent carvery and an infamous pudding trolley with cream-laden trifles and gateaux.

'Come on, Mum,' he was urging her now. 'I've booked us a table on the terrace. It's a beautiful day.'

But she shook her head.

'I've got one of my headaches,' she replied. 'I wouldn't be able to enjoy it. It would be a waste.'

For a split second Bruno felt a surge of anger. Why wouldn't she let him try to make her happy? He was sure if he could persuade her out, she might enjoy it. Even if it was only for a nanosecond. He looked at her as she folded up the wrapping paper from his present neatly, smoothing it out with her fingers. Did there come a point where guilt became a habit? he wondered. An indulgence? Should he shout? Should he force her?

No, he thought. Look what had happened last time he'd been overbearing.

'Fine,' he said wearily, getting to his feet.

She smiled up at him, her blue eyes watery.

'Thank you for the jumper. It's lovely.'

Then bloody wear it! he wanted to shout, suddenly knowing it was going to be shoved in a drawer.

'You're welcome,' he replied wearily, dutifully, and walked out of the house.

'Less than two weeks today!' said Lisa, looking at the calendar. 'I can't believe it. Will we pull it off, do you think?'

'You don't have to worry about the party,' Victoria assured her. 'I do this kind of thing in my sleep.'

'It's my worst nightmare. I hate giving parties.'

'Just stick to getting the hotel ready. That would be the real crisis – if all the guests turned up and there was still a skip in the drive and decorators everywhere.'

'We're right on track,' Lisa assured her. 'They're doing the carpets on Monday and Tuesday. Wednesday as well if they overrun, which they will because the stairs are fiddly. Then the furniture arrives on Thursday. Which leaves us another whole week to hang the curtains, put up pictures, train up the staff . . .' She trailed off, looking panicky. 'Oh God . . .'

'Trust me. It'll be fine.'

George came in with the post. It never arrived until gone midday, another aspect of Devon life which took some getting used to. Sometimes the postman didn't wander up till gone two, if he'd been waylaid at the Mariscombe Arms.

'Bills, bills and more bills.' He chucked most of the letters on the desk and picked up a large A4 envelope. 'I expect these are the proofs for the brochures.'

Victoria hovered over him as he slid his finger carefully under the flap.

'I can't wait! I hope they've done a good job.'

He pulled the contents out carefully.

'Oops,' said Victoria, backing away.

'What is it?' asked Lisa. 'Have they made a mistake?'

'Have a look.' George dropped the contents on his desk in distaste.

It was a sheaf of colour photographs. Of Lisa. Lisa with her top off, smiling invitingly for the camera, in nothing but a pair of bikini bottoms. Lisa cavorting in a pair of high heels, licking an ice cream. Lisa bending over to pick up a beach ball, her rear stuck up in the air. Her hair was longer, almost to her waist, and she was about ten years younger. But it was undeniably her.

As Lisa looked at the photos, her face drained of any colour. Then she grabbed the envelope, shook it open, then tore it apart, looking for a clue as to who could have sent them.

'You kept that quiet,' said George accusingly.

'They weren't a secret,' she insisted. 'I'd have told you if I thought it was important. To be honest, I'd forgotten all about them.'

'You'd forgotten that you'd posed naked?'

'Topless.'

'Topless. Sorry.' His voice dripped sarcasm.

'There is a difference.'

'Oh, is there? Well, sorry, but I'm not up on the finer points of pornography.'

'This isn't porn!' Lisa's eyes flashed with fury. 'This is the sort of thing that's in national newspapers every day. It's perfectly acceptable.'

'That's a matter of opinion, surely?'

Lisa squared up to him.

'I'm not ashamed.'

'Then why haven't you ever mentioned it?'

'I don't know! It was a long time ago. It was what I had to do at the time.'

'Take your clothes off for money? Very nice, I'm sure.'

Lisa's voice was trembling. 'I was seventeen. All I had going for me was my looks. I'd failed my exams, because my mother

289

had just died. I had to stand on my own two feet and this was the quickest way of doing it.'

George looked at the photos again with distaste, unswayed by her defence.

'It's not the first thing most seventeen-year-olds think of.'

Lisa looked as if she had been slapped.

'I didn't have the benefit of a private education,' she spat back. 'I didn't get the chance to go to university. I couldn't become an architect or a lawyer.'

'Not everyone who leaves school at sixteen ends up taking their clothes off for money.'

'Well, I'm sorry if it offends you.'

'You could at least have done me the courtesy of telling me.'

'Like you told me you were married?'

Lisa kept her voice light, but her barb hit its target.

'That's entirely different,' George snapped.

'How is it different?'

'It just is.'

'For Christ's sake, George. Back off.'

The two of them turned to stare at Victoria. In the heat of the moment they had almost forgotten she was there.

'The question isn't whether Lisa was right to do this. Or whether she should have told you, George. The question is, who sent them?'

There was a deathly silence. Lisa finally spoke.

'I wonder?' she said sarcastically and swept out of the room, slamming the door behind her.

Victoria caught up with Lisa just as she was about to go out of the front door.

'Lisa!'

Lisa just looked at her, her face expressionless.

'I know what you're thinking. But it wasn't me who sent those photos. I promise you.' Victoria screwed up her face, looking genuinely worried. 'I don't want George back. I did him far too much damage the first time around. Irreparable damage. And I think you've been fantastic for him.'

She put out a hand to touch Lisa's arm.

'He always wanted something more when I was with him. He hated his work. But he was too busy wasting his time on me to spend any time realizing his own ambitions. Lucky for him someone came along who wasn't so self-obsessed. You've let him realize his dream.'

'Just a pity about my murky past,' said Lisa bitterly.

'I'm sure he didn't mean what he said. I think he was just a bit shocked. He is a bit of a prude, George.' Victoria gave a low, throaty laugh. 'I think the photos are fantastic. Trust me, if I'd got the body for it, that's what I'd be doing now.'

Lisa just about managed a smile. She realized that Victoria was doing her absolute very best to be genuinely nice, something she probably didn't do very often.

'You wouldn't want to do it, if you didn't have to,' she said in a shaky voice. 'But thanks.'

'Come on,' said Victoria, putting a conciliatory hand on Lisa's arm. 'I think you two should talk about this. Don't let somebody's petty prank spoil what you've got.'

'No.' Lisa was firm. 'I think I'd like to be on my own, if you don't mind.'

She wasn't going to cry in front of Victoria, no matter how nice she was being. She slipped out of the door, down through the garden, and scrambled down the rocky path to the beach, remembering with a bitter irony the first time she and George had climbed down it. It seemed a lifetime ago.

In which case, the photos must have been done two lifetimes ago. As Lisa trudged along the beach, all the memories came flooding back. That hideous, horrible frightened feeling, of being all alone, of having to make her own way in the world. Of thinking that if this was what she had to do, then she'd do it. She'd only been seventeen. OK, so that wasn't a scandal in itself, but it hadn't been an easy decision to make. And she'd had no one to confide in. No one she could weigh up the moral issues with. Never had she wanted her mother more. But then, if her mother had been there, she wouldn't have found herself in that situation.

She'd seen an advert in the paper, asking for models to come and audition at a local hotel. She decided to go, just for a laugh, though she didn't hold out much hope. She'd worn a pair of jeans, a low-cut top and boots, her hair loose. Everyone else had been done up to the nines, in tight dresses and high heels and full make-up. The queues were endless. Lisa had been about to leave, convinced she would get nowhere. As she went to push open the door of the function room, a hand had grabbed her arm.

'I hope you're not going anywhere, sweetheart?' a swarthy man in an Italian suit had asked, his white teeth glinting.

That was her first brush with Tony Lavazza. He'd whisked her upstairs immediately. Fast-tracked her, he called it, to a suite where the shortlisted candidates were sitting round drinking white wine and soda while they were scrutinized by Tony and his associates. In the end, only Lisa and another girl called Candy had been signed up.

Her assignments had been straight to start with. Some modelling, some promo work, often quite dull and dreary. She did some knitting patterns and a jodhpur catalogue. Lots and lots of exhibitions. Then came the offer of some glamour work. Which by then Lisa knew meant topless. Tony kept insisting it was just a bit of fun.

'It's seaside postcard stuff. Saucy. Think *Carry On*. Or Benny Hill.'

Neither of these examples meant anything to Lisa. But the substantial fee they were offering did. And in the end, it was the money that convinced her. She could earn as much in one session as she did in a month. You couldn't argue with that. Her teeth had chattered on the first shoot. Not with cold, but with fear. She had been racked with nerves. In the end, the photographer had forced a few glasses of Pernod and blackcurrant down her. Funnily enough, it had worked. Her qualms dissipated and before long she actually got caught up in the spirit of the shoot. Everyone had been delighted with the results, and there and then Lisa decided it was just mind over matter. She didn't need to get drunk. It would be far better if she kept her head and found her own way of relaxing. That way no one could ever take advantage of her.

So after that, it was easy. The photographers were usually a laugh, and because she was good at her job it was a fairly painless process. Certainly easier than standing on your feet all day handing out leaflets. Although it was rather an irony calling it glamour work, because glamorous it was not – there was never anywhere proper to change, she usually ended up doing her own hair and make-up in the toilet mirror and she had to remember to bring a sandwich if she wanted lunch. She never knew where the photographs were destined – catalogues and calendars and magazines – but she didn't care because she was earning.

Meanwhile, she saved furiously. At the end of three years, she had enough for a deposit on her first flat. When she was quite certain she was secure, that even if she had to take a job as a secretary she would still be able to afford her mortgage, she told Tony no more topless. He was hopping, of course. But he couldn't do without her. She was incredibly popular. And she had the sort of looks, the sort of body that meant it didn't really matter if she was clothed. She almost looked more inviting with her kit on. So he'd agreed. And as the years passed by, she became more and more choosy about her assignments, until it was her calling the shots.

But somehow, her past had caught up with her.

As she walked, Lisa realized that the azure blue sky was clouding over. The weather on the coast could change in an instant. Blue skies could become black, and black blue. A heavy mist could roll across the beach in seconds. A bit like life, really, she thought moodily. Everything had been sunny that morning. She had been full of excitement that they were

293

only two weeks away from their launch. But now she felt filled with gloom.

Who had sent the photographs? And why? Of course, the prime suspect was Victoria. But Lisa was certain that her protestation of innocence earlier was quite genuine. She could tell when someone was trying to cover something up: the girls she had worked with over the years were adept at fibs and equivocations; the mistresses of deception. She would have been able to see straight through Victoria if she had been lying.

Maybe it was a set-up? Maybe it was George? Perhaps George, too cowardly to dump her, was deliberately sabotaging their relationship in order to bring about a break-up that would leave him with clean hands? And allow him to get back with the real love of his life?

Now she really was being paranoid, decided Lisa. There was one very obvious suspect, with motive and opportunity and access to the photos, and that was Tony Lavazza. Egged on, no doubt, by Milo. She imagined them cooking up the plan in some flash bar in Birmingham, falling over with laughter at the thought of their revenge. It would be typical of their nasty, small-minded attitude to life. They were the type to bear grudges. They would never wish anyone well. They would both be eaten up by the fact she had walked out on them. They only knew how to take.

Lisa felt vaguely comforted by the possibility that it was them. What further damage could they do, after all? She decided that their vendetta would probably stop there, that they would have got a sense of satisfaction from their anonymous package which would hopefully quench their desire for revenge.

Big, fat raindrops started to fall. She looked up and realized she was more than halfway down the beach. Huge black clouds had rolled in over the horizon. She'd been so immersed in her own black cloud she hadn't noticed how far away from shelter she was. This wasn't going to be a quick shower. There was absolutely nowhere to take cover. As the rain began in earnest she shivered. Within seconds her sleeveless top and knee-length skirt were wet through.

A huge, tawny dog came lolloping up to her. Through the sheeting rain she saw his owner come closer, whistling furiously. Then she recognized him. It was Bruno.

'Hi!' he shouted. 'This is torrential. Come inside while it lasts.'

He pointed a thumb over his shoulder. Lisa saw she was at the bottom of the dunes just outside his house. She looked doubtful.

'I'm OK,' she insisted. She wanted to be on her own, not to have to be polite, no matter how welcoming the prospect of Bruno's shelter was.

'You're crazy. You're going to catch your death.'

She could barely hear him through the downpour. But she knew he was right. Her soaking skirt flapped round her legs, stinging her as viciously as small boys armed with wet towels in the school changing room.

The next moment Bruno was beside her, taking her arm.

'Come on,' he insisted. 'Come and get dry. I can drive you home afterwards.'

Short of wriggling out of his grasp and running off down the beach, there was nothing she could do. It was at least half a mile back up to The Rocks, and she didn't fancy attempting the cliff path in this maelstrom.

'OK,' she relented, and allowed herself to be steered towards the steps that led to his veranda.

'I think you're being a complete wanker.' Victoria was standing in front of George's desk, her hands on her hips.

He looked up from his paperwork, irritated.

'There aren't many men who would be delighted by such a revelation, I can assure you.'

'Get real, George. Most men would give their eye-teeth to go out with a former topless model.'

George looked furious.

'Well, not me.'

'She was seventeen. And, personally, I think she was jolly brave.'

'Yes, well, we all know about your moral code, Victoria.'

Victoria glared at him through narrowed eyes.

'And what about yours?' she asked softly.

George sighed, screwed the top back on his pen and laid it down carefully.

'I think it would be better for everyone if you left. I should never have let you stay in the first place.'

'Don't worry.' Victoria was arch. 'I'm not about to tell Lisa what we got up to. Not least because I'm completely disgusted with myself. Wild horses wouldn't drag it out of me.'

'Good,' said George lightly. 'Because I don't know what you'd get out of it if you did.'

Victoria leaned down and pushed her face right up close to George's, scrutinizing him in disbelief.

'What?' he asked indignantly.

'You've got no idea how lucky you are, have you?'

'Me?'

'Lisa is a lovely, lovely girl. She's worth about ten billion of me. And you have to rub her nose in something she did years and years ago, when she was a frightened kid whose mother had just died? Do you know, I'm almost tempted to confess, even if I do come out of it badly. Because at least she'd know what a hypocrite you are. And maybe I'd be doing her a favour.'

'I want you out of here by this afternoon,' thundered George.

'What's going on?' Mimi appeared in the doorway, alarmed at the raised voices.

'Why didn't you remind me what an arsehole he is?' demanded Victoria. 'Go and pack your stuff. We're leaving.'

'What?'

Victoria marched across the office and picked a bulging file off the top of the filing cabinet. She threw it on the desk in front of George.

'There's the party file,' she hissed. 'The invitations went out yesterday. Second class. Because for once I've managed to stick to my budget.'

She swept out of the room. Mimi stared at George, who had his head in his hands.

'What's happened?' she asked.

'Don't ask,' he replied wearily.

Mimi scanned the room for clues and spotted a familiar-looking brown envelope poking out of the bin. She gulped nervously.

'Where's Lisa?'

'I don't know. She's stormed off as well.' He heaved an enormous sigh. 'Why does it have to be so difficult, Mimi? I don't understand why I suddenly get turned into the enemy when I'm only trying to do my best.'

Mimi couldn't look him in the eye. Shit, she thought. This has majorly backfired. She had hoped to bring her mother and George together, not drive them apart.

Lisa stood in the middle of Bruno's kitchen, dripping on to the slate floor. He handed her an enormous towel.

'There's a cloakroom just off the hall.' He pulled some dry clothes from an airer hanging over a French range, handing her a shirt and a pair of shorts. 'You can stick these on. You won't win any fashion awards, but I'll drive you back so no one will have to see you.'

'Thanks,' said Lisa gratefully, trying not to shiver.

She slipped into the cloakroom, which was colossal, with the same slate floor as the kitchen. On one wall was a triptych: three large square canvasses each with an identical photo screen-printed on to it of a beautiful boy with long eyelashes, his head back, laughing. The same image repeated in royal blue and black, in the style of Andy Warhol. This must be Bruno's brother, she realized. The one who had driven off

Mariscombe Point. If Leonard was to be believed, she thought wryly. Had it been another of his fairy tales?

By the time she'd dried herself and dressed, Bruno had lit the fire in the living room and a delicious smell of woodsmoke filled the air. He'd made them both Irish coffee. Thick, sweet espresso with a slug of Paddy's and a dollop of Devon cream on the top.

'Was that your brother, in the bathroom?' Lisa asked.

Bruno looked at her warily.

'In the photos? Yes.' His voice sounded strained.

'They're beautiful.'

He'd had them done after Joe died. To erase that last memory of Joe's hurt, scornful gaze, so full of hatred and resentment. He'd wanted to remember Joe carefree and laughing, because that's what he so often was.

'He was beautiful,' he replied carefully. 'Sickeningly beautiful. I think that was half his problem. If he hadn't been, he wouldn't have got away with half of what he did.' He looked at Lisa, then looked away again. 'You obviously know what happened to him.'

She nodded.

'It must have been awful.'

'Awful . . . ?' Bruno tried out the word, but it didn't seem to suffice. 'The awful thing was not knowing what was going through his head that night. Joe was wild. And he was pissed. But to do that . . .'

His jaw tightened.

'I shall never forgive him,' he said through gritted teeth. 'For what he's done to Mum. He was always selfish; he always had to come first. And just because he thought he wasn't going to get his own way for the first time in his life . . .'

Lisa watched in horror as Bruno put his head in his hands. A strangled noise came from him and she realized it was choking sobs; choking sobs that he was desperately trying to suppress.

'I'm sorry . . .' He looked up and his face was contorted

with the effort to control himself. 'It's been a difficult morning. It's my mother's birthday. I tried to get her to go out to lunch, but she refused point-blank. She's . . . never going to get over it. And I keep blaming myself.'

Lisa came over to sit by him. She took his hands in hers.

'You mustn't blame yourself,' she soothed. 'Joe was a grown man. It was his decision.'

'But it was me who pushed him.' Bruno was calmer now, able to articulate. 'I taunted him. But I was only trying to make him realize . . . I loved him. We all loved him. But he was going off the rails. I wanted to save him. I wanted him to make something of himself. And I would have helped him in the end. But first he needed a shock. He needed a wake-up call, and he needed to make the decision to change. He couldn't be forced . . .' He ran his fingers through his hair despairingly. 'How was I to know he couldn't take it? No one had ever given it to him straight in his life. He always had it cushy. And I had to come along and give it to him with both guns.'

'You weren't to know.' Lisa desperately hunted around for something to say that wasn't a cliché or an empty platitude.

'And now I look at Mum and I blame myself. She's got nothing to live for.' Bruno looked down into his coffee cup. 'She's an empty shell and it's my fault.'

'Why?' demanded Lisa. 'Why are the self-indulgent actions of someone who got his own way all his life *your* fault?'

'It was my fault for goading him. My fault for leaving the keys. My fault for being everything he wasn't and making sure he knew it. You name it.'

'Well, I'm sorry, but I don't see the point in blaming yourself,' declared Lisa. 'If Joe couldn't handle the truth, that was his problem. He was obviously a loser. Why should you have to suffer for that?'

Bruno looked at her in astonishment.

'Do you know, no one's had the nerve to say anything like that before?'

Lisa shrugged.

'Joe's dead. He's not bothered, is he? Don't beat yourself up on his account.' She twizzled one of her curls round her finger. 'You obviously haven't had counselling.'

'Counselling?' Bruno snorted. 'No, I haven't. It's not really my thing.'

'It's not mine either,' Lisa replied. 'But I have to admit, it did help when I finally got round to it. Not that it changes anything. But you get to understand that it's OK to feel the way you do. And to have the guts to put things into perspective. And not go round apportioning blame. Feeling guilty isn't going to bring Joe back.' She took a sip of her coffee. 'In my case, I didn't blame myself. I blamed everyone else, which is just as bad. I've just about come to terms with the fact that it wasn't actually *anybody's* fault. It was fate.'

'So why . . . ?'

'Why did I have counselling?' Lisa leaned forward and put her cup down on the coffee table. 'My mum died when I was seventeen.'

'Ouch.'

'Very ouch. I didn't bother seeing anyone for ages, because I thought counselling was for pussies. But you can't bottle everything up for ever. And you can't dump on your friends all the time.'

Bruno put his head back and shut his eyes for a few moments.

'Actually,' he said, 'it's the first time I've really talked to anyone about it.'

Lisa didn't answer at first.

'You can talk to me any time,' she offered eventually. 'I can be an objective ear. I don't mind, because I know what it's like.'

'Thank you.' Bruno looked genuinely touched. 'Though to be honest, I don't really give a toss about myself. It's Mum I feel bad about. She doesn't seem to be getting over it at all.' He paused. 'How did your father cope?'

'Dad?' replied Lisa grimly, then couldn't help a rather cynical smile. 'He ran off with my mum's sister.'

'Ah.' Bruno looked embarrassed. 'Sorry. I shouldn't have asked.'

'He . . . didn't even have the decency to wait until Mum had died.'

'Shit.'

'So I kind of lost my dad as well.'

'You fell out with him over it?'

Lisa nodded.

'We still don't speak. They live in Spain, him and my aunt. He doesn't even know I've bought The Rocks.'

'Doesn't he even have a phone number for you? In case . . .'

'In case what? He dies?' Lisa was aware that her voice was scornful. 'I really don't care what happens to him.'

There was a long pause.

'Don't you?' asked Bruno gently.

'No!' replied Lisa vehemently, but she couldn't meet Bruno's eye. She pressed her fingertips to her eyelids for a moment, then looked over at him. 'Yes. Yes, of course I bloody do. But it's been too long now. Thirteen years. I mean, if he really cared about me, he'd have tried to get in touch, wouldn't he? Maybe even just once. Like when I was eighteen. Or twenty-one. Or thirty . . .'

She'd never told anyone how painful those milestone birthdays had been. How she had approached the letter box with a dry mouth, hoping for a card. Hoping for something that said he still cared about her. But there was nothing. She'd imagined him stretched out on a sunlounger by the pool, Andrea next to him with her belly bulging out of a white bikini, with no idea that this day was any different to any other in the glorious Spanish sunshine.

Suddenly Lisa felt tears streaming down her face. She tried to compose herself, dabbing desperately at her eyes with the back of her hand.

'Hey . . .' Bruno leant towards her. 'Hey, I'm sorry. I didn't mean to be tactless.'

He put a concerned arm around her. For a moment Lisa was tempted to throw herself against his chest and howl. His presence felt so comforting. Or was it something else? She was keenly aware of his warmth; she could feel the hardness of his muscles through the fabric of his shirt. For a second she thought it would be heaven, to have his arms wrapped round her, breathe in that scent . . .

She drew herself away hastily, before she made a fool of herself.

'I'm sorry,' she said, beside herself with embarrassment. 'Honestly, I haven't even given him a thought for years. I guess . . . it's been a stressful couple of weeks, trying to get things ready.'

She smiled at him and he held her gaze solemnly. The two of them sat still, keenly aware that there had been a moment between them that transcended mere friendship. It was Bruno who broke away, standing up and running his hand through his hair with a rueful grin.

'Maybe we should start our own support group.'

'I'm fine,' said Lisa. 'Honestly, I don't need any more counselling or therapy. I'm over it. But any time you want to talk, that's all right,' she added hastily. 'If you want a shoulder to cry on . . .'

'I'm OK too, generally speaking,' insisted Bruno. 'It's just that little things get to you every now and again. But thanks for listening.'

He moved away swiftly, clearing away the coffee cups. 'What were you doing walking on the beach in the pouring rain, anyway?'

Lisa decided it was too trivial to go into.

'It was just a silly argument that got blown out of proportion. I think I probably overreacted.'

She stood up.

'I better get back. I've got a mountain of stuff to do.'

'Let me give you a lift.'

Lisa looked out of the window. The rain was still pounding relentlessly against the glass. Everywhere she looked it was grey: grey sand, grey rocks, grey sea, grey sky.

'Actually,' she said, 'if you could just lend me an umbrella. I'd rather walk.'

Bruno put his head to one side and looked at her quizzically.

'You're very independent, aren't you?'

'Yep,' she replied, thinking that was probably where she had made her mistake. She'd relinquished her independence and now she was paying for it. Now she was accountable to other people. Well, that was going to change, she thought, as she took the umbrella from Bruno. She didn't have to explain herself to anyone, least of all George.

When Lisa had gone, Bruno went into the cloakroom. Ostensibly to take a leak, but in reality to see if he could look the photos in the eye. And he could.

'Sorry, Joe,' he said to them all. 'I'm not going to let you ruin the rest of my life.'

Joe stared back at him, laughing, as he always did. But this time the look wasn't quite so scornful and triumphant. He didn't seem to be taunting Bruno any more. And perhaps that was because Lisa's words had sunk in. Bruno might not feel totally absolved from guilt, but she was right; there was no point in beating himself up about it for the rest of his life.

He walked back into the living room. Bruno was used to being on his own, but suddenly without Lisa it felt incredibly empty. Her presence there that afternoon made him realize he had all this space, and no one to share it with. He really should start entertaining, he decided. This was a house for sharing, for parties. Not an exile for some sort of eccentric recluse. He plumped up the cushions where Lisa had been sitting, then strode over to the sound system and put on some music.

Suddenly, he couldn't bear the silence that until now had been his solace.

George shot out of his office as soon as he spotted Lisa walking across the drive under her umbrella.

'Thank God you're back!' he exclaimed as she came in through the front door. 'I was worried you might have gone off and left me to it. And I wouldn't blame you if you had. I behaved like a complete . . .' He searched round for a word, but couldn't find a better replacement for Victoria's epithet. 'Wanker,' he finished.

Lisa managed a smile as she shook out her damp curls.

'Yes,' she said. 'You did.' She wasn't going to give him an inch.

'I was shocked,' he admitted. 'I don't like to think of anyone having to do that for money. Especially you. But I took it out on the wrong person. It wasn't your fault. You were exploited, by some greasy little oik who took advantage of your age and your vulnerability. I've a good mind to go straight up to Birmingham and find Tony bloody Lavazza—'

Lisa put up a hand to stop him.

'It's OK, George,' she said briskly. 'Let's just put it behind us, shall we? We've got enough on our plate without worrying about spiteful, anonymous packages from people whose noses have been put out of joint.'

George looked hugely relieved.

'By the way, you might be glad to know Victoria and Mimi are going tomorrow. It's another added pressure we could do without, having them around.'

'What?' Lisa looked rather alarmed.

'Victoria's phoned her mother. Who's doing the decent thing for the first time in her selfish life and is going to give them a roof over their heads.'

'Hang on a minute!' Lisa panicked. 'Who's going to organize the launch party?'

'We can manage.'

'No, we can't! We'll be lucky if we get everything done in time as it is.'

'We'll cancel it, then. We weren't going to have a party in the first place.'

'But the invitations have already gone out. It'll look as if we've got something to hide if we cancel. We've got to go through with it. And it's got to be spectacular.'

'OK, OK!'

'Victoria's the only person holding it all together. Ask her if she'll stay. At least until the party. If you won't, then I will. I can't take organizing that on board as well. I'll have a nervous breakdown.'

Life, George decided, was weird. Two weeks ago his ex-wife and girlfriend had been at each other's throats. Now it seemed they were best friends.

'OK,' he sighed. 'But can you ask her? I don't think she's in the mood to do me any favours at the moment. But she thinks the world of you, all of a sudden.'

Fifteen

Just under two weeks later, Bruno sat in his kitchen drinking coffee and looking at the invitation pinned to the cork board.

Lisa, George and Justin
Invite you for cocktails and canapés
to celebrate the launch of
The Rocks Hotel
Mariscombe

The accompanying brochure was on matt cream paper, printed with turquoise and silver ink. 'A chic maritime hotel where you can relax in style,' it read.

> Rediscover your childhood on the beach, paddling in the rock pools and building sandcastles, then trail sand up the stairs to your room, safe in the knowledge that someone else will sweep up after you. Wallow in one of our freestanding baths with their breathtaking views, then feast on seafood in our alfresco dining room. End the day by watching the sun set over the beach while you sip champagne, then collapse into the softness of your feather bed and fall asleep to the sound of the pounding surf.

Bruno felt a stab of envy. He would have to spend millions before the Mariscombe Hotel could offer that sort of ambience. Yet again he felt regret that he hadn't persevered with his bid for The Rocks. He would have enjoyed putting a package like this together; it would have got his creative juices flowing. But then he would have got in the way of Lisa's dream, and he wouldn't have wanted to do that.

Since their conversation a fortnight ago, her words had rung in his head often, and he had determined to stop putting his life on hold. He decided he'd had enough of being a recluse. He'd invited some friends down from London for the weekend, two couples that he used to hang around with when he had dated Serena. They'd all had a great time: the blokes were fiercely competitive about their surfing, while the girls lounged on the beach reading *Heat* and *Hello!* and Marian Keyes. Then Bruno had barbecued whole sea bass on the veranda, whizzing up strawberries in the blender and topping it up with Prosecco for the girls, and chucking the blokes endless bottles of beer.

It had been a carefree weekend, and what cheered Bruno the most was that he had felt no compulsion to follow them back to the city on the Sunday night. He was living the life that was right for him, and if the Mariscombe Hotel was never going to have the chic allure of The Rocks, it was getting there. Frank had done a fantastic job in turning the restaurant around – they were about to embark on a speedy makeover of the dining room that would turn it from old-fashioned and gloomy into airy and modern, hopefully in time for the summer holidays. They'd gradually introduced Frank's revamped menu and the lighter, fresher meals seemed much more popular even with the older guests. Gradually the dreariness of the place was lifting.

And so was Bruno's mood. He was looking forward to the party that evening. He wasn't sure what to wear. He stood in front of the mirror in his best jeans and a tan leather belt, holding up shirts. In the end he went for a sober blue and white stripe, but left it hanging out – it wouldn't do to look too formal. As he did up his buttons, he realized this was the first time he had socialized in Mariscombe for nearly two years, and he wanted to look right. He knew he would be under scrutiny, even if people pretended he wasn't. The invitations themselves had already caused consternation, those who had been summonsed lording it over those who hadn't. So he knew the party would be dissected and discussed ad infinitum. He sighed – such was village life.

As he sloshed Marc Jacobs cologne on to his wrist, he realized he had butterflies. He gave himself a wry grin in the mirror – he really did need to get out more. Once upon a time he'd have been to a launch or a cocktail party or a dinner every night of the week. There was nothing to get excited about.

Lisa lay up to her neck in coconut-scented bubbles and decided that they had been absolutely right to sacrifice the two smaller bedrooms and convert them into bathrooms. This was heaven, lying in an enormous tub that stood in the centre of the room on a small raised platform, looking out at the sea. She had a glass of champagne in her hand and she sipped it slowly. It was the only drink she was going to allow herself until all the guests had gone. She would have gone without altogether but George had insisted on opening a bottle for all of them at four o'clock, so they could enjoy a toast together. The five of them – George, Lisa, Justin, Victoria and Mimi – had stood by the reception desk and clinked glasses, almost unable to believe their surroundings and hoping that this evening's guests would be equally delighted.

The walls shone white as moonbeams. Down the centre of the stairs ran a coir runner held in place by pewter stair-rods. The reception desk was built from an S-shaped concrete curve, the front emblazoned with silver and white mosaic tiles shot through with turquoise. From the centre of the ceiling hung a spectacular chandelier that sparkled and twinkled, offset by recessed lighting installed just above the skirting boards. Muslin embroidered with fine silver thread fluttered at the windows.

Behind the reception desk were chunky driftwood shelves

lined with piles of thick turquoise and white striped beach towels and a row of tin buckets and spades. They gave a humorous edge, reminding the visitor that this was the British seaside, that there was much fun to be had, that the essence of the place was to kick off your shoes and rediscover your childhood. It was an inspired marriage of period and modern, cutting edge but unthreatening; a sense of luxurious calm pervading the atmosphere, but with the occasional witty twist.

There was no doubt it was stunning, but they were all too fraught with nerves to be complacent. The time for congratulation would be after the guests had gone. Lisa had taken her champagne upstairs to enjoy in the bath. She and George had decided to treat themselves to the master suite for the weekend, before the real guests arrived. So they could experience it for themselves, make sure that there was no tiny detail missing.

She had a whole two hours to get ready. Victoria had insisted that she was going to supervise all the party preparations; Lisa had nothing to worry about except herself. For the first time in weeks, she gave herself a top-to-toe pampering, putting on a face mask and a conditioning pack for her hair. When the water was cold, she climbed out of the bath and carefully painted her toenails bright red, reflecting that this routine had once been gone through two or three times a week. And although today it was luxury to take the time to pamper herself, she hadn't missed the rigours of maintaining perfection one little bit.

Lisa was in her dressing gown, waiting for her nails to dry, when there was the faintest rap on the door. She walked gingerly over the carpet, trying not to smudge her varnish, and opened it. Mimi was standing there looking ashen.

'Mimi! Whatever's the matter? Has there been an accident?'

Mimi shook her head.

'No.' She was deathly white under the mass of freckles she'd acquired over the past few weeks. 'I need to talk to you. Can I come in?'

'Of course.' Lisa was perplexed. 'You'll have to excuse me. I'm having a major overhaul. I can't believe that I haven't shaved my legs for over two weeks. You should see the bottom of the bath. It's disgusting.'

Mimi gave a ghost of a smile.

'Sit down.' Lisa pointed to the wicker chair by the window. 'Do you want a drink or anything?'

'No.' Mimi sat obediently. 'I've got a confession to make.' She clasped her hands in her lap. 'I wanted to tell you before we left. Just in case you were still worried. That someone might be out to get you. Because they're not. It was me.'

Lisa stared at her.

'What was?'

'All the cock-ups. And the photos. I sent the photos.' Her little face crumpled. 'I wanted you and George to split up. I wanted him to get back together with Mum.' Tears were spilling down her cheeks and she rubbed her knuckles into her eyes. 'I know it was wrong. I know he belongs with you. And I wanted to say I'm sorry . . .'

The next moment she had broken down completely. Lisa rushed over to her.

'I know he's not my real dad,' Mimi sobbed. 'But he looked after us. He was brilliant. And he's the only person that really knows how to handle Mum. Except me. But she needs more than me. I can't look after her for ever. I just thought . . . If George would have her back . . .'

Lisa scooped her up in a big hug.

'Hey, hey, hey,' she crooned soothingly. 'You don't have to cry. It's all right.'

'It was a horrible thing to do to you. You didn't deserve it.'

'Look, you'd had a really hard time. You probably weren't thinking straight. People do crazy things under stress.' She rubbed Mimi's back comfortingly. 'It was very brave of you to come and tell me. I appreciate it.'

'You won't tell George, will you?'

'Of course not.'

'And . . . you'll look after him for us when we've gone, won't you?' Mimi asked anxiously. 'He's ace.'

Lisa found tears prickling the back of her eyelids.

'Of course I will,' she said softly. 'And you know, any time you want to come and stay, just call me.'

Mimi gave a sniff.

'I better go and get ready,' she declared. 'I'm on canapé duty and if I don't look immaculate Mum will kill me.'

Lisa stood up and realized that in the middle of the drama she'd smudged her toenails.

'Bugger,' she said. 'I'll have to do them again.'

'I'll do them for you,' offered Mimi. 'It's impossible to do your own properly. And I always do Mum's.'

'Thanks.'

Five minutes later George walked in to find Mimi painstakingly applying varnish to Lisa's toes.

'Welcome to the beauty salon!' said Lisa gaily.

Mimi waggled the brush at him.

'Are you next, George?' she asked impishly. 'It's the in thing for men to have their toes painted.'

'No, thanks,' George grinned. 'Red's not my colour. OK if I use the bathroom?'

'Sure,' said Lisa.

A moment later he came out of the bathroom, a look of utter disgust on his face.

'What the hell is that in the bottom of the bath?' he demanded. 'There's hair and stubble and toenail clippings and scum . . .'

'Oops,' said Lisa. 'Sorry . . .'

She caught Mimi's eye and the two of them burst into laughter.

Half an hour later, clad in a pale yellow Irish linen suit, George walked into the drawing room. Victoria was sitting in the retro rattan egg seat that hung from the ceiling, gazing out of the French windows. She was wearing a pair of wide-legged white linen trousers and a navy-and-white striped top with a square neckline; her only jewellery a long string of pearls. She looked very Chanel, very thirties. Almost like a heroine from an Agatha Christie novel, thought George, as he walked across the room towards her. The one who's found strangled by her necklace in the library.

'Are you OK?' he asked.

'Just enjoying a moment's peace before the chaos.'

George checked his watch.

'Half an hour to go. I better go and check the kitchen—'

Victoria put out a hand to stop him.

'No. Don't. Everything's under control. Stay here a moment. I need to talk to you.'

George came and stood by her. She looked up at him, her eyes large and serious. He saw that her knuckles were white on the edge of the chair, where she was clutching it tightly, as if for support.

'Are you sure you're all right?'

She nodded.

'I finally spoke to a solicitor this afternoon. About our divorce.'

'Divorce?' George looked alarmed.

'Don't panic,' she reassured him. 'It's going to be very straightforward. He promised me it could be whizzed through in a matter of weeks, if we're both in agreement.'

George swallowed.

'But we haven't discussed a . . . settlement.'

'There isn't going to be a settlement. I don't want anything from you, Georgie.' She managed a wan smile. 'And if you want anything from me you're out of luck. Maths was never my strong point, but I know half of nothing is nothing.'

'But . . .' George's mind was racing.

'I just wanted you to know, you're going to have a clean slate. I owe it to you. And Lisa. You've both been very good to me.' She smiled up at him. 'You'll be a free man by the end of the summer.'

George looked down at his shoes. There seemed to be a lump in his throat. He tried to clear it.

'Thank you.' It came out as rather a pathetic croak. He coughed again. 'I will always be here for you, if you need me.'

'You've got enough on your plate with this place. It's going to be a huge success, I can feel it in my bones. And Mimi and I will be fine. The only danger will be if I end up killing my mother. Which is quite likely, of course.'

Victoria slipped out of her chair. She put her arms around him and held him to her, holding him tightly as if her life depended on it.

Gardenias. She smelt of gardenias.

Then she let him go. She clapped her hands together briskly, as if to indicate that chapter was closed.

'Right. I'm going to go and give one of my famous pep talks to the waiting staff. Make sure they know exactly how I like things done. And woe betide them if they don't.'

A dazzling smile and she was gone.

George stood at the window looking out at the sea, his hands in his pockets. In the splendour of the drawing room, with the magnificent coastal view, he felt a bit like the Great Gatsby.

He turned and looked at the white sofas, wide and deep and low. The vintage travel posters, framed in black, immaculately lined up on the wall. A phalanx of glass vases stuffed with spiky pink and orange flowers. Towering lamps with feather-trimmed shades that threw pools of soft light. In four days' time the first of their guests would be booking in, coming in here to curl up with a book or a magazine. Had he thought of every eventuality? There were magazine racks with the latest issues of all the glossies – no celebrity tat, if they wanted that they could buy it for themselves. There were playing cards and backgammon, a marble chess set. A supply of already stamped postcards with a photograph of the outlook. Mother of pearl binoculars on the windowsill for spotting birds or checking out the surf. The French windows gave out on to the decking, which was lined with bench seating. Huge square copper planters filled with palms were dotted around, and alternate cream and black parasols blocked out the fiercest sun. Hanging between two trees was a striped hammock. At the end of the garden was a summerhouse, painted in a dusty pink, for romantic encounters on the heap of cushions thoughtfully placed inside.

It was all as close to perfect as he could hope.

A waiter came in with a single glass on a tray, which he presented to George rather obsequiously.

'Would you like to try the cocktail, sir?'

They were serving Sea Breezes as the guests arrived. George took a tentative sip, then nodded.

'Perfect.'

'Thank you, sir.'

George waited until he had left the room, then raised the glass to his lips and drained the rest in one swallow.

Lisa had dried her hair carefully and waxed it so that it fell in perfectly coiled, glossy ringlets, which she piled loosely on top of her head so some of the curls fell down. She swept a shimmering, metallic green powder over her eyelids, curled her lashes and carefully applied a concoction of lip liner and gloss to her mouth. Finally, she slipped on her dress, a white, Grecian-style tunic. The silken fabric was tied in a halter-neck which left her nut-brown back bare, then draped itself tightly over her breasts, falling away in pleats to just above the knee. She bent down to put on her shoes: strappy gold sandals, with laces that tied up her legs.

She stood in front of the mirror, examining herself anxiously. It was so long since she had pulled out the stops, she barely recognized herself. She wondered for a moment if the overall effect was too much, whether she should opt for some less ostentatious footwear to tone herself down. Then she thought no, this was her evening. She deserved to look glamorous.

She looked at her watch. Quarter to six. She slipped out of the room and walked along the corridor, getting used to the sensation of high heels again. She'd been in flip-flops and trainers for so long, it felt alien. It was hard to believe that she used to live in stilettos. She came down the stairs to the hallway. Victoria was standing at the reception desk, fiddling for the millionth time with the huge vase of birds of paradise. She looked so self-assured, as if she belonged here as mistress of the house, the arbiter of good taste in navy and white. For a moment, Lisa panicked. In contrast to Victoria she felt as if she was dressed for a hen party. She was about to rush back to her room and change, when Victoria looked up and spotted her. Her eyes widened in surprise.

'Lisa. You look absolutely stunning!'

Lisa hesitated, her hand on the banister.

'You don't think it's too much?'

'God, no. You look completely gorgeous. Utterly edible. And, anyway, who cares? This is your night.'

Victoria rushed over to the bottom of the staircase as Lisa walked down the last few stairs self-consciously.

'That dress is divine. You look like a goddess.'

'You look lovely too.' A little over-awed by the compliments, Lisa felt obliged to return them. But Victoria didn't seem to need reassurance. She took Lisa by both hands as she reached the bottom of the stairs.

'This place is going to be fantastic. You know that, don't you?'

'I hope so.'

'You and George have got it absolutely right. It's going to be a massive success. And I just want to say . . .'

For a moment, Victoria looked rather tearful.

'I really appreciate how good you've been to me and Mimi. There aren't many women who would have put up with the situation.'

The two women embraced. As she hugged Victoria, Lisa realized that she had become almost fond of her. That she might actually miss her. That she almost, but not quite, thought of her as a friend.

George came out of the office and into the hallway and stopped dead in his tracks at the sight of Lisa and Victoria in each other's arms at the bottom of the stairs. His heart was in his mouth as he looked at the pair of them. Lisa, shimmering, radiant and voluptuous. Victoria, elegant, aloof and serene.

Justin loped in through the front door, wearing rolled-up jeans, a white Aertex and espadrilles. Lisa giggled.

'Glad to see you've made an effort, Justin,' she teased, knowing he wouldn't be offended. He was known for underdressing.

'Well,' he said cheerfully. 'This is it. The moment of truth. And by the way, there's someone I'd like you to meet.'

A tall figure stepped into the hall behind him, with a breathtaking cloud of blond ringlets, golden skin and a cherubic mouth.

'This is Joel. He's been teaching me to surf,' said Justin lightly, taking Joel's arm.

'Hi, guys,' said Joel, revealing his Antipodean origins and a row of pearly white teeth.

'Hi,' the three of them chorused back, as Justin smiled proudly, giving the faintest of winks as he met Victoria's astonished gaze.

At the Mariscombe Hotel, Molly was doing the late-afternoon shift. Tidying the rooms and turning down the beds; making them again if necessary because guests often had an afternoon nap. Emptying the bins, wiping the basins and loos, polishing the taps. She was just puffing up the pillows when her mobile phone vibrated in the pocket of her overall. Staff weren't supposed to have their mobiles with them while they worked, but Molly kept hers on in case there was a problem with Alfie. She pulled it out, frowning. It was number withheld.

'Hello?' she said cautiously.

'Molly?' The voice was rough. 'It's Cal.'

Cal. Cal was one of her sister's circle of friends. He was rough, but kind, a big, ugly brute of a man with dodgy connections and a heart of gold. He had a soft spot for Molly, and she knew that if she had ever wanted to succumb to his advances he would look after her and Alfie. But Cal wasn't her type. Not that she had a type . . .

'What do you want?' She didn't mean to sound brusque, but she prayed he wasn't going to try and ask her out. She didn't want to hurt his feelings.

'I've had a tip-off. From a mate. The DS are going to raid your place.'

'DS?' For a moment Molly wasn't with him.

'The Drug Squad. They reckon Zen might be stashing his gear there.'

'Gear?' Molly realized she sounded stupid as soon as she said it. Of course Zen was a dealer. Not just a user. Why hadn't she clocked it before? It would explain the cash Siobhan sometimes flashed around, why she never felt the need to get a proper job but somehow always had the latest skirt, the latest boots, the latest phone.

'Get yourself and Alfie out of there, love.' Cal's tone was urgent. 'If they find any stuff, it might mean they'll take the baby off you.'

'How do you know all this?' Again, Molly knew she sounded sharp but she was frightened.

'Contacts. And for Christ's sake don't tell anyone I told you, or I'll be found in the bottom of the harbour. Bleeding fish food.'

'Thanks, Cal.'

But the phone was already dead. Molly thrust it back into her pocket with trembling hands. She had to get home. She tore along the corridor and down the stairs, two at a time, no time to wait for the lift. Hannah was at the reception desk. She looked up, startled, as Molly pounded across the hall, wild-eyed.

'Hannah – I've got to go. It's an emergency. Can you get someone to do my rooms for me?'

'Sure. Molly – what's happened?'

'Family crisis.' Molly pulled off her overall and as good as threw it at a speechless Hannah. Then she flew out of the door, fumbling for her purse to see if she'd got enough for a taxi. By the time the bus got to Tawcombe the whole place could have been turned over. She had a fiver and some change. Probably just enough. She felt panic rise up in her chest. Stay calm, she told herself as she pulled open the door of the taxi at the front of the rank and hurled herself into the front seat.

'Uffculme Road, Tawcombe, please. And can you be as quick as you can. My baby . . .' She trailed off, not sure what to say. 'My baby's ill,' she finished definitely, praying that it wasn't tempting fate to lie like this. But it seemed to do the trick, as the driver fired up the engine and pulled away, scattering disgruntled tourists in his wake.

It was five to six. Everyone was quiet with nerves. A waiter passed through carrying a tray loaded with gleaming glasses, a waitress following in his wake with two jugs; the only sound was the clinking of the ice cubes. As they watched anxiously out of the window, a car pulled in, cautiously at first, then commandeered a parking space by the front door. A bearded man emerged, scanning the front of the hotel curiously before making his way in through the front door.

He held out his invitation.

'Christopher Tate. From the Tourist Office?'

For a moment there was silence as everyone stared. Then George stepped forward, holding out a welcoming hand with a broad smile.

'Welcome to The Rocks.'

Sixteen

As the taxi pulled up outside her house, Molly fought back tears, scrabbling for the fare.

'Seven pounds eighty, love.'

Shit. She didn't have enough. She thrust her fiver at him, choking back a sob as she shook out her change.

'Hang on . . .'

'It's all right, love.' The taxi driver could see she was distraught. 'You go and find your little one.'

Molly didn't have time to be grateful. She jumped out of the car, slammed the door and ran up the steps. She felt sure she was in time. If anything had happened, if there had been a raid, the pavements would be full of rubberneckers gawping at someone else's misfortune. Raids and arrests were what counted as street entertainment in Tawcombe.

The drawing room, the dining room and the reception area of The Rocks were bursting at the seams. Waiters and waitresses glided amongst the guests, bearing oversized white platters stuffed with tantalizing nibbles inspired by the seaside – scallops wrapped in bacon, tiny Devon pasties filled with lamb and potato, coriander-flecked crab cakes, crispy goujons of sole served with big fat chips studded with sea salt for dipping into glistening pools of aioli, mini cups of chowder. Greedy hands reached out repeatedly and lips were licked as the delicious morsels were washed down with a never-ending supply of cocktails and champagne. The walls reverberated with chat and laughter, against a background of specially chosen music: 'Here Comes the Summer' by the Undertones, 'Echo Beach' by Martha and the Muffins, 'Rock Lobster' by the B52s – sounds redolent of summer, the seaside, holidays, sunshine.

'Much as I hate to admit it,' said Justin, lounging in the door of the French windows, 'you know how to throw a good party.'

Victoria smiled.

'I know. And by the way, congratulations.'

Justin looked momentarily sheepish.

'I decided it was hypocritical of me to slag you off, when I wasn't being honest with anyone either. You always were too observant for your own good.'

Victoria glanced over at Joel, who was deep in conversation with a dark-haired man in a blue and white shirt.

'Well, I must say he's completely divine. I wish I'd seen him first.'

'You're not his type, darling.'

'He would be by the time I'd finished with him,' Victoria twinkled, and wound an arm round Justin's scrawny neck. 'Truce?'

Justin kissed her cheek.

'Truce.'

Victoria looked thoughtfully back over to Joel.

'Who's he talking to?'

'That's the legendary Bruno Thorne,' said Justin. 'But I'm not worried. He's a hundred per cent heterosexual.'

'Good,' replied Victoria.

She plucked two full glasses of champagne off the tray of a passing waiter and glided across the room until she reached Bruno and Joel.

'Justin's looking for you, darling,' she purred to Joel, then turned to Bruno with a dazzling smile. 'And I'd like to introduce myself. I'm Victoria Snow.'

And with that, she handed him a glass of champagne.

*

Molly unlocked the door to her flat cautiously, almost bracing herself to be pounced on by uniformed officers. Inside it was eerily silent. Perhaps they'd taken Alfie to the park? But no . . .

She spotted Siobhan immediately, crashed out on the floor. Zen was sprawled on the sofa. For an awful moment she thought they were dead. But then the acrid scent reached her nostrils and she realized they were just out of it. God knows what they'd been doing. Molly wasn't interested in drugs, but she sensed this wasn't just a recreational mid-afternoon spliff. The air hung heavy with not just decadence but desperation. These two had reached the end of the line.

Hot fear pooled in her stomach as she ran past them, to be replaced by sweet relief as she saw Alfie fast asleep in his cot. How the hell could her own sister do this? Be more worried about her own gratification than the welfare of her nephew? Molly knew Siobhan was a waster, but she'd thought she could trust her to look after Alfie. But then, under the influence of Zen and whatever it was they'd been smoking . . . Molly knew enough about drugs to know they induced self-absorption and a total disregard for anyone else's needs.

She picked Alfie up carefully so as not to wake him, and cuddled him to her. He snuggled into her shoulder sleepily. Her heart contracted simultaneously with love and fear. What the hell was she supposed to do now? She knew she had to get out because of Cal's warning – she couldn't risk it being an empty threat or a false alarm.

The only person she could think of to turn to was Hannah. Hannah had always been kind to her; Hannah had common sense too. And although it would be risky bringing Alfie to the hotel, Molly was desperate. She'd think of a good cover-up. No one would suspect the truth, after all, as it was too far-fetched.

Swiftly she packed up their things: nappies and babygros and a packet of wipes, jeans, underwear and a couple of tops – stuffing them all into a big carrier bag with sturdy handles.

Then she stood in the middle of her room, her heart hammering. Should she wake up Siobhan and Zen, warn them? Siobhan was her sister. She didn't want to see her banged up. Then she remembered that Siobhan had been quite happy to neglect Alfie. The fact that Molly had been able to sneak in the way she had proved that anything could have happened and the two of them would have been oblivious. If they got done, that was their problem. She had to look after herself first.

She pulled Alfie's blanket out of the cot and wrapped it round him. It was a warm evening, but she didn't want to disturb him by going out into the fresh air. If she kept him wrapped up, he would stay asleep. As she tiptoed out of the flat, she saw Zen's denim jacket slung over the arm of the settee. His wallet was poking out of the pocket.

Should she?

Molly had never stolen anything ever in her life. But as she stood there, she reasoned that whatever lay in Zen's wallet was ill-gotten gains. And she thought of all the times she'd cooked them tea, or gone to get chips, without any thanks or ever being repaid. Carefully she laid down her bag, pulled out the wallet, whipped out the wad of cash and hastily replaced it – a difficult manoeuvre with a heavy toddler in her arms, but she was used to doing things with one hand.

Shit – Alfie was waking up, disturbed by the movement.

'Mumma?'

Please don't let them wake, she thought desperately. She rammed the cash in her pocket, picked up the bag and left. By some miracle, the cab driver who had dropped her off earlier was making his way back down the other side of the street. She waved at him frantically.

'I've got enough money to pay you now.' She bent in through the driver's window as he slowed down. 'Can you take me back to Mariscombe?'

*

Halfway through the evening, there were groans of delight as 99s were handed out; cornets filled with the super-sweet swirl of soft ice cream garnished with a Flake. It was a salutary reminder, thought George, of how clever Victoria was, playing on nostalgia to seduce her audience. He looked for her amongst the crowds, wanting to thank her. The party was a resounding success, and he doubted he could have pulled it off. She had done her homework on the guest list, researching who the local bigwigs were on the council and the tourist board, sniffing out celebrities who had second homes nearby, as well as local artists and musicians. And, of course, the press. Added to which, she'd asked local restaurateurs and hoteliers – anyone who might have felt threatened by their opening – so they could see exactly what they were up against and therefore prevent idle speculation. And Leonard Carrington, the biggest mouth in Mariscombe. It made for an eclectic mix that, had she not been so good at her job, might have been hard to gel. But George had a feeling they weren't going to get rid of this crowd before midnight.

She was standing by the window, deep in conversation with a striking-looking man with dark curls. From her gesticulations, they seemed to be talking about the hotel, but the way their eyes were locked, the way they each had a smile playing around their lips, there was obviously some subtext going on. George worked out, via a process of elimination, that this must be Bruno Thorne. For some reason, he felt a hideous curdling in his stomach; a sensation that was both icy cold and searingly hot, that bubbled up and hit him in the back of the throat. He thought for a moment that he was about to be sick, then realized that what he was feeling was jealousy, that the liquid in his gullet was deep green and poisonous.

They looked fabulous together. She was shimmering and golden and delicate; he was dark and strong and magnetic. Of course they would make a fairy-tale couple. He had wealth and standing; she talent and beauty. He would be able to give her opportunities. George could just imagine her leaping on to the infamous helicopter, the two of them flying off somewhere. The jetset lifestyle.

George tried to tell himself that at least that would be the end of his problems, that he wouldn't need to feel guilty any more. Then he plucked another Sea Breeze from the tray of a passing waitress and knocked it back.

Lisa came through into the drawing room from the hall, then stopped in her tracks. Framed against the setting sun were Bruno's dark head and Victoria's golden one, as he whispered something in her ear. She laughed in response, and a flash of complicity sparked between them. No one who saw them could fail to notice the attraction. The air round them was pulsating with sexual tension.

Lisa felt her throat tighten inexplicably. Her mouth felt dry; she couldn't swallow. What was the matter with her? She grabbed a glass from a passing waiter and gulped thirstily.

Hannah had just finished packing her suitcase. She'd only packed comfy clothes, because she planned to go and stay on her parents' farm after the operation in order to recuperate. She'd thought about it long and hard. She could have checked in somewhere, put herself in isolation for a week while the bruises faded. But she didn't see the point in forking out when she had a perfectly good bedroom at home, and fresh air and her mum's home cooking.

Her parents would be shocked at first, she knew that. She'd decided not to tell them about the operation before-hand, because she was afraid they would be upset, and would ask her so many bewildered questions that she might bottle out. After all, she knew that they loved her unconditionally, that when they looked at her they saw a loving daughter, and didn't notice her nose. And if they knew the truth about the misery she'd learned to hide, the anguish, they would be devastated. And guilty.

Her mother was the least vain person she knew. She had

been forty-two when she had Hannah, and thus well into her fifties by the time Hannah became aware of her own looks. By which time her mother's hair was thick, wiry and iron grey, her complexion ruddy from being outside, her figure bulky from a lifetime of cooked breakfasts, meat and two veg and proper puddings, full-fat milk and clotted cream. Hannah didn't think she bothered to look in a mirror from one day to the next, which was why she would be so perplexed, so horrified, at the thought of her own daughter having plastic surgery.

If she turned up with it as a fait accompli, she would still have to explain her motives, but the deed would be done. And she hoped they would understand, especially when they saw the transformation. Her stomach gave a flutter as she remembered the computerized image of herself with her new nose. Not Kate Moss obviously. But not a beaky freak.

She left the lid of her case open and her sponge bag just inside, waiting for her to pop her toothbrush and toothpaste in the next morning. Suddenly there was an urgent knock on the door. She hurried to open it.

Her mouth fell open as she saw Molly standing outside her room, her face streaked with tears, laden with bags and a small boy in her arms.

'I didn't know where else to go,' she sniffed. 'Let me in quickly, before someone sees.'

Hannah stood to one side as Molly squeezed past her.

'Molly . . .' she looked aghast. 'You haven't . . . kidnapped him or anything?'

'Of course not.' Molly sat the toddler on Hannah's bed and stood up straight. 'This is Alfie. He's my son. My little boy.'

George took up his position by the fireplace and tinged the edge of his glass to call for attention.

Everyone crowded into the drawing room, looking at him expectantly. He looked incredibly debonair. Apart from a couple of men from the council, he was almost the only person wearing a suit, but because it was loose, despite being impeccably tailored, he didn't look overdressed. His cocktail glass hung between his fingers as he smiled around the room.

'I just want to say a few words, to mark this evening. Firstly, thanks to all of you for coming. I'm afraid we've been up to our necks in dust and paint for the past few weeks, but I'm looking forward to starting a social life, and hope we'll be seeing more of you over the summer. Secondly, a huge thank you to Victoria Snow, who organized this party. If it had been down to me it would have been lukewarm Sangria and sausages on sticks, but Victoria knows me only too well and thankfully took over. So a big round of applause, please.'

He pointed his glass towards Victoria, who gave a gracious nod in response to the enthusiastic clapping that followed his vote of thanks. He held her gaze for a moment before carrying on.

'When Lisa first suggested to me that we buy this place, I laughed at her. I told her that everyone in the country dreams of running a hotel by the sea; that it's the ultimate escapist cliché. But she asked me one very good question. Why should that stop us? For that reason, there is something very important I have to say. Apart, of course, from welcoming all of you to The Rocks.'

He paused for a moment, his eyes scanning the room until he found Lisa, and he smiled.

'I want to say to Lisa: thank you for helping me realize my dream. There is no way I could have done it without you. You're the one who squashed all my fears, ignored all my objections, found solutions to every problem. Who got her hands dirty when I was faffing about choosing paint colours and doorknobs. Whose grit and determination is what lies beneath everything you see here. Without her, none of this would be possible.'

He paused to take a breath and a quick slug of his cocktail. His throat felt dry.

'And that's why I thought this was the appropriate moment to say not just thank you to Lisa, but . . . will you marry me?'

Lisa felt as if time was standing still. She stood rooted to the spot, conscious of a roomful of eyes upon her.

What on earth was she supposed to say?

Even though she had made a huge commitment to George, and to all intents and purposes they were in it for the duration, she just wasn't the marrying kind. The idea of it filled her with dread. Maybe it was an irrational fear. A phobia she had developed because of what she had suffered. Marriage was the last thing on earth she wanted. Ever.

But how could she reject him in front of a room full of people who were eagerly anticipating her reply? She couldn't even begin to explain how she felt. She'd have to accept, at least for the time being, because to refuse would create such consternation. It would turn a hugely successful evening into an unmitigated disaster; everyone was holding their breath waiting for her response.

She would have to let George down later, tell him that on reflection it wasn't right, it wasn't what she wanted. After all, he'd been rather unfair, springing a proposal on her in front of an audience, leaving her with little choice but to say yes.

She smiled her widest, most professional, most charming smile.

'Of course I will,' she replied, and the room burst into rapturous applause.

Seventeen

'Bloody hell!' Hannah gazed at the sleeping child in amazement. They'd tucked him into Hannah's bed and given him a cup of milk. He'd gone off to sleep quite happily. 'So this is why you never come out with us. We all thought you were having an affair with a married man or something. You've always been such a dark horse.'

'Well, now you know.' Molly gave a crooked smile.

Hannah frowned. 'But why did you keep him a secret? I mean, having a baby's not a crime, is it? No one would mind. You should have said, Moll. I mean, I'd have helped you out if I'd known. No wonder you were so knackered all the time. No wonder you looked ill. I would have babysat for you—'

'Hannah . . .' Molly's chin was trembling. 'It's not that simple.' She looked at Hannah, her eyes enormous in her heart-shaped face, which was white with anxiety. 'I just need to stay here the night, if you'll let me. But nobody else must know I'm here.'

'Why not?' An awful thought occurred to Hannah. 'He's not beating you, is he? The dad?'

'No.'

Molly was so definite that Hannah was reassured.

'His dad's not around,' Molly went on. 'Which is why it's been so tough, working here. I've had to bring him up on my own. It's been a nightmare, Hannah. A real struggle. And I don't know if . . . if I can cope any more . . .'

Molly had never come close to admitting defeat before, but she couldn't pretend any longer. Suddenly she seemed to deflate, sitting down on Hannah's bed, her head in her hands, her thin shoulders shuddering with a lifetime of tears that were suddenly unleashed. She desperately tried to contain her sobs, as she didn't want to wake Alfie, but the more she tried to suppress them the more determined they were to escape, until she found herself positively howling.

Hannah very wisely didn't press for any more answers. She sat on the bed next to Molly, wrapped her arms around her minuscule frame and held very tight until the crying subsided. Gently she stroked her hair, rocking her.

'You shouldn't have to cope on your own,' she whispered. 'You've got rights, Molly. Haven't you heard of the Child Support Agency? You should let the father face up to his responsibility. They'll backdate it, as well. You'll get money from right back when Alfie was born . . .'

She looked at Molly, who was looking at her doubtfully. Hannah sighed inwardly. She suspected it was going to be a difficult job persuading her.

You've got to get tough, Molly. Not just for your sake. For Alfie's. You don't have to contact him yourself, if you don't want to. They do it all for you. But you shouldn't have to struggle. It takes two, remember?'

Molly shook her head. Hannah grabbed her by the arms, as if to shake her.

'Don't be frightened,' she said urgently. 'It's your *right*.'

'There's just one problem,' Molly replied, matter-of-factly. 'His father's dead.'

Hannah's mouth fell open.

Molly closed her eyes. She felt so weary. All she wanted to do was to fall into a deep, dreamless sleep, so she could be free from her troubles. But somehow she knew that the time had come to share her secrets. That if she was to find a way out of the mess she was in, she had to confide in someone. And she knew Hannah well enough to know that she trusted her. Hannah was calm and sensible. Hannah would know what to do.

'Darling,' murmured Victoria in George's ear. 'What an absolutely wonderful stunt. I wish I'd thought of it. You had the whole room eating out of your hand. They positively swooned with the romance of it all. Very clever.' She leaned forward to kiss him. 'And by the way, congratulations.'

George felt her hair tickle his cheek, then the warmth of her lips.

'Thank you.'

The energy levels in the room had moved up yet another gear after Lisa had accepted his proposal. Champagne had appeared as if from nowhere; guests he didn't know from Adam had toasted and congratulated him. Lisa was in the middle of the melee, laughing, glowing, accepting kisses from total strangers. She looked more radiant than ever, as if she had been lit up from within. Victoria was right. There was no way people wouldn't leave this party and go on to talk about it. As a way of grabbing the limelight, it took some beating.

But that wasn't why he had done it.

Victoria was bidding him farewell.

'I'll see you in the morning.'

The guests were leaving in dribs and drabs, clutching their tin goodie buckets, which Victoria had filled with seaside nonsense. A stick of Mariscombe rock, a copy of *Five Go Down to the Sea*, a bottle of suntan lotion, a pair of child's Lolita sunglasses, a bag of pink, sugary candy shrimps. Clever, witty, stylish . . .

George watched as she drifted over to Bruno's side. He had clearly been waiting for her. The two of them slipped out amongst a gaggle of chattering, inebriated guests. Typical Victoria, to slither away when the hard work was about to start. The unglamorous, thankless bit. But, as she was always quick to point out, she didn't do washing-up.

It had been the only answer. Absolutely the only way to get Victoria out of his system. By betrothing himself to Lisa, he had put up an impenetrable barrier that would protect him from her once and for all. Otherwise, Victoria would have carried on haunting him. He might have been tempted. Correction: he *would* have been tempted. Just seeing her with Bruno had made him candescent with fury inside. While he was engaged to Lisa, he was safe. It was like a spell, a magic spell that would save him from himself.

Besides, he told himself, it was the right and proper thing to do. After all, he and Lisa would be under the same roof, sharing the same bed, for many years to come. It made sense to make it official. And he did love her. He felt a glow of pride at the thought of having her as his wife. Added to which, there was another thought at the very back of his mind, the thought that Mariscombe would be a wonderful place, a very wonderful place, to bring up children . . .

George watched as Victoria and Bruno walked across the drive. He saw her slide into the front seat of his car, then they exchanged a few words and a smile, before the car swept out of the driveway.

In the end, Molly told Hannah everything. She was too tired to work out what to leave out.

'Joe Thorne,' breathed Hannah in amazement. 'He's a legend. People still talk about him. But I don't get how you managed to keep it a secret.'

'You never met Joe,' said Molly wryly. 'If you had, you'd never believe he would bother with someone like me. Joe could have anyone he wanted.'

'You poor, poor thing.' Hannah couldn't take it all in. 'Did you . . . did you love him?'

'Love?' Molly was brusque. 'I thought I did. Till I had Alfie. And now I know what love really means.'

She turned to look at Alfie, who was sprawled on his back, long lashes curved over his cheeks. Hannah reached out a hand in wonder to stroke the back of his hand and his fingers twitched in his sleep at the contact.

'You've got to tell Bruno,' she said.

'No.' Molly sprang to her feet, her eyes blazing. 'Hannah – you don't understand. They mustn't find out. They'll blame me . . . they'll blame me for his death.'

'How? Why? I still don't understand why you had to keep it a secret. I mean, we're not living in Victorian times. No one can throw you in the workhouse.'

Molly was silent for a moment. There was just one bit of the story she'd left out. A rather crucial detail. It was weighing like a huge stone on her conscience. Sometimes she couldn't breathe with the pressure of it. Maybe to share it would ease the burden just a little. To tell someone else would be such a relief, even if it merely confirmed her belief that she'd done something dreadful. She took a deep breath in.

'After I saw Joe with Tamara that afternoon, I didn't just tell him we were finished.' This was the story she'd given Hannah. 'I told him I'd had an abortion.' Tears began streaming down her face. 'That's why he drove off the cliff, Hannah. Because I told him I'd killed our baby. It's my fault he died. It's my fault . . .'

Hannah hugged Molly, trying to make sense of what she'd just told her. Privately, she was shocked by the horror of it all. The way two young people had played with each other's lives until one of them had died. But Molly was still alive. Molly and Alfie. She had to do her best to get Molly to see sense; salvage what she could of the situation.

'Molly – you weren't to know what he was going to do. He'd treated you like dirt. Anyone might have done what you did to teach him a lesson. Anyway, he was drunk. He'd had a massive row with Bruno. It all came out at the inquest. It wasn't just because of what you'd done.' Hannah had heard the story a thousand times. It was legend in Mariscombe. And no matter how many different versions you heard, there was one thing that remained constant: Joe was crazy, a loser. Hannah didn't say it, but she felt certain that the story wouldn't have had any prettier an ending if Joe had lived.

'Anyway,' said Molly, sniffing hard. 'That doesn't matter

now. Thanks to my useless family, I'm homeless.' She fell back on the bed, looking up at the ceiling in disbelief. 'How do you manage to live such a normal, sane existence, Hannah? I don't know how I drew so many short straws.'

'You've got a very beautiful baby,' said Hannah softly.

Molly sat up suddenly.

'Yes,' she said. 'You're right. And, actually, he's all that matters.'

There was a small pause.

'Which is why I still think you should tell Bruno,' said Hannah.

Victoria lay on the zebra-skin rug, feeling Bruno's six-o'clock shadow brushing against her thighs.

Bruno heard her take a sharp breath in; felt her fingers raking through his curls, her muscles tense.

He smiled. That was the art. Starting and stopping. Teasing. Prolonging the agony. It made for a more powerful crescendo in the long run.

He moved up her body, kissing her, his lips still bearing her scent. By the time he got to her mouth, she would be begging. Only then would he give in to her pleas. Only then would he give her himself.

He was level with her eyes. But she wouldn't meet his gaze. She was away on her own journey somewhere. She didn't seem to want to share the experience. Maybe looking at him would imply some sort of commitment; perhaps it was a level of intimacy she didn't want to go to.

Suddenly, he found his appetite had gone. The idea of screwing Victoria suddenly seemed sordid, whereas moments ago it had been a wild need. She was leaving the day after tomorrow, she'd told him that earlier. Why the hell was he indulging in a one-night stand? Sex meant more to Bruno than just physical contact. He had to be emotionally engaged. Was he emotionally engaged with Victoria? Absolutely, definitely not. He thought she was stunning, sexy, witty . . . but he didn't think for a second that she was after anything meaningful.

She looked up at him, confused by his hesitation.

'Sorry,' he said softly. 'I don't think I can.'

'It's OK,' she said, a dullness in her tone.

Outside, the moon gazed through the glass at them, an eerie silver disc.

'I think I'll go,' said Victoria.

'I'll drive you back.'

'No.' She pulled her sweater back over her head. 'I could do with a walk.'

Her head was held proudly. Bruno felt guilty.

'It's not you,' he said gently. 'It's me.'

'Sure.' She managed to say it without a trace of bitterness.

Hannah pulled her duvet up the bed and tucked it firmly around Molly and Alfie. The two of them were snuggled in together, fast asleep at last, looking more like brother and sister than mother and son. In the end, Hannah had persuaded her that what she needed was a good night's sleep, that things would make more sense in the morning, and Molly had agreed. She'd fallen asleep within seconds.

Hannah herself was exhausted, yet felt wide awake. She'd made up a bed for herself on the floor with a sleeping bag and a spare pillow. As she tried to get comfy, Molly's revelations whirled round and round in her head as she tried to find a solution. As well as that, she was beginning to feel butterflies over her impending operation. She shut her eyes but her brain was whizzing at a million miles an hour, leaping from one subject to the next. She decided she'd go to the kitchen and make herself some hot milk to help her sleep.

Frank was standing at the sink drinking a glass of water, wearing nothing but a pair of white boxer shorts. His back was a mass of scratches.

'What have you done to your back?' Hannah was horrified.

'I got thrown off my surfboard,' Frank replied quickly. 'Should have had my wetsuit on.'

Hannah looked at the marks doubtfully. They looked like fingernail marks to her.

'You should put some antiseptic on. You don't want them going nasty.'

She went over to the first-aid box and pulled out a tube of Savlon.

'Come here. Turn round.'

Frank turned his back to her obediently as she squeezed out some of the soothing cream and rubbed it gently into his skin. It was like running her hands over a sculpture, the muscles chiselled out by a master craftsman. She could feel each sinew, each tendon, each knot under her fingers. Each scratch was like a blemish on a marble statue. It was sacrilege. This must be Caragh's handiwork, thought Hannah. How could she inflict such damage upon him? How could she want to rip apart his smooth golden skin? If he was hers, thought Hannah, she would want to kiss and caress every glorious inch of him.

Frank gave a little groan of appreciation.

'That feels great. Don't stop.'

'Why do you let her do it?'

Immediately she felt Frank's muscles tense underneath her fingertips.

'Who? What?'

'Caragh. Why do you let her hurt you?'

Frank moved away from her suddenly.

'I told you. I fell off my surfboard. Thanks for the cream. I'll . . . see you tomorrow.'

He strode out of the room. Hannah watched after him longingly, admiring his broad shoulders, his slender waist. He deserved to be worshipped, not mauled.

Victoria stood at the water's edge, her trousers rolled up to her knees, her shoes in her hand. She wondered about walking in. Walking and walking and walking until the waves closed over her head. Someone had once told her drowning wasn't all that painful; that once you had made up your mind to succumb . . .

She kicked at the water petulantly. Who was she trying to kid, making some kind of melodramatic gesture? For a start, she was too much of a coward. Secondly, she didn't like the thought of a bloated corpse. And thirdly, she thought self-pityingly, who would the gesture be *for*? Who would care?

Actually, she couldn't afford the luxury of the last objection, because obviously Mimi would care. Very much. Which was why her mawkish wallowing was totally pointless. And there was a fourth snag, which was that her three-hundred pound Nicole Farhi linen trousers wouldn't take kindly to sea water, and if she failed in her bid to drown herself she would have ruined one of the key items in her wardrobe, and she couldn't afford to abuse her garments any longer. Once a red-wine stain or a tiny tear would have meant relegation to the bin or the charity shop. Now she was having to *manage* her wardrobe.

She reflected that in the few weeks she had been in Mariscombe she had changed. She admitted to herself that subconsciously she had arrived with all intentions of wooing George back. The moment she set eyes on him she knew it was within her powers. But as the days evolved, she realized that it would be wrong, that to manipulate things to her own ends might have meant her getting her own way, but it would have been no guarantee of happiness. Not her own, not George's – and certainly not Lisa's.

Victoria had gone from being dismissive of Lisa, regarding her as a minor inconvenience to be disposed of, to admiring her very much. And she didn't mind admitting that she was envious of Lisa's sunny nature, her ability to get people to do things for her by being *nice* – Lisa would never be manipulative like Victoria, or throw a complete tantrum if things didn't go her way. She could, she decided, do worse than take a leaf out of Lisa's book in future.

She sighed. Resolutions were all very well, but she was frightened. Frightened of a future where she had only herself to depend on, frightened of rebuilding a relationship with her parents – that was going to be weird. But in a funny way she was looking forward to it. She had been amazed when her mother had acquiesced almost immediately. Why, after all these years, were she and Mimi suddenly welcome? Perhaps it was because her mother and father were getting older and realizing their mortality, realizing they had a chance to rectify mistakes before it was too late.

Too late. Victoria gazed at the moon dancing on the water and hoped that *she* hadn't left it too late, to rebuild a life for herself and Mimi that wasn't based on self-gratification and cheap thrills. She wanted, desperately, a life that meant something. Watching George and Lisa tonight had taught her a huge lesson. They had built something together, they had had a dream and made it reality because of the strength of their convictions and their belief in each other. Which was why they had everything and she had . . . nothing. Her entire life up until now had been superficial, meaningless and destructive.

She turned and looked back at Bruno's house. She'd been clutching at straws earlier that evening, hoping for one wild moment that he might be the answer, that he might give her the chance to stay in Mariscombe. But she realized now that she had to make her own way. Victoria was keenly aware that it wasn't just a question of pinpointing where she had gone wrong up until now – she had a long and painful journey ahead of her.

She breathed the salty night air in deeply, summoning up her strength, trying to fill herself with hope rather than fear, anticipation rather than dread. It was going to be all right, she promised herself. She had her parents, she had Mimi, she still had her skills and talents – tonight's success had reassured her of that. She would survive.

There was only one tiny thing niggling at her, a minute worry in the back of her mind, but she batted it away. It would probably come to nothing and if it did – well, she had dealt with it before and she could deal with it again.

As Bruno went to close the veranda door before going to bed, he saw Victoria standing on the beach in the moonlight, looking out at the ocean. She looked so still and small and alone; he could sense her dejection even from a distance. For a moment he felt a trickle of fear. Had he misjudged the effect his rejection had had on her? He knew bloody well what a magical pull the sea had when you were feeling down and alone. Almost as strong as the lift it could give you when the sun was bright and your spirits were high. People often underestimated the power it had on your mood. They didn't always appreciate that it could evoke melancholy as well as euphoria.

He put his hand on the door handle, about to rush down the steps and reassure her, when she turned and walked back along the beach. Her shoulders were back, her head was high and she was swinging her shoes in her hand – she seemed carefree and confident. Relieved, Bruno turned the key in the lock.

Minutes later, as he slid between the sheets, he felt glad that he was alone. He knew for sure that he and Victoria could have shared a night of wild passion, but his gut had told him that it wouldn't have been no-strings, that something wasn't quite right. Was it something in her or in him that had set off a warning signal?

As he drifted off to sleep, he told himself not to kid himself. He knew precisely why he'd brought Victoria back. She was a displacement, a knee-jerk reaction, an antidote to the rather ungentlemanly envy he had felt when George had proposed to Lisa, and she had accepted . . .

*

George and Lisa lay on the cushions in the little summer-house that perched at the end of the garden overlooking the cliff. A bottle of champagne and two glasses sat on the floor beside them.

'I'm just sorry I didn't have a ring.' George was anxious, realizing his faux pas.

'That doesn't matter,' Lisa reassured him. 'It's only a bit of old metal. It doesn't *mean* anything.'

'That's not what most women think. Most women look upon the engagement ring as an exact measure of how much they are loved.' George knew this from experience.

'Well, maybe I'm not most women.' Lisa lay back on the cushions. She looked amazing, her hair wild and unruly, her eyes sparkling.

She'd decided not to say anything just yet. It seemed rather unkind, to tell him straightaway that she had merely stage-managed her acceptance, that she had no intention of marrying him. There would be plenty of time for them to discuss their future together more seriously, once they had come down from the high of the evening. The euphoria of its success was making her blood fizz in her veins. She stretched her arms over her head, her full lips curled upwards in a wicked, teasing smile of invitation. George needed no further encouragement. He leaned over and undid the clasp at the back of her neck, gently sliding the silk fabric down.

The two of them fell back together on the cushions, limbs entwined, kissing passionately as the cool night air caressed their limbs.

Neither of them noticed Victoria emerge from the top of the cliff path, slip silently past the summerhouse and in through the French windows.

Eighteen

The next morning, Molly awoke with a start, bathed in sweat, her heart hammering. Alfie was snuggled up in the crook of her arm, dead to the world. It was his proximity that had made her so hot; the two of them were stuck together. Gently she edged away from him, anxious not to wake him just yet.

She looked around the room, confused for a moment, then the memory of last night came back to her as she saw Hannah curled up on the floor in a sleeping bag. She sat on the edge of the bed. She could just about make out the hands of Hannah's watch on her wrist – it was quarter past five. Outside it was dawn, the already blue sky signalling yet another beautiful day. But Molly didn't have time to admire the weather. She had decisions to make, and fast.

Why the hell had she broken down like that last night and told Hannah everything? It had been a huge, huge mistake, Molly decided now. The momentary relief of sharing the truth, of finally confessing, wasn't worth the panic she was now feeling. The secret she had kept for so long was out. And she couldn't get it back in. You couldn't untell a secret.

Not that Molly didn't trust Hannah. She would never have confided in her if she hadn't. But she'd let her guard down now. Confiding in Hannah meant she was vulnerable. And Hannah had been so adamant that she should tell Bruno that Molly was no longer sure of herself. If she stayed any longer, she feared that she would succumb to Hannah's persuasions, that she might be tempted to confess all to the Thornes and throw herself on their mercy. And then she would no longer be in control.

No, she decided as she pulled on her jeans as quietly as she could. Life would be much easier if it was just her and Alfie. She wasn't going to be compromised, no matter how tempting it was. Hannah had painted a very inviting picture of life in the bosom of the Thorne family, and Molly couldn't pretend that there hadn't been several moments when she'd nearly capitulated.

But now, in the cold light of dawn, after a night's sleep, she had made up her mind. She'd go and find Skyla. She knew there would be a warm welcome for them, and although the alternative scene wasn't really Molly's bag, she had always admired their sense of sharing, their acceptance of personal circumstances, the fact they didn't judge . . . She smiled to herself. She could do dreadlocks and rainbow clothes if she had to. And Alfie would love it, though she thought he might struggle with rice cakes.

She checked her bag for Zen's wad of cash, only allowing herself a moment to wonder if he and Siobhan had been raided, if they'd woken up and realized she'd done a runner, if they knew the money was missing. She'd turned her phone off the night before, in case anyone had tried to contact her. She didn't really need it now, she mused. She wasn't going to let Alfie leave her side.

She scooped the little boy up in her arms. He was still fast asleep, for it had been quite late before he'd settled again, and he liked his twelve hours – thank goodness. She picked up the plastic carrier bag containing their things and sneaked out of the room. She was desperate for a pee, but she didn't see how she could go without putting Alfie down and disturbing someone, so she decided to hold on until she'd reached neutral territory, where no one would question what on earth she was doing with a toddler in her arms.

She left the digs just in time, as she heard the first alarm trill at half past five. It must be for the breakfast staff, she decided.

Eager guests could be known to be waiting at their tables at seven. She hurried along the sandy path that led through the trees around the outskirts of the grounds, coming out at the back of the town. She reckoned she might be able to hitch a lift to the coach station. It would be at least another hour before the bus started, but there were often people about at this early hour – crazy surfers who'd been to catch an early wave before work. Or people who'd been tempted to tag another day on to their holiday and were setting off home early.

Molly stood on the kerb and stuck out her thumb. The fresh air had woken Alfie up and he was looking around, rather dazed. At least with a baby in her arms people might take pity, and wouldn't assume she was some drug-crazed lunatic about to hold them up with a knife. She kept her eyes steadfastly on the road out of Mariscombe, knowing that if she looked back and caught a glimpse of the sea she might change her mind. Mariscombe had always been her dream home, the place she would have loved to bring Alfie up, but it wasn't meant to be and therefore she mustn't look back.

Hannah came to at about half past seven. She struggled to wake, trying to filter through the various bits of information that were forming in her head. The first thing she remembered was that today was the day of her operation. Which meant that this was officially the last day she would ever have a big nose. The thought made her smile to herself as she stretched sleepily.

Then she sat up with a start. Molly! Where was she? How on earth could she have forgotten last night's bombshell, the bombshell that had kept her awake into the wee small hours worrying? That was why she was in a sleeping bag on the floor.

But her bed was empty. Molly and Alfie had gone.

Hannah scrambled to her feet and pulled open the curtains so she could see round the room. Their stuff had gone. There was no note. Which meant, Hannah realized with a sinking heart, that Molly wasn't going to listen to her advice. She'd done a runner.

What time had they left? she wondered. She'd still been awake at half past three, and they were both sleeping soundly then. It had now gone half seven. Which meant she had to get her skates on. She had to be at the hospital for half nine and it would take over an hour for her to get there. She needed a shower – no breakfast, of course, because she would be having an anaesthetic later. Lucky she'd packed everything the night before. Even her clothes were ready.

But what about Molly? Where was she going? Had she decided to go back home, perhaps? Hannah thought not. She'd been pretty definite that yesterday had been the final straw. So where were she and Alfie . . . ?

Hannah didn't have time to worry about it now. She grabbed her towel and her sponge bag, cross with herself for not having set her alarm the night before. If she was late she might miss her consultation and then they might cancel the op . . . she couldn't bear the thought. This was the day she'd been waiting for nearly all of her adult life, since the day her nose had chosen to keep growing and overshadow the rest of her features, since the day she'd become a freak, a laughing stock, the girl no man wanted to go near.

She leaped into the shower, turning it on to full blast, hoping that the early morning staff had left enough hot water. Even though she'd have a bathroom adjoining her hospital room, she wanted to be pristine when she arrived. She tipped up her shower gel, squeezed a generous blob into her hand and starting scrubbing.

But as she stood under the water, the image of Molly and Alfie out there alone somewhere wouldn't leave her mind. She guessed they would try to find Skyla, the New Age friend Molly had mentioned, but a tent in the middle of a field was no place for a young girl and a baby. Molly had no money to speak of, just the measly bit of cash she'd admitted to stealing from her sister's junkie boyfriend.

Hannah stepped out of the shower with a sinking heart. She couldn't just let Molly go off like that. Not after everything she'd told her. She realized she'd probably sneaked out before Hannah was awake because she knew Hannah would put her under pressure to talk to Bruno.

Because that was the right thing to do. Hannah was absolutely sure of it. Bruno was a good, kind man. He would be horrified to think of Molly in the situation she was in – even without realizing that Alfie was his own brother's baby. Bruno would want Molly rescued and saved. Bruno would work out a solution for her regardless. As a mere employee, he would give her a place in the staff accommodation at the very least. As the mother of his nephew . . .

Hannah looked at her watch. It was quarter to eight. What should she do? Molly wouldn't have got far yet without her own transport. She'd mentioned heading for Bristol, before going on to Wales to find the festival site. Hannah didn't know what time the coaches started from Bamford, but probably not this early.

Hannah grabbed her phone and dialled Bruno's number, which all the senior staff had in case of emergencies. He answered on the first ring.

'Hello?'

'Bruno? It's Hannah.'

'Hannah. Is everything OK?' His voice was warm and friendly, but tinged with concern.

'No. Not exactly.' She cleared her throat. How the hell was she going to explain the situation over the phone? He'd think she was barking mad. Or playing a practical joke. She had to explain it to him in person, so she could convince him she was genuine. She glanced at her watch again and did a quick bit of mental arithmetic. If she took her stuff with her, then went straight to the hospital, assuming it only took twenty minutes to convince him of Molly's plight, then she would be forty minutes late for her checking-in time. As long as there were no other hold-ups, she might be OK.

She'd have to risk it. She couldn't just turn her back on Molly. Molly and Alfie's future versus her nose job? It was a no-brainer. After all, her nose wasn't going anywhere.

'Can I see you? Urgently?'

'Of course. What is it?'

'I'll come straight over.'

Hannah jumped into the tracksuit she'd taken off the night before – she didn't have time for the blouse, tights and skirt she'd hung up on the back of her door – and bolted out of her room, grabbing her handbag and her overnight case. She paused for two seconds to make sure she had her admission details and left without even locking the door.

As she bombed her little car along the track that led to Bruno's house, she wondered for a moment if she was doing the right thing. Molly had pleaded with her to keep her revelation secret. For some reason she was convinced that Joe's family would blackball her, that they would think she was on the make and blame her for his death to boot. Hannah felt sure that given what she knew of Bruno, that wouldn't be the case.

She reassured herself that, although she was breaking her promise, she was doing it for the right seasons. She'd read enough moral dilemmas in women's magazines to know there were times when a betrayal of confidence was right and proper. Molly couldn't be objective about her situation. And Hannah knew Bruno better than Molly. At least she hoped she did . . .

Bruno ushered Hannah into the living room. For a moment she felt totally overwhelmed, both by the splendour of the room and the import of what she was about to say. She turned to Bruno, who smiled at her kindly.

'What is it, Hannah?'

He was probably expecting her to spill out some sort of

petty hotel problem. A spat with another member of staff. A run-in with a guest.

'It's Molly.' Hannah managed to find her voice. 'She's got a baby. A little boy. None of us knew. He's . . . nearly two.'

Bruno nodded gravely. There was understanding in his eyes.

'I thought there was more to Molly than met the eye. That explains a lot.'

'That's not all.' Was he going to believe her? She bit her lip. 'The baby . . . it's Joe's.'

For a moment Bruno looked totally confused, as if he was trying to work out which member of staff she meant.

'Your brother,' Hannah added.

Bruno looked thunderstruck. His skin went quite pale.

'Joe?' He repeated. 'Joe's the father?'

Hannah nodded.

'Molly used to work on the campsite. She and Joe had an affair, just before he died. Molly . . . caught him with Tamara, after he'd promised to finish with her. So Molly ended it.' She paused. 'But then she realized she was pregnant.'

She was aware she was giving him edited highlights. Slightly manipulating the sequence of events, but there was a lot for him to take in. And no time to lose.

Bruno was filtering what she'd told him so far.

'She's had Joe's baby all this time?'

Hannah realized that wasn't the point of her story.

'The thing is, Bruno, she's done a runner with him. Her sister's boyfriend was dealing drugs in her flat; she was afraid she might be busted, that they'd take Alfie away. So Molly's gone . . .'

She trailed off, aware that she was gabbling, aware that Bruno was completely flummoxed by the revelations. He put up a hand.

'Just tell me one thing, Hannah. Why didn't she come to me?'

Hannah swallowed.

'Because . . . she was afraid that you wouldn't believe her. That you'd think she was just after money.'

Bruno's lips tightened.

'Is it definitely Joe's baby?'

Hannah hesitated for a moment. She had no proof, after all.

'Yes,' she said definitely. 'Molly wouldn't lie to me. We need to find her, Bruno. She can't survive on her own. She's got no money; nothing.'

Bruno ran a hand through his curls, trying to think rationally.

'Do you know where she might have gone?'

'I think she's getting the coach to Bristol. She's got this friend who goes round the festivals—'

Bruno didn't need to hear any more. He strode around the room gathering up his keys, his coat. Hannah stood rooted to the spot. Bruno looked at her.

'You'll have to come with me,' he said flatly. 'She'll freak out completely if she sees me waiting for her. I need you with me, Hannah.'

Visions of an empty hospital bed flashed through Hannah's mind. A surgeon waiting, tapping his scalpel against his hand impatiently.

Then she thought of Molly, with little Alfie in her arms, both of them pale and tear-stained and frightened.

She sighed.

'OK.'

Ten minutes later, Hannah sat back in the cream leather seat of Bruno's Range Rover which seemed to mould itself to her body, and felt the cool of the air-conditioning on her face. In that single moment, Hannah suddenly understood luxury. She had never felt such total comfort before. She felt like a princess. Or a superstar being chauffeured to an important engagement. Dream on, she thought to herself. This would probably be the first and last time she'd sit in a car like this.

They made the junction of the motorway in a record forty

minutes. Hannah looked at her watch. Exactly thirty minutes after she should have turned off in the other direction, had she kept her appointment. She hadn't even had time to phone up and cancel, and she didn't want to do it now in front of Bruno.

Bruno spoke suddenly.

'Tell me about Molly,' he said. 'What's she like?'

Hannah considered her reply carefully.

'I don't know her that well. But I like her. A lot. She's quiet. But quite tough. And she's very loyal.' She had a sudden recollection of Molly in the corridor, eyes blazing, hands on hips, standing up to Caragh. 'She stuck up for me once. She was amazing. She's not afraid of anyone.'

The corner of Bruno's mouth lifted in a wry smile.

'Except me?'

Hannah looked down at her hands.

'Yes, well, you live in a different world to Molly.'

Hannah noticed Bruno was drumming his fingers on the steering wheel and that his thick brows were meeting in the middle.

'Are you OK?'

He nodded.

'I'm just angry. Furious, in fact.'

Hannah felt hot with discomfort.

'Not with me? Should I not have told you?'

'Not with you. God, no. I'll be eternally grateful to you.' Bruno paused. 'I'm angry with Joe. As ever. Bloody Joe, for not facing up to his responsibilities. For not thinking about anyone other than himself. Just when I thought I'd come to terms with his selfishness . . .'

Bruno broke off. Hannah could see his jaw was clenched. She thought about the other part of the story, the bit she didn't feel was hers to tell him, and wondered if she ought to reveal it now. But she decided that it was up to Molly. She didn't want to scupper her friend's chances of a brighter future, just to let Joe off the hook.

She saw that the speedo was nudging up and marvelled at how smooth the car felt. The coach from Bamford was due in to Bristol at eleven. She prayed that they would make it and that Molly would be on it, that she hadn't decided to hitch a lift or go somewhere else.

Hannah kept her eyes fixed firmly on the road, and tried not to think about the fact that by rights she should be lying on the operating table while the surgeon prepared to change her life for ever. Or how long it was going to take her to save up for another operation. It was only money, she consoled herself. Whereas this was Molly's future.

Half an hour later, Bruno sat in the waiting room at the coach station. They'd decided it was best that Hannah would wait for Molly to come off the coach.

Bruno remembered talking to Molly about the house-keeper's job and how frustrated he'd been by her reluctance, which he had written off as a lack of ambition. God, if he had known. If only he had known. Hannah had filled him in on what she knew of Molly's background and her feckless family. Her life sounded like sheer drudgery – a hell of squalor and measly handouts. And all the time there he had been, living like a lord in his luxurious surroundings, oblivious.

Bruno stared at the filthy floor scattered with cigarette butts and burns, his hands clasped, praying they hadn't missed Molly, praying that in a few minutes' time he could atone for his brother's behaviour, and realizing that he felt almost sick with the anticipation of meeting his own flesh and blood.

The coach was ten minutes late, but it felt like ten hours. Engines thrummed, doors opened and closed, the tannoy babbled meaninglessly overhead. When Molly finally stepped down the stairs, with Alfie in her arms, she didn't look surprised to see Hannah.

Hannah was nervous. She'd seen Molly turn. She knew she had fire inside her, that she might tear into Hannah for betraying her. But she just stood there, straight and proud, her face impassive as she waited for Hannah's explanation.

'I told Bruno,' Hannah said flatly. 'I think it was only fair. For him and for you. And for Alfie. And for Joe.'

Molly gave a deep sigh.

'You're probably right.'

She'd known in her heart of hearts that running was futile. How did she expect to manage? Over Hannah's shoulder, she saw Bruno approaching from the waiting room. She was mesmerized by his expression. There was hope, fear, compassion. Sorrow. Expectation. And when he set eyes on Alfie, Molly didn't think she'd forget the look on Bruno's face for as long as she lived.

'I didn't tell him everything,' Hannah was saying urgently, sotto voce. 'I didn't tell him . . . what you told Joe. About the abortion. He thinks you found out you were pregnant after Joe died. It's up to you to tell him the rest if you want to.'

Bruno had reached them. He stood in front of Molly, put a gentle hand on her arm and looked in wonder at his nephew's pale freckled face.

'Hey, Alfie . . .'

Molly, being Molly, had to come clean. She couldn't live with the burden of a single secret any longer. She wanted a clear conscience. So she spilled out the whole story, not leaving out any of the detail, kneeling on the floor in front of Bruno's fireplace, Hector flopped down beside her. Bruno sat beside her, his arms wrapped round his knees, trying to absorb the implications of everything she was telling him, trying not to judge, even though he was shocked by the harshness of the various twists and turns. And now he was able to look back on the dreadful night that Joe died with different eyes, knowing that he had carried an extra burden.

'I can't tell you how much I respect you for telling me the truth,' he said finally. 'Being totally selfish, it kind of lets me off the hook, because I've been blaming myself for what I said and did all this time. Just like you have.'

Molly nodded solemnly.

'The bottom line is, Molly, I guess we're both a bit to blame. We both did and said things that maybe we shouldn't have, on reflection. But we're not as much to blame as Joe. If Joe hadn't behaved like he did, if Joe hadn't driven us both to the edge, then none of it would have happened, and he'd still be here now.'

She looked down at her fingers, clenched tightly in her lap.

'Maybe what you said to him was wrong,' Bruno continued. 'But you were frightened. And hurt. And maybe what I said to him was wrong. But I was frustrated. And angry. And why should we carry the guilt round for the rest of our lives? That's certainly not going to do Alfie any good. And he's the one positive thing to come out of it.'

Molly gave a glimmer of a smile. Bruno thought she understood what he was saying. He leaned forward.

'Molly . . . there's something I'd like you to do. But you have to trust me. And if you decide you don't want to, I won't force you.' Bruno swallowed. 'I know . . . that if my mother knew about Alfie, it would mean more than anything in the world to her. Because if anyone *wasn't* to blame for Joe's death, it was Mum, and I think she's suffered more than any of us. Would you . . . would you let her see him?'

Molly gulped.

'Would I . . . have to tell her everything?'

Bruno thought carefully. The whole situation was incredibly delicate. There were so many people's sensibilities to take into consideration, not least Molly's.

'I think . . . it might be better for everyone if she doesn't know the whole truth. I think she'd be ashamed of Joe's behaviour to you.'

He saw a flicker of gratitude in Molly's eyes, that he'd avoided making her look bad by making Joe the scapegoat. Bruno certainly didn't want Molly to have to go through the shame of telling her side of the story again. Not that he felt that she had been so wrong. But he knew how painful the confession had been for her. And he knew his mother would be appalled by the sordidness of it all, no matter whose side she came down on.

'What if . . . we tell her you only found out you were pregnant after Joe died?' he suggested. 'And that you were too afraid to come forward until now? That's what Hannah told me.'

Molly bit her lip.

'You don't think that's lying?'

Bruno was touched.

'I think it's a very, very white lie. And, frankly, I can't see any benefit to anyone in telling the truth.'

Molly thought long and hard. She stroked Hector's ears, then sighed.

'Yes,' she said. 'I'd like Alfie to meet his grandparents. Very much.'

Bruno walked up the path to his parents' bungalow with his heart in his mouth. How on earth was he going to break the news? Joanie was incredibly fragile emotionally. Would she be able to cope with the shock?

He walked into the kitchen without knocking. She was standing at the sink, still in her dressing gown.

'Mum?'

'Bruno, love . . .' Her face was wan. She managed a fleeting smile. Then she frowned. 'Is something the matter?'

He could see the anxiety in her face and he rushed forward to reassure her.

'No, Mum. There's nothing the matter. But I have got some news. You'd better sit down first.'

He pulled out a kitchen chair. She sat, looking flustered.

'What? What is it?'

He sat down next to her and picked up one of her hands.

'Listen carefully. I don't know exactly how to tell you this, it's all a bit complicated. But . . . Joe was seeing someone, just before he died.'

Joanie nodded.

'Tamara . . .'

'Not just Tamara. There was another girl. Her name's Molly. She worked on the campsite.'

Joanie's face clouded as she tried to put a face to the name. She shook her head.

'I don't remember . . .'

'It doesn't matter. She was Joe's . . . I don't know what the word is. They were having an affair, anyway. And Molly got pregnant.'

Joanie was staring at him with a bewildered expression, not knowing what the punchline was going to be. Bruno rushed to get the words out as quickly as he could.

'Mum, Molly found out she was having Joe's baby, not long after he died. She had a little boy. Alfie.' Bruno swallowed hard, realizing that he had tears in his eyes. 'He's your grandson, Mum. You've got a little grandson.'

Joanie closed her eyes. She seemed to sway slightly with the shock. She gripped Bruno's fingers in hers.

'Where is he?' she whispered.

'Molly and Alfie are at my house. I only found out the whole story today. Molly was frightened to come to us. She was frightened . . . we might think she was lying. That she was after money.'

Joanie released her grip. Her hands were shaking. She took in a few deep breaths.

'Can I see him?'

Bruno nodded.

'Of course you can.'

For a moment, Joanie didn't move.

'Does he look like Joe?' she whispered.

Bruno considered his answer carefully.

'A little bit. He's got Joe's eyebrows, I think. And his mouth.'

Joanie buried her face in her hands, completely overwhelmed. Bruno took her in his arms.

'Give yourself a few minutes. To get used to the idea. Then go and get yourself dressed. I'll drive you over. You can see him for yourself . . .'

Nineteen

Mimi was amazed. When she'd left Bath, none of her friends had turned a hair. But she'd only been in Mariscombe a matter of weeks and her mates were throwing her a farewell party that afternoon. They'd brought crates of beer down to the beach, rigged up a sound system and cooked sausages and burgers on a fire that Matt had built.

All of which made the fact that they were leaving the next day so much harder to bear. Mimi was dreading going back to Bath, dreading even more having to live with her grandparents, whose motives she mistrusted. It was all very well them welcoming her with open arms now, when she was virtually old enough to leave home. Mimi was as old as her mother had been when she had her. Talk about shutting the barn door after the horse had bolted.

As much as both she and Victoria had loved Mariscombe, on a practical level there was nothing there for them. And Mimi was keenly aware that Victoria probably wanted to put as much distance between herself and George as possible. Mimi realized now that you couldn't force two people who didn't belong with each other together.

Like her and Matt? Picking up a bottle of Smirnoff Ice, she looked over at him changing the music. She knew it was him who'd arranged all this for her; he'd put the word round, collected money for a kitty to buy food and booze. So he must care about her. But she still didn't know exactly where she stood. They'd been as thick as thieves, out together every night. He didn't go out with anyone else. They ate together, drank together, danced together. But that was it. It was like having a very best friend.

Mimi wanted more.

'Come for a walk with me.' She put her head to one side coquettishly and smiled up at him. She realized she was a little bit drunker than she'd thought – not quite slurring her words, but everything in her head was slightly fuzzy. Though actually, it helped.

They walked down the beach. Mimi slid her arm through Matt's, feeling a little bit unsteady on her feet as she drew him round past the rocks, round the corner to a sheltered spot where they were out of sight. Feeling braver, she pulled him towards her, then slid her arm around the back of his neck and kissed him.

His response told her everything she needed to know. He kissed her back fiercely, entwining his hands in her hair. She slid hers under his T-shirt, exploring his skin. They fell on to the damp sand, oblivious to anything but their passion.

'Make love to me, Matt,' she said softly.

He pushed her hair back from her eyes and gazed into them.

'I can't, Mimi,' he sighed. 'Not if you're leaving. It wouldn't be right. You'd only regret it.'

'I wouldn't.' She pressed herself against him.

'Mimi, you're drunk. I'm drunk.' He stroked her hair. 'Let's wait. Wait until we both know what we're going to do with our lives.'

She fell back on to the sand, deflated.

'You don't fancy me.'

'Are you kidding?' He stroked her cheek. 'You've no idea how long I've been wanting to kiss you. But I always knew I only had you on borrowed time. I didn't want to start something we couldn't finish.'

Mimi blinked away a tear.

'It's not fair. I don't want to go.'

'I know. I don't want you to go. But maybe—'

She sat up, filled with hope.

'Maybe what?'

'Maybe you can come back and visit.' Matt wasn't going to make her any promises. He'd been through it all so many times before. Holiday romances. Vows to return. Passionate encounters that seemed so intense in the sunshine but faded away after a couple of weeks' half-hearted texting. His reluctance was as much to protect himself as it was Mimi. That was the price you paid for living in Mariscombe. A temporary paradise.

'Come on,' he coaxed her. 'The food should be cooked by now. Let's go and get something to eat.'

He took her hand and they walked back round the rocks, where the barbecue was pronounced ready. Sausages and jacket potatoes and corn on the cob were handed round. Mimi didn't want food, however. In her misery, she downed three Smirnoff Ices in quick succession and had more than her fair share of a fat spliff that was being passed around.

Feeling slightly anaesthetized, she wandered down to the water's edge. The tide was on its way in and had nearly reached a big inflatable crocodile that one of the group had abandoned. Mimi pushed it into the water, wading out until she was past the line of waves that fringed the shore. When she was up to her waist, she clambered in. She lay back, sculling the water gently with her hands, looking up at the sky. It had been a glorious afternoon and the sun was just starting to edge down between the two clusters of rocks that stood guard either side of the inlet.

She stopped sculling and closed her eyes. As the sun slipped further, it started getting cold, and she was wet, but she didn't mind. Out here there was nothing to think about, just the sea below her and the sky above. Her head was spinning slightly. Her mind felt numb at the edges, her limbs heavy. The crocodile bobbed up and down in the water. She felt like a baby being rocked to sleep in its cradle.

Dimly, she noticed that she was drifting out past the rocks

and into the open sea. But she didn't worry. She was safe in her little boat. She could paddle back in when she wanted. A dark cloud passed over the sinking sun. A raindrop fell and landed on her stomach. Then another.

So what if it rained? She was wet already. Besides, rain suited her mood. Perhaps she'd changed the weather with her gloomy thoughts?

An unexpectedly large wave caught the underside of the crocodile, nearly tipping her up. Mimi sat up in alarm. Maybe she'd go back into shore now. The sky that had been blue all afternoon was now a steely, unforgiving grey, and she could see a line of driving rain advancing in. She started to paddle with her hands but the crocodile drifted determinedly in the opposite direction, as if it knew better. Another wave blew in and this time she was tipped out.

She bobbed to the surface, spluttering, and grabbed the plastic handle on the edge of the inflatable. But it was too large and unwieldy for her to turn it over while she was treading water. She tried to hook her arms over the edge, but she kept slipping off. The waves were getting bigger. The sky was getting darker. The rain was getting heavier. Mimi clung on to the plastic handle and started to swim for the shore. It seemed an awfully long way off all of a sudden. And somehow it seemed to be getting further and further away.

Matt was throwing wet sand over the last of the barbecue to damp out the coals, even though rain was starting to fall. He looked round for Mimi, thinking he'd walk her back home. He couldn't spot her anywhere. Maybe she'd gone off in a sulk. He didn't think that was her style, but you didn't know with girls. They could be incredibly touchy.

'Any of you guys seen Mimi?' he asked the others.

'Didn't she go out on the croc?'

Matt hastily ran down to the shore, scanning the water for signs of the crocodile. By now the rain was coming in thick and fast. He couldn't see out past the rocks. The waves had got up. They were over five foot, easily. No one in their right mind would be out in the sea now.

If the crocodile was nowhere to be seen, and neither was Mimi, then there was only one conclusion to come to. Matt ran back up to the others, trying not to panic, trying to work out how long it was since he'd seen her.

'Has anyone got a signal down on this beach? I need to call the coastguard.'

Half an hour later, a thick mist was closing in fast. The rain was coming in horizontally, fine but determined. As the rocks on the horizon vanished from view, Victoria whimpered and George drew her in close to him, wishing fervently that he had enough conviction to reassure her. But as he looked vainly out to sea, he felt any hope he had evaporating. Mimi could be anywhere on her inflatable crocodile – if indeed she was still on it. A wave could have turned her over and would she have had the strength to retrieve her life raft? Or was she even now desperately treading water?

He looked behind him and could see gaggles of people gradually turning out on to the esplanade as word got round. The kids Mimi had been hanging out with were loitering at the far end, pale with uncertainty, smoking furiously. One of them had run up to the hotel to tell them what was happening, and for that he was thankful, even though he felt quite help-less.

George noticed that Lisa was nowhere to be seen, that she had discreetly slipped away, and he was grateful to her for her sensitivity. She knew that Victoria needed him and she wasn't going to object. Lisa, he thought with a wave of shame, was too good for all of them.

The coastguard helicopter arrived, an incongruously cheerful bright yellow. It swooped overhead, cruising over the shoreline, then disappeared between the cliffs, heading purposefully out to sea. George felt reassured. They knew what they were doing. They did this kind of thing every day of the week . . .

They found Mimi, exhausted and nearly unconscious, still clinging to the crocodile. They flew her straight to the hospital outside Bamford. George drove Victoria there in Lisa's car, where they found Mimi in A&E, wrapped in a foil blanket and on a drip.

'I'm sorry, Mum.'

Her little face was drained of any colour. Victoria bent down to kiss her. Her skin felt incredibly cold.

'You silly girl . . .'

George watched as the two of them hugged each other tightly. His stomach was still churning with anxiety. How easily this could have turned into a tragedy. A fact that was under-lined to them by the doctor, who came into the little cubicle with a grave face.

'She's had a very lucky escape. The combination of alcohol and cold water is deadly. If she'd fallen unconscious, she wouldn't have had a hope. Not in those waves.'

'But she will be OK?' Victoria looked up anxiously.

'Yes,' the doctor reassured her. 'But I want to keep her in tonight, just for observation. She was bordering on hypo-thermia.'

'Can I stay?'

The doctor shrugged.

'If you want. But there's no real need. I suggest you go home and come back for her first thing in the morning. Obviously we'll call you if there are any complications in the meantime.'

Victoria hesitated, reluctant to leave her daughter.

'Mum, I'll be fine,' said Mimi. 'There's no point in you staying. All I want to do is go to sleep.'

'I don't like the thought of leaving you. You might need me.'

Mimi grinned.

'What are you going to do to help? You're useless at first aid, you hate needles, you faint at the sight of blood. Go home and come and get me tomorrow.'

Victoria finally relented. Outside in the corridor, she burst into tears. George put his arms around her. A couple walked past and gave them a sympathetic glance, assuming they'd had bad news.

'Hey,' he said gently, as she buried her head in his chest, her shoulders convulsing. 'Mimi's going to be fine. I know you've had a shock, but there's no need to get yourself into a state.'

'It's not Mimi,' Victoria croaked.

'Then what is it?'

She clung on to his lapels, looking up at him.

'I think I might be pregnant.'

'Oh.' It took George a couple of seconds to digest this news. 'How . . . pregnant?' he asked lightly, an uneasy feeling growing inside him.

'I'm a day late.'

Even George, whose knowledge of women's cycles was sketchy, could do the maths on this one.

'You mean . . . ?'

Victoria nodded, her face crumpling as she dissolved into sobs again.

'I'm sorry. I wasn't going to tell you.'

'What were you going to do?'

'I don't know!' Victoria wiped her nose with her sleeve like a small child and took in a deep, juddering breath to calm herself down. 'I . . . don't know. I mean, I can't even be totally sure. I haven't done a test or anything. But I'm pretty sure. I feel . . . I *feel* pregnant.'

George suddenly felt the need for a very large drink.

'I thought you were on the Pill. I'd never have touched you if I'd thought . . . You've been on the Pill for ever. You're neurotic about not getting pregnant.'

'I stopped taking it after Nick dumped me,' said Victoria flatly. 'I wasn't ever going to sleep with another man again.'

George looked at Victoria. She looked about twelve, her face white, her eyes huge.

'What am I going to do?' she asked him, her voice very small and plaintive.

He was silent for a moment.

'What are *we* going to do?' he corrected her.

'I can't get rid of it. Even I couldn't do that. Even I couldn't be that selfish.'

'Of course not!' George was appalled at the suggestion. 'That hadn't even occurred to me.'

'I've got no money, no job, nowhere to live . . .'

George looked up at the ceiling for a moment, as if the answer might be lurking there.

'You've got me.'

'But I haven't, have I? Lisa's got you.' Victoria babbled on. 'I can go away. Have it in secret. Bring it up somewhere – Lisa need never find out.'

'Absolutely not.' George was adamant. 'That's positively Victorian. We're in this together. This is *our* baby . . .'

The relief on Victoria's face was palpable.

'George . . . ?'

'What?'

'I didn't do this on purpose. I know that's what everyone's going to think. I know that's what Lisa will think. But I honestly didn't.'

'No,' said George. 'I'm sure you didn't. If I remember rightly, you didn't exactly force me into it.'

He wiped a bead of sweat from his forehead. Suddenly it seemed incredibly hot in the hospital.

'I suppose you'd better do a test first. Make sure you are pregnant. There's no point in pushing the panic button if it's a false alarm.'

Victoria pressed her lips together until they were nearly white in an effort not to cry again.

'We can get one from the all-night supermarket in Bamford,' she whispered. 'Will you come with me?'

'Of course I will . . .'

*

Half an hour later, George found himself pacing the fruit and vegetable aisle while Victoria did her test in the loo. There had been quite a few tests to choose from. True to form, Victoria had grabbed the most expensive.

'I won't be long,' she said. 'It says it only takes two minutes.'

Now here he was staring at a pile of gleaming aubergines, thinking how peculiar life was. This situation was completely surreal. All because of a moment of weakness on his part. Of course, Victoria might not be pregnant. Her period might be late for all sorts of reasons. It had been a stressful time for her. And maybe her body was adjusting to not being on the Pill after all these years. After all, people didn't get pregnant that easily, did they? It had been very quick, all of thirty seconds, if he remembered rightly. Yes, George reassured himself, it was very unlikely . . .

He looked across the aisles into the entrance area just as Victoria came out of the loo. She looked around for him and their eyes met. Her expression told him nothing. She just stared as he rushed over to her.

'Well?'

She gave a wobbly smile as her eyes filled with tears. What did that mean? She looked . . . happy. That must mean negative.

'Positive.'

George's heart gave a little flip.

His stomach filled with butterflies.

As he stood there under the harsh lights, customers barging past him with their trolleys, he realized that was the answer he had been hoping for.

Lisa was at the door before he'd even opened it, anxious for news of Mimi.

'Is she all right? Why didn't you phone me? You've been ages. I've been so worried.'

George walked into the hall with a heavy tread.

'Mimi's going to be fine. They're keeping her in for observation, that's all.'

'Thank God.'

'Lisa . . .'

Lisa looked at him. His face was grim, his mouth a hard line.

'Lisa, I don't quite know how to tell you this.' He cleared his throat in an effort to get the words out more fluently. 'Victoria's pregnant.'

Lisa blinked in surprise. 'How did she manage that? That's all she needs at the moment. And I suppose that means we can't just kick her . . .'

She trailed off as the realization dawned on her.

'It's yours.'

'Yes,' said George. 'And I'm sorry.'

Lisa stared blankly into space for a few moments.

'I don't think I'm surprised,' she said eventually. 'And I don't think I'm even angry.'

'You should be. I can't tell you how disgusted I am with myself.'

She gave a deep sigh. George looked agonized. He couldn't think of anything to say that would make it any better.

'I love you, Lisa. I think you're amazing and fantastic and I'd never have got this place off the ground without you.' George ground one fist into the palm of his other hand as he searched for the right words. 'But—'

'But you love her.' Lisa's voice was matter of fact. 'You never got over her. I know you tried to convince me and her and yourself. But the truth is, the minute she walked back in through that door you were hooked.'

'What do we do now?'

He was looking to her for answers. Because he knew she was stronger than he was. Because if anyone could find a solution to this mess, it would be Lisa.

Lisa looked around the reception area. In two days' time

the first guests were due to check in. She gave a despondent shrug.

'Sell up, I guess. We should get our money back. We've got a healthy stream of bookings already.'

'It's a bloody shame. After all that hard work.'

'You could buy me out.'

George couldn't help wishing that Lisa would scream and cry, hit him even. She was so incredibly down to earth. So practical. It was unnerving. And it made him feel more guilty because he knew that no one was really that tough, that inside she was probably devastated. Not that he flattered himself that he was a heartbreaker.

'I don't think I can afford to.' Not with a baby on the way, he added to himself as an afterthought. 'And it doesn't seem fair. You've put such a lot into this place.'

'Not as much as you've put into Victoria.' Her crudeness made him flinch. But at least she was showing some sort of reaction. 'Where is she now?'

'I've booked her into a hotel.'

Lisa scoffed.

'That's a bit pointless, isn't it?'

'I could hardly bring her back here.'

'Why not? The damage has already been done.'

A trace of bitterness had crept into her voice.

'I never meant to hurt you.'

'No, I'm sure you didn't.' Her tone was brisk. 'But perhaps it was meant to be. And, anyway, I wouldn't want to be second best.'

'Lisa, you are not second best. You've got to believe that. No way. You are beautiful and talented and sexy and . . .' George shrugged helplessly, at a loss for the right words. 'Amazing. You're amazing.'

'But I'm not Victoria.'

Lisa always had a knack for getting straight to the point.

George sighed.

'No.'

She squared her shoulders.

'I don't know where Justin's got to. I think he's out with Joel. I'll tell him when he gets back. You better go and find Victoria.' She paused. 'Let's have a meeting tomorrow, when we've all had a chance to think about what we want to do. Say . . . ten o'clock?'

Christ, how could she be so businesslike when he'd just blown her whole world apart? He gazed at her, her chin lilted defiantly in that gesture he'd come to know so well. She was blinking rapidly and he realized she was trying not to cry. She wouldn't want to do that in front of him; he knew her well enough for that. He drew away hastily.

'Ten o'clock, then . . .'

As George turned and walked out of the door, Lisa squared her shoulders and managed a rueful smile. She'd been looking for the right moment all day to tell George she didn't actually want to marry him. She'd been berating herself for agreeing in front of all those witnesses, wondering how on earth she'd managed to find herself engaged and how she was going to get out of it while not hurting his feelings.

Now, she didn't have to worry. Telling him she'd never intended to marry him would only look like sour grapes. Besides, she didn't think she wanted to do anything to ease his conscience.

Bloody men, she thought. Why didn't she ever learn? Suddenly blinded by tears, she ran through the drawing room and out of the French windows. She'd go down to the beach. Things never seemed so bad on the beach, somehow.

Twenty

It had been decided that Hannah would break the news about Molly and Alfie to the rest of the staff, as discreetly as possible. It was a dubious honour, as it was very hard to drop a bombshell like that without looking as if you were relishing everyone's reaction. But she understood that Bruno would feel uncomfortable announcing it to all and sundry, and they obviously couldn't keep it quiet for any length of time.

She was standing now, in the staffroom, her fists clenched, her nails digging into her palms, as Caragh marvelled at the revelation.

'What a brilliant scam.' She exclaimed. 'I wish I'd thought of it.'

'Scam?' frowned Hannah. 'What do you mean, scam?'

'Well, how do they prove it is Joe's baby? I wouldn't take that little scrubber's word for it.'

Hannah stepped forward.

'What did you call her?'

'Molly Mahoney's a little scrubber.' Caragh stood her ground. 'A scheming little scrubber, coming out of the woodwork two years later. It's perfect. They're hardly going to dig up his body for DNA, are they?' She cackled. 'It's like a Catherine Cookson story. Bastard son born on the wrong side of the blanket. Though if you ask me it could be any Tom, Dick or Harry's baby from here to Tawcombe.'

Hannah was trembling with rage.

'Take that back.'

'What?'

'Take back what you just said. About Molly.'

Caragh's mocking eyes danced.

'Oh yes, of course. What it is to inspire such loyalty. But then she stuck up for you, didn't she? All the losers and the misfits stick together in this place.'

Frank stepped forward.

'Shut it, Caragh.'

Her eyebrows shot skywards.

'I beg your pardon?'

'Apologize to Hannah.'

'Why is it everybody wants me to apologize to her? The only one who should apologize to her is God, for giving her that conk. That's unforgivable.'

Caragh sat back in her chair, looking very pleased with herself.

Frank looked uncomfortable.

Hannah stared at her evenly.

'It was you,' she said.

'What was me?' Caragh gazed back innocently.

'When I called the hospital, to apologize for not turning up for my operation. They said I'd already cancelled. Two weeks ago.'

'Did they?' Caragh shrugged nonchalantly. 'Nothing to do with me.'

'Don't worry,' said Hannah sweetly. 'Because actually you did me a favour. If I'd cancelled on the day, I'd have lost all my money. But because you gave them two weeks' notice, they'd found someone else to take my place. I got a full refund. And they've booked me in again for a fortnight's time.'

'What operation?' asked Frank, bewildered.

'Do you have to ask?' Caragh looked scornful.

'I'm not ashamed,' said Hannah. 'I was booked in for a nose job.'

'Why?' Frank really thought he'd missed something. Two minutes ago they'd been on abandoned babies.

Caragh snorted.

368

'Why?' She collapsed, helpless with laughter. 'Why stop there, do you mean?'

Frank looked down at her.

'You bitch.'

'Oh, for God's sake,' said Caragh. 'Get over it. I saved her nearly four grand.'

She held out her hand to look at her nails. Frank stared at her in disgust, then turned on his heel and walked out of the room.

Hannah bent down until her face was on a level with Caragh.

'You can say what you like about me,' she said evenly, 'but if you don't take back what you said about Molly, you'll be the one needing surgery.'

Bruno was in the back office. He felt quite light-headed, from too much coffee and not enough sleep. It had been an extra-ordinary couple of days. His heart soared every time he thought of his mother's face when she'd first seen Alfie. Of course, there had been tears. Lots of tears. It had been painful in some respects. Incredibly emotional. Even his father had cried, and Bruno didn't remember him crying once, not even when Joe had died. Molly had been cautious, wary, protective, but that was to be expected. And there were bound to be difficult times ahead. There were too many emotions involved to expect a totally smooth path.

But otherwise, it had been quite wonderful.

There was a knock at the door. Bruno sighed. He'd hoped to sneak off, grab some lunch at home and get some sleep.

'Come in.'

The door opened and Frank stepped inside. He looked anxious.

'Frank. Come and sit down. What can I do for you?'

Frank took the seat in front of his desk. Bruno saw his hands were trembling.

'What's the matter?'

Frank folded his chef's hat in his lap.

'You're not going to like any of this. You're going to be down a manageress and a head chef by the end of it. And to be honest, I don't care if you end up suing me. Or if I end up in prison. But I can't keep quiet any longer.'

Later that afternoon, Hannah had come off duty and had gone to flop on to her bed. She was shattered after the emotional rollercoaster that had been the past couple of days. Her confrontation with Caragh had drained her – she'd made a dignified exit in the end, as the girl had refused to apologize. Hannah felt rather hurt that Frank had slunk off and left them to it. She couldn't believe what a coward he was.

The knock on the door was so faint she didn't hear it at first. But then a louder one came.

'Hello?'

She sat up, wondering who it could be. The door opened and in came Frank, looking rather shaken.

'Oh,' she said, rather curt. 'What?'

'She's gone,' he said, in wonderment.

'Who?'

'Caragh.' He came and sat down on the bed without being invited. 'I told Bruno everything. Every scam and fiddle she'd been up to. I had to tell him about the one I was involved with as well, because I knew she'd dump me in it, given half the chance.'

'You're kidding!'

'I couldn't stand her any longer, Hannah. She was doing my head in. She was such a total bitch. To you. To everyone. But she had me by the balls. The only way I could get away was to turn myself in.'

Hannah put a hand on his shoulder.

'So – have you been sacked?'

'No!' Even as he said it, Frank couldn't believe it. 'He reckoned if I was brave enough to own up then I was basically an honest person.'

'And Caragh?'

Frank grinned.

'Half an hour to pack her bags. And a taxi to the station.'

'No!' Hannah threw herself back on the bed laughing, kicking her legs with glee. 'Well done you.'

'I thought I'd had it. I thought that would be it. I thought I'd be out on my ear. But I couldn't take another night of it.'

Hannah remembered his scratches and sat up.

'How is your back?'

Frank was staring at her.

'Fine.'

Hannah stared back at him.

'What?'

Hannah blinked. The next thing she knew, she was in Frank's arms. They were kissing and she knew this wasn't out of sympathy, or kindness, or desperation. She slid her hands up under his shirt and this time his skin was hers to feel, and she revelled in every inch of it. And Frank revelled in the pleasure of being stroked and caressed. It was heavenly.

'You're beautiful, you know that?' Frank whispered to her.

'Now I know you're lying,' Hannah laughed. 'You don't have to say that.'

'Seriously. I mean it. Don't have an operation. You don't need an operation. I don't want to change one little bit of you.'

Hannah lay back on the bed and stared up at the ceiling. Frank sat up.

'Honestly. Cancel it. Just think what you could do with the four grand.'

Hannah was silent for a moment.

'You're not going to talk me out of it, Frank.' She was quite determined. 'I've thought and thought and thought about it. And even though my dream has come true today –' she smiled up at him, trailing a finger down his arm – 'my absolutely wildest dream, it doesn't change the fact that I don't want to live with this nose. And I don't have to. I'm going ahead with it.

And there's absolutely nothing you can do to make me change my mind.'

In his office, Bruno came off the phone to his lawyer. He had to laugh: the man had been rather taken aback by his agenda, which had involved long-lost illegitimate nephews, fraudulent manageresses and trust funds. He rubbed his jaw. He needed a shave, a drink and a sleep, not necessarily in that order.

There was another knock on the door. He wasn't going to get any of them at this rate.

'Come in,' he sighed.

It was Lisa. Bruno felt cheered at once. He didn't mind her interrupting him in the least.

'Lisa – hi. That was a fantastic party, by the way. I'm sorry – I haven't got round to doing my thank-you letter yet. It's . . . been a hectic couple of days.'

'Yes. It has for us too. I won't keep you long.'

Bruno frowned. There was something very odd about her manner. She seemed unnaturally businesslike and upright. Not her usually sunny self.

'Is something wrong?'

'I thought you'd like first refusal. As you were interested in buying it in the first place.'

'First refusal?'

'On The Rocks. We're . . . selling up.'

Bruno nearly fell off his chair.

'What? Why?'

Lisa shut her eyes and recited her reply, in a monotone, as if it was something she'd learned by heart.

'Victoria's pregnant. It's George's baby. Justin's going off to Sydney with Joel. So he wants his cash out because he doesn't want to touch The Rocks with a bargepole if Victoria's got anything to do with it. And I can't afford to buy either of them out so . . . well, I don't know what I'm going to do, but that doesn't matter. I like a challenge.'

She smiled at him brightly.

'R-i-i-i-ght.' Bruno nodded.

'So there you go. I said I'd ask. Are you interested? Because if not, my next stop is the estate agent.'

'Lisa, Lisa – slow down. You're going at this like an express train. Let me get you a drink, at least. God knows I could use one after the day I've had.'

He didn't want to drop into the conversation the furore of *his* weekend. He didn't want to look as if he was upstaging her, though it sounded as though it would be a close-run battle. Instead, he poured them each a tumbler full of whiskey.

Lisa grabbed hers gratefully and drank. Bruno thought she was only just holding on to her sanity. She looked quite shaken, underneath the brisk exterior. Poor girl – what on earth had been going on? He thought he'd get the gory details later, but the only thing he could be grateful for at that moment was that *he* hadn't slept with Victoria. That really would have made things complicated.

'So.' Lisa was anxious to get back to business. 'What do you think?'

He swirled the whiskey round in his glass, thinking carefully.

'I can't afford to buy The Rocks outright,' he said eventually. 'Not at the moment. I want to spend a good deal more money here. And there's a few . . . commitments I need to sort out.' He took a deep slug. 'But . . . I might be interested in a partnership. I might be able to buy say . . . two-thirds.'

Lisa looked down into the bottom of her empty glass.

'It's not really what we're looking for. I think we're looking for an outright buyer. But I could tell George to come and have a chat.'

'No. You misunderstand.' Bruno held out his hand for her glass to top it up. 'I'm not remotely interested in going into partnership with George. The only person I'd want to do business with is you . . .'

Lisa looked up sharply.

'Me?'

'Why should you have to give up The Rocks, when you've put in all that hard work? After all, you love it here, don't you?'

'Well, yes, but . . .'

'But what?'

'I can't run it on my own.'

'I wasn't suggesting you did. I've got plenty of staff here – bags of talent looking for a new opportunity.'

Bruno's mind was racing. He felt like his old self, that trader on the shop floor, buzzing from lack of sleep, putting deals together. Frank would be perfect for The Rocks. And Hannah – she was too inexperienced to take Caragh's place, but she could handle a small hotel. He felt a surge of adrenalin.

'What do you think?' he asked Lisa.

'I don't know. I hadn't really thought of it as an option.'

'I think it makes fantastic sense.'

Lisa chewed on her thumbnail. He did have a point. She was rather aggrieved at having to give up the hotel when everyone else seemed to be ending up with what they wanted. She'd been a little hurt that Justin hadn't stuck by her; she'd hoped he might buy George out, but he was champing at the bit to start a whole new life and, anyway, she wasn't sure he'd be an entirely reliable business partner on his own. But Bruno. Bruno was solid and sensible. He understood Mariscombe and how it worked. He had the flair that she lacked – the sense of style that The Rocks needed.

He would, Lisa decided, be the perfect partner.

Twenty-one

Lisa woke terribly early on Christmas morning. She always had done. Ever since she had been a small child. Even though she was now over thirty, and alone, the anticipation of the day wrenched her from her sleep and she felt a tingle in her stomach.

Her eyes sought out the luminous figures on her alarm clock. It was only just gone five. She must try and get back to sleep. There was nothing to get up for yet and if she got up now she would be exhausted later. The hotel was full; it surprised her how many people wanted to be away from home over the festive season. They could have filled it several times over, thanks to numerous mentions in glossy magazines and Sunday supplements who rated it as the ideal venue for a quiet Yuletide retreat. They were mostly young couples who wanted to escape the tyranny of a family Christmas and the drudgery of doing all the work themselves. Thus The Rocks was offering them a week of luxury and indulgence, which had begun the day before with a pair of beauty therapists treating each guest to a relaxing massage, followed by salmon coulibiac and white chocolate chestnut gateau and a screening of *It's a Wonderful Life* on a flat screen in the drawing room, the fire lit and liqueurs or champagne discreetly served.

Breakfast was going to be wild mushroom brioches with scrambled eggs, and at each place was a present that Lisa had chosen carefully: exquisite leather-bound travel journals for the men and heavenly scented candles for the women. Impersonal but tasteful gifts that would be appreciated and used, wrapped in matt gold paper with dark purple grosgrain ribbon. She smiled to herself – George would have been proud.

It had been an incredible few months. She adored running the hotel. Dealing with guests suited her nature perfectly. She had accrued a wonderful set of staff who were loyal and reliable and took as much pride as she did in The Rocks. So she'd barely had any time for self-pity. And Bruno was there to support her. He left her to run the place as she wanted, but was always on hand if she wanted advice or another opinion. Once a month they had taken to going out for dinner, to discuss the previous month's performance and chew over ideas for the future.

Meanwhile, George kept in touch, dutifully, faithfully. He and Victoria were back in Bath – he'd managed to get his old job back, as they hadn't found a satisfactory replacement for him, and Victoria was opening a 'design emporium', whatever that was. Mimi was at college, and Lisa had already promised her a job as a chambermaid the following summer. George phoned regularly to make sure Lisa was all right, both in herself and in her dealings with the hotel. She didn't bear him a grudge. There was no point in histrionics. Besides, she didn't have time to feel sorry for herself. She buried herself in her work and found it incredibly fulfilling. She didn't need anyone else. She was best off on her own. She should have trusted her own instincts in the first place and never allowed herself to be seduced into a relationship.

Lisa pulled her covers back up to her chin and went to turn over. As she did so she felt something rustling at the bottom of the bed. She moved a foot experimentally and realized there was something there; something that definitely hadn't been there when she went to sleep. She sat up in consternation, pushed back the covers and cautiously reached out an arm to investigate. She pulled a soft object back up the bed, then snapped on her bedside lamp.

It was a parcel. A present wrapped in white tissue paper tied with gold ribbon. There was no tag. She tore it open. Inside was a pair of white silk pyjamas and a matching dressing gown, soft and screamingly expensive.

Lisa sat surrounded by scrumpled-up tissue paper and discarded ribbon. She found her heart was beating rather faster than it should be. Common sense told her it was the staff who had clubbed together, knowing that she was going to wake up on her own without a present. She instilled that sort of loyalty and consideration. After all, she'd given each of them carefully chosen and personal gifts, to mark her appreciation of their commitment to her.

But try as she might, she couldn't imagine any of them having access to the sort of shops that stocked this calibre of present. And even if they'd bunged in twenty quid each, which Lisa would have considered more than generous, the total wouldn't cover this.

Bruno phoned her at eleven, to make sure everything was going smoothly with the guests.

'Perfectly,' Lisa assured him. 'Most of them have gone off for a walk on the beach to work up an appetite for lunch.'

'Good. Just ring if there are any snags.'

'I will.' She paused. 'By the way, Father Christmas came,' she said lightly.

'Of course he did.' Bruno's tone was serious. 'He always knows where you are. You can't hide from Father Christmas.'

Lisa found unexpected tears in her eyes, but hastily brushed them away. It was nothing to cry about, for heaven's sake.

'Why don't you come over here for tea?' Bruno went on. 'They won't need you at The Rocks. Lunch will be over and everyone will be snoring in their bedrooms. You don't need to be back till cocktail time.'

Lisa hesitated. He was probably right. She wouldn't be missed for a couple of hours. There would be staff on hand to cover for her. And she had to admit it would be nice to get out, to be off duty.

'OK,' she agreed.

'I'll come and pick you up at four. I can have you back for half six.'

Lisa put the phone down with a slightly trembling hand. She didn't want to think about the significance of the present. About Bruno wandering from shop to shop, thinking about what she might like. He'd probably got one of his staff to get it. From a catalogue. Putting it to the back of her mind, she went off to make sure that Frank was happy in the kitchen. He had taken over at The Rocks a month ago and was looking forward to a chance to really show off over Christmas lunch with an Italian-influenced menu – delicious smells were already beginning to waft into the hallway.

Later that afternoon, the atmosphere at Bruno's house was seductively relaxing. Lisa sank on to the sofa and allowed herself to be waited on. She'd been on her feet nearly all day, making sure that her guests wanted for nothing. Bruno brought her a huge mug of steaming Earl Grey tea.

Bruno's mother Joanie was sitting on the sofa with a glass of wine. She wore a knitted skirt and cardigan in olive green, which suited her honey-blond hair. She was watching her husband on the floor, assembling the most elaborate train set that Lisa had ever seen.

'Who's it for?' she asked teasingly, watching Graham carefully show Alfie how to use the controls.

Molly was sitting cross-legged on the floor, watching her son proudly. When Lisa had first met her, she had been painfully thin and drawn, with dark circles under her eyes, the weight of the world on her shoulders. Now she had filled out and had some colour; her hair was thick and shiny, her eyes had some sparkle. She was wearing jeans and a thick red polo-neck sweater sprinkled with snowflakes.

Molly had paid a duty visit to her mother that morning. Despite her changed circumstances, she hadn't had it in her heart to cut her mother off. But now she wasn't dependent on her in any way, she could handle her. Teresa had made a spiteful remark about her going off to the big house.

'It's all right for those who can afford it,' she griped.

She was going to the pub for her Christmas dinner, to get slaughtered with her cronies. But Molly didn't feel guilty. She wasn't going to the Thornes for the extravagant gifts and the sumptuous food, although she knew that would be there. She was going for the love, the incredible love that they lavished on Alfie that was worth more than any money. Joanie and Graham spent hours patiently answering his questions and showing him things and playing endless games of snap and dominoes, or colouring in. They wouldn't leave him in his pushchair in the corner of a pub with a beaker full of pop and a dummy.

She had finally agreed that they should buy her a house. Bruno had persuaded her that it was only right; that Joe would have provided her with a roof over her head. There was money in his trust fund that would have gone towards a house for him eventually, if he had lived. So by rights that money was Alfie's. Reluctantly, Molly was persuaded. They had put in an offer on a tiny terraced house in Mariscombe. Molly felt ill with excitement whenever she thought about it.

She was determined to keep her independence. She had carried on working at the hotel and Bruno had finally persuaded her to take on the position of housekeeper. But the best of it was that Joanie looked after Alfie during the day, and she knew he would be loved and cared for and fed. It had taken her a while to surrender him. After all, Molly had protected herself with a wall of wariness for over two years, had lived a life shrouded in secrecy and become adept at keeping people at arm's length. But the Thornes were incredibly kind and considerate. They seemed to understand that Alfie was hers first and foremost, and didn't put her under undue pressure to share him. They took her guidance on what he was allowed and not allowed, and they tried very hard not to spoil him, preferring to give him their time. But actually Molly didn't mind if he was spoiled; the first couple

379

of years of his life had been a time of such deprivation, of making do and going without.

They spoiled her, too. Today she had been given a pair of ceramic hair straighteners – Molly was touched because she knew Bruno must have done some serious research to work out that was what she wanted. It would have been Hannah who'd given him the clue.

Hannah had blossomed beyond belief since going ahead with her nose job, despite Frank's protestations that had lasted right up until the minute she had gone into the hospital. Still solid and reliable, she now had a patina of confidence that had grown not so much from her surgery as from her relationship with Frank. Her dress sense, her hair, her posture had all become more confident. She had lost weight and become more toned, thanks to Frank forcing her into the sea. She was almost a beach babe. Bruno was grooming her as his right-hand girl at the hotel. When Caragh had left with her tail between her legs, Bruno had taken over as manager, but was looking for someone to delegate to. Hannah had told Molly, in gleeful tones, that she and Frank were moving into a little flat together. They wanted some privacy, away from the communal staff accommodation they were growing out of.

In the kitchen, Bruno pulled a tray of mince pies that his mother had brought out of the Rayburn and tipped them on to a plate. It had been a wonderful Christmas, he reflected. At last, Joe's ghost had been laid to rest. The burden of guilt they all felt equally between them had rolled away and they could look to the future. More than anything, Bruno couldn't believe the change in his mother. Between the day he had introduced her to Alfie and now, she had altered immeasurably. She had recovered her zest for life, rediscovered her old friends and hobbies. She'd gone to the hairdresser's and had a radical cut and change of colour which had rolled back the years. And her renaissance had given his father back his *joie de vivre*. Graham seemed to be discovering his second childhood, forever messing about with train sets and kites and doing silly card tricks – Bruno had forgotten what an endlessly patient father he had been.

Of course, they would never forget Joe. With his parents' permission, Bruno had made a small speech before they began lunch, and they had all raised a glass in a toast to Joe, the wild one, the *enfant terrible*. The one who had brought them all together.

Lisa woke with a start. She'd nodded off on the sofa and it was nearly six o'clock. Two hours had seemed like two minutes, and she realized with regret that she was going to have to leave this haven and get back on duty. She scrambled to her feet.

Bruno looked troubled.

'I'd drive you but I'm way over the limit now. Too much of Dad's claret and far too much Paddy's.'

'I'm happy to walk.' The fresh air would do her good.

'I'll walk you. Hector needs a good run.'

'OK.'

The night was cool and crisp and even, as all good Christmas nights should be. Hector bounced along the beach, as full of energy as ever, retrieving sticks good-naturedly. The stars in the sky looked as if they had been positioned there by an Oxford Street window-dresser, sprinkled evenly across the velvet black and winking in sequence. The moon hovered, milky white and luminous. Lisa shivered slightly and tucked her scarf in more tightly.

'Cold?'

She nodded and the next moment found Bruno had put his arm around her.

She stopped in her tracks. He pulled his arm away hastily.

'Sorry.'

'No.' She smiled up at him. 'It was . . . nice.'

She stepped forward to be closer to him. This time he put both arms around her. She melted into his chest. She could hear the gentle pounding of the waves, feel the cold of the night air around her. And his warmth. Tentatively, she slid her arms around his waist. They stood, locked together, for what seemed like an eternity.

'Lisa . . .' Bruno stroked her cheek gently with the back of his forefinger. She tilted her head back, looking straight into his eyes as he kissed her. She could feel him, taste him, smell him, the Bruno-ness of him: there was Earl Grey tea and Irish whiskey and the scent she had smelt that first day she'd met him that now made her weak with longing.

She marvelled at how right it felt, despite her reservations, despite her caution, despite her rules. She'd never experienced this combination of emotions: wanton desire; hot, desperate urgency; a compulsion to devour and be devoured – all under-pinned by a glow of warmth and security that was like coming home.

Trembling, they parted and gazed at each other. Her curls were blowing wildly about her face. He smoothed them down with his hand and she closed her eyes at the very bliss of his touch, wanting to nudge at him for more caresses like a demanding cat.

'New Year's Eve,' he said gently. 'Come for supper. I know you've got a mad week ahead of you. You deserve to be pampered.'

'But—' She was about to protest. The hotel was full for New Year's Eve. But he put a finger to her lips.

'Shush now,' he commanded, smiling. 'I've already sorted it. Frank is in total control. The staff are perfectly capable of overseeing his gourmet dinner. Hannah will be on duty at the Mariscombe and she can be at The Rocks in two minutes if there's an emergency. For heaven's sake, Lisa. When did you last have a day off? Or a night out?'

She couldn't actually remember.

'I don't mind. I love my job.'

'That's not the point.'

They kissed again. It was fervent, passionate. For one wild moment Lisa felt like throwing off her clothes and pulling

382

him down on to the wet sand. But duty called – at six thirty her guests would be in the drawing room ready for yet more champagne. She tore her lips away.

'I must get back.'

'I know,' said Bruno regretfully. 'Come on.'

He grabbed her hand and pulled her along the last stretch of beach. She followed after him, breathless, laughing, Hector springing along behind them wondering what on earth was going on but happy to join in.

All evening, as she poured champagne and passed around canapés and made polite conversation with her guests, Lisa couldn't keep the smile off her face.

At last it was time for bed. The final guest had been despatched up the stairs, the staff had gone home, the tree lights had been turned off. It wasn't quite midnight. Lisa stood in the reception hall, gazing round at its white walls, at the ivy garlands entwined with chiffon ribbon, at the enormous flower arrangement studded with tiny dark red rosebuds, the wrought-iron candelabra filled with church candles. She flipped through the bookings' register, marvelling at the reservations she already had for the coming year. She picked up the champagne glass she had been carrying around all evening but barely touched, and finally allowed herself to drink. She didn't usually use alcohol to fortify herself, but on this occasion she needed to summon up some fortitude.

There was one more thing she had to do before bedtime.

She picked up the phone and dialled. Although she'd never used the number, she'd learned it by heart, for fear of losing it. She glanced at the clock – what was the time difference? Ahead or behind? She couldn't be sure, but nor did she care. If she didn't do it now, she never would.

Someone picked up the phone at the other end.

'Hello?'

The voice was so familiar, even after all this time, even from so many miles away.

'Dad . . . ?' That was the only word she could manage as a huge lump in her throat choked her.

'Oh, Lisa, love.' The words came out almost as a sigh. And in that sigh was a myriad of emotions: grief, relief, shock, love. And anxiety. 'Are you all right?'

'Yes.' She could only manage a croak, before the tears came. She valiantly tried to control her sobs. 'Happy Christmas, Dad.'

'Oh, Lisa, love,' he repeated, and this time there was joy in his voice. 'Happy Christmas to you too.'

Twenty minutes later she put the phone down with a slightly shaking hand. To her amazement, she'd agreed to fly over to Spain, in less than three weeks. Her father had wanted to jump on a plane the very next day to come and see her, but she'd been firm. She needed time to prepare herself for their reunion, to make sure she was strong, that she had things straight in her own mind. Besides, she had other things to attend to before then.

She carefully snuffed out the candles, taking care not to let any hot wax drip on to the floor. She walked into the drawing room to check the French windows were closed. Her eyes raked along the dark outline of the beach, until they came to rest at Bruno's house. There was a light on and she wondered if he was still up, or if it was just left on for security.

She turned and left the room, walking back across the hall to the telephone. She picked it up and dialled a number hastily, before she could change her mind.

He answered after the third ring.

'There is absolutely no way,' she said firmly, 'that I can wait until New Year's Eve. I'll meet you on the beach in ten minutes.'

For a taste of summer, read on for

VERONICA HENRY'S

A Sea Change

One

The M5 motorway on a Friday afternoon in August was enough to drive you mad. It took Craig forty minutes just to get out of the city. Then the traffic would be nose to tail all the way from Birmingham to Taunton. Stop–start. Stop–start. A slow crawl that had him drumming his fingers on the steering wheel.

Craig looked longingly at the hard shoulder. It was so tempting. If he got stopped, he could just flash his badge. He'd probably get away with it, except he wasn't that sort of copper. He didn't abuse his position. He had mates who had no problem with doing that kind of thing – breaking the rules – but Craig liked to stick to the letter of the law. He always played it straight, even if it wasn't always the easy option.

He could feel his T-shirt sticking to the back of his seat. He wasn't going to be a pretty sight by the time he got to the beach at Everdene, nor a pretty smell. The air-con didn't seem to make any difference, and opening the windows didn't help. He took a swig from the bottle of water he'd stuffed in the cup holder. It was warm, but it took the edge off the dryness in his throat. He wiped his brow with the back of his arm and looked at the sweat. Gross.

After Taunton, the traffic cleared and he put his foot down, keeping at a steady seventy miles an hour until he turned off the motorway. The car headed over Exmoor – its high, bleak landscape parched and brown from the summer sun. Away from the traffic Craig started to relax. He had a whole week off. A whole week to do what he liked. All he had with him was a few clothes, a wetsuit and his surfboard. And the key to the beach hut.

There were eight of them from the police station who'd clubbed together to rent the hut. Young people who were all into beach life and loved surfing, rock climbing, walking and kayaking. It was cheaper than going on holiday. It took just over three hours to get there, if you put your foot down, so between them they made the most of it.

Craig was the only one going down this weekend. All the others had different plans. After all the stress he'd had lately, he was looking forward to the peace and quiet. He couldn't wait to get there.

As he drove past the last supermarket before Everdene, he decided to pull over and pick up some food so he wouldn't have to venture out for a day or so. He bought a hot chicken and some rolls, a bag of salad, fruit, biscuits, some beers and bottled water. By six o'clock he would be sitting on the step, sipping a beer and looking at the sea.

As he left the car park he turned up the radio, grinned from ear to ear and gave a whoop.

Let the weekend begin.

Two

Jenna ran a damp cloth over the counter of her ice-cream kiosk for the tenth time that afternoon. She liked to keep it spotless. Behind her the radio was blaring, and above her the sun was shining in the sky. She adjusted the cones waiting to be filled, smoothed out the surfaces of the tubs and washed her scoops again. She looked down at the cabinet, pleased with the way it looked.

Inside there was a rainbow of ice creams to choose from. There were the usual, of course – chocolate and strawberry and vanilla. Then there were the more exotic flavours. Maple and walnut, rhubarb and ginger, Mississippi mud pie, peanut-butter cluster. The one that most kids seemed to hanker after was bubblegum, bright blue and sickly sweet. Dream Ices certainly didn't leave you short of choice.

The kiosk was situated at the top of the row of shops that led down to the harbour. Tawcombe had once been a thriving holiday resort, bursting at the seams with tourists. Now, in the recession, it was feeling the pinch. The hotels were closing down one after the other, as were the restaurants. Eventually the empty places got boarded up, then covered in graffiti, which didn't make the place very inviting.

The fishing boats still came in and out of the harbour, but there was a run-down air to the seafront, which had once bustled with life. Now it was deserted most of the day, until evening when gangs of bored youths collected there with cans of lager. The coastline was spectacular with its craggy rocks and crashing waves, but the town itself had become grey. A handful of attractions remained – a merry-go-round circled on the front, its horses in need of repainting. The arcade beeped and flashed with fruit machines.

And Dream Ices sold twenty-nine varieties of ice cream, which you could have in a waffle cone, or in a cone coated in sprinkles, or in a cone dipped in chocolate. You could also have chocolate, raspberry or butterscotch sauce on top. Then if you still wanted more, there were chocolate flakes and fingers of fudge and a squirt of whipped cream to finish.

Twenty-nine flavours had always annoyed Jenna. She would have made it thirty, but one of the tubs was filled with water for washing the scoops. Three rows – two of ten and one of nine – of brightly coloured, mouth-watering ice cream. She had noticed over the past week that some of the tubs were nearly empty and hadn't been replaced. Usually they were filled up before you could see the white plastic at the bottom. They'd almost run out of rum and raisin, and mint chocolate chip, and Devon clotted-cream fudge. There wasn't any in the freezer, which was strange. When she mentioned it to her boss, Terry, he just nodded and said he'd get onto it.

Dream Ices had done OK. Even though times were hard, it seemed like people still had money for an ice. There were just enough day trippers to keep the place ticking over. Sometimes Jenna scooped away all afternoon. All the same, she should have sensed trouble coming. For some reason, she hadn't.

So when the owner of Dream Ices, Terry, came up to her on Friday afternoon, Jenna hadn't expected to be sacked.

'I've got some bad news, love,' he said. 'I was hoping this wasn't going to happen but times are hard. I'm going to have to let you go.'

Her eyes widened in shock. 'You're not closing down, surely?'

'No. Not yet.' He looked gloomy, as if this might happen. 'But I can't afford to keep you on. I'll have to run the place myself.'

She wasn't sure how he was going to manage that. Terry

spent most of his time in the pub or at the bookies. Maybe that explained why he was in difficulty.

'Things will pick up,' she said hopefully. 'We've been busy today. And the forecast for the weekend is great. Nearly thirty degrees, they reckon.'

Terry was always moaning that the glory days were over. He was always telling her about the life he used to have, when the town was in its heyday and his pockets were stuffed with cash.

He shook his head. 'Even if we doubled the takings in the next month, I can't afford you. I'm sorry.'

'Surely we've done all right this summer?' she asked. 'I've been rushed off my feet some days.'

He shook his head. 'Not like the old days. I could clear five hundred quid cash, no problem, on a bank holiday. I struggle to get that in a week now. And the rent's gone up. And the wholesalers have put their prices up.'

Jenna didn't know what to say. Terry looked out to sea and cleared his throat. 'I can't give you your wages, either.'

Jenna's heart skipped a beat. He owed her over two weeks' money.

'You're kidding me.'

'I haven't got it. I had to pay the supplier. There was nothing left.'

There had been enough for him to have a few pints at lunchtime. She could smell the beer on his breath.

'I'll bring it round when I get it,' he promised her. 'If we have a good weekend . . .'

She'd never see it. She knew that.

'You could have told me before,' Jenna told him. 'You must have known you couldn't pay me, but you let me carry on working.'

'No,' he said. 'I promise you. I was hoping for something to happen. I was hoping . . .'

'For a win on the horses?'

Terry gave something between a shrug and a nod. Jenna felt hot with fury.

'Gambling is a game for mugs. Surely you know that by now, Terry? If it was that easy, everyone would be doing it.'

Terry just walked away and stood by the harbour railings. He lit a cigarette.

Jenna couldn't believe what Terry had done. She had been so loyal to him. She'd kept the place afloat all summer, smiling and laughing with the customers. She talked them into having two scoops when they only wanted one. She persuaded women who were watching their figure that just one wouldn't hurt. And the locals came here to buy ice cream from her too. She'd become a bit of a local landmark over the summer. It was her banter rather than the ice cream that they came for. And her singing.

She'd started off singing along to songs on the radio, using a cone as a microphone. Then she started singing whatever she felt like, her own favourites that she could belt out behind the counter. It kept her sane even if she did look mad, but people seemed to enjoy it. Her mood was catching.

She was known as the Ice Cream Girl. She didn't mind being called that at all. It was a happy name. People had started making requests. They were always telling her she should go on *The X Factor*, or get an agent, or join a band. But Jenna knew there was a big difference between mucking about and doing it for real. She wasn't convinced she had any real talent. She just wanted people to have a good time.

She wasn't going to be the Ice Cream Girl any more, though. In the past two minutes she had been turned back into a nobody. That would teach her to have trusted Terry, and to have done her best for him. She had genuinely thought he would look after her and see her right, but no. As soon as things got tough he had dumped her. He was just like everybody else. Out for himself and what he could get.

She felt tears pricking the back of her eyelids, but she

refused to cry. Terry Rowe wasn't going to see the effect he'd had on her.

She took off her apron and folded it up carefully. Then she picked up the strawberry sauce and squirted it all over every tub of ice cream in the cabinet. She followed it with the chocolate. Then she sprinkled a shaker full of hundreds and thousands over the lot.

She felt sick with anger. She remembered the number of times Terry had rung her, begging her to do a shift because he'd had a skinful. The days she'd stayed late because he couldn't drag himself out of the pub. He had repaid her loyalty by sacking her the minute things got tough.

He came back when he had finished his cigarette. She could smell the tobacco on him and it turned her stomach.

'What have you done?' he asked, outraged.

She shrugged.

'You can pay me back for all of that! There's a couple of hundred quid's worth there.'

'Take it out of my wages,' she told him.

It hadn't been a dream job. No one dreamed about selling ice cream the way they did about being an actress or a supermodel or a singer. She'd enjoyed it, though. Ice cream brought a few moments of pleasure. She loved watching people's faces as they looked at what was on offer, dazzled by the choice. She loved their smiles as they took their loaded cones. There were worse jobs.

She walked away from the kiosk without looking back or bothering to say goodbye.

By the time Jenna got to the end of the quay, her anger had turned to fear. She felt anxious. So anxious that it felt like her insides were being eaten. It was turning out to be a bad summer. Three weeks ago, someone had broken into the house where she had a room. They'd smashed in all the doors and taken everything they could. Jenna didn't have much in the way of valuables. But she had had three weeks' worth of wages tucked into the back of a drawer, waiting to pay the rent.

Her landlord hadn't been at all understanding. He reckoned it wasn't his fault the house had been burgled, even though everyone said the locks hadn't been strong enough. He'd agreed to wait for the rent until Jenna got her next lot of wages, which should have been today.

How was she going to pay now? Her landlord was going to kick up, she knew he was. He wouldn't be interested in reasons or excuses. She'd promised him the rent she owed in cash by the end of the week, which was today. Friday. Otherwise he was going to boot her out. She knew he would. He knew people who would come and pack up her stuff and throw it out of her room, then drag her out afterwards. She'd seen it happen before.

It didn't matter where she stood legally. People like her landlord didn't take any notice of the law. They knew the system wouldn't look after her. She was a nothing, a nobody, and no one cared.

Jenna trudged into the centre of Tawcombe, past the chip shop and the arcade and back to her house. She'd never call it 'home'. Home was somewhere you were glad to come back to. Somewhere you felt you belonged. She was yet to feel that about anywhere.

Three

The last five miles of Craig's journey were along a winding road lined with hedges. On either side the fields were full of sheep and cows. At last he reached the roundabout that led down the hill to Everdene. After another half a mile and then, around the next corner, was the sight that lifted his heart every time he saw it.

The sea. Endless and blue, yet never quite the same colour. That first glimpse was always a thrill. He could see the pinky brown of the beach, too, which was more than a mile of soft, soft sand. Then when he got closer, he spied the candy colours of the beach huts lined up in a row. The one that he shared with his copper mates was the seventh one along. Pale blue and white and in need of a lick of paint, but they never complained. Who cared about the state of the paint-work when there was fun to be had?

He left his car in the public car park, took his overnight bag and his shopping from the boot and headed off down the slipway next to a small arcade of shops. They were all just closing for the night but he had time to buy himself a bag of chips from the cafe. He sat outside and ate them, one by one. Craig usually ate healthily, but he always treated himself every time he came down here. He'd soon burn off the calories.

He kicked off his shoes and made the last part of his journey barefoot. The heat of the day was still in the sand, although as he sank deeper it was cool beneath the surface. It was hard going with everything he had to carry, but at last he reached the seventh beach hut along, with its faded blue door.

He pulled out the key and slid it into the padlock, unlocked it and stepped inside.

It always smelled the same, of damp and wood and salt. He breathed in and his stomach did a flip. It was like coming home. This was the place in the world where he felt most happy. It was basic. Some of the huts on the beach had been done up like show-homes, but this one had hardly been touched since it was put up over thirty years ago. It had four wooden bunks, a kitchen area with a couple of cupboards, a tiny sink and a Calor gas stove. There was also a makeshift shower and a toilet. It was furnished with a giant old settee that sagged in the middle and a rickety table with four wobbly chairs.

The blokes who shared it made no effort to decorate the hut, but sometimes the girls tried to add a feminine touch. One had bought a set of matching spotted mugs, tired of the chipped and stained ones. Another had put up some surfing pictures, and another had strung up some fairy lights. They had an ancient ghetto blaster on which they played old cassettes. They had a competition to see who could dig out the most cheesy tape. Most nights the hut rocked to the sounds of Herb Alpert, Barry Manilow and Boney M.

Tonight, though, it was going to be peaceful. Craig preferred quiet when he was on his own. He needed to be alone with his thoughts, because he knew he was going to have to make a tough decision this weekend. As he looked out across the shore, he felt the worries and tension of the past few weeks gradually start to ease.

It was all very well knowing you were innocent, but that didn't always count for much, especially when it was your word against someone else's. And when the video evidence against you looked bad, you didn't have much of a chance. Craig knew he would never treat a police suspect with unnecessary violence. But he'd been set up by a gang of blokes with a grudge against him. He'd been responsible for arresting one of their mates who'd been sent down for a long stretch.

As a result, they'd stitched him up and had him accused of police brutality. He'd been suspended while there was an investigation. Craig had spent the entire three months leading up to his case convinced he was going to lose his job – or, maybe, even worse.

In the end, justice had been done and he had been found innocent, but the stress had taken its toll. He lived in fear of it happening again and now faced every day with dread. He was fine with his close friends, but felt awkward with other work-mates he came into contact with. He could tell they were wary, wondering if he had been guilty. After all, there was no smoke without fire.

The whole episode had made him question what he was doing with his life. He'd been longing to escape back to Everdene, so he could clear his head. Now that he was here, he felt more hopeful. As he sank into a deckchair outside the beach hut and looked at the view with a bottle of beer in his hand, the future didn't seem quite so bleak.

Jenna finally arrived at the terraced house where she lived. She had a bedsit on the third floor. She shared a bathroom and kitchen with six other people. Six other people who didn't know how to use a dishcloth or bleach, or even flush the toilet, sometimes. She ended up cleaning up herself, even though they were supposed to take turns. It was either that, or live in squalor.

She'd tried to make her room as nice as she could, but it was difficult. The carpet was green with mould in the corners. The wallpaper was ancient and coming off the wall in clumps. The windows let the cold in through the cracks in winter and turned the place into a sauna in summer. She couldn't afford proper curtains, so she'd hung a pair of old sheets from the rail. On the walls, she'd stuck photos of her heroines: Marilyn Monroe and Dita von Teese – both glamorous pin-up girls not afraid to show off their curves. She tried to copy their image, but it was hard to look the part when you barely had enough money to keep body and soul together. Still, she always tried to wear a dress, and lipstick, and put her hair up, and this look usually helped to lift her spirits. If things were going badly, and you slobbed about in jeans and no make-up, you were bound to feel bad about yourself.

No amount of dressing up took away her fear, though. She sat in the middle of her bed. It would only be a matter of time before the landlord came knocking. She didn't have the money for her rent. Her stomach churned with dread. Where would she go if he kicked her out? She didn't think she could get any lower. She'd left her mum's house a year ago when their rows had got out of control. She'd thought she could stand on her own two feet. It was much harder than she thought.

Jenna thought about phoning her mates and meeting them at the pub, then she remembered she wouldn't be able to afford a drink. She was penniless. Someone would buy her one, of course they would, but she didn't want to feel like a scrounger. She flopped back down onto the mattress. The room smelled stale. The air was almost too hot to breathe. Everyone was saying what a fantastic weekend it was going to be, with soaring temperatures and fun in the sun.

There wasn't going to be any fun on the third floor of 21a Boscombe Terrace.

It was after his second beer that Craig began to miss Michelle.

He knew it would happen. The first drink relaxed you. By the second, your defences were down and emotions started to kick in. It would take another two or three beers to blot out the feelings altogether, but Craig didn't want to get drunk. He was going to have to put up with how he felt.

They'd gone out for five years, Craig and Michelle. It had been a very easy relationship with no drama. They enjoyed each other's company and liked the same things. Then six months ago she'd been offered the chance to run a hairdressing salon at a big glitzy hotel in Dubai.

The salon she had run in Birmingham city centre was struggling. She'd had to let valued staff go. She'd cut back on the cleaning and the number of towels they used. She hated cutting corners but she had no choice. People just weren't spending the money any more. They were going three months, even longer, without having their colour done, or doing it themselves at home. She was worried that the shop was going to go under. Then the opportunity of a lifetime had come along. Craig had had no second thoughts.

'You have to take it,' he told her. 'You hate your job at the moment. It's depressing. Dubai will be an awesome chance for you.'

Michelle and Craig were sensible enough to realize that their relationship wouldn't survive the separation. Neither of them wanted the pressure or the guilt of trying to maintain it in the long term.

'I don't want you to get out there and feel you can't have fun,' Craig told her.

'And I don't want you to mope around because I'm not there,' said Michelle.

So they agreed to part, but as friends. He drove her to the airport. She hugged him tight at the departure gate, and cried a bit, but he could tell she was excited about her new life. They'd agreed he would go out there at Christmas if neither of them had found someone else. Neither of them had so far, but Craig didn't think he would go. Long-distance relationships never worked. He'd seen the pictures she'd posted on Facebook and it felt as if he was looking at a stranger. They went on Skype from time to time too, but he found it upsetting. It just reminded him of what he was missing.

He'd been too caught up with the investigation to find anyone else. His mates egged him on when they went to the pub in Everdene for a drink. They thought he should find someone new, but he didn't want to force it. He wasn't one for one-night stands, not like some of his friends who went out with a different girl every time they came down to Devon.

Maybe this weekend he should start to have a look round, he thought.

Not tonight, though. He wanted to wind down and get a decent night's sleep so that he could make the most of the weekend. Craig watched the waves roll in towards the shore. There would be plenty of time for pulling. He had the whole week, after all.

At half past nine, there was a bang on Jenna's door. It was so loud that she jumped off the bed, her heart thumping. She realized she had fallen asleep. She did that a lot these days. Being asleep was so much better than being awake. Her mouth went dry with fear. The knock came again, even louder. She thought about pretending that she wasn't in.

'Oi!' There was a shout from the other side of the door. She knew that voice only too well. 'I know you're in there. Open up.'

The landlord probably did know she was in there. He had spies everywhere. She didn't trust any of the other tenants in the house.

'OK!' she called out, and hated how weedy her voice sounded.

She opened the door. The Prof was standing there. They called him The Prof because of his thick, black-rimmed glasses. Not because he was clever, unless you counted ripping desperate people off as clever. He was wearing a grubby white shirt, jeans and scuffed black slip-on shoes. Anyone would think he was on the breadline too.

'You got something for me?' He wandered in as if he owned the place. Which – technically – he did, but it was her room. He should respect her privacy.

Jenna swallowed hard.

'I'm really sorry,' she stammered. 'My boss wouldn't pay me. I haven't got the rent money. I'll get it for you by Monday. I promise.'

He made a clicking noise with his tongue behind his teeth.

'You're already behind. I'm going to have to start charging you interest.'

'I can't afford to pay you interest. I can't afford the rent as it is.'

He shrugged.

'It's not my problem.'

He walked over towards the window and looked around, then nodded.

'It's a big room, this. Too big for one. I could probably get a family in here. Not waste it on someone who won't pay up.'

He was threatening her, Jenna realized. How did he expect her to find the money? There was no point in asking him for sympathy. Men like him didn't care. How did he sleep at night, she wondered? Better than she did, probably.

She looked at him, and her stomach turned. He must rake in a fortune with all the money he took. What did he spend it on? He certainly didn't spend it on his clothes, or his hair, which needed a good cut, not to mention a wash. Or his car either – she'd seen him drive around in a battered old Ford Mondeo. She wondered where he lived, and if he had a wife, or any kids. She pitied them if he did.

Sometimes Jenna wondered if there were any decent men in the world.

He was walking towards her wardrobe, opening it up, looking through her stuff with that stupid grin on his face.

'Get out of my wardrobe,' Jenna told him.

He looked up. His hands were mauling her clothes, all the vintage dresses she'd bought in charity shops and at jumble sales and from eBay. 'Just seeing if there's anything I could take instead of cash . . .'

She stepped towards him.

'There isn't anything. I've told you. I'll get the rent money.'

He raised an eyebrow.

'Yeah?' He looked her up and down. She shuddered as she felt his gaze undress her. She knew what he was thinking. She folded her arms across her chest. She didn't have to take this unspoken threat. He was a bully.

'Where do you get off, treating people like this?'

The Prof took a step back, surprised by her outburst.

'Like what?'

'Bullying them. Not just me, either. I've seen you bully that woman downstairs – the one with the baby. Does it make you feel good?'

He scowled, slamming the wardrobe door shut.

'All I want is what's owed to me. Nothing wrong with that.'

He came towards her with a smile. He reached out his hand and ran the back of his fingers down her cheek. His breath was stale and sour.

'Get me the rent. By Monday. And if I were you, I'd keep your opinions to yourself.'

Jenna jerked her head away. She could see that she'd rattled him. Something she'd said had touched a nerve. At least he hadn't mentioned interest. Even so, she still didn't have the rent. She hadn't got anything to sell. No jewellery, no nice watch, no computer, fancy phone or iPod. Those had all gone ages ago. At least she'd bought herself some time, though.

He looked at her steadily. She could see the stubble starting to poke through on his chin.

'I'll be back first thing on Monday.'

She thought he was probably enjoying torturing her. It's not as if he needed the money that much. He owned several houses around the town. He must be coining in thousands a week. He could afford to wait. If she pointed out that fact, she knew what he'd say. 'If I let you get away with it, they'll all want to pay late.'

At last he left the room. Jenna hadn't thought that she was going to get rid of him that easily, but maybe he had some one else to pick on. Her landlord was scum. He wasn't the only one of his kind around, though. There were quite a few 'entrepreneurs' in Tawcombe who'd bought up the big old Victorian houses that had been so splendid in their heyday. Especially now the town was a run-down seaside resort filled with unemployed and disillusioned people with no hope of escape. The landlords slapped up chipboard walls and cheap kitchens and crammed in as many tenants as they could find.

Jenna certainly wasn't the only person struggling. There were no decent jobs out here in the sticks. You could pick up casual work during the summer season if you were lucky, but there was slim chance of a proper career. She'd wanted to go to college but her mum had just laughed. She'd refused to support Jenna while she studied.

Cheers for that, Mum, she thought bitterly, though she shouldn't have been surprised. Her mum had never gone out of her way to help her with anything. Jenna had thought she'd be able to make a better life for herself on her own, but her plan had backfired big time. She was worse off now than she'd ever been, but no way was she going to go crawling back home. She knew she could just step outside and get on the bus that would take her two miles up the road to the estate where her mum lived, but she couldn't bear the thought of the look on her mum's face.

'Look what the cat's brought in,' she could hear her mother saying gleefully.

Never, thought Jenna. I'm never going back there. Instead, she had to find nearly four hundred quid by Monday morning, or she'd be out on the pavement surrounded by what little she had left.

Her landlord, The Prof, didn't make idle threats. She knew that for certain.

When night had fallen, the beach was wrapped in a soft navy-blue blanket spattered with stars. Craig unrolled his sleeping bag and curled up on one of the bunks in the beach hut, leaving the door slightly open. It was unlikely that anyone would try to get in, and he loved to go to sleep with the sound of the waves in the background. It was so soothing, more soothing than any lullaby. He loved the sound of the constant 'shushing' as the tide went in and out.

He checked the weather forecast on his phone before he fell asleep. Tomorrow was set fair. He'd get up early and hit the surf before anyone else.

Two minutes after his head hit the pillow, Craig was asleep.

Jenna was still wide awake at midnight. Her room was stifling, but if she opened her window the noise came in from outside the pub opposite. Her mind was whirling as she thought about the unfairness of the day. The full weight of being sacked was gradually beginning to hit her. Not only did she not have the money for the rent – her immediate problem – but what was she going to live on?

As she closed her eyes and tried to shut out the laughter of the pub-goers, her mind began to wander. What was the point of playing by the rules? It didn't seem to get you anywhere. The people she knew who'd done best in life, like The Prof, didn't seem to bother. Her family had never played it straight, any of them. They were on to every scam going, and they were all as happy as Larry. If you played it straight, it seemed as if you just sank to the bottom.

How was she going to get out of this trap? There would be no work going in Tawcombe for the rest of the summer. All the jobs were already taken. Maybe she could move to a bigger place? Bamford was the nearest big town, but she couldn't see a life for herself there. She didn't know anyone, for a start. Or a bigger city? Plymouth? Exeter? The thought of that terrified her. She'd only really known Tawcombe her whole life.

Jenna sighed. She was stuck here. She couldn't even afford a lottery ticket.

She turned onto her side and curled her legs up, tucking herself into a ball. All she could think about was The Prof's face on Monday morning. She bet he was hoping she wouldn't have the money. She was sure he enjoyed kicking people out of his scuzzy rooms so that he could lure someone else in and get the deposit from them.

Even if she found a job tomorrow morning, she couldn't get the money she needed in time. Nobody would pay her in advance. There were girls she knew who would know how to get that kind of money quickly. In a seaside town, there were always ways that you could supplement your income. Jenna wasn't going to take that path. Once you got into that, there was no way out. Anyway, the thought made her skin crawl. If she'd wanted to sell herself, she'd have made a deal with The Prof already . . .

As she felt the music from the pub pound through her body, she began to turn over possibilities in her mind.

Five minutes later, Jenna sat up as an idea occurred to her. Her heart thumped. Was it crazy? It seemed so simple. Of course it was wrong, but in the grand scheme of 'wrong', it was way down the scale. There were far, far worse things she could do.

She asked herself which was better – to be straight and penniless, or crooked and in the black, as far as money was concerned? She'd spent enough time already being the former, and it had nothing to recommend it. She'd always had a clear conscience, but you couldn't eat a strong set of moral values.

The more she thought about it, the more enticing her idea became.

As she went over the details and eventually drifted off to sleep, she told herself she only had to do it once, just once, until she got herself back on her feet.

Four

There was nothing more perfect than waking up by the sea and watching the sunrise.

Every time he saw it, Craig couldn't believe how lucky he was. By six o'clock in the morning, the copper from the Midlands was walking towards the sea with his surfboard tucked under his arms, his footprints in the damp sand the first of the day. He reached the water's edge.

The white frill of surf had looked like nothing from the hut, but once he got up close he realized the waves were pretty big. He ran straight into the water without stopping. His breath was taken away for a split second by the cold, but he carried on, paddling out behind the waves.

He surfed for nearly an hour. Craig was no expert and he envied the surfers who cut through the water with grace and elegance, as if they were at one with the waves. He knew that came with years of practice. These guys were devoted. They surfed every day, in all conditions. They were fanatics.

He'd heard their tales in the bar often enough. They told him about the surfing hot spots as far away as Hawaii, India and Australia, and their stories inspired him. He admired their devil-may-care attitude to life. They lived to surf. That was it. They picked up work when they could, where they could. They didn't worry about anything else. They had no responsibilities.

That kind of mindset didn't really suit him, being in the police. Until recently, Craig figured he had the best of both worlds. Where were these guys going to be in their old age?

None of them would have a pension, just their memories. It was only now that he'd started to have doubts, to begin thinking differently, that he wondered about whether he'd really got it right.

Craig had given everything to his career. He loved his home town, and he'd wanted to contribute to its future. He wanted to make it a safe place, to protect his fellow townspeople from harm, to give them hope. Someone had once given him hope, after all, which was why he was lucky enough to be here now, enjoying the crystal-clear water.

By the time he got back to the beach hut with his surfboard, the early-morning sun had nearly dried him off after his dip in the sea. He pulled on his jeans and walked up the beach to the cafe in the arcade, taking a table outside. He ordered a surfer's breakfast of bacon, sausage, egg, mushrooms, tomato, beans, hash browns, toast and a pot of tea.

A guy he knew vaguely, Rusty, pulled up a chair next to him and sat down. That was the great thing about Everdene. You didn't see someone for months, but when you bumped into them, it was as if you'd seen them yesterday.

'Hey, buddy, how's it going?'

Rusty was from South Africa and was a photographer. He took pictures of the sea, blew them up onto canvas and sold them out of a camper van on the front. The tourists loved these shots, which funded Rusty's lifestyle. He didn't have to answer to anyone. He'd helped Craig out when he'd started surfing last summer. And Craig knew he would never be as good as Rusty could be in the water.

'Good, thanks,' replied Craig. 'Though I've had a rough time of it the past few weeks.'

He didn't know if Rusty would even remember he was a copper.

Rusty nodded. He looked up at the sky. 'Bad times, man.'

His hair was bleached blond by the sun. His skin was tanned, and his bright blue eyes shone out. Craig felt a twinge of envy at his lifestyle. Rusty would never have experienced the stress that Craig went through on a daily basis because of his job. The dryness in your mouth because you didn't know how things were going to turn out, or whether you were going to make the right decisions. And even if you did, whether you were going to make a difference.

And even if you did make a difference, whether it was then going to backfire.

Craig sighed. He didn't want to turn into a cliché of the disillusioned cop.

'So what have you been up to?' he asked.

Rusty took a tiny roll-up cigarette out of a tin in his pocket and lit it. He took a drag, sucked in the smoke, then blew it in a thin stream up in the air. Then he began to tell Craig what he'd been doing. He'd spent two months in Goa, then a month in Ireland, playing at festivals with some friends who had a band. Now he was back in Everdene to spend August teaching surfing to the tourists until the days grew short.

Craig put his head back and let the sun warm up the skin on his face as he listened. Rusty's life was as far away from his own as you could get. Every minute of Craig's life was accounted for. He didn't have a choice from the second he woke up.

Did he envy Rusty? He had very little, just his camper van, his surfboard and some worn and faded clothes, but he took opportunities as they presented themselves. Craig thought of his one-bedroomed apartment by the waterfront. The furniture he'd filled it with was all bought and paid for. He had a car, a wardrobe full of clothes and a top-of-the-range entertainment system. They were all the rewards of a tough job. Yet somehow the thought that nothing was going to change was constantly nagging at him. In the future, Craig would get a promotion, then probably a wife and kids, then maybe a house. There was nothing wrong with any of that, but would he ever see the world, like Rusty? Would he ever wake up in the morning and think, 'What now? Where next?' Who knew?

Even when he was down here at Everdene, he knew he was

on borrowed time. It wouldn't be long before it was time to get back into the car and drive up the motorway. Then he would have to get back into his uniform and clock on. He'd be out in his police squad car, patrolling the streets, never knowing how much trouble the day was going to bring. He rarely came home feeling he'd done a good job. It wasn't that he was shocked by what people did, far from it. It was because he knew why they did it. The saying, 'There but for the grace of God go I' was often in his thoughts.

Next morning, Jenna woke at seven and listened to the sound of seagulls circling. She knew they would be feasting on the packets of leftover chips and kebabs dropped in the streets. They were scavengers to the end, those seagulls. She lay for a moment looking at the ceiling. There was a huge brown stain in the middle of it that seemed to bulge. She lived in fear of the roof caving in, imagining the bloke upstairs falling through the floor and landing on top of her, leaving a man-shaped hole.

She gave herself five minutes to decide whether she was going to go through with her plan. Even though it would mean she had failed. She had been so determined to prove herself.

'You think you're better than I am, don't you?' This had been her mother's parting shot.

'Yes, I do,' Jenna had told her, and her mum had just laughed. She could hear the cackle now, fuelled by fags and cheap bottles of supermarket own-brand vodka. Her mother's bloke went and bought a bottle of vodka every morning from the corner shop, and by four o'clock in the afternoon the pair of them would have polished it off, just in time to head to the pub.

Of course she thought she was better than that.

Jenna had dreamed that, if she got away from the grimy house where she had been brought up, she could make something of herself. She had to escape the lazy, drunken woman who had given birth to her and four other kids. Her mum had never been a proper mother to any of them. If anything, they had to look after her. There were days when Jenna hadn't gone to school because her mum was so drunk that she was scared to leave her.

Jenna could remember going back to her friends' houses sometimes. She had looked on, wide-eyed, as their mothers fussed over them, made them tea and asked about their day. She had sat in the bedrooms of her schoolfriends, with their crisply ironed duvet covers and matching curtains, and fluffy dressing gowns and slippers. They had clean towels hanging in the bathroom and toilet paper on a holder. There were proper mealtimes when the whole family sat round the table. They had fathers who came home and hugged them. They had fathers who would never raise a voice, let alone a hand, to their wife or kids.

Jenna wasn't jealous, but she never invited anyone back to her house. She would have been too ashamed because their house was a hovel. The tiny front yard was studded with dog turds that baked hard in the sun or turned to mush in the rain. Sometimes, Jenna cleared them up but she ended up gagging. Inside the house, the lounge was covered in dog hairs and the wallpaper had been scratched off the wall. Every surface in the kitchen was covered in dirty cups and plates, cereal boxes and takeaway cartons. There were empty bottles everywhere, but no glasses. Her mum just poured vodka straight into a can of 7Up and glugged it. In the hall, there were tins of dog food upended straight onto the floor. Her mum argued that the dogs only took two seconds to eat it, because they were always starving, so what was the point of dirtying a dish?

Whatever happened, Jenna wasn't going back there.

She blinked back the familiar tears. It was up to her now. She had no one else, and that was how she liked it – even though it was hard. She forced herself to get out of bed. She could lie there all day, but then she would be just like her mother. She had to keep going, even though she knew that what she was about to do was wrong.

Jenna got herself dressed – before she could change her mind. She put on a bikini, then chose a dress. She didn't want to stand out, so she picked out one with a simple white halter neck. In a bag, she put a towel, some suncream, a bottle of water and a book. She tied her hair in a high ponytail and finished off the look with a pair of sunglasses and some flip-flops decorated with big flowers.

As she left the house, she looked like any normal young girl about to spend a day on the beach.

Jenna had just enough money for the bus fare to Everdene. It was only five miles away, but it might as well have been a thousand. Her heart lifted every time she went down the hill towards the bay. It was as unlike Tawcombe as you could get. Everywhere you looked there was beauty, from the rolling hills to the sea to the sun on the distant horizon. There were shades of green and blue and shimmering gold.

She'd come here before – sometimes with her mates. They ate chips on the beach, washed down with bottles of cider, and got the late bus back. They never went in the sea. That was for tourists and surfers. As far as Jenna was concerned, the sea might look nice – but it was cold and wet.

She got off the bus in the centre of the village where the traffic was insane. On a hot day, in the height of summer, you had to find a parking space by nine o'clock or you had no hope. The pavements were crowded with people heading to the beach, lugging their beach bags, buckets, spades and body boards. It was a nightmare getting through, dodging push-chairs and dogs on leads, but Jenna kept her head down and pushed on. In the end, she walked in the road, because it was easier. The traffic was so slow that she was unlikely to get run over. She didn't think about what she was going to do. She had no choice, she told herself – over and over.

She passed the Ship Aground, the pub in the middle of

Everdene where everyone hung out. There was a huge poster outside, advertising their end-of-season pop-singing competition. The first prize was a hundred pounds. For a moment, Jenna hesitated. Her friends were always trying to persuade her to enter competitions like this. They were always telling her she had an amazing voice, but she didn't have the confidence. It was one thing mucking about in the ice-cream kiosk, but it was quite another walking out on stage.

Anyway, even if she did enter, and even if she won, what then? She'd have a hundred quid in her pocket, but that wasn't enough to live on or to pay the rent she owed. Her current plan was going to make her more money. She turned away and walked on.

As she passed the coffee shop in the arcade at the top of the beach, she realized that she hadn't eaten or drunk anything since she'd left the ice-cream kiosk yesterday afternoon. She pulled out the last of her change and estimated she had enough for a cup of tea. With three sugars in it, it might keep her going for a while. She ducked inside and ordered a takeaway cup. As she paid and turned to leave, she was just taking off the plastic lid when she bumped straight into a man heading for the counter.

Luckily she hadn't been holding the cup close to her, or it would have spilled all down her front. Instead, it went all over the floor.

'Oh my God, I'm so sorry.' The man put out his hand and touched her arm. 'Are you OK?'

'I'm fine,' said Jenna, looking up, right into the most incredible eyes. Eyes that were silver-grey, with the longest lashes she had ever seen on a man – and set in a kind face, too.

'I wasn't looking where I was going . . .'

'Neither was I.' She managed a laugh. Wow! This guy was really good-looking, she thought. There were always a lot of good-looking guys in Everdene, but he was even hotter than most. He had dark curly hair, cropped close, and was lean and muscular in his T-shirt and faded jeans.

'Let me get you another.' He looked at her, his dark brows meeting in a frown. 'Seriously. Go and sit down and I'll bring you one over.'

Jenna bit her lip, thinking how wonderful it would be to sit down while he brought her a fresh drink. Then she remembered what she was doing here, and realized that today of all days she didn't want to bring attention to herself. The last thing she needed was to strike up conversation with a handsome stranger who might remember her.

'It's OK. It's fine. I'm in a hurry. Honestly. I have to go.'

She smiled and walked away as quickly as she could, throwing her empty cup into the nearest bin.

Eventually Jenna made it onto the sand. The tide was in, which meant at the moment there was little room for people to set up camp. As the sea inched out again, the visitors began to spread out their rugs, putting up their windbreaks and laying out all the things they needed for the day. The sun grew ever more sparkling, welcoming the crowds with its rays.

Jenna spread out her towel at the bottom of the bank beneath the beach huts. She'd chosen her pitch carefully. She wanted to be on the edge of the crowds, so she could watch, but she didn't want to stand out. Everyone was so busy having a good time that they weren't going to notice her.

Five

Craig noticed Jenna straight away.

She was the girl he'd bumped into at the coffee shop. She was sitting at the bottom of the bank outside his beach hut. She looked as if she'd stepped out of a 1950s film set, with her curves and her high ponytail and her retro dress. She really was very pretty, and he wondered why she was here on her own. Maybe she was waiting for her mates, or her boyfriend? Maybe that was why she hadn't let him buy her a drink, because there was another bloke in the picture.

Craig told himself to stop staring but he wasn't sure what else to do. There was certainly no point in trying to surf while the beach was this busy. Even though there were supposed to be separate areas for surfers and swimmers, Craig could see it was chaos in the water. He wasn't a good enough surfer to avoid hitting someone if they got in his way. He'd wait until later this evening, when the crowds had gone. The waves would still be good. In the meantime, he put up his striped deckchair in front of the hut and sat watching all the people on the beach. He wondered who they were and where they had come from as little dramas unfolded. A teenage boy fussed over his gran, making sure she was comfortable. Two small toddlers fought over a spade until their mother intervened. A young couple stretched out on a rug together, sharing the headphones on an iPod.

His eyes kept straying back to the girl with the ponytail. She was still on her own. Maybe he should go and talk to her, or offer her another drink? If his friends were here, he knew they would be encouraging him, but without them he felt shy. Maybe she wanted to be on her own and didn't want company? Craig decided in the end he would leave her alone. He picked up his book instead and started to read.

Jenna spread her things out around her, then rubbed some suncream on her arms and the back of her neck. She didn't want to burn in the heat of the sun. From behind her sunglasses, she examined all the groups of people around her. She made sure she knew exactly who was in each group, and how the dynamics worked. Small families with toddlers would be the best target. The parents of small children were always distracted.

Jenna had never stolen anything in her life before, but she knew plenty of people who had. Members of her family were always coming home with knocked-off gear or things that had 'fallen off the back of a lorry'. Her mum was always sticking stuff in her pockets when she was out shopping. It was a way of life for them, but Jenna hadn't had to stoop that low before.

She felt sick that it had come to this, but she was desperate. Her mum's words came back to her time and again. 'You're no better than the rest of us.' Well, maybe not, but at least she'd had a go at getting out there and trying to make a better life for herself. Anyway, she reminded herself, this was a one-off. She told herself she was only getting back what had been stolen from her a couple of weeks ago. She knew deep down that was no excuse, of course, but she didn't know what else to do. It was either this or be thrown out of her room by The Prof on Monday.

Jenna looked around the beach again. She knew all the rules of pickpocketing. When you came from the kind of family she did, you picked up these things along the way. She knew how to identify an easy victim, a 'mark', and the best conditions to steal from them. You had to wait until they were off their guard and weren't paying attention. The beach was perfect for that, because people were concentrating so hard on having a good time that they forgot to look after their valuables. Of course, it was better to have an accomplice, a partner in crime, but that was out of the question. Jenna could hardly have asked one of her mates to come and help her.

She decided to try the ice-cream queue first. There were three vans parked along the beach, and the searing heat meant that the lines outside them were already long. She waited nearby until she saw a harassed-looking father join the queue with two small children in tow. She slipped in behind him, guessing it was going to be at least ten minutes before they got to the window. By then, everyone would be more hot and bothered than ever.

She examined her target. She could see his wallet in the back pocket of his shorts. He was doing his best to control his two children, who were bawling in fury that their ice cream wasn't coming sooner. When he bent down to tell off one of them, she whisked the wallet out of his pocket and into her own.

Before the children had stopped arguing, she left the queue. Anyone would think she was just bored with waiting. She didn't wait to see the man's reaction when he discovered his loss. At first he would assume he had dropped his wallet on the walk over, or that he'd forgotten to put it in his pocket. It would probably be at least twenty minutes before he figured out he'd been pickpocketed, and by then he wouldn't be sure where it had happened. Jenna would be long gone.

Her heart was hammering and her mouth was dry as she made her way back to her towel. She felt slightly sick, too, although she wasn't sure whether that was a combination of the heat and the fact that she still hadn't eaten. She opened the wallet, pulled out three twenty-pound notes and a crumpled fiver and put them in her bag. All she had to do now was get rid of the evidence. She walked a couple of hundred yards back up the beach to where six big black bins were regularly emptied throughout the day. She lifted the lid, recoiling slightly from the stench of chip wrappers and dirty nappies baking in the sunshine, and dropped the wallet in. She wasn't going to touch the credit cards. That wasn't her level of crime at all, although she knew people who would have found them useful.

So far, so good, she thought. She didn't want to think about whether she'd ruined the family's day out. Feeling guilty was not going to help with the task in hand. She went back to her blanket for a few minutes and waited until her heart had stopped hammering. Then she decided to head up the beach in the other direction. She'd spotted a young couple walking down to the water, hand in hand. The girl had very carefully placed her handbag under a towel before they left, as if that was going to fool anyone. Some people, thought Jenna, were very stupid.

Craig woke with a start, realising he'd fallen asleep in the heat of the midday sun. There was sweat trickling down his forehead, and he was dying of thirst. He should probably go back into the hut, into the shade. He sat up and glanced around, mostly to see if anyone had spotted him dribbling while he was asleep. He looked down to the bottom of the bank to see if the girl with the ponytail was still there, but her towel was empty. Her stuff was still there, though, so she had to be around.

He scanned the crowds, looking for her, and thought he could spot her ponytail and white dress further up the beach. He reached down for the pair of binoculars he kept by him. There were always interesting things to look at – a passing ship, a hang-glider, a bird of prey – and it also meant he could keep an eye on the surfing conditions when the tide was out. At last, he caught sight of the girl through the lenses. Was he being a bit of a stalker? Surely it wasn't normal, to spy on someone like this, but the girl had fascinated him. He watched her as she walked further up the beach.

A few moments later, Craig couldn't believe his eyes as she approached someone's empty rug, reached under a towel, found a bag and took out a purse, all in one fluid movement that took less than five seconds. Then she walked calmly away, back up the beach towards him.

He didn't know why he was so shocked. After all, he was used to this sort of behaviour. He arrested people like this girl every day of the week in the town centre. Admittedly, they usually worked in gangs rather than on their own. There would be one on lookout, and one causing a distraction. Maybe he was shocked because he viewed Everdene as an escape. He'd built it up in his mind as some sort of romantic hideaway where nothing bad ever happened, but of course it did. A crowded beach was the perfect place for a petty thief.

He followed her progress back up the beach. He watched her take money out of the purse, stuff the notes in her pocket, then ditch the purse in the bins as she walked past. His heart sank as he realized that this meant she was definitely guilty, although if he was going to confront her he needed proof.

He felt a sour taste in his mouth. He didn't want to deal with this, but now that he had seen it happen, he couldn't ignore it, even if he was off duty. Of course, he could just turn a blind eye, but that wasn't in Craig's nature. He'd never been one to stand by and let people do wrong. Even after what had happened to him lately, he was still a policeman, first and foremost.

Or maybe he'd just imagined what had happened. It was certainly hot enough to make you see things, and the heat of the sun made everything hazy. He'd had a beer as well, from the fridge, which might have impaired his judgement. Maybe he should just carry on reading. It was too beautiful a day for trouble. Then he sighed and picked up his binoculars. He would sit and watch her to see what she did next. If she just sat on her towel and did nothing else, he decided, he would give her the benefit of the doubt and leave her alone.

Jenna drank half a bottle of water and lay back down in the sun. She couldn't believe how easy it had been. She mustn't get carried away, though. Word might start spreading on the beach. She would just do one more today, then go to the other beach around the point tomorrow. One thing she had learned from her family as she grew up was never go back to the scene of the crime.

The other thing she knew was that even if someone did call the police, they wouldn't come out. They weren't going to bother to respond to a crime where the victims had been stupid enough to leave their stuff unattended. On a busy Saturday in the summer, when they were already understaffed, there were far more important things they could be dealing with.

She just had to hold her nerve. There was over a mile of beach to choose from. She was anonymous. Everyone looked right through her. If Jenna needed proof that she was a no-body, this was it. She sat up again. The heat was intense, as if the sun was burning a hole in the sky. It was hard to look at the sea without squinting. The light reflecting off the water was almost white.

One more, Jenna decided. She'd spotted a family. Earlier she'd seen the dad take his wallet out and give the three kids money for ice creams. They looked well off. They had all the kit. UV tents and thick, plush beach towels and a sleek spaniel on a lead, as well as a cool box brimming with all manner of treats. Jenna's stomach rumbled and she realized that she still hadn't eaten anything. She watched as the mother opened the cool box and rummaged inside, handing out drinks.

She wondered if they knew how lucky they were. She'd never been on holiday. 'What do you want to go on holiday for?' her mum had asked. 'We live by the sea. People pay to come here. Why would we want to pay to go somewhere else?'

Jenna knew she shouldn't sit there feeling sorry for herself to justify her actions. This wasn't about self-pity, or feeling bitter. This was about survival. Besides, thought Jenna, this family could definitely afford to lose a few quid. She watched while the mother zipped up the children's wetsuits and gath-ered up the towels to take down to the water, then applied suncream to the backs of their necks. The dad shoved his wallet in the cool box, obviously thinking that no one would look in there for something to steal. She shook her head in disbelief.

The tide was at its lowest, so the family had a long way to walk to get to the sea. She watched until they were three-quarters of the way there, then made her way over to their encampment. She plonked herself casually down on the rug, then lifted the cool-box lid. She rummaged about inside, looking for all the world like a young girl finding the best thing to eat.

She pulled out an egg roll, oozing with mayonnaise, and a giant chocolate-chip cookie. She looked down to the shoreline where the family had reached the water. It would take them at least ten minutes to walk back, even if they remembered that they had forgotten something vital. She devoured the roll, then rifled through the wallet as she munched on the biscuit. There was over a hundred quid in there. Three credit cards. A photo of the family, the kids in posh uniforms outside a massive house. For some reason this made her feel better. They weren't going to miss the money.

She might as well take the whole lot. There was no point in leaving them any. They were obviously loaded. The man would be furious for about an hour, then he'd go to the cash-point and get some more money. It was no big deal. It was his own fault for leaving his wallet unattended. She folded up the notes and stuffed them in her pocket, then put the lid back on the cool box. She felt slightly sick from eating so fast in the heat of the sun. Then she stood up and walked away.

Six

Craig's heart was thumping, which was crazy. This wasn't some stake-out on a dodgy estate where things could go badly if he made the wrong move. So why was he worried? He should just march over, collar the girl and make people aware that this kind of crime could happen, even somewhere as carefree as Everdene. That might make them take more care of their valuables.

Something was stopping him, though. He'd felt drawn to the girl the moment he had bumped into her in the cafe. He wanted to know why she was doing this. Instinct told him this wasn't her usual behaviour. She didn't have the air of a hardened pickpocket, and the way she had taken food out of the cool box told him she was hungry. Although being hungry didn't excuse what she was doing, far from it.

Craig knew that if his mates were here they wouldn't give her a chance, and that they'd call him soft. Well, maybe he was soft, softer than he admitted even to himself. In fact, he had to face up to it now. He'd lost his killer instinct. He'd been dragged over the coals, and even though he'd been cleared of blame, the experience had soured him. Where once he had felt it was his duty to see justice done, now he was asking himself questions. And a good cop shouldn't hesitate.

He sighed, put down his binoculars and got out of his deckchair. He could see her without them now, weaving her way among the holidaymakers back to her towel. He paused for a moment, and watched as she sat down, then put her head in her hands. He could see by her body language that she felt guilty. Her shoulders were hunched and she moved slowly as she started gathering her things up ready to leave. Smart move, thought Craig, because it was about time she moved on. That last family looked as if they would cause a fuss, and it would be better for her if she wasn't around when they raised the alarm.

He watched as she stuffed the last of her things in her bag and stood up. He walked down the last few feet of the bank and made his way towards her as she moved off. He fell into step beside her and put a hand on her arm.

'Hey,' he said, not loudly, as he didn't want to cause alarm. She stopped.

'What?' She looked straight at him. There was a moment of confusion, then she recognized him. 'You were in the cafe.'

'I saw what you did,' he told her.

'What?' she repeated, frowning this time, and he saw that her eyes were amber speckled with gold. 'Spilled my tea, you mean?'

For a moment, in the heat of the sun, he doubted himself again. He felt awkward. This was far more difficult than an arrest, when he was in uniform. He wasn't quite sure what to say.

'No. I saw you nick that wallet out of the cool box. And take that purse out of that woman's handbag earlier.' He pointed back down the beach.

She shook her head. 'I don't know what you're talking about.'

She moved away and carried on walking. He walked beside her.

'I've got photos.'

She hesitated for a moment. 'Of what?'

'Good enough evidence for a court of law.'

She turned on him. 'Go and hassle someone else, will you? You're being weird.'

'I should have you arrested.'

'I should have *you* arrested. You've been following me since this morning, taking pictures. That's stalking.'

He was impressed by the way she stood her ground. On the surface, she seemed defiant. A passer-by would believe her innocence, but Craig had been trained to read body language. Her fists were clenched, and she refused to make eye contact. He was going to have to be more forceful to get her to admit her guilt. Yet somehow his heart wasn't in it.

Maybe he should just let her go and be done with it. Thinking she had been caught would probably put her off doing it again, and this was supposed to be his week off. He just wanted to chill and get things straight in his head. This was like being back at work, if not worse. All he really wanted to do was sit back down and have a beer and maybe fall asleep again.

Craig nearly gave up and let her go, but something inside him wanted to know more about her. He wanted to know why she was on the beach nicking money. He never had time, when he arrested people, to go into the whys and wherefores, and he was interested.

'I don't want to make a big scene,' he told her. 'But I can't just let you walk off with all that money.'

She spread her hands, laughing. 'There is no money. I haven't even got enough for an ice cream.'

He held her gaze.

'Open your bag. Let me have a look.'

'Leave me alone. Or I'm going to call for help.'

He looked around and then took his wallet out of his shorts. 'You better take a look at this.'

He flipped it open and showed her his police identification.

She stared at it for a good five seconds before she finally dropped her eyes to the ground. She sighed and turned away.

'I didn't have any choice,' she said, her voice tight with tears.

'We all have a choice,' he replied. 'I've got a choice right

423

now. I can take you into the nearest station. Or we can talk about it.'

'What are you, my counsellor, all of a sudden?' she asked, crossly.

He raised an eyebrow. 'Normal girls of your age don't come to the beach on their own and spend the day nicking money.'

'You think I don't know that?' She raised her voice, and he realized that people were looking.

'Look,' he said. 'I'm a cop. By rights it's my duty to turn you in. But I'm on holiday. I don't want a load of hassle.' He looked at her. She was staring down at the sand. The fight seemed to have gone out of her. 'And I bet you don't either.'

She looked up and put her hands on her hips. 'So what are you going to do? Give me some big lecture? It's not as if I don't know it's wrong.'

'So why did you do it?'

She stared at him. Her eyes were huge in her face. He reached out a hand and touched her arm.

'Come on. Come inside and have a drink. We can talk about it.'

Jenna stood there. She didn't know what to do. All she knew was that the heat was suddenly unbearable and she felt sick. She wasn't scared. She didn't feel like running away. In fact, she almost felt a sense of relief. Her future was now going to be out of her hands. Someone else was going to be in control.

She looked up at the bloke again. He was going to decide her fate. She didn't have to make the decisions any more. She couldn't read the expression in his silver-grey eyes. She'd expected harshness and accusation but they seemed almost understanding.

'Come on,' said the man, nodding his head up towards the faded blue beach hut behind him. 'We don't want to have this discussion in public.'

For a moment Jenna was tempted to run. She was wearing flip-flops, which were impossible to run in, but she could kick them off. How far would she get? Not far, she knew. And he looked fit.

She followed him obediently up the slope towards the beach hut. He had broad shoulders tapering down to a slender waist. He was wearing red surfing shorts decorated with flowers although there was nothing girly about him. He was lightly tanned, and his skin glistened where he'd put on sun-cream. Despite her heart thumping, she managed a smile to herself. Nice work, Jenna – you've been caught red-handed by the hottest cop you've ever seen.

Seven

Jenna followed her captor up to the beach hut. She could see where he'd been sitting, in a red and white striped deckchair. There were a couple of empty bottles of beer, and a pair of binoculars.

'I've been watching you all afternoon,' he said.

Jenna said nothing. She knew from experience that was the best policy. Don't confess or deny anything.

He led her into the hut. Inside it was surprisingly cool. He poured her a glass of water without asking, and she drank thirstily.

'So do you do this a lot?' he asked.

Whatever she said was going to sound like a line. If she told him this was the first time she had ever nicked anything, he would say, 'Of course it is', in that nasty voice coppers kept specially for such occasions.

'Easier than getting a job,' she told him defiantly.

'How much did you get?'

'I don't know . . .'

He held out his hand to take her bag. She had no choice but to give it to him.

'So,' she asked him. 'Where are your handcuffs? Are you going to march me back up the beach past everyone?'

He pulled out the money. When he saw how much there was, he raised his eyebrows.

'Quite a bit,' he said, and started to count it. Jenna felt sick with humiliation. Seeing all that money that belonged to other people made her feel even worse than she already did. She just wanted to lie down and curl up into a ball, then go to sleep for ever.

He was nodding as he counted.

'Two hundred and seventy-five quid,' he remarked. 'Beats working for a living, I suppose.'

His cool grey eyes stared at her.

'No,' she said. 'Actually, I'd much rather be working.' The stress of the last couple of days boiled up inside her. 'Do you think I want to do this? Do you think I felt good about myself, sitting there on the beach, looking for the people who I thought wouldn't miss the money?'

Suddenly her knees went weak and she saw black dots at the corners of her eyes. She swayed for a moment and shut her eyes. She was going to throw up. She looked around in a panic, her hand on her stomach.

'Here.' He grabbed the washing-up bowl from the sink and thrust it at her just in time. She took it from him and vomited, her cheeks burning. She wiped her mouth, sweat breaking out on her forehead. It didn't get any worse than this. Meeting a hot guy, then him catching you stealing, then puking up in front of him.

What a class act, Jenna thought. She couldn't look at the bloke. She wanted to crawl away into a corner and die.

'Sorry . . .' she managed at last.

'You've had too much sun,' he told her, and took away the bowl. 'Go into the bathroom and clean yourself up. There's mouthwash.'

She did as she was told. In the tiny bathroom she gripped the edge of the sink and looked at herself in the mirror. Her hair was plastered to her forehead and her cheeks were burning. Her head felt as if it was held in a vice. She felt too terrible to worry about what was going to happen to her. She washed her face with cold water, rinsed out her mouth and found the mouthwash. Then she ventured out again, not sure what was going to happen next.

*

While she was in the bathroom, Craig looked at the money and tried to decide what to do. He should turn her in, but what good would that do? She'd go up before the magistrate. Even if they were lenient she would have a record that would make sure no one gave her a job.

When she came back out she looked terrible. She was shivering, even though it was hot. He thought it was probably a mixture of sunstroke and shock. He went over to put the kettle on. What a cliché, thinking a nice cup of tea could solve anything, but it seemed the best thing to do.

She sat down on the settee without being asked, then leaned back and shut her eyes. Her hair was damp where she had washed her face.

'I'm Craig, by the way,' he told her. 'Do you want to tell me your name?'

'Jenna . . .' she replied, faintly. He thought she was telling the truth.

'OK, Jenna,' he replied, opening the cupboard to find the tea bags. 'What do you think we should do about this situation?'

She shrugged. 'You're the policeman.'

He lobbed a couple of tea bags into two mugs.

'Why?' he asked. 'It's a pretty rubbish thing to do, don't you think? Nicking people's money when they've come for a day out on the beach?'

She stared into the middle of the room, sullen.

'Where do you suggest I go, then? Up to the hospital, where people are having a shit time anyway? So my nicking their money won't make any difference to how they feel?'

He had to hide a smile at her logic. He poured water onto the tea bags, got the milk out of the fridge and added a splash to each mug. He walked over and handed her one. She took it from him without a word of thanks, just held it between her knees, her shoulders hunched again. Her hair had come loose from its ponytail, falling onto her shoulders, and he thought again how pretty she was.

'How about not doing it at all?' he asked.

She slammed her mug down on the coffee table in front of her.

'Those people aren't going to miss that money,' she told him. 'They're just here to have a good time. They haven't got a care in the world, any of them. I was watching. They've got everything they could possibly want.'

Craig looked at her. 'Does that make it right, then?'

'No, of course it doesn't,' she shot back. 'I know it's wrong. I don't need you to judge me. You with your job, and your beach hut, and your surfboard, hanging out by the sea. You don't know what it's like, to have no hope, no money. Nothing. I've got nothing!' she shouted at him. 'I've got the clothes I'm standing up in, but that's it. I lost my job and my boss never gave me my wages. I owe my landlord four hundred quid, and if I don't get it, he's going to kick me out. Tell me what I was supposed to do, Mr Policeman?'

She spat the last few words out with real venom. Craig was silent for a moment.

'Actually,' he told her, 'I do know what it's like to have absolutely nothing.'

She gave a snort of disbelief. 'Yeah, right.'

'I was brought up on an estate on the outskirts of the city. My brother was a drug dealer, but my mum thought the sun shone out of him because he brought her things. Things he'd nicked. She never took any notice of me. So I decided I'd start nicking things too.'

The girl looked up in surprise at this confession. Craig gave a wry smile. He didn't think he'd ever admitted this to anyone before. It wasn't something he was proud of.

'Lucky for me, there was a teacher at my school who could see I had potential. He gave me a really hard time. He went on and on at me until I realized he was right: that I would have more of a chance if I passed my exams. When I got my exam results, eight GCSEs, my mum didn't take any notice. She was too busy watching the big-screen telly that my brother had got her.'

Craig still remembered his anger now – the feeling of hopelessness, wondering what on earth was the point – and he'd thrown the letter with his results in the bin. His teacher had come to find him, told him how proud he was, showed him everything that piece of paper would allow him to do.

'Three weeks later, my brother got shot in a drive-by shooting and I decided to join the police. My mum never spoke to me again, because my brother had taught her to blame the cops for everything.' Craig paused for breath. The memory was still painful. 'So don't give me your sob story. I could have followed in my brother's footsteps. I had every opportunity, I can tell you. But I didn't.'

Jenna didn't say anything. She stared at the floor. Eventually she looked up.

'I'm sorry about your brother,' she said. 'But it's not that easy, you know. Just because you found a way out doesn't mean that we all can.'

Craig frowned. 'So that's it, is it? You feel justified?'

Jenna jumped to her feet. 'No. I never felt justified. I felt desperate.' Her amber eyes were flashing as she crossed the room to stand in front of him. 'How am I supposed to pay my rent? It's no good telling me to go to the council. He wants cash. Now.' She was trembling with fury. 'Of course, there's one way I could pay him. I know that. But I kind of thought nicking a few quid from people who wouldn't notice was a better way to go than sleeping with some sleazebag . . .'

'Hey, hey, hey.' Alarmed by her reaction, he went to put his arm round her shoulder. She shook it off.

'Just get off me.' She pulled away from him and threw her bag across the room so that its contents spilled on the floor. 'I'll leave it up to you to do what you think is best with the money.'

The next moment, she was gone. The door of the beach hut swung shut behind her. Craig stood in the middle of the room with no idea what to do. Going after her would do no good. He didn't have a solution to her problem. If he did, he would be running the country by now. There were thousands like her, stuck in a trap. He saw them every day, saw the results of their desperation and what they did as a result. He'd made the classic mistake, of thinking that just because he had pulled himself up by his bootstraps, anyone could change their life for the better.

He went to the fridge and pulled out a beer. He took off the top with the opener someone had screwed to the wall and took a sip. It tasted bitter. He put the bottle down. Getting drunk was no solution when you felt bad. He saw the results of substance abuse every day. People who took drink and drugs to forget, not to have fun.

He walked over to the settee and sat down. So much for a quiet, relaxing week. Instead, what had happened today had brought everything into sharp focus, highlighting all of the things he felt unhappy about. He had, he knew, joined the police for all the right reasons, but now he wasn't sure he was doing the right thing any more. When he looked at people like Jenna and sympathized with their plight, how could he carry on? Maybe it was time for him to make a difference in some other way. Turning a blind eye today was one thing, but he couldn't do that when he went back to work.

The incident had only confirmed for him what he already felt in his gut, that the day was coming closer and closer when he would have to walk away.

Eight

Jenna ran all the way back up the beach to the road. Running on the sand was hard work, and she was soon out of breath.

She slowed down to a walk as she went through the village towards the bus stop. She passed the Ship Aground again, and saw the band bringing in the gear for that evening's singing competition. She stopped for a moment, wondering whether she had the nerve to enter.

'Don't be stupid, Jenna,' she told herself. 'You're not good enough.'

She remembered her birthday, a few years ago now. Everyone had piled round to her house, all her brothers and sisters and their mates and her mates. The house was heaving, the booze was flowing and the music was pumping. There was a real party atmosphere, even though she hadn't sent out any official invites. For once, the mood in the house was light. Even her mum was happy – she'd done herself up to the nines, and was dancing and laughing and flirting with all Jenna's brothers' mates.

Someone had brought round a karaoke machine. Nicked, no doubt, but everyone started to take it in turns to have a go. Jenna felt too shy at first, but her friends encouraged her. They'd heard her sing and they thought she was great. They weren't going to stop, so Jenna picked up the microphone.

She sang 'Beautiful' by Christina Aguilera. Everyone else had chosen upbeat singalong songs, from bands like the Spice Girls and Take That, so for a moment she felt awkward when she realized everyone had stopped talking and laughing, and was actually watching her. She wasn't note perfect, not by any means. Every time she made a mistake she cringed inside and wanted to run off, but she carried on. When the last note died away, there was silence. Then suddenly everyone broke into wild applause.

Jenna couldn't believe she'd actually done it, sung on her own in front of a roomful of people. It felt amazing. She felt . . . beautiful, just like in the song.

Then her mother had stepped in front of her, grabbed the microphone, put on another song – something rowdy and upbeat. In the blink of an eye she had the whole room singing along with her, cheering and clapping. Jenna was forgotten. Overshadowed. She'd felt invisible again. How could she have thought she was any good? Everyone was drunk. They were just playing along with her. The applause had been empty. They'd have clapped for anyone . . .

The memory burned inside her, and she turned away from the pub and headed to the bus stop. Five minutes later she was on the bus to Tawcombe, leaving Everdene and the horrors of the day behind her.

As soon as she got back to her house, she went into her room, shut the door and leaned against it. She felt numb, unsure whether to laugh or cry or just throw herself onto the bed and go to sleep. She wanted to block out everything that had happened in the past twenty-four hours. She wanted to block out the future, too. Just one more day and The Prof would be knocking on the door, an oily smile on his face, knowing full well she didn't have the rent.

She looked around at the shabby furniture and the few things she had that made the room her own. She wouldn't be sorry to leave. Her time here had not been happy. The other tenants in the house had been in no hurry to make friends. She had never felt comfortable bringing anyone back here. Her friends would have been shocked, even though they might not live in palaces themselves.

As she looked around, Jenna understood that she had no choice but to go back home. She would go now, tonight. She would save The Prof the pleasure of evicting her. She couldn't stand the thought of his face as he made her pack up her stuff. And this way, she wouldn't have to owe him the money. He might try to track her down and chase her for it, but at the end of the day how could you get money out of someone who didn't have any?

For the next half-hour, Jenna went through her wardrobe and her drawers, sorting out everything she wanted to take with her. Then she piled it all into two black bin bags. That was it, everything she had in the world. She put them by the door. She'd call a cab. Her mum would have to pay the fare when she got there.

She picked up the bags and stood in the doorway for a moment. So much for making her own way in the world. She'd reached rock bottom today. Her mum was so right. Of course she wasn't any better than any of them. She belonged right back there with the rest of her family. How could she possibly have imagined there was a better life out there?

She thought about Craig. Why couldn't she have ended up with someone like him? Someone decent and honest who'd made his way in the world, even though he'd had no better a start than she had.

The door slammed shut behind her. She stepped out into the street, blinking at the early-evening sun that shone in her eyes, and trailed up the road to find a taxi.

No one batted an eyelid when she walked through the door. Her mum was lying on the settee watching telly. She grumbled a bit when Jenna asked for a fiver to pay the cab driver, but she gave it to her.

'You're back, then?' she asked. 'You can't have your room. Your brother's using it as an office.'

'An office?' Jenna frowned.

'Yeah. He's set himself up in business. Delivering pet food. He keeps it all in the garage. He's doing all right for himself.'

Her mum sat up. Jenna looked at her more closely.

'What?' her mum asked.

'Nothing. You look . . . different, that's all.' She did. She looked slimmer, younger, not so puffy. And she wasn't drunk. Usually by this time on a Saturday she'd have started the second bottle of vodka.

'I've got a new bloke, haven't I?'

Jenna put down her bags and glanced around the room. Everything looked tidy. There were no dog hairs. There were no empty glasses, no ashtrays. In fact, her mum wasn't smoking.

'Have you given up the fags as well?' she asked.

'Most of the time,' her mum admitted. 'I have the odd sneaky one every now and again. I wouldn't want to be perfect, would I?' She grinned at Jenna, then looked away.

Jenna felt a lump in her throat. She turned away before her mum could see her tears and think she was soft. Instead, she lugged her bin bags upstairs and put them in her old room. All her stuff had gone, but she could sleep on the floor for the time being. Compared to her old flat, it would be luxury.

Her mum appeared behind her in the doorway.

'I'll give you a hand shifting his stuff out. Your brother can do his paperwork in the kitchen.'

'Thanks.'

Her mum traced the pattern of the carpet with the toe of her shoe, then cleared her throat.

'I'm cooking a chilli tonight, if you want some. You can meet Arnie.'

Jenna looked out of the window onto the front garden that she'd stared out at so many times during her childhood. She noticed that the lawn had been cut, and there were two pots of flowers on either side of the front door. Whoever Arnie was, he'd certainly made some changes happen. She couldn't remember the last time her mum had cooked a proper meal.

'I'd love that,' she managed finally. 'But there's something I've got to do first. Can you lend me a tenner?'

Her mother rolled her eyes. 'You've only been back five minutes,' she grumbled, but she rummaged in her purse and handed Jenna the money.

Five minutes later, Jenna rooted through the bin bags until she found her favourite dress – a vintage sundress with a full skirt covered in red cherries. She pulled out her make-up bag and drew a sweep of black liner over her eyelids, added mascara, then finished with a slick of bright red lipstick. She brushed her hair out, backcombed it and tied it back up in a high pony-tail. Then she walked out into the street, made her way down to the main road and jumped on the bus. Twenty minutes later she was in Everdene.

By the time she got to the Ship Aground it was jam-packed. Tourists and locals mingled, the tourists pink from the sun. The bar staff poured pint after pint and filled up jugs of sangria. The competition was in full swing. The in-house band provided the music from a list of favourites as contestant after contestant got up to sing.

Jenna signed herself up for the competition before she could change her mind. She read the list of songs to choose from and made her choice. She sat in a corner of the bar and listened. The range of talent was quite varied. Some murdered their songs with good humour, while others took their attempts very seriously.

She was as good as any of them. She knew she was. And suddenly it was her turn. As she stood at the microphone, she remembered all the people who had listened to her sing over the summer, their smiles and their encouragement. She could do it, she knew she could.

She heard the opening bars and her mouth went dry. She grabbed her water and took a quick drink. Then she started to sing. Her voice wavered at first, and no one took any notice of her, thinking she was just another wannabe singer who